UNTIL
THE
MOUNTAINS
FALL

Books by Connilyn Cossette

OUT FROM EGYPT

Counted with the Stars
Shadow of the Storm
Wings of the Wind

CITIES OF REFUGE

A Light on the Hill
Shelter of the Most High
Until the Mountains Fall

CITIES OF REFUGE · 3

UNTIL
THE
MOUNTAINS
FALL

CONNILYN COSSETTE

BETHANYHOUSE
a division of Baker Publishing Group
Minneapolis, Minnesota

© 2019 by Connilyn Cossette

Published by Bethany House Publishers
Minneapolis, Minnesota 55438
www.bethanyhouse.com

Bethany House Publishers is a division of
Baker Publishing Group, Grand Rapids, Michigan

Printed in the United States of America

Library of Congress Cataloging-in-Publication Data
Names: Cossette, Connilyn, author.
Title: Until the mountains fall / Connilyn Cossette.
Description: Minneapolis : Bethany House, division of Baker Publishing Group, [2019]
  | Series: Cities of refuge ; 3
Identifiers: LCCN 2018048924| ISBN 9780764219887 (trade paper) | ISBN
  9780764234064 (cloth) | ISBN 9781493418756 (ebook)
Subjects: | GSAFD: Christian fiction.
Classification: LCC PS3603.O8655 U58 2019 | DDC 813/.6—dc23
LC record available at https://lccn.loc.gov/2018048924

Scripture quotations labeled NIV are from the Holy Bible, New International Version®. NIV®. Copyright © 1973, 1978, 1984, 2011 by Biblica, Inc.™ Used by permission of Zondervan. All rights reserved worldwide. www.zondervan.com

Scripture quotations labeled ESV are from The Holy Bible, English Standard Version® (ESV®), copyright © 2001 by Crossway, a publishing ministry of Good News Publishers. Used by permission. All rights reserved. ESV Text Edition: 2011

Cover design by Jennifer Parker
Cover photography by Mike Habermann Photography, LLC
Map illustration by Samuel T. Campione

Author is represented by The Steve Laube Agency.

Baker Publishing Group publications use paper produced from sustainable forestry practices and post-consumer waste whenever possible.

To Nicole and Tammy
Thank you both for being not only an important
part of the stories I write, but precious additions
to my own story as well. Neither would be the
same without you.

Perfume and incense bring joy to the heart,
and the pleasantness of a friend springs
from their heartfelt advice.
– Proverbs 27:9 NIV

"If brothers dwell together, and one of them dies and has no son, the wife of the dead man shall not be married outside the family to a stranger. Her husband's brother shall go in to her and take her as his wife and perform the duty of a husband's brother to her."

Deuteronomy 25:5 ESV

Part I

CHAPTER ONE

Rivkah

25 Av
1380 BC
Kedesh, Israel

I'd been here before. Seated on this same three-legged stool with the same two girls plaiting the black locks around my head, their hands fragrant with sweet almond oil as they entwined tiny white flowers into the braids. Only this time, their matrimonial blessings rang hollow and the smiles they offered were tinged with grief instead of joy.

Fidgeting in my seat, I tugged at my white linen dress, the whisper-smooth fabric I'd once delighted in now constricting and raspy against my skin. How absurd this day was even called a celebration—my husband, Gidal, having been laid to rest just a month before. If only my father would've had the decency to hand me off like a broodmare quietly. But as the head priest of our city, nothing my father did was without fanfare, so naturally he'd determined we would not keep this transition to ourselves but make my obedience a shining example of steadfast commitment to the Torah.

"You are as beautiful as always, Rivkah," Abra said, her tone stilted. "My brother . . ." She cleared her throat, false smile wavering. "Malakhi will be pleased." I pushed aside any thought of her twin brother and what he might or might not think of me. I may be forced to endure a levirate marriage, but no one could strong-arm me into being glad of it.

At sixteen Abra might soon find herself ensnared in a betrothal as well. With sleek black hair and silvery eyes, the exotic shape of which attested to the strength of her mother's half-Egyptian heritage, the girl was already generating interest from the young men of Kedesh and beyond. But with a father who commanded a contingent of spies and an older brother also counted among that well-trained group of warriors, none had been so bold as to approach her yet.

Chana, two years younger than her sister, was as much a beauty but lacked the outward vibrancy that defined Abra. She peered shyly at me, her gaze catching mine in the wavy image of the polished copper mirror. Her lips parted as if to say something, but then she turned away, a glimmer of tears in the corners of her eyes. Of the two girls, she'd been the apple of Gidal's eye, a constant shadow of her older brother, and his near image in so many ways. Therefore, in the month since he had died, I'd avoided her as much as possible. My late husband had been nothing but kind to me, but her grief far eclipsed my own.

A vision of Gidal's pale face, shining with sweat as he lay dying in our bed, arose to jeer at me. If I'd been the wife he'd deserved, more attentive and less demanding, or if I'd gone to search for him in the orchard when he hadn't returned by dusk, my husband might still breathe.

A knock sounded at the door and my heart clattered an uneven response as I stood, spine straight and chin high, poised to accept my lot. Moriyah, Gidal's mother, entered the room, her gaze meeting with mine. Although there was no accusation in her expression, I glanced away, but she approached to place warm hands on my shoulders.

"Rivkah," she said. "Daughter. Look at me." I cringed at her choice of words, but obeyed nonetheless. "I understand that this day is difficult for you, and I above all others wish you had been given more time to grieve. But I want you to know that I am grateful to you." Her voice faltered, her silver eyes filling with tears. "Through you, a piece of my precious son will live on, and his name will not be forgotten."

A sharp response sprang to my tongue, but I had no cause to disrespect Moriyah. She had welcomed me to her family, treated me as if I were one of her own children, and advocated that instead of being given directly into marriage after the customary thirty days of mourning, I be allowed at least a three-month betrothal before being claimed by Malakhi. However, the idea that my submission to this arrangement would somehow protect Gidal's legacy was beyond preposterous. Not only was his inheritance of little value— the firstborn status claimed by his adopted oldest brother—but the man was dead. Nothing remained of him but memories.

"I am pleased to do so." The words were bitter on my tongue, but she accepted the falsehood with a gracious nod. Then, as was my duty, I followed Moriyah out into the courtyard of her inn, as prepared as I would ever be to enter into a betrothal with my husband's younger brother.

Although tempted to latch my eyes on the ground to avoid the inevitable stares, I affixed a bland smile on my face as I followed Moriyah through the courtyard, keeping my head high. If only my own mother were here to hold my hand and whisper reassurances as I marched toward the destiny chosen for me. Instead, Yahweh had ripped her from my life, leaving me with nothing more than the faint memory of her face, older siblings who were entirely wrapped up in their own lives, and a father whose priestly duties took precedence over everything.

Since my grandfather Dov had been the first priest to settle in Kedesh twenty years ago, our ever-expanding clan had taken root and flourished here. A large number of the crowd in attendance were members of my own family: cousins, uncles, aunts, nieces, and nephews. But although every few steps I was stopped by another relation offering a kiss or a quiet blessing, the atmosphere was significantly more subdued than when I'd married Gidal four months ago. There would be no seven days of feasting, no dancing, no lighthearted teasing about the wedding night. I hoped by the time Malakhi claimed me as a bride that I could dissuade my father from making another fuss over the confirmation of our marriage covenant, but in all honesty I did not expect to be successful.

My oldest brother, Tal, and his wife, Prezi, stepped forward to embrace me, and three of their five daughters trailed behind me, carrying baskets of flowers to hand to well-wishers along the way. Only missing were the second- and third-born sons in our family, Kolel and Alon. They'd each departed for Shiloh when they turned twenty to be trained for their role as *kohanim*, priests in service to Yahweh.

Seated on the stone stairs that led to the upper level of the inn, my future bridegroom lounged back on his elbows as he held court with three young women his age, a sultry smile curving his lips as he listened to their flirtatious chatter. With his shaggy black hair and well-defined features inherited from some Egyptian ancestor— including bronze skin and silver eyes that brimmed with mischief— Malakhi was widely regarded as the most handsome young man in Kedesh.

Since the age of thirteen, when he'd begun the transformation into manhood, Malakhi drew girls to him like drunkards to choice wine—something he'd barely seemed to notice at first. But then, a little over a year ago, around the time I'd become betrothed to Gidal, something changed. Suddenly he reveled in the attention, taking full advantage of the effect his looks and innate, roguish charm had on females. More than a few angry fathers had shown up at the family inn to demand that the boy stay away from their daughters or offer up a bride price. His father, Darek, a master of negotiation after years of spying among our enemies, somehow convinced each girl's father that his wayward son was not yet prepared to support a wife and that indeed they were fortunate to avoid such a match.

I huffed a silent laugh at the irony, for none such excuse was given to my father when Darek agreed to a levirate marriage. Within a week of Gidal's death, it was determined that I would be passed along to his brother for the sake of continuing my husband's line through my body. Of course Malakhi could have refused, could have demanded the town elders release him from the obligation, but the longtime friendship between our families was a cord of many threads. Darek had agreed to the match without condition, and though he was under no obligation to do so, offered up an additional bride price to secure the bond.

Malakhi caught sight of me trailing after his mother and sat up, brushing back the unkempt hair that perpetually hung into his eyes. The simpering girls at his feet were seemingly forgotten, and his carefree expression became sober. His gaze met mine, and something passed across his too-handsome face that I could not decipher.

Although Gidal and Malakhi shared a mother and a father, their similarities were few. Gidal's hair had been a rich reddish-brown, his form tall and lanky, and his eyes dark like Darek's. Malakhi's build was only now beginning to broaden, and although we'd rarely been in close proximity in past years, I guessed he would stand barely three fingers taller than me. I was only two years older than him, but I had the distinctive sense that I was marrying a boy, not a man. The thought curdled my stomach as I turned my face away.

I did not even like Malakhi. He'd spent much of his childhood pulling my hair, throwing pebbles at me, and sticking all manner of insects down the back of my tunic. Although Gidal had participated in some good-natured teasing when we were small, he'd always come to my rescue whenever Malakhi stepped over the line, ordering his younger brother to leave me alone and then making his parents aware of the offense.

But in spite of the many consequences Malakhi received because of such instances, my complaints only served to encourage his beastly behavior, especially after my mother died, and he'd become nearly relentless in his provocation. The harassment abruptly ended a few years ago, not long before I was betrothed to his older brother, but nothing could wipe away the distaste I had for the boy who'd tormented me for so long.

It was because Gidal had been my champion in such matters that I'd agreed to my first marriage—although my father had given me little say, finding in me the perfect vehicle to strengthen ties with Darek and Moriyah's family, since we were not affiliated by tribe.

"Rivkah!" My older sister, Lailah, approached, arms outstretched and saffron-colored headscarf billowing around her. "You look lovely." She kissed both my cheeks, then leaned to whisper in my ear, "Smile. You look as though you are headed to your execution, not your betrothal."

Are they not one and the same?

I attempted to comply, wiping away any trace of trepidation in favor of a passably bright expression. She curved her palm over my cheek, as if to emphasize the four-year gap between us and the maternal role she'd slipped into since our mother died. "I know you miss Gidal, but this union will be pleasing to Yahweh," she said. "And I am sure you and Malakhi will be blessed with children very soon as well."

With a smile that bordered on condescension, she laid a hand over her own rounded belly, her second child with her husband, Oded. I'd once adored my older sister, but when our *ima* died seven years ago, she'd transformed from sibling to authority overnight, and the sisterly bond between us was gradually ground to dust. Her public display here now served only to sharpen the ever-present ache for my mother. Keeping my expression placid, I accepted her well-wishes but inwardly questioned why I must be passed off like a used sandal in order to please the Almighty—especially to Gidal's smug, irritating younger brother.

"That she will," said my father. "Her obedience to the Torah will be rewarded." He smiled down at me warmly, but his rebuttal to my arguments against this marriage would linger in my memory. They cycled over and over in my mind as my family and Malakhi's gathered around us.

"I have chosen what is best for you, daughter, even if you do not understand all my reasons now. You must trust that Darek and I have only your good in mind. Malakhi is able and willing to take on this responsibility, so the betrothal will go forward. And you, my daughter, have a duty to honor your husband, your family, and your God in this manner."

However, even as I prepared to declare my willingness to be bound in covenant to the boy across the courtyard, my heart vowed differently. If there were even the slightest opportunity to escape this prison my father had built for me, I would take it.

CHAPTER TWO

Malakhi

"Are you ready for this, brother?" Eitan's large hand landed on my shoulder, pulling my attention from my future bride across the courtyard, now hidden by a flock of women encircling her with eager exclamations.

"As ready as I will ever be," I said, affecting a tone of begrudging acceptance as I waved away the three girls who had been fruitlessly vying for my attention all morning.

My oldest brother watched them scatter before peering at me, his hazel eyes piercing my falsehood. "No one is forcing you, Malakhi. Abba will understand if you refuse this arrangement."

Panic shot through my body, but I gave an indifferent shrug and offered a half-truth. "I owe this to Gidal." I'd not honored my brother enough during his lifetime; I would not let him down for the length of my own.

Eitan folded his arms, which were marked by a multitude of burn scars from years of metalworking. He said nothing as he stared at me with the same preternatural patience that caused our enemies to spill their secrets in sheer terror.

But as I had a lifetime of practice standing firm against his interrogation tactics, I would not reveal how my heart was surging impatiently against my rib cage at the thought of standing next to Rivkah today. How even the scornful glance she shot my way as she walked past with my mother caused my pulse to stutter and my palms to sweat.

Apparently satisfied with my answer, Eitan smiled and slung his arm around my shoulder. "All right then, little brother, let's go see to your bride. Perhaps someday you'll be nearly as happy as I am with my own." His hold tightened around my neck as he roughly tousled my hair with his knuckles.

I struggled against him with a laugh and a jab of my elbow to his gut. Sofea, his foreign wife, had been kidnapped from an island across the Great Sea and brought to our city eight years before, but she returned his adoration with enviable ardor. My brother—a warrior, master metalsmith, devoted husband, and father of four children—was blessed indeed.

After a few more teasing remarks, Eitan led me to the gathering around Rivkah, which parted as we approached, leaving the woman I was to pledge my life to standing alone, her gaze downcast as I moved to her side.

She refused to look at me, but I knew every line of her face: the regal curve of her dark brows, the way her full lips twitched when she was holding back a sharp retort, the elegant sweep of her cheekbones, those wide amber eyes that missed nothing—nothing except how much I desired her.

Even now, standing within the circle of our family and friends, ready to pledge my commitment to take her as my wife in three months, shame curled an iron fist around my lungs. Could they see? Did they know how double-minded I was over having everything I'd ever wanted at the expense of my older brother's life?

Her father, Amitai, held high the *ketubah* document and began reading aloud the terms of our betrothal. Rivkah's expression was indecipherable as the *mohar* my father had put forward was outlined, the bridal gifts equal to those he'd offered with Gidal's marriage, even though it was neither necessary nor expected. But when the special circumstances surrounding our marriage were recited—that the first son conceived of our union would be counted as Gidal's heir, as his own flesh—her jaw went hard and her shoulders tightened.

Was her grief so acute that even the mention of his name caused her body to tense and her breath to catch? They'd only been newly wed when my brother had passed from this world, had only just begun their life together when it was cut short. How could I possibly take the place of a man as upright and honorable as Gidal? Would she ever find me worthy of filling the void he'd left behind or welcome my touch when the time came? Blinking away thoughts of Gidal and Rivkah together, along with the disturbing mixture of envy and anticipation those images conjured, I instead focused on my father and the basket of household goods, pieces of silver, and jewelry near his feet—the mohar destined for my bride.

"Do you agree to the terms set forth within this ketubah?" Amitai asked as he handed me the rolled papyrus. "Will you take my daughter as your wife, treat her with the respect and care the Torah prescribes? Will you commit to ascribing the firstborn son of your union to your brother Gidal?"

My affirmative answer was swift and strong. "I will." Although Gidal and I had been opposite in so many ways, no two brothers had loved each other more. If I could have died in his place, I would have. Fulfilling my duty to his widow had never been a question in my mind.

Amitai turned toward his daughter, his expression surprisingly stern. "And will you accept Malakhi as your husband and treat him with the respect and care the Torah prescribes? Will you commit to ascribing the firstborn son of your union to your husband Gidal?"

An extended pause echoed through the courtyard, one that ampli-
fied my thudding heartbeats and the restless shuffle of some child's
sandals behind us—most likely my youngest sister, Tirzah, for whom
stillness was as much a burden as it was for me. Amitai frowned at
his daughter's delayed response. Although Rivkah held her posture
straight, a faint flutter of her dark eyelashes made it clear she was
agitated. When finally her lips parted to speak her agreement, her
flat tone told me more than her sharp tongue ever could—this marriage was begrudging fulfillment of a duty for her, nothing more.

As well-wishers crowded around us after we'd shared a cup of
wine to confirm the binding contract between us, I watched her from
the corner of my eye. Although her mouth curved into a semblance of
a smile as she graciously accepted each embrace and blessing for our
betrothal, it was evident that she wanted nothing more than to flee.

I had known Rivkah before I could even walk. Our mothers had
raised us all in tandem, and nearly every childhood memory I had
included her. Granted, for the first fourteen years of my life she'd
been more of a sister to me than anything, but one chance moment
beneath a flowering terebinth two years ago had changed everything,
transforming Rivkah from the girl I'd teased to exasperation into
one whose beauty enthralled me nearly as much as her intelligence
and spirit. I'd gone from devising ways to provoke her ire to dreaming up ways to draw closer to her.

For months after that I'd tried to make amends for my behavior
toward her, but she rebuffed my every awkward attempt. She saw
me only as the boy who'd antagonized her for so long. And then,
only a year later, my father announced she was to marry Gidal, and
all hopes of making her mine someday were dashed to pieces. So
I'd stepped away, determined to respect my brother no matter the
cost to my heart. But now that Rivkah would soon be my wife, I'd
do everything in my power to make her understand how much she
meant to me.

Rescuing us from the crush of friends and family, my mother

ushered Rivkah and me to the low table in the center of the court-yard. Seated cross-legged on plump cushions, our knees brushed together only once before my betrothed scooted a handbreadth away. Yet even that contact was enough to set my blood racing.

After handing me a loaf of flatbread, my mother gave my shoulder an affectionate squeeze before moving on to serve the rest of those who'd gathered around the table and in groups all over the courtyard, breaking bread together in honor of our betrothal.

Taking the pillowy round of barley loaf in my hands, I tore it in two, handing one half to Rivkah. The rich aroma of the fresh bread wafted through the air, and my eager stomach snarled. A small bowl of spiced and salted olive oil sat on the table between us, so I nudged it toward her with a finger. With a tight smile that more resembled a grimace, she dipped her bread into the oil and I did the same. We were expected to offer a bite to one another, another sign that our covenant was binding for life.

Leaning nearer, I lifted the offering to her lips, my hand shaking slightly as my fingers neared her mouth. I'd not been this close to her since I was a boy. Wordlessly, she accepted, using only her teeth to swiftly snatch a bite and still refusing to look into my eyes as she did so. She reciprocated the gesture with jerky movements, and then looked away, taking a long draft of her wine, her discomfort so obvious that I half expected her to jump up from the table and flee.

Determined to use these next few months to win her over, I edged closer, hoping that the overlapping voices encircling us would afford a measure of privacy. "There is no need to be uneasy, Rivkah. You and I have known each other our whole lives."

Her attention snapped to me, her golden-brown eyes traveling over my face and her mouth pursing. "I am not uneasy."

"A lie if I've ever heard one."

Her lips parted in shock at my brazenness.

I shrugged a shoulder. "When you are anxious your eyelids flutter."

Her eyes narrowed. Had I given my obsession away with my too-sharp observation? To cover my misstep, I spread a wide smile across my face, one that seemed to entice many young ladies to linger near the foundry whenever I was at work there with Eitan. Instead of returning the gesture, she scowled and mumbled something under her breath about me "not having changed in the least."

Apparently the long history we shared, along with my childhood follies, would be a stumbling block to my pursuit of her favor. Three months was a short time to change her ingrained opinion, but I loved nothing more than a challenge. I would chip away at her walls, help her forget her grief, and pray that someday she would come to love me.

"I am sorry," I said.

Rivkah seemed dumbstruck by my words.

"I was unkind to you as a boy."

"You were hideous."

"That I was." Leaning closer, I pinned her with a knowing look and a smirk. "But you were all too fun to rile."

And indeed, for years I'd made it my duty to vex her until her amber eyes would flash, her fists would slam to her hips, and her pretty mouth would bunch into a furious little pout before she would tear off, black braids streaming behind her as she ran to tell her father, or mine, about my misdeeds.

Entranced by that pursed mouth now, even as she pretended to ignore my teasing remark with a haughty lift of her chin, I could not help but remember the moment I'd begun to wonder what it would be like to press my lips to those rose-colored ones.

"Tell me, Rivkah . . ." I ignored the way her body stiffened at my nearness as I bent to whisper into her ear. "Will you sing for me when we are married?"

"I don't know what you are talking about," she snapped, taking another sip of wine and turning away.

Until the day I'd followed her out to the very edge of Kedesh's boundary two years ago, I'd never heard her voice lifted in song, nor had I since then. Perhaps it was something she only did in solitary moments. Unmerited jealousy washed through me as I wondered whether in the privacy of their chamber, she'd sung one of those secret songs to Gidal.

"What were you writing that day beneath the terebinth tree?" I asked, confident that she would remember the moment she caught me spying on her as she'd alternated between singing and scribbling on a scrap of papyrus. Her mind was too keen to forget such a thing. She was the only woman I knew who'd been trained as a scribe, assisting her father as he tended to the administration of Kedesh, and she was able to speak more languages than I'd even known existed. There was no woman like Rivkah in the territory of Naftali, perhaps in all of the tribes of Israel—brilliant, beautiful, and with a voice as rich and smooth as date honey.

"That is none of your concern," she said, giving credence to my assumption, even as she kept her gaze latched on some far point across the courtyard instead of meeting my eyes.

Deciding it was better to goad her than endure her shunning, I reached over and slid a finger across the back of her hand. "A poem, perhaps? Or a love song?"

She gasped and yanked her hand away, nearly knocking over her wine cup in her haste. When her eyes finally met mine with golden fire, I grinned and leaned even nearer, glad that no one would question our proximity on the night of our betrothal. I breathed deep, taking in the floral scent of her hair and skin, my entire body humming with the pleasure of being so close to her and wishing that these next months of waiting would pass quickly. "Perhaps one day you'll even write such words for me."

Silence vibrated between us, blocking out the buzz of conversations all around, and for one shining moment I wondered whether anyone would notice—or care—if I stole a kiss from my bride. But then she went rigid. Her mouth hardened into a firm line, and the voice with a capacity for singing dulcet tones came out like the edge of a rusted knife. "It's not too late to undo this."

THREE

Rivkah

"You don't want me as a wife." I tilted my head toward the group of girls, heads together, whispering and watching the two of us from across the courtyard. "Besides, there seem to be plenty of other brides eager to take my place. Ones your own age."

"We are but two years apart," he said, his voice husky, his expression unreadable.

I'd been married, and then widowed, over the last five months. Those two years seemed a lifetime in my opinion. In truth, even at eleven years of age my very bones had felt ancient as I watched my beautiful, gentle mother be carried away to her grave, the stillborn child she'd given her life for wrapped in her eternal embrace. My mother had been my soft place, the one person who'd understood me. Surely if she were here she would be on my side. A flash flood of loneliness roared though me, but just as swiftly I swept it aside. She was not here to stand up for me, so I must do it for myself.

"You should end this, Malakhi."

He responded with a stretch of silence so long that I searched his countenance with elevated hopes. But then he took those hopes and destroyed them as thoroughly as if he'd tossed them over the wall of Kedesh to the rocks below.

"No. I will fulfill my duty to my brother," he said, the depth of his voice belying his youth.

"Your duty," I repeated.

"Of course. I loved my brother, Rivkah."

"This is no reason for us to be trapped together for a lifetime, making each other miserable."

A hint of a grin curved his lips, and his eyes took on a distinctively mischievous glint. "We won't be miserable."

I scoffed. "You and I are oil and water. We have despised each other since we were children. Misery is all but guaranteed."

His playful expression dissipated. "I don't . . . I've never despised you."

I waved a hand. "Indifference is the opposite side of the same stream." His eyebrows came together in a swift move that I would interpret as a flinch on anyone besides Malakhi. "And I have no interest in being a wife who sits at home while her husband makes of fool of her with other women."

Now he did recoil. "I would never—"

"Oh, spare me your protest. You are the most faithless person I've ever known. You cannot sit still for an hour. You were forever running off on Gidal when he needed your help. There is not a female form you don't ogle." I waved a hand at his all-too-handsome visage. "And none of those females would turn you away from their door and you know it. Your brother I trusted to be loyal. But you"—I scoffed—"you won't last a month."

I'd seen Malakhi arrogant before. I'd seen him excited and carefree and petulant when he did not get his way, but I'd never seen him so stricken, unable to form words on that glib tongue of his. The sight of it was nearly enough to make me apologize for my harshness. Instead, I plowed forward, his gaping mouth and blank eyes assuring me of victory. "Surely this cannot be what you want either."

He said nothing, his attention seeming to have been drawn away by the sight of his mother and father across the courtyard, their heads close together. Darek's hand was on his wife's hip as she spoke, his gaze intent on her face. Among the many marriages arranged by parents eager to secure tribal connections or familial ties, theirs stood as a testament to steadfast love that crossed impossible barriers, withstood the test of time, and weathered storms, separation, and heartache. How the two of them could even stay upright, could walk through this day that seemed such an affront to the son they'd lost, was far beyond my comprehension.

"This betrothal *is* what I want," he said. "We will be married. We will honor Gidal, and I will never be unfaithful to you. To do so would be the same as treading on my brother's grave." I'd not dreamed that Malakhi would consider this travesty as truly honoring to his brother.

"And someday . . ." His sober expression transformed into that same smile he'd given those girls before the ceremony—the one I'd imagined myself impervious to, and yet caused a flicker of something traitorous in my pulse. His gaze traveled back to his mother and father, their focused attention on each other as intimate as any embrace. "Someday you'll look at me just like that."

◆ ◆ ◆

How dare he refuse to release me.

I fumed as I took down the name of the farmer in front of me on a sheet of papyrus with neat, compact marks, along with the amount of produce he'd brought to the Levites as yearly tithe. Then I directed the man to take the baskets into the storehouse, even as I continued muttering to myself about Malakhi's audacity. It had been over two weeks since the betrothal ceremony, and I'd not seen much of him. Ignoring my plea, he acted as though we'd never even had the conversation in the first place and instead offered me knowing smiles that suggested I would all too soon capitulate to his charm. Without looking up, I gestured for the last person in line to join me under the black goat-hair canopy where I'd been writing names and cataloging offerings all afternoon.

From the moment I'd discovered the magic of written symbols I'd been smitten. I'd spent my early childhood watching my father craft words from a mysterious series of lines and curves as he tended to the administration of Kedesh, and eventually he'd given in to my pleas and taught me as well. The dance of ink over finely woven plant fibers became an act of worship, a connection to the Creator of language himself, especially when the words of a new song spilled from my heart onto a sheet of papyrus. But I rarely indulged in that pastime anymore. Singing only made my heart ache for my mother, and as much as I enjoyed serving as a scribe for my father, I'd been inordinately tired lately, both in body and soul. I massaged the ink-stained crook of my thumb, glad that the offering line had dwindled and my job was nearly complete.

A waterfall of multicolored apples thudded to the ground in front of me, bouncing in the dirt and rolling in every direction. A young woman about my age knelt down to retrieve her fruit, uttering a low curse. Setting aside my scribing tools and the slab of olive wood that served as my writing surface, I reached to help her toss the red and yellow globes back into her basket.

"Thank you," she said as she pushed her thick dark braid back over her shoulder with an exaggerated sigh. "My cousins were supposed to carry this for me, but as usual they've taken off somewhere." She scowled as she scanned the marketplace surrounding us. "I don't know why my father trusts them to accompany me into the city. I could be kidnapped and sold to Egypt and they most likely wouldn't notice for days." Once her basket was set back to rights, she sat back on her heels, a bright smile on her lips. "I've never met a woman scribe before."

"Neither have I," I said. "But my father is the head priest of Kedesh. He taught me." A small bubble of pride welled up. Once I'd become proficient in my own language, I'd focused on learning Egyptian and other trade languages as well, some that not even the Levites who'd been trained under my father could decipher. I'd even begged Sofea, Eitan's wife, to teach me to speak the language of her people from across the Great Sea.

"Your father is the head priest here?"

"He is. As was my grandfather Dov before him." My oldest brother, Tal, would succeed my father when his time of service was over.

"I'm Nessa," she said. "I live down in the valley." She waved a hand toward the east, where farms and orchards covered the fertile basin around a shining blue lake. She must be from one of the ever-expanding clans who'd settled there over the thirty years since we'd come into the Land of Promise.

"Rivkah." I offered her a smile as she folded herself down on the ground in front of me. She reached into her basket and handed me a golden apple. Since she was the last person in line and my stomach growled at the delicate scent of the fruit, I accepted with a nod of gratitude.

"I am glad to meet you, Rivkah," she said as she waved her own apple toward the headscarf that covered my hair, indicating that I was no longer a maiden. "Does your husband approve of you working as a scribe?"

My teeth ground together. "I am a widow."

Her brow furrowed with pity. "May his memory long endure. How long ago?"

"Not yet two months." I twisted the stem off the apple with an aggressive flick of my wrist. "But I am already betrothed to another."

"Oh?" Her eyes widened. "Who are you to marry?"

"My husband's brother."

Her jaw gaped. "You are to be given in *levirate* marriage?"

I let my grimace respond for me and bit into the apple with a satisfying crunch.

"You are upset over this arrangement? Is this brother cruel?"

Although it was tempting to exaggerate, I acknowledged the truth. "No. Aggravating, but not malicious."

"Ah, then he is ugly?" Her dark brown eyes twinkled in mock sympathy. My mind wandered back to the other night, when Malakhi had been seated all too close and the shiver of awareness I'd felt as his strange silvery eyes had been trained on me. He'd not seemed a boy in that moment, but rather a young man with an inexplicable draw that he knew how to wield on women. On me. Not trusting myself to utter the words "extremely handsome" out loud, I shook my head.

"Then why do you seem so hesitant to marry him?"

I had few friends in this town. Either they avoided the daughter of the head priest, as if association with me was somehow distasteful, or they feigned friendship with me to garner favor. And ever since my mother had died, I'd avoided even the friends I'd had before, annoyed by both their overwrought tears or awkward words of sympathy. Strangely, only Malakhi had treated me no differently than before I'd lost the most important person in my life, becoming even more of a nuisance instead of acting as if I were some fragile rose petal. But this girl had no preconceived notions about me or my family—or Malakhi's, for that matter. So I told her about how my father was deaf to my arguments, insisting it was to my benefit that I marry a boy who'd given me so much grief over the years.

"My own father recently announced that I too will be wed," said Nessa. "To some ancient, toothless farmer."

"Have you voiced your opinion of the match?"

"My father cares nothing about who he marries me off to." Her deep brown eyes went as dark as obsidian. "The man need only be willing to take me off his hands and out of his house."

Somehow I sensed that beneath the razor-edged words ran a deep vein of sadness, as if this was not the first time Nessa had felt like an unnecessary appendage. "Surely he values you enough to make sure you are well cared for?"

"I am not a son and therefore of little worth to him."

The bleak words touched a tender spot in my soul, making me feel an instant kinship with this girl I'd only just met. "What can either of us do?" I asked. "All authority lies with our fathers, and then, when the time comes, our husbands."

"But your betrothed can still change his mind, isn't that true?"

"Yes, he could appeal to the council of elders at the city gates and release me." Although the severing of the betrothal would be akin to a writ of divorce and likely rule out any future marriage prospects, at least I'd be free.

"Then perhaps . . ." She stood, tossing her apple core toward a goat tied up nearby, then hauled her basket of apples to her hip. "You could do what I plan to do when I meet this 'grandfather' my abba plans to sell me off to during the Festival of Sukkot in a few weeks. You can *show* him just how ill-matched you are." Her little grin was pure mischief, a stark change from the gravity of her expression as she spoke of her father. "I'd best deliver these apples to the storehouse and then return home before the sun goes down. I'd like to make it back before my cousins realize I am gone or my aunt will give them no end of grief for leaving me unescorted."

I laughed as she winked and walked away. It was not until she'd disappeared from sight that I realized I'd forgotten to take down her family name and the amount of her offering. But hopefully I'd see her again soon, for although the conversation had been brief, I'd found encouragement in our shared grievance with our fathers' high-handedness.

As I packed away my inks and reeds, rolled the papyrus, and headed for home, I considered her idea about showing Malakhi that our match would be a disaster. Plans began to form in my mind, and for the first time since my father had announced I would marry again, I felt a small measure of hope.

FOUR

Malakhi

11 Elul

I yanked on the branch, twisting it back and forth until it snapped free. After tossing it atop the pile that had grown all too slowly at the foot of the tree, I brushed slivers from my palms and then wiped the sweat and dirt from my eyes.

Why had Gidal ever found working in the orchard a pleasant occupation? I slid to the ground and leaned back into the shade of one of the larger quince trees that stood in this hidden grove on the hill above Kedesh, closing my eyes against the glare of sunlight overhead. It had been a few hours since I began the arduous task of pruning, and I'd only completed five of the twenty or so bushy trees in this recently harvested grove. I'd much rather be hauling their carcasses into Kedesh for one of Eitan's carpentry projects. This task would take me days, and it was only one of the many varieties of fruit trees my brother had tended around the city over the last few years.

As boys Gidal and I had been inseparable, flitting around Kedesh with the slings Eitan made for us tucked in our belts, racing through the marketplace as if chased by wolves, and, of course, aggravating our sisters and Rivkah. But the older he'd gotten, the more serious he'd become, sometimes disappearing for hours as he puttered in the dirt around tree trunks or tended his beehives. I'd never understood his excitement over crop yields or new fruit varieties brought by traders from far-flung places, nor why he seemed so content to poke around in the soil like a mole.

Rivkah spoke the truth; I had made myself scarce whenever Gidal needed me. In fact, the day he'd surprised a viper coiled beneath a fallen branch, I had brushed off his request for help in favor of hunting with some other young men. It should have been *my* arm that deadly snake sank its fangs into, not Gidal's. Not my solemn, kind, honorable brother. I could not undo my choices that day, could not bring back my best friend, but at least I could tend his fruit trees and keep them alive.

Groaning, I rose to my feet, picked up my iron-toothed handsaw, and once again set myself to the task of shearing off the diseased or damaged limbs from the trees that had recently bowed low to the ground with golden-skinned pomes. If only I'd listened more closely when Gidal described how to ensure the trees would bear the most fruit in the coming year. I had much to learn, but I would do it. For him.

As if conjured by the loud protestations of my empty stomach, Rivkah appeared in the orchard a few hours later, a basket on her hip that I very much hoped was full of food from my mother's kitchen. If I were not all but certain she would slap my face, I would have thrown my arms around my betrothed and kissed her lips at the prospect of a fresh meal.

She regarded me warily as she approached, almost as if she'd divined my thoughts. "What are you doing out here?" she asked.

My brow wrinkled at her odd question. "Tending the orchard."

"But you despise these trees."

I blinked at her astute assessment. "They've been neglected for the past months." I did not point out that it was Gidal's death that had led to their abandonment, but the purse of her mouth told me she heard the silent words all too loudly.

"I brought you some food," she said, holding out the basket with a brusque motion.

My stomach growled in appreciation, so I gave her a warm smile that I hoped might melt the icy expression she maintained. She turned, as if to head back to the city, but I grasped her wrist before she could take a step. "Please stay," I said, desperate to spend more than just a few moments with her. "Eat with me."

Although she twisted her arm from my hold, she nodded, and once I was settled on the ground, folded herself down a couple of paces away. Plucking a twig from the ground, she proceeded to scrawl symbols in the earth, reminding me of the many hours I'd seen her practicing letters on shards of pottery, on rocks, even on strips of bark. I knew only the rudiments of our written language, but her single-minded commitment to learning not only Hebrew but so many strange and foreign tongues only deepened my regard for her.

Reaching into the basket I pulled out two large rounds of bread, still warm from the oven, and breathed deep of the rich smell. I offered her one, but she shook her head. "I made them for you," she said, continuing to scratch lines in the dirt.

"You made this?" Warmth curled in my chest.

She lifted her shoulders in a shrug. "If I am to be your wife, I'd best get used to providing your meals. You eat more than I've ever seen any one man consume."

"My mother says the same thing." I took the bread in both hands, but instead of tearing with steamy ease, it snapped in half like a shard of flint. Flipping it over I realized that although one side of the loaf was gently marked with brown spots, the other was charred black.

I flicked a glance up at Rivkah. She was watching me intently, so I kept my expression even and took a bite. The bread was hard as slate and tasted like a hunk of coal. But she had made this for me, of her own free will, so I refused to hurt her feelings. That would be no way to ease her into a life with me, nor to overcome the obvious reservations she had about our marriage. I chewed the mealy mouthful and then took a great swig from the waterskin she'd brought. The water was tepid, with a slightly gritty aftertaste, but I forced myself to react as if it were the freshest water from the spring nearby.

Reaching into the basket again, I discovered a large bowl of lentils, barley, and chickpeas, seasoned with cumin and coriander, just the way my mother prepared it. Murmuring my appreciation, I used one of the stony pieces of bread to scoop the fragrant concoction into my mouth. The instant it hit my tongue, I sucked in a breath through my nose.

Salt. So much salt that it nearly brought tears to my eyes.

But it was either spit out the foul mouthful or brazen it out for Rivkah's sake. I chose her. Keeping my mind on the prize of her affection, I ate the awful mixture, drinking tepid water every few bites to rinse the layer of brine from my battered tongue. Had she always been such a terrible cook? I did not remember Gidal complaining of it, but my brother was the best of men, full of magnanimous grace. He would never shame his wife by voicing such a thing, so I vowed to do the same.

She sprang to her feet, turning away from me as she scanned the orchard, then tugged absently on one of the leafy branches. "Do you even know how to maintain quince trees?"

I restrained the impulse to bristle at her sharp question. "Gidal taught me which branches need pruning after harvest. And I am certainly capable of cleaning away the brush and weeds." To my relief there were three green apples in the bottom of the basket, along with a hunk of soft cheese and some olives. Nothing that Rivkah could ruin. I nearly sighed with relief at the burst of tart flesh in my mouth as I bit into one of the apples.

"Cultivating fruit is far more complicated than simply pruning and weeding," she snapped. "Your brother was forever going on about the challenges involved. Since you refused to help him out here, I doubt you learned enough to follow in his footsteps."

Stricken by her insult, I chewed thoroughly and swallowed the bite of apple before responding with a measured tone. "Perhaps I listened more than you realize. I—"

She cut me off with a shake of her head. "Why don't you let one of the men deal with this grove?"

I felt the blood drain from my face. *One of the men.* Which meant that in her estimation I was not to be counted among them. She considered me a child. I squared my shoulders, feeling a swift defense of my maturity surging forward. I may only be nearing my seventeenth year, but I had been working alongside Eitan for years now, forging weapons, crafting tools, felling trees, and swinging an adze with proficiency. And my father had been training me in the art of war and stealth since I was fourteen. I could wield a sword as well as many of the soldiers in his command, if not better, and had a talent for spying that rivaled his own. I was no mere boy.

But just as I opened my mouth to plead my case, I remembered the grief on her face during the betrothal ceremony, the way she so bravely held her body still as the ketubah was read, and the way she questioned my resolve to honor both my brother and the Torah by caring for his widow.

So instead I smiled at her, popped a couple of olives in my mouth, and then worked to keep my voice soft. "Whatever I do not know I will learn. You are right that I was not attentive enough to my brother's tutelage, but I will do my best to maintain his trees and continue his work. Following in his footsteps, no matter how unworthy I am to do so, will be an honor." My response seemed to shock her. Her mouth gaped for a moment before she rolled her eyes skyward and huffed out an exasperated groan. "Fine. I'll leave you to it," she bit out. Then she whirled around and stalked off, forgetting the empty basket on the ground.

I kept my eyes pinned on the woman who would soon be my wife as she strode toward the city like a soldier bent on breaching the walls. Obviously, I had much to prove to her and a long way to go before I could break down her defenses, but much as I vowed to learn the secrets of Gidal's orchards, I would learn hers as well. I would work to clear away the thorny weeds of our childhood and tend our marriage with the same attention I would give a delicate sapling. Even if she never loved me like she had my brother, I would do my best to earn her trust and respect.

And thankfully, my mother was the best cook in the entire city—perhaps in all of the tribe of Naftali. Surely Rivkah would glean some skills from her along the way. As I turned back to the never-ending task of pruning the quince trees, her meal laying like a mud-brick in my stomach and the taste of ash still on my tongue, I fervently prayed it would be so.

FIVE

Rivkah

I clamped my lips together until I was well out of Malakhi's hearing before releasing the hard spurt of laugher I'd been suppressing. It must have taken a will of iron to choke down that lump of char. A note of begrudging admiration for my betrothed's newfound restraint struck me. The boy I'd known my entire life would have spat it out, wiped his mouth with his arm, and then mocked my cooking skills. I'd been braced for just such a reaction, ready to make it clear I had little intention of putting forth any great effort into preparing meals for him. And yet to my great surprise, he'd accepted my burnt offerings without complaint. And he'd been almost *honorable* in his determination to continue Gidal's work in the orchards. But whether or not he had gained a modicum of maturity over the years, it did nothing to change my opinion about this marriage.

Lost in my thoughts, I'd nearly forgotten that the women of Malakhi's family were gathered at the stream to launder clothing and bedding and that I was expected to join them. I shifted my course away from the city gates to search them out among those filling waterskins and washing in the sweet water that flowed from the spring deep beneath the foundations of Kedesh.

"Did Malakhi enjoy his meal?" Moriyah asked as I approached the place where she and her daughters knelt by the stream. Not pausing for my answer, she returned to her task, her strong arms and capable hands making easy work of scrubbing one of Darek's tunics. "That boy eats even more than Eitan ever did. I am sure it won't be long before he's under my feet asking for more, but hopefully you gave him enough to stave off his ravenous hunger . . . for an hour or two." Her easy laughter made it clear that she hadn't suspected my scheme against her son. She would be horrified that I'd ruined her lovingly prepared food when her back was turned, but I had to induce him to break the betrothal by whatever means necessary.

The girls laughed too, well acquainted with Malakhi's unparalleled appetite, then delved back into discussing when Darek and his men would return from whatever mission they were on at the moment. Disinterested with chatter of soldiers, spies, and enemies, I let the words fade into the background as I retrieved a tunic from the basket between them and knelt on a flat rock at the water's edge, putting my hands to work scrubbing the grime and soot from the filthy garment.

Three small boys with light brown hair and a multitude of freckles between them bounded into the stream, sending up a spray of cold water that soaked the front of my dress and dripped from my eyelashes. "Boys, do not splash the ladies!" Sofea called out as she approached with her tiny daughter on one hip, her rounded belly causing an uneven gait. Although it had been years since she'd learned Hebrew, her lilting accent always strengthened when she was frustrated with her active brood. "And stay near the edge or you'll get swept downstream!"

She repeated the warning in her original language, which always made the threat more substantial, and added a command to greet their grandmother. They sheepishly sloshed back to the bank, where Moriyah offered each an exuberant kiss and a fresh date roll from a basket tucked near the roots of a nearby willow tree. Collecting a few fallen willow branches, they set off to explore with Tirzah, Malakhi's youngest sister, who seemed to much prefer playing with wooden swords and climbing trees with the boys to spending time with girls her own age.

"I apologize for the dousing," Sofea said to us as she handed her daughter to Moriyah and rubbed the small of her back. "And I would have been along to help sooner but the boys begged to help their father sand a cedar beam, so it took much longer than I expected. And of course once I let Eitan hold Mari he refused to give her up."

"That man is smitten," said Moriyah, nibbling her granddaughter's fingers, which instigated a shrieking laugh from the two-year-old.

"That he is." Sofea grinned, running her fingers through Mari's soft curls. "And he insists that this next one will be another girl for him to dote on as well."

Sofea's daughter had the same golden-brown hair and blue eyes that made her mother stand out among the mostly dark-haired, dark-eyed Hebrews. It was said that Eitan had been enraptured by her from the moment she walked into the inn after being rescued by Darek and his men during one of their missions. And from the way the two of them still gazed at each other as if they were newly married, nothing much had changed. Of course they were a rarity, a match formed by mutual admiration, *not* by machinations of overbearing fathers.

Grabbing another soiled garment, Sofea knelt next to me with surprising grace for a small woman heavy with child and began scrubbing at the cloth with a smooth stone. "Malakhi was not at the foundry. Where has he taken himself off to today?"

Brushing the wet hair from my eyes with the back of my hand, I waved back toward the grove. "Up there on the ridge with Gidal's trees."

Her delicate brows arched as she followed the direction of my gesture. "Oh?"

"Apparently he's decided to care for the orchards." I allowed skepticism to color my tone.

"He has? I thought he had no interest in them."

I picked up a stone and focused on a particularly deep-set charcoal stain instead of meeting her curious gaze. "He thinks to take up Gidal's work as a tribute."

Sofea placed a dripping hand on her chest. Tears seemed to choke off her words until she cleared her throat. "How lovely. I can think of no better way for Malakhi to honor his brother's memory."

Resentment flared. "Aside from filling my belly with an heir to continue his line, of course," I mumbled.

Sofea's blue eyes went round at my crass retort, and my face burned with regret that I'd spoken such a thought out loud. But I held back the apology that leapt to my tongue and scrubbed harder at the tunic.

After a tense silence, Abra let out a sudden chuckle. "Remember when Gidal and Malakhi ate almost an entire basket of figs?"

Sofea nodded, her eyes sparkling with humor. "Oh yes! Right after Eitan and I married. And their bellies were so sick! I've never seen little boys turn that particular shade of green."

Moriyah joined in the laughter as she bounced Mari in her arms. "I figured they earned their own natural discipline after that poor decision."

"But Malakhi insisted on taking the blame, remember, Ima?" said Abra. "Even though they snuck the basket into their room together, he vowed over and over that it had been his idea alone. He always did that, even though I know for certain that Gidal was no innocent in their mischief."

"No, he certainly was not," said Moriyah, her tone wryly wistful for her firstborn. "Even if he was the quieter of the two, and not nearly as reckless, he had his moments of disobedience. But you are correct in that, more often than not, Malakhi usually stepped forward to accept responsibility for whatever trouble they'd gotten themselves into."

"He may have been reckless," said Abra, "but there was that time they climbed to the top of the storehouse—"

"Oh!" Chana interrupted. "I remember that! And Gidal was so scared that he refused to come down. But Malakhi stayed with him, talked him through each step, and gripped his tunic so he would feel secure." Pride shone on her round face. "He didn't even seem frightened at all, even though one of the Levites had fallen from that very place a year before while mending the roof and had broken both of his legs."

"I thought my own ribs would shatter from the pounding of my heart as those two scoundrels descended," said Moriyah with a grimace. "And your father had much to say when their feet hit the ground. But after I began breathing again, I was ever so proud of my Malakhi for watching over Gidal that day."

Annoyed and still flushed with embarrassment for my ill-timed remark, I kept my eyes locked on my task as the women reminisced about Malakhi's more valiant deeds, including the way he'd saved two of his nephews from a runaway steer in the marketplace by throwing himself in its path, and the time he shimmied into a small dark cave to rescue a trapped goat. Of course I smiled appropriately and murmured affirmations of his bravery, but my frustrations grew with every scrape of rock against wool. When they finally moved on to stories about Eitan's childhood escapades, I wrung the garment tightly, enjoying the release of violently wrenching the fabric in my fists.

Although none of the women had breathed a word of censure, or even directed a look of scorn in my direction, their message echoed like a shofar at dawn. They acknowledged Malakhi's failings but would tolerate none of *my* opinions about their beloved son and brother.

I had no ally among these women, nor even among those in my own family. Lailah lauded my father's commands as the height of wisdom and chided me whenever I had the audacity to speak my mind. Prezi, Tal's wife, was the most gracious of women and would never say a contrary word to anyone, let alone my father, whom she revered. And my mother, the only person who'd ever understood me, truly saw me, was gone. I could rely on no one but myself in this fight.

Shaking out the tunic, I lifted it high to check my progress. It was then that I realized that I held one of Malakhi's garments in my hands, one sullied by soot, charcoal, and wood-pitch from his work in the foundry. Glancing around to ensure that none of the others were watching, I plunged the tunic back into the water, felt around on the stream bed for a sharp-edged stone, and renewed my task with a vigor that I hoped no one would take note of.

Malakhi may have charmed the women in his life into championing him, but I would make him understand that I would not be the fawning, compliant wife he undoubtedly imagined. He'd not walk to the elders and beg for release from the betrothal—he would run.

◆ ◆ ◆

Nessa, the girl I'd met in the tithing line, reappeared numerous times as I took down tithes over the next three weeks. Joining me beneath my canopy as she waited for her cousins to barter in the market, she became something of a confidante, as well as a collaborator in my underhanded plots. She'd laughed until tears rolled down her cheeks as I related the sight of Malakhi's face as he choked down the burnt bread and strained to swallow the over-salted lentils. She'd gasped in mock horror as I described the holes I'd ground into his tunic with my sharp stone and applauded when I told how I'd used one of his favorite obsidian knives to saw through a tree branch, leaving it shattered beyond repair. And, like me, she marveled that in spite of everything I'd done, Malakhi refused to walk away.

I'd been hoping Nessa would appear today, anxious to tell her how I offered to cut Eitan and Malakhi's hair yesterday, since Sofea had been suffering in bed with ever-lengthening contractions. I'd left Eitan with a neat trim just below his ears and my betrothed with a lopsided shearing that forced him to cut the remainder of his black waves nearly to his scalp.

But unlike before, when she'd appeared in the afternoons to sit beside me as I worked, this morning she was first in line, holding a basket half full of bruised apples that were nowhere near acceptable as an offering. It looked as if she'd simply taken whatever she could find as an excuse to seek me out.

I took one look at the stricken expression on her face, packed up my scribal tools, and asked a young Levite to take my place, pleading illness. I then followed my friend around the corner and into an alley, all humor at Malakhi's expense dissipated.

"I am leaving," she said, her jaw set like granite and eyes sharp as obsidian. "I will not stay here. I will not lie down and accept these dictates from my father any longer. He won't even notice I am gone, since he barely looks at me now." The vibrant girl with whom I'd found a kinship over these past weeks, usually so easy to laugh and quick with a jest, had been replaced by a hardened woman.

"What happened, Nessa?"

"I dared question my father's choice of husband," she said, her back stiff and her tone oddly detached.

"And he refused to listen?"

"He said he fought alongside the man for years and that I would do well to marry a man of such *honor*." She sneered at the word. "Not only is he old, nearly twenty years my senior, but he's a widower with four sons. Four! I would be nothing but a servant to the children of his dead wife and a breeding sow for more of his brats. But when I said as much, my father became enraged, screaming that I would marry whomever *he* chose and that silver had already exchanged hands—as if I were no more than an omer of barley."

I slung my arms around her and pulled her close. "Oh, my friend, I am so sorry."

She shrugged me off. "I am leaving in three days. There is a festival in Laish and I mean to find work with some of the tradesmen there. I have been bartering for three years now in that city for my father, so I have friends there. And I know how to drive a hard bargain. How to make myself useful."

"But you cannot go alone."

"My cousins Yoash and Kefa have agreed to accompany me. Of course they think we are only sneaking away to attend the festival, but we can easily escape them and hide until they leave."

"We?"

She pinned me with a determined look. "Come with me, Rivkah. If you don't you'll have to marry that awful boy. You'll wither away and never know what it's like to be free. I've traveled to Laish, and I know your skills as a scribe would be valuable there. You could make your *own* wealth, choose your *own* destiny. No one could make you marry unless *you* chose to do so. You'd finally be out from beneath the thumb of your father—of any man. You can go where you want, when you want."

The picture she painted was a wild one. One I'd never even thought to consider before. To thwart my father's authority and step out from beneath his protection, and that of Gidal's family, would be the greatest of risks. I stood blinking at her like a fool, mouth agape. "But my family . . . I could not walk away from them. . . ."

"It need not be forever. Stay away for a few months, perhaps a year. Malakhi will marry someone else and then you can return, if you so choose."

"But isn't it dangerous?"

She swept away my concerns with a flip of her hand. "It's only a few hours' walk from here, and the people of Laish are known as peaceful. They tolerate everyone regardless of heritage or allegiance as long as they have goods to trade and don't create problems for others. Many Hebrews live there too. We will find good people to work for. My friends can give us direction. They'll watch out for us." ·

"I don't know. . . ."

"Please!" She gripped my hands, her expression a desperate entreaty. "I don't want to go alone, but I will if I have to. I cannot marry that ugly old grandfather, no matter what my father says."

My thoughts jumbled together in a heap. "I must think on it. I am not sure I can—"

She ignored my indecision. "I am leaving on the fifth day of the week, at dawn. I'll wait for you at the farthest boulder on the boundary line near the olive grove. If you aren't there, I will take that for your answer. But please, Rivkah. Come with me. Let's make our own path."

CHAPTER
SIX

Malakhi

With her head bent over her work, Rivkah's long, graceful fingers gripped the reed pen. I followed their swift, yet precise movements as they flicked over the papyrus to detail each farmer's tithe as they approached the head of the line.

When I was a boy, the crowd of people bringing portions of their goods on days like these stretched nearly fifty deep, but every year the lines were shorter, the baskets smaller, and the stock less robust. For the Levites who depended on the tithe to sustain themselves and their families, the trend was a concerning one indeed. I'd heard rumors that in other Levitical cities the situation was truly desperate, and some were forced to abandon their homes to seek out a trade or watch their families starve. The more prosperous we'd grown, the less generous we'd become with those who'd been appointed to serve Yahweh and were therefore unable to inherit land of their own.

Rivkah pointed to the storehouse behind her, directing a man to carry his basket of goods to the Levites inside, and then, as if she'd suddenly sensed my presence, her attention snapped to me. Her brows drew together in displeasure before she gestured for the next person in line to approach. What I wouldn't do to have her offer *me* a welcome like she did the strangers in her line. Even the toothless old man carrying a braying brown-speckled goat in his arms received a kind greeting and a semblance of a smile. Yes, I had been awful to her as a boy, but nothing I'd done since would warrant the tricks she'd been playing on me since our betrothal.

I could tolerate a few holes in my tunic, a broken knife, and even the shearing of my head, but today Eitan had seen me trying to choke down yet another meal Rivkah had delivered to the foundry and revealed—after he'd stopped laughing—that in no way was Rivkah a terrible cook and it was obvious she'd been ruining my food on purpose. She'd deliberately made me look a fool in front of my brother. My future bride was much wilier than I'd given her credit for, but I intended to find out exactly why she'd been inflicting such mischief.

She continued to ignore me, taking each man in turn without looking my way again, but the stiff set to her shoulders did not soften. She gripped her reed with near vehemence, attending to her task with militaristic precision. She was determined, but I would wait her out. I would never give in—and she knew it. The cord of tension vibrated between us like a plucked string. She may not be watching me, but she was just as focused on my presence as I was on hers.

However, the awareness between us was sliced in two the moment her father appeared at her side. Amitai patted her shoulder and then pointed at something on her list, asking a few questions. When I shifted my position against the wall, the movement somehow snagged the priest's attention. With a pointed lift of his heavy brows toward his daughter, he gestured at me. Rivkah's lips pursed and she shook her head. A swift, near-silent argument happened between the two of them and then, to my surprise, Rivkah stood and followed her father. I pushed away from the wall, straightening as the honored leader of our city approached. I'd known Amitai my entire life, and although he was nothing but kind, in truth he'd always intimidated me—and even more so now that he was to be my father by marriage.

He reached to grip my shoulder with a firm paternal grasp. "Shalom, Malakhi. Has Sofea given birth yet?"

"No, but Ima says her time is close. Eitan was so distracted in the foundry he hammered his fingers twice. I insisted he go home."

"Ah yes. I remember well those uncertain days of waiting for my own children's births. So, you've come to visit your betrothed, I gather." He glanced back at his blank-faced daughter, who seemed more interested in the milling crowd of the marketplace than the conversation between her father and me.

"Yes." I cleared my throat, hoping she would not notice the warble of my voice. "I thought to walk her home when she finished for the day."

"Excellent," said her father. He reached over and nudged Rivkah toward me. "She is finished now."

Rivkah was skilled at keeping her face devoid of emotion, but I knew every twitch of her lips, every quirk of her brow, every flutter of her sooty lashes, and fury was in every single one of them. Any thought of confronting her treachery was obliterated from my mind. I did not want to push her away further. I simply wanted to understand why.

Without a word, Rivkah stalked off toward home, head high and stride long, obviously determined to get as far away as possible. Was the prospect of marriage to me truly so abhorrent? Was I so lacking that she thought nothing of making a fool of me? I'd thought I could persuade her, show her the esteem I held for her, and prove that I'd provide and care for her as well as Gidal had done. But if she was this set against our union, then what profit was there in holding on? The thought of asking the elders to free me from the commitment I'd pledged leached the strength from my bones. I placed my palm against the mud-brick of the building beside me to steady myself. Perhaps I *should* set her free after all.

"I know she can be difficult," said Amitai, as if he'd heard my conflicted thoughts. His gaze was full of understanding and compassion. "She's quiet but headstrong, as you well know. And after her mother died I thought I'd never see her smile again. But she is worth the effort, son. *You* are what she needs, even if she does not see it now."

I remembered the days when Rivkah smiled and laughed freely, sometimes even paid back my brotherly teasing with taunts of her own when she played games with Gidal, Abra, and me, before her mother's loss hovered over her like a constant death-shroud. What would it take to get her to laugh with me again?

Amitai tipped his head toward the direction she'd fled. "Don't let her get away."

After a swift farewell, I ran to seek her out in the marketplace, where she seemed to have gotten distracted from her mission to escape me. Although she gave an admirable show of pretending I did not exist when I finally caught up to her, I was given fresh determination by Amitai's encouragement and stayed by her side as she explored the stalls. All around us, the bustle of commerce stirred the air. What had started out a desolate market when my mother first came to live here nearly twenty years ago had blossomed into rows of teeming trade. Caravans from Damascus, Tyre, and even as far as Egypt and Hattusa crossed through our city now, bringing with them a cacophony of languages and a wide assortment of foreign goods.

Rivkah stopped to converse with a Mitanni trader. A slender mahogany box with a row of blossoming trees carved into the lid had caught her eye. Her clever fingers slid over the design in reverent exploration before she lifted the top to reveal five small alabaster inkpots. Opening each one in turn, she lifted them to her nose. Then she dipped the tip of her smallest finger into the last and smudged the iridescent green color across her palm before asking another question of the man. Nodding her satisfaction at whatever answer he gave, she closed the pot and replaced the lid, then with a gesture of thanks, walked on, weaving through the mass of bodies as she headed toward the inn with me in her wake.

"What were those dyes made from?" I asked, returning to her side. "I've never seen such brilliant colors."

She did not respond and kept her eyes trained ahead, as if my words were merely a brush of wind against her ear. She would likely keep silent until she reached the inn unless I gave a nudge toward provocation.

"Leaves of some sort, dried and ground into powder?" I nodded my head, as if impressed with my own conclusion. "Yes, that must be it. . . . But what kind of plant dye could be that bright? A grape vine? A root of some sort?"

Handing me an easy victory, she groaned at my ignorance and stopped to glare at me. "It's malachite. The ink was made from finely ground copper ore. No color from a plant could be so rich." She lifted her palm, tilting the glittering streak back and forth in the sunlight.

Pulling together every bit of courage I possessed, I reached for her wrist and bent to examine the swipe of color across her skin. "Hmm. Yes, I see it now," I said, determined to keep my tone unaffected even while my heart pounded like a signal drum and fire coated my veins. My hand curled around her wrist, shackling it gently as I brushed a finger along the green line. Beneath my thumb, her pulse fluttered and she seemed to be holding her breath. I lifted my eyes to hers and held the gaze, unwilling to relinquish the simple pleasure of touching her.

After a few delicious but fleeting moments, Rivkah twisted her arm away from my grasp. "You need not walk any farther with me. I am sure you have much to do." Her voice was hushed, nearly lost in the melee of the market.

"When Eitan went to be with Sofea, I closed up the foundry for the day so I could come see you. I wanted to talk—"

"So you've abandoned Gidal's trees already, have you?" The interruption was knife-edged, but I ignored the cut.

"Actually, I do have something that needs tending in the grove today. . . ." I looked up, gauging the angle of the sun in the sky. "And there is something I'd like to show you as well. A surprise."

"What?" Suspicion colored her tone.

"You'll see." I smiled, savoring the look of interest that had stolen into her amber eyes, and lifted a note of challenge into my entreaty. "Come. You know you are curious."

She pursed her mouth, seeming to dig in her heels.

"It will be worth it, I assure you." Opting for an underhanded tactic, I took a few steps back toward the storehouse. "Shall I ask your father first?"

"No." She released a huff of annoyance. "That isn't necessary. I'll come."

Smothering a grin of satisfaction, I walked away, only the smallest bit repentant that I'd goaded her into following me out of the gates of Kedesh.

"Well?" she said as I led her up the western ridge and into the quince grove. "Why have you dragged me out here? The sun will be going down soon. I should help your mother with the evening meal." Her lips were still pressed together in a tight line. She was either unimpressed or simply did not notice all the progress I'd made over the past weeks.

Pride pricked by her dismissal, I took a moment to survey my own handiwork and was filled with surprising satisfaction at the sight of the well-pruned grove, now devoid of underbrush and stray saplings. Perhaps Gidal's obsession with his trees was not so incomprehensible after all.

"This is why I brought you here." Pulling back a few branches to open a path, I led her into a small hidden clearing at the very center of the grove. I gestured to the three mounds there that I'd painstakingly reconstructed from straw and mud. A lifted brow was her only response.

"Gidal had been working to establish these hives for nearly two years, and they'd finally started producing. But when he . . ." I paused, the truth still so painful to speak aloud. "When he died, they were forgotten and left out here during those storms last month. They should have been brought into the shelter." I was ashamed that it had taken me until recently to remember the hives. Gidal would have been horrified to see his hard work had been undone by heavy rainfall and his once-thriving colonies abandoned.

"One of the Levites is the grandson of a master beekeeper from back in Egypt. From the wealth of knowledge he gleaned from his grandfather's stories, knowledge passed down through the generations and then carried through the wilderness into the Land of Promise, he taught Gidal the art of beekeeping. The same man showed me how to restore them."

"I've never heard of such a thing," she said. "Can one tend bees like one tends a herd of sheep?"

I laughed at the imagery. "I had not either. But one of the few things I do remember Gidal telling me was that whenever honeybees are near fruit trees, those trees seem to be more productive, although he did not know why. My mother will be thrilled to have access to fresh honey this summer if I can entice the bees to repopulate the hives."

She murmured her agreement but glanced back toward the city, looking anxious to return.

"The bread you brought me last week might have benefitted from some honey, don't you agree?" I said. "If only to make that charred mess a bit more appetizing."

Her attention whipped back to me, immediately defensive. "Are you mocking my cooking skills?"

"Not at all." I widened my eyes in false innocence. "I am lauding your skill as a mischief-maker. I didn't know you had it in you anymore." Although she did not say anything and her face remained remarkably blank, the tiniest corner of her mouth twitched.

"Truly, you are a master." I dipped my chin, a palm to my chest in a gesture of homage. "If Eitan hadn't revealed that your cooking skills are perfectly respectable, you might have succeeded in dragging out the ruse for a week or two more. I'd gotten quite adept at holding my breath while partaking of your meals—when they were actually edible."

I stepped closer, the amusement in her eyes making me bolder. "Although nothing could salvage that vileness you called 'fish stew.'" The concoction had been little more than a few paltry hunks of dried fish, green olives, and some bland root vegetable boiled to death in vinegar. "I'm known for being willing to eat anything that is placed in front of me, but even *I* would not put that slime in my mouth." Just the reminder of the atrocious smell that had emanated from the dish made me shudder.

She rolled her lips inward, a paltry attempt at disguising the humor she'd been squelching, but a sudden bubble of laughter betrayed her before she could slap a palm over her mouth. Her body trembled, and she squeezed her eyes shut, tears forming at the corners. I could do nothing to restrain the sharp burst of laughter that practically exploded from my mouth.

At the same moment, and for the first time in my memory since her mother had died, Rivkah actually let go. She tipped her head back and laughed with gusto, the sound so full and lovely that my own amusement crashed to a halt and I could do nothing but stare. The notes of her laughter twirled through the air like butterflies alight on the breeze.

It did not matter that she'd been trying to push me away, or that'd she'd made a fool of me to do so. It did not matter that my brother had married her first. All I could see were rosy lips, smooth honeyed skin, and amber eyes sparkling with unshed tears of mirth.

The sharp-witted, vibrant girl I'd played with as a boy had trans-formed into this beautiful, brilliant woman who was soon to be my wife. Every bit of restraint I had dissolved. I slid my arms around her slender waist, pulled her to me, and kissed her, triumph and joy and relief entwining as I explored her lips with mine.

For a brief, weightless moment she allowed the embrace. But then instead of melting into me, or returning my kiss, her body suddenly went rigid, a pillar of resistance in the circle of my arms. With her mouth set like stone, her hands fisted on my chest as she used her forearms to push me away. The laughter in her eyes had been swept aside by outrage so palpable I tripped backward two steps in cowardly retreat.

"Why would you do that?" Her words pressed out through gritted teeth. "I did not give you permission to touch me . . . to kiss me."

Shame lay heavy on my shoulders. Gidal would never have done that to Rivkah, would never have just grabbed her like some animal. My eyes dropped closed. "Please . . ." I choked out, my throat burn-ing. "Forgive me. I had no right. . . ."

"No. You did not. How dare you lure me out here just to paw at me! You *don't* own me. Yet." These last words were tipped with venom.

I lifted my palms in surrender. "No. Please . . . that was not my intention. You must believe me. I only wanted to show you the hives, explain my commitment to building trust between us, just as I did these mounds of mud and straw. I want you to see that I *will* honor my brother's memory and that I will be a good and faithful husband to you, for his sake. I know you are grieving, but in time I hope that something good can come of this." I gestured between the two of us. "I know you loved him—"

"You know nothing of me, Malakhi." She aimed an accusing finger at me. "You are the same spoiled boy you've always been, wanting nothing more than to torment me and get your way. I don't want this. I will *never* want this. I never should have agreed to this in the first place."

She spun around to flee, pushing aside a heavy branch that whipped back and lashed me across the face when I tried to follow. But still she fled, leaving me battered and bleeding among the only remnants of my brother's life, each of her parting footfalls another blow to the dream I'd not deserved, but had foolishly dared to hope for.

SEVEN

Rivkah

I found my father on the roof, on his knees. Bent in supplication toward the south, he faced Shiloh, where the Mishkan resided with the tablets of the Covenant at its heart. For my entire life, this had been his habit at the end of each day, his private prayers accompanying the sun to its resting place. Although normally a silent ritual, this evening his lips moved quickly, his whispers barely audible but full of such strong emotion as his body swayed in rhythm that my arrival went unnoticed.

I'd gone straight to my childhood home from the grove, unwilling to cross Malakhi's path at the inn after I'd left him so abruptly among the trees, but the stricken expression on his face followed me anyhow, as did the memory of that unexpected kiss. . . .

The shock of Malakhi's lips against mine had caused every rational thought to flee, leaving only the traitorous one that found the sensation all too pleasant, the one that called for more. But just as quickly, sense had washed over me, and I'd awakened to the certainty that the embrace was nothing more than another manipulation, an attempt to sway me toward this unwanted marriage. I shuffled my feet, as much to alert my father to my presence as to distract myself from the reminder of those brief moments when my body had nearly betrayed me.

"Rivkah." My father stood. "I was just praying for you."

I startled. It had been *me* he'd be laboring over in prayer with such passion?

"How was your time with Malakhi?" he asked, his smile expectant. "He seems quite taken with you."

Ah, it must have been my capitulation he'd been supplicating for. I scoffed inwardly; not even Yahweh's heavenly host could persuade me to be at peace with this decision. There had been hints in the grove today that perhaps Malakhi had matured beyond what I'd assumed—the way he'd taken my misconduct in stride and how he'd tended to Gidal's trees and rebuilt the hives with such determination. But he'd not changed enough to overcome my misgivings, or the past.

"He is little more than a child," I said.

His dark brows drew together. "He may be younger than you, daughter, but he is no child. He is already well on his way to becoming a warrior. He is fiercely loyal and a hard worker who will provide well for you and your children. And most importantly he is willing—"

"To do your bidding," I interrupted, a shade surprised at my own audacity, for although I'd made it clear the night before my betrothal to Malakhi that I was none too pleased with the arrangement, I'd submitted to my father's authority. "He won't question a command from a priest, nor from his own father."

"Rivkah." The censure in my father's tone made my mouth snap shut. "I understand you have reservations, but I would not have agreed unless I felt that Malakhi would be a good husband to you. And I would be remiss in my duties as a father if I did not ensure you were protected, my girl."

"What dangers are there in this city? This place may harbor manslayers, but there has not been a serious incident of violence here since I was a child."

"That may be true. But you have been surrounded by these high walls your entire life. You are oblivious to the perils outside Kedesh—dangers that you as a woman, as a widow, are far more vulnerable to. There are even rumblings that war may be on the horizon. Malakhi has been training with Darek and Baz for the past two years and is already rumored to have extraordinary skill with a sword. If something happens, I have full confidence that your husband will protect you and your children."

"But—"

"Malakhi also understands the importance of honoring his brother. If he married another woman, his firstborn son would be counted as his own. It is to his credit that he would sacrifice that right in order to ensure Gidal's legacy continues. Yes, he is young, but the simple fact that he would submit to the Torah in this matter shows that he will continue to grow in honor and uprightness."

He pointed downward, where beneath our feet lay the small chamber he and my mother had once shared. "I also have a chest full of silver and jewelry that shows just how much Malakhi and his family esteem you. They did not have to offer such riches a second time, Rivkah. But they wanted to make it clear to us—to you—that they do not consider this some leftover marriage, but a new and valuable union between you and their beloved son. Although the mohar is in my safekeeping for now, if something happens to Malakhi, you would be provided for. This is why I had *you* be the one to write out the ketubah agreement instead of one of my other scribes, so you could see just how treasured you are."

The reminder of Nessa's father bartering her away for silver made my stomach sour. It didn't matter whether my father saw the bridal gifts as some sort of insurance; I'd been purchased like a heifer, and Malakhi would have complete authority over me once he claimed me as his bride. It would be up to him whether I could even continue my scribal duties.

"Am I not a help to you? Can I not just stay here, continue working as a scribe? You can keep Gidal's mohar so I would not be a burden to the household. I vow to be more of a help to Lailah as well—"

He sighed, shaking his head. "This house is already stretching its seams, daughter. With Lailah's family now growing again, there is barely room for all of us as it is. This conversation is a fruitless one anyhow. You already committed yourself to the betrothal in front of many witnesses. You can either choose to struggle against this marriage and make both of you miserable or embrace the gift you have been given and seek joy in your life together. And whether you believe it or not, Malakhi is not entering this marriage solely for the sake of his brother; I see it in the way he looks at you. You are well matched—in truth, much better paired than you and Gidal ever were. I have faith that you will come to believe that in time as well."

I nearly laughed out loud at the absurdity. How could I possibly be compatible with the boy who tormented me nearly every day of my childhood?

"At times you are willful," my father continued, his tone softening as he brushed his callused palm down my cheek. "But you have the capacity to be a good wife to him; a compassionate help-meet for a young man who is still grieving the loss of his brother. You of all people understand what it is to mourn the death of someone you cherish."

He slipped an arm about my shoulders and turned me toward the stairs. "Now, come. Let us cease arguing over a decision that has already been made and join the meal. Your sister has prepared my favorite dish, and I would hate to see it go to waste."

My father would never bend. Would never *hear* me. It had been useless to even try. There was only one choice left that gave me any sort of control over my own future. Tomorrow I would meet Nessa at the boundary and determine my own path.

◆ ◆ ◆

"I did not think you were coming." Nessa's disembodied voice met my ears just as I neared the boundary stone. "We were almost ready to leave."

I peered into the dim, seeing three shadows against the predawn. "I had to wait until the gates opened for the morning," I said. "And also convince the guard that I was merely delivering an urgent message to my sister's husband out among the sheep." Thankfully, my paltry explanation seemed not to have raised suspicions, but I'd held my breath until I'd passed the tree line and was out of sight of the city walls.

Nessa approached, her features gaining clarity with each step. "I am so glad you decided to come!" She gestured at the two large shadows a few paces behind her. "These are Yoash and Kefa, my cousins who will be escorting us to the festival and back."

Nessa had assured me that the two young men were trustworthy, and in fact quite fiercely protective over her, but knowing that we meant to slip away from them at some point put me on edge, so I avoided meeting their eyes as they greeted me.

"We'd best be on our way. It will take us a few hours to walk there, but we should arrive just after the noon hour," said Nessa. "Lead on, cousins."

Yoash and Kefa complied, leading the way through the last of the olive grove and down over the eastern ridge into the basin. Nessa slipped her arm through mine as we trailed in their wake, leaning close to speak. "You've made the right choice, Rivkah. Together we will do well." She squeezed my arm and launched into a multitude of details about Laish from the many times she'd been there before, but I heard little of it. Every step away from Kedesh felt like fighting against a rushing river. I could practically feel my home calling, beckoning me to return.

However, my mind turned to the meal with my family the night before. My siblings and their spouses and children had all been there, filling the house with animation and good-natured banter. But as much as I loved them all, not one of them noticed that I barely spoke, or that I'd slipped out to my father's chamber halfway through the meal to collect Gidal's mohar—a large number of silver pieces, three copper rings, and a beautiful lapis lazuli necklace that looked to have originated in Egypt. The secret weight of it in the leather purse I wore beneath my tunic was assurance that even if Nessa and I did not find work right away, we would be able to feed, shelter, and clothe ourselves for some time.

But I'd left the silver and jewelry that had been given as Malakhi's portion, along with a note telling my father to return it to him for his next bride. I felt entitled to nothing more than the wealth meant to sustain me as Gidal's widow—the only semblance of inheritance I would ever receive—so I felt no guilt at taking it. It was my best means to freedom.

Even so, I wondered how Malakhi would react when he found out I'd left him. Surely this was best for him as well. He would find another bride, one worthy of all the things my father believed him to be. As I'd tossed and turned on my bed last night, I conceded that much of what my father had said was true.

Yes, Malakhi had kissed me without my consent, but he'd also been more than gracious when our fathers demanded the marriage, and he'd obviously loved his brother very much. The stories the women of his family had told at the stream had made that very clear, as had the pride on his face as he showed me the hives he'd rebuilt in Gidal's honor.

And a fleeting memory from just before I'd been betrothed to Gidal rose to the surface as I'd hastily packed a small satchel of belongings last night. I'd been tempted to take my writing board, the one I'd used for nearly the past two years—the one Malakhi had made me. He'd only been an apprentice to Eitan for a few months, so when he arrived at my door one morning, feet shifting nervously, with a piece of sleek olive wood beneath his arm, I'd been speechless. With little more than an assertion that the board, with its angles smoothed to perfection and polished to a shine, was a gift for me, Malakhi excused himself from my presence so quickly that I'd not even had time to thank him.

Any attempt to reconcile the shift in his behavior toward me, one I'd noticed since the day he'd come across me beneath the red-flowering terebinth tree, was swiftly brushed aside by my father's announcement that I would wed his older brother. And once I was betrothed to Gidal, Malakhi had become so scarce that I'd eventually forgotten the incident altogether. And yet I'd used that writing board on my knees nearly every day, a sturdy foundation upon which I crafted letters and words. I truly loathed leaving it behind for the sake of traveling light.

I still did not understand why Malakhi had become so exasperating after my mother had died, nor why he'd avoided me so pointedly once Gidal and I had been bound together, but at least in that moment—and if I was honest, a few others from my childhood—he'd been kind. No matter how he'd acted when we were children, he *did* deserve a wife who could give him a sympathetic ear as he grieved, not one who'd failed the brother he mourned and who resented them both.

"Are you already regretting leaving?" Nessa's question cut into my thoughts. Apparently she'd been trying to get my attention for a while. She pulled me to a stop and peered at me curiously. "Do you want to turn back?"

For one breath I almost relented, almost gave in to the pull of the city at my back. But I'd made my choice. My father would not reconsider, and this way Malakhi would be free to make his own choice of bride. One day he'd thank me for such a gift. And if last night was any indication, my family would barely notice my departure and would forget me soon enough.

I shook my head, lifting a wide smile to cover any hint of hesitation. "No. I have not changed my mind."

Her narrowed eyes told me that she was not fooled. She called to Yoash and Kefa to pause for a few moments, and they obeyed without question, settling beneath the shadow of a sycamore. "I'm not my father, Rivkah. I won't force you to come. I'm excited to have you with me, but if you want to stay here then say so."

"I don't feel forced, Nessa, truly. The conversation I had with my father last night made it abundantly clear that he does not care what I think or feel. I *want* to go with you. I want to be free."

She finally returned my smile, a spark of adventure brightening her countenance as she clapped her hands twice. "Good! And besides, Laish is less than a day's walk. If you get there and you are not enjoying yourself or you decide that you do want to marry that boy after all, you can go home with my cousins at the end of the festival."

The knot of tension that had been coiling at the base of my throat since I stepped foot out of the gates began to loosen. This decision was the right one, I was certain of it, and like she said, it would not be so difficult to return in a day or two if I changed my mind. This time I slipped my arm through hers to tug her onward. "Come, tell me more about your friends in Laish. . . ."

EIGHT

Afternoon gold filtered through the trees, which reached so far into the sky that I had to tilt my head back to catch a glimpse of their tips through the thick canopy above. Tiny streams forked through the rocky ground, all hurtling toward the headwaters of the mighty Jordan River. At one point, we were forced to hop from stone to stone in order to cross over the ribbons of icy water that originated on the slopes of Har Hermon to the northeast. The closer we came to Laish, the louder the many-voiced rush of waters grew, until the sound surrounded us and blocked out all birdsong in the dense forest.

I breathed deeply, uplifted by the fragrance of green overgrowth all around me. A family of furry coneys scurried across our path, heading toward one of the multitude of tributaries we'd passed over, noses twitching as they caught sight of us and then darted into the underbrush.

I was so transfixed by the beauty of the area that I barely noticed when we began to climb the road up to Laish, but soon other travelers joined us, the clatter of hooves on stone and the babble of different languages around us making it clear that we were nearing our destination. Outside the city, a number of shrines greeted visitors. Being raised in Kedesh, where such things were outlawed, I was perversely fascinated by the sight of travelers kneeling before the stone carvings, some kissing the ground in front of the idols as if in gratitude for their safe journey to the city.

The road wound its way upward, and the agitated bray of donkeys and camels spoke to the difficulty many of our fellow travelers faced as they prodded their animals up the steep, roughly cobbled incline. One donkey sat down on his haunches, not caring when his owner began to beat him with a switch. Oblivious to the cart of goods he'd toppled, the poor animal simply refused to go any farther. Our little group veered away from the scene, and after a small wait when a glut of visitors became jammed together at the entrance, finally made it through the gates of Laish.

The air of festival was thick in the city, lending a buoyancy to the overlapping voices of merchants calling out their wares. The excited urgency of this marketplace contrasted with the relative calm of the one in Kedesh. My attention bounced between stall after stall of foreign goods: spices, vibrant fabrics, dye powders, and varicolored produce stacked precariously high in baskets and pots.

But the biggest difference between this market and the one I'd known my whole life was the stalls offering idols of every sort—wood, clay, stone, some overlaid with copper or silver, some painted with such bright colors that the statues seemed to have a life of their own. A trickle of something dangerous entered my mind, a warning of some sort, but I pushed it away. I had no desire to worship idols like those dickering here for the lowest price, but it was certainly interesting to see the enormous variety offered, the skillful designs, and the animated faces of each customer as they bartered over their gods.

Nessa urged me to follow Kefa as he led us toward the heart of the city. I was thankful that Yoash had taken to walking behind us. He was a quiet man a couple of years older than Nessa, but burly enough that no one seemed eager to bother us. And although I'd wondered if I would feel unsettled in this foreign place, there was such a sense of camaraderie among the people here that I felt calmness descend upon me.

Nessa had told me this was a peaceful city, one where everyone was welcome without regard to heritage, and seeing it now for myself I believed it. I caught sight of Sidonians, Arameans, Mitanni, Egyptians, and many others whose dress and skin colors gave me little clue as to their origin. But although the city was filled with such a variety of cultures, some of whom I was well aware were at bitter odds, everyone seemed to be caught up in such a spirit of revelry that all was civil.

A young woman approached Nessa, an inviting smile on her face and many tiny yellow blossoms braided into her hair. "Hello, travelers! You are here for the festival, yes?"

"We are," replied Nessa. "But first I am looking for some friends, traders who I hope might be here." She listed off a few names and, although the girl did not seem to know most of them, she responded to the last one.

"Thalma! Yes, I know her! I saw her group around the corner from the temple. They've set up a few stalls there."

"Oh thank you!" said Nessa, visibly relieved. She must have been much more anxious about finding friendly faces here than she'd led me to believe.

"Not at all," said the blossom-braided girl, her smile having grown impossibly wider, revealing deep dimples in each cheek. "My name is Lina. You must come find me tonight; I know the best place to view the festivities, one where no one will bother you." She lifted her grin to Yoash, who stood beside me. "Although with this big handsome one with you, I doubt you'll have much trouble."

As Nessa introduced her cousin, Yoash dipped his chin, a swipe of red deepening on his cheeks, strangely shy for a man of his height and girth. Kefa sidled up beside his brother, a flirtatious tilt to his grin. "I'm Kefa, the *more* handsome brother."

Lina giggled, brushing her small hand down his bare arm as she looked back and forth between the two, wide-eyed. "Oh, now I think it's a fairly equal match. But I hope that both of you will join me and my friends tonight."

She pointed to the corner of the street a few paces away. "Just look for the gap between the potter's shop and the barber. There is a staircase that leads to the rooftop where we will celebrate together atop the villa of the richest man in Laish. There is a wonderful view of the temple porch from up there, so we'll be able to see the sacrifices quite clearly. And then afterward we'll join the dancing. Since you don't seem to be from this area, I'll teach you the dances you don't know."

I cleared my throat, unsettled by talk of sacrifices. I'd heard a few hushed rumors about the way some of the surrounding nations conducted such rites—and I was the daughter of a priest of Yahweh, after all. "We are Hebrews. We don't worship in the same manner."

She waved away my concern with a palm decorated in swirls of henna. "Oh, that matters not to any of us. There are people here from all over the world, and few of us worship the same gods. Everyone is welcome to join the celebrations, regardless of whether you take part in the rituals. In fact, there are quite a few Hebrews who live here in Laish and worship Yahweh."

We left Lina with the promise to find her later in the evening and headed toward the place where she'd indicated Nessa's friends had set up their trading booth. Thalma, who Nessa had told me was a half-Hebrew, half-Moabite woman only a few years older than me, greeted Nessa with jubilant affection. "It's been so long, my friend. Where have you been?"

With an exasperated groan, Nessa explained that since her father had forced her betrothal to a stranger, she'd been allowed to travel no farther than Kedesh. "Apparently all the trading I've done for my father over the past two years means little," she said. "But I am here now, and I've brought my brilliant friend Rivkah with me."

She slung her arm around my waist. "She is a scribe, Thalma, a very talented one. And she speaks a number of languages with astounding fluency for a girl locked in one city her entire life."

Thalma's eyes widened as she scanned me from head to toe and back again. "Truly? A female scribe? Come," she said, leading us toward a group of three stalls set up nearby, which were full of pottery from the east, spices from the north, and even perfume and unguents from Egypt. "I'll introduce you to our group and you can tell us more about your skills."

The afternoon passed by quickly as I got to know Thalma's fellow merchants, most of them Hebrews from the tribe of Gad or Reuben to the east of the Jordan. We ate a meal with them and listened to stories of their travels. They'd gone as far northeast as Harran, where our ancestor Avraham had lived for a time, and down into Moab, where Thalma's mother still had family connections. I told Thalma more about my informal training with the Levites of our town, and she tested me by stopping a few passersby and making me translate their various languages. Her eyes grew larger with every successful interaction.

"And you can write these languages as well?" Her tone was awestruck.

"A few. Hebrew, of course, and Egyptian, along with the language of the Tyrians and Hurrians. I've only just begun to learn the language of the Sea People, but it's so different from the symbols we use that I can only decipher the most simple of terms."

Later, Thalma pulled me aside, telling me that Nessa had confided our desire to travel with them. "I know plenty of tradesmen who would pay well for your services, my dear. I think you would be in high demand. And of course it doesn't hurt that you are a lovely young woman," she said with a wink. "A bit of novelty goes a long way when commanding a higher price for your valuable skills."

If I'd stayed in Kedesh, the only time I would be able to exercise my knowledge would be in the service of my father, and even then

I did little more than take down names of local farmers and their offerings, or once in a while compose a missive to a priest in another city of refuge or at Shiloh. It had been a long time since I'd even scribbled down a song in secret. Thalma's confidence in me inspired a heady mixture of nerves and anticipation to pump through my limbs, washing away the last of my hesitations. I *had* made the right choice in coming here.

The four of us were invited to join their camp for the night, and with thanks for their generosity, Nessa explained how we'd been invited to join Lina and her friends atop the rich man's villa and that we'd be back as soon as the festivities concluded for the evening. Thalma laughed at the suggestion. "The dancing will last until dawn. In fact, once the celebration begins, it will not slow down for three days—or until everyone is too drunk to go on."

Nessa surreptitiously glanced my way but covered any unease in her expression with a laugh of her own. "Well, none of us are used to those sorts of revelries, so I am sure we will return tonight."

"You are certainly welcome back anytime," said Thalma, sweeping her hands through the air, brushing us away. "Go, my friends. Take it all in!"

NINE

A few hours later, led by Kefa and followed by Yoash, Nessa and I climbed the deeply shaded stairway between the potter and the barber. A chill moved across my shoulders, but as soon as we emerged onto the roof, the odd feeling faded in the sunlight.

Canopies had been lifted across many of the flat-topped homes that encircled this extravagant villa, reminding me of the upcoming Feast of Sukkot, when we Hebrews remembered our ancestors' time in the wilderness by setting up temporary shelters for seven days and nights. The sight of those fluttering canopies and the memories of the annual celebration caused a small ache to lodge beneath my ribs, but I pressed the thought away to focus on the unfolding scene before me.

The parapet that surrounded the villa's rooftop was low, barely reaching my knees—much lower than any I'd seen on a Hebrew home. Revelers could move from rooftop to rooftop with ease. Three boys sat on a ledge nearby, their feet dangling over the side as they covertly tossed pebbles into the crowd below, seemingly oblivious to the danger of their precarious position. Their easy laughter caused a flicker of memory to surface from my eighth year, one when Gidal and Malakhi had fruitlessly attempted to teach me how to use the slings their older brother Eitan had made for them. Frustrated with my lack of skill in the endeavor, I'd stomped away, insisting I had no interest in tossing pebbles around. To my surprise, neither boy said a thing about my tantrum later, nor did they stop inviting me into their games.

Beneath one of the white canopies perched atop this home, which rivaled the size of Moriyah's inn, a small group was playing some sort of game that consisted of a wood board and many small pegs. Underneath another, revelers partook of food from communal bowls. A few servants milled around, filling and refilling cups of wine, their eyes downcast as they darted from guest to guest. Other servants were setting out flickering oil lamps all around the roof ledge and on a few scattered tables, preparing for nightfall.

"Nessa! Rivkah!"

We turned to find Lina, dressed in airy white garments that billowed behind her as she moved toward us, giving the illusion that she floated across the roof. Three young women trailed behind her, all dressed in similar fashion, with curious looks on their heavily painted faces as Lina kissed our cheeks in greeting and then slipped an arm around both Nessa and me. "I am so glad you've come," she said. "You were right on time. The rituals are about to begin." After breezily introducing Yoash and Kefa to the ladies who'd accompanied her, she steered us away from Nessa's cousins. "My friends will keep them sufficiently occupied," she said as she winked conspiratorially. "Let's find a good place to watch the spectacle."

She called for a servant girl to bring us a fresh pot of wine and led us to the edge of the building nearest the temple. Gazing over the parapet, I felt a moment of dizziness until she gestured for us to sit on pillows so finely woven that they glimmered. I sank down gratefully and looked toward the temple complex, where what seemed like hundreds of torches had been lit all around the plaza in anticipation of the setting sun.

"When the sun hits that point on the horizon"—Lina pointed to the tip of a hill in the west—"the ritual will begin."

"And which god does this celebration revere?" I asked.

"Why, Astarte!" she replied. "Don't you know that this city is allied with the Sidonians?"

I shook my head, feeling chastened in my ignorance. I'd heard of the coastal city far to the north, rumored to be wicked in the extreme, but knew nothing of a treaty between them and Laish.

"When Sidon graced us with protection twenty years ago, we gratefully elevated their primary goddess over the rest we serve," said Lina.

Astarte, or Ashtoreth in our tongue, was a consort of Ba'al, and I'd been raised on stories of how our people drove her worshipers out of Canaan. It seemed that about the time the Hebrews were moving into the Land of Promise, this city had allied with Sidon.

Although my father and the Levites railed against such practices, secretly I'd always wondered what was truly so repugnant about them. Lina and her friends seemed kind—not the wild-eyed, raving idol-worshipers and baby-murderers I'd imagined such devotees to be. The stories must have been exaggerated to ensure that we Hebrews were not tempted to pursue other gods. And while I had no interest in turning from Yahweh, I could not help but be curious. Anticipation pulsed as the entire city seemed to hold its breath while watching the sun touch the tip of the farthest hill and then slowly melt behind it.

Then, as the torches took over the job of illuminating the celebration in the plaza, drums began a low, steady beat. My heart echoed the rhythm. A line of white-robed men and women emerged from the temple, their crimson and purple headdresses the only flash of color in the torchlight. When they stopped, so did the drums, leaving an eerie silence filled only by the rush of breeze through the many trees that encircled Laish.

A voice rang into the emptiness, one lone female voice singing an unfamiliar song, the notes sliding up and down in a way I'd never heard before. Behind her, priests and priestesses began a soft chant, their bodies swaying with each word. The distance swallowed up its meaning, but something about the eerie song called to me, tapped at an empty place at the center of my being, as if it were speaking only to me and vocalizing my deepest desires. I held my breath, wishing the song would go on forever. The singer held the last note for an impossibly long few moments, until the echo died away and the drums struck up a frantic beat. Another line of about twenty priests emerged from the temple, each one carrying a young pig. I'd never traveled to Shiloh with my father to experience the daily sacrifices at the Mishkan, but our law forbade the eating of swine flesh and considered the offering of a pig an abomination—an affront to the Almighty God. Disgusted, yet compelled by morbid curiosity to keep watching, I fidgeted in my seat as the pigs were brought before a two-horned altar, slain, and butchered, and then their mutilated carcasses tossed into the flames. The sweet-acrid smell of burning flesh caused my stomach to lurch. I glanced over at Nessa to gauge whether the violent sight bothered her as much as it did me, but she was caught up in conversation with Lina.

A servant girl returned to fill my wine cup, which I'd already drained to douse the roiling of my stomach, and although I thanked her, she darted away swiftly without meeting my eye.

The darker the evening grew, the wilder the revels became. Soon all the bodies pressed into the plaza swayed and bounced in rhythm, loud laughter and shrieks of jubilance filling the air, along with the smoke from the sacrifices and sickly sweet incense. Two of the white-robed people on the temple porch were entertaining the crowd with some sort of dance I'd never seen before. I leaned forward to make sense of their movements and was struck by the dreadful realization that they were performing intimate acts together, in plain sight of everyone in the city. I lurched to my feet, horrified, sick to my stomach, and flushed with embarrassment down to my toes.

Startled, Nessa jerked her head to stare at me, annoyance crimped between her brows. "Rivkah, are you well?"

Torn over what to say, since she clearly was not as bothered by what we'd witnessed and seemed eager to please Lina, I cleared my throat and forced a tight smile. "I am fine. Need to move away from the incense. It's making me queasy."

"You do look a bit pale." Lina waved a hand at the far side of the rooftop with cool dismissal. "The air will be fresher on the other side of the canopies. Go, have something to eat. Rejoin us when you feel better."

Glad to turn my back on the depravity, I crossed the rooftop, avoiding the canopy and the food beneath it. I sank down in a shadowed corner, my head on my knees and my hands pressed to my churning belly.

What had I gotten myself into? The exhilaration of walking away from Kedesh, breaking free from my father's authority and marriage to Malakhi, had withered to nothing. Even the flattered euphoria I'd experienced after Thalma complimented my skills seemed foolish. I did not belong here. The liberation I'd imagined back in Kedesh, had craved so much that I'd turned my back on everything, was nothing like the reality of the debauchery here.

"Are you well?" A deep voice drifted down from above me.

I lifted my head, blinking at the shadowed figure against the bright torchlight. "Can I bring you something?" asked the man. "A drink of water?"

"I am well, thank you," I said, dropping my head back to my knees, hoping that the man would walk away if I ignored him, and determining to stay in this position until Nessa came to look for me.

"You are Hebrew?" asked the man in a voice completely devoid of foreign accent—a Hebrew voice.

Shocked, I lifted my eyes. The man had shifted so I could see his face more clearly. The full beard gave testament to our common heritage, and he dressed similar to most other men in my acquaintance, but he was uncommonly handsome and broad-shouldered, with a reddish hint to his wavy hair and light eyes that shimmered in the flickering light. He looked to be a few years older than me, perhaps twenty-five or so. "From which tribe?" he asked, his words nearly overtaken by the music and drums that had grown louder as I huddled against the low stone parapet.

Sheer relief at the familiar question caused the answer to tumble out of my mouth. "Levi. My father is one of the *kohanim.*"

"A priest? Truly? And what brings you to Laish?"

Foolishness. "I am here with friends for the festival."

"It does not seem that you are having a pleasant time," he said, amusement in his tone.

I pressed my hands tighter to my abdomen and pulled in a deep breath to settle my stomach. "It is not what I expected."

"And what did you expect? Have you not been told of Canaanite worship practices?"

"Yes . . . but truthfully I thought they were exaggerated."

"Ah," he said, with a lift to his brows. "An innocent."

Annoyed by the gentle tease in his laugher, I scanned the rooftop behind him, and my eyes were drawn to a few of the revelers who seemed to be imitating what they'd seen on the temple porch. Bile coated my throat, and I dropped my head back to my knees with a gasp. "I never should have come."

If only I could squeeze myself into a tight ball and somehow wake up in my bed at the inn. The drums kept pounding, each beat adding to the rhythm of my regret, and the titillated laughter wafting from dark corners mocked my stupidity.

Tears gathered in my eyes. The things I'd seen tonight could never be washed from my mind. I now fully understood why the Torah forbade that we even *know* what the nations did during their repugnant rituals. How would I face my father upon my return? How could I stand before the priest who so faithfully taught the Torah to the people of our city after coming here?

When the Hebrew man spoke again, I realized he'd folded himself down next to me, his tone soothing. "I know this is different from our ways, and some of this may be a shock to you, but it's all just a harmless celebration," he said. "There is even beauty in some of the things they do."

I thought of the singer from earlier and how her haunting melody had touched a place in my soul, a place I'd not realized was so hollow. But then a waft of heavily perfumed smoke from an incense burner nearby caused me to cough violently, my eyes burning as I attempted to catch my breath. I placed a hand on my chest, over the hidden purse I carried beneath my tunic, and was glad that the noise around me muffled the clink of the remaining silver pieces against the rings inside the bag.

When I'd revealed my treasure to Nessa earlier, she'd talked me into spending some of it on cosmetics, which we'd done our best to apply like a few of the girls we'd seen in the market, and then cajoled me into wearing the lapis lazuli necklace. Pressing aside the reminder that the last time I'd worn the piece was on the day of my wedding to Gidal, I'd given in to her argument that there was no better night to display such a trophy. Then, intoxicated with the freedom of spending the mohar, I'd also purchased new kid-skin sandals for both of us and new leather belts for Yoash and Kefa as thanks for their escort. Perhaps I had been a bit reckless with the silver today, but I vowed to ration it more carefully from now on.

Oblivious to my musings, the man handed me his own cup, encouraging me to drink as he rubbed a comforting circle on my back. The wine was strong, filled with fruit and spiced heavily, with a faintly bitter aftertaste. However, it did soothe the irritation in my throat.

"All better?" he asked, once I'd stopped choking and my body had begun to relax. His tone was gentle and his smile encouraging. When I attempted to hand back his cup, he lifted a palm in refusal. "That one is yours."

I took another sip of the drink, which was not as bitter after a few more swallows. "I should find my friends."

"The two young women you were with went down to the plaza a while ago," the man said. I flinched, surprised that he'd been watching me.

He seemed to divine my thoughts. "I saw the three of you together earlier." He smiled, a bit shyly it seemed, and then set his gaze on me. "Or rather, I saw *you* and happened to notice there were other ladies beside you. I am doubly pleased that you are a fellow Israelite." His warm smile caused my former anxiety to sidle backward a step. What an odd coincidence that a Hebrew would find me here in this foreign city.

Noticing that I'd already drained his cup, the man gestured for a servant. The same woman from before approached, eyes downcast. "Bring more of the spiced wine," he said. The servant's gaze cut to mine briefly, a flicker of something moving within their dark depths. But just as quickly, her expression went blank and she nodded.

"Tell me your name," the Hebrew man said, without a second glance toward the girl as she backed away, head down. I stared back into his eyes, the weighty moment stretching long. It was a question and a challenge in one. Would I stay? Or would I go? After the things I'd seen here I was still tempted to run, to beg Yoash and Kefa to take me home, but here was a handsome man interested in talking with me, not a vexing boy who had been pushed on me to fulfill some ridiculous law that benefited no one but my dead husband's family. I'd had enough of others making decisions for me, enough of being pushed around and passed over.

"Rivkah," I said, before I could change my mind again.

"Ah, Rivkah." He slanted a grin at me. "And you are no doubt even more lovely than your namesake." Although I knew his statement to be little more than flattery, I flushed at his assertion as I opened my mouth to ask his name, but he spoke first.

"Tell me, Rivkah," he said, settling beside me with one elbow leaning on the parapet and his cheek resting on his fist. His attention on me was complete, as if nothing existed outside the circle of our conversation. The piercing focus of his light eyes was exhilarating "How is it that a daughter to a priest came to be in Laish?"

His calm demeanor and the familiar cadence of his voice encouraged me to relax, the raging panic that had threatened to choke me earlier fading further into the background. The servant girl returned to fill my cup, her lips pressed in a flat line, but she did not look at me again as she padded away on bare feet. I took another sip of the wine and hummed in pleasure as the liquid left a warm trail down my throat. "What spices are in this? I've never tasted the like."

The man waved a palm. "Oh, cardamom. Cinnamon. Honey, of course, and some sort of citrus fruit. And special seedpods imported from the coast."

"It's delicious," I said, taking a deep inhalation of the fragrant mixture. It smelled like bliss and cozy firelight. "It makes my tongue tingle."

He laughed, his eyes dancing in a way that enticed me to make him laugh again. The kindness in his expression and the way he'd maneuvered his body to block the depravities from my line of vision made me feel safer than I had in some time. Perhaps I had been too hasty in considering a flight back to Kedesh.

A pleasant sensation descended over me as I considered my reasons for coming to Laish in the first place. Lina *had* told us there were many other Hebrews here in the city, and if they were all as welcoming as this man, Nessa and I might yet find a place among them. I could still be a scribe, still find my own way. I'd simply turn down any more offers to be a part of these awful celebrations. I was strong. I knew how to take care of myself. I could worship Yahweh even if no one around me was doing so.

All the earlier fears that had threatened to waylay my plans dissipated like smoke, and I stood, feeling the need to shed my inhibitions fully, to throw wide my arms and embrace the freedom I deserved.

"Where are the stars?" I asked the man with the lovely eyes as I tilted my head back to peer into the blackness above. "I want to see them. . . . No, I should *dance* with them! Like Nessa and Lina are dancing!" Words dripped from my mouth and lifted into the sky too, swirling like me . . . around and around and around . . . floating like a leaf on the water . . . melding with the drums and the laughter in a swirling pool of happiness and freedom.

Something collided with my calves, and I wobbled, my arms wheeling, grasping at nothing as my vision blurred and swooped. But strong arms locked around me, preventing me from toppling backward over the parapet. My heart pounded a frenetic pace as I clung to my rescuer, my body plagued with the sensation of falling even though my head knew my feet were planted on the rooftop.

"There now, you are safe," the man said, his tone soothing as he traced circles on my back again, his warm body lending me strength. "I've got you."

"Thank you!" I said, my words coming out on a giggling exhale. "I could have fallen to my death!"

"Not to worry." He guided me back to the ground, then sat next to me, cross-legged, and peered at me with concern in his gaze as I waited for my head to stop spinning. This man was so kind. I was glad he'd found me. He saved my life. He would not hurt me. Or trap me like my father and Malakhi. Nessa was a good friend to bring me here.

"Where is Nessa and . . . that other girl?" The words emerged stitched together, as if my teeth and tongue could not separate the sounds. I laughed at the silliness.

"Don't you remember Lina took your friend down to the plaza to dance?"

"Yes! Yes I do!" My lashes fluttered, making the oil lamps dip and sway in a strangely fluid way. "But . . . do you know Lina?"

He blinked twice. "No, you told me your friends' names."

Of course I had. He had such a nice face, I could tell him anything.

I smiled at him, my lips stretching so wide my cheeks hurt. "Thank you for stopping me from falling off the roof."

He shifted, leaning closer, his voice gentle and his breath enticingly sweet. "Well now," he said, a slow smile moving across his lips and his hand curving around my hip. "That was *my* pleasure."

The noise of the celebration and whatever foolish thing I'd been worried about before faded away, leaving only the two of us in this world of shadows. A flood of warmth pooled in my belly, and a feeling of bone-deep calm spread through my body like wild honey.

"Now . . ." He reached to smooth my hair behind my shoulder, the move sending a wave of delicious shivers across my skin. "I want to know everything about you."

TEN

Metal on metal clanked against my growing awareness, the sound clawing into my ears with bone-jarring steadiness. My blurry thoughts attempted to place the hideous racket, but the throbbing at my temples warred with any semblance of order. Flinging my arm over my face, I rolled to my side, caring nothing that the ground beneath me was hard as cobblestones, or that my aching neck seemed to have been at an odd angle all night. I only needed to sleep a few more hours. Or days, perhaps.

Someone nudged my elbow, and I jabbed at the intrusion, muttering a demand to let me be. Pain knocked around the walls of my skull, nothing left inside it but shards of glass and fiery arrows that stung the backs of my eyes.

Another rude nudge was accompanied by a low grunt near my ear. My eyes seemed too large for their sockets and my eyelids far too heavy, but I cracked them open. A violent spear of sunlight pierced me through, pinning the back of my head to the ground. I moaned, my parched tongue clinging to the roof of my mouth with alarming tenacity.

This time the jab to my thigh was painful. "Whatever you people do at night is of no concern to me," croaked a raspy voice. "But at least have the decency to leave when you've finished."

My eyes flew open to see a wrinkled woman hovering over me, a frown of disapproval adding to the deep creases around her ancient mouth. "Get up, girl," she ordered, with another hard stab of her broom handle. "I need to feed my pigs. So unless you want to share their meal, move away from the trough."

Disoriented and fighting the blur of my vision, I pushed myself up on my elbows, coming face to face with a mud-encrusted snout. Horror and paralyzing confusion slammed into me with the force of a lightning bolt.

Not just one, but five pigs shuffled around me in a small courtyard in front of a mud-brick house, nosing my skin, and mouthing the tunic that was pushed up past my knees. One clamped down on my sleeve and I shrieked, jerking my arm away and flailing helplessly.

The pigs skittered away, grumbling and squealing as they scattered.

The old woman glared, shaking her broom at me. "Leave my pigs alone, girl. Should I call for someone to haul you away?"

"No . . . No . . ." I blinked hard and then slowly stood, the entirety of my body stiff and sore. "I can't remember—" I gripped my forehead in my palm. "I must find—I must go home." My mouth seemed at odds with my mind, the words disjointed and tasting of sour wool.

The old woman frowned harder, her gray brows lowering as she shook the broom at me menacingly. "Well, go on now. And take your trysts somewhere else next time." Hot embarrassment crawled up my neck at the insinuation. What would cause her to say such a thing . . . ?

Realization poured over me like a pitcher of icy water, along with a river of fragmented memories from the night before. The Hebrew man. His potent gaze. Laughter and shadows and my third cup of wine, or perhaps my fourth. Grasping hands. A hot mouth pressed to mine.

Horrified, I looked down at myself. The laces at my neckline were untied, the fabric gaping wide. My palm slapped against my chest, a futile attempt at covering what was left of my modesty. It took only two stuttering, gasping breaths to realize that the purse beneath my tunic that held the silver and jewels Gidal and his family had gifted me—along with the beautiful lapis necklace—was gone.

Eyelids fluttering against searing tears, I stumbled away from the woman's house, my thoughts becoming more lucid with every step. I was in Laish. Nessa was nowhere in sight. And although the memories of last night were very hazy, as if I were peering at them through murky water, one thing became very clear: I'd betrayed my family, Gidal's family, and most of all, Malakhi.

I could never, ever go home again.

CHAPTER ELEVEN

Malakhi

Four days she'd been gone, each one more excruciating than the last. Every door in Kedesh had been knocked upon. Every grove and field around the city searched. My father and his men had visited nearly every neighboring village, but the only thing we knew was that Rivkah had left just before dawn the morning after I'd kissed her, claiming to have a message for a shepherd as a means to slip out of the gates and vanish.

Beneath the shade of the foundry roof, my body moved by rote, lulled to mindlessness by the rhythm of my sanding stone traveling back and forth across the wood. Before she left, the sharp smell of cedar had been a pleasant one, one I'd breathed in deeply while imagining the look on my betrothed's face as she beheld the bed I'd made for her with my own hands. Our marriage bed. Now the smell made my stomach turn, fragrant wood shavings and bitter disappointment clinging to me in equal measures.

Designed by Eitan and constructed beneath his expert supervision, the bedstead was nearly ready—only a bit of sanding and a final oiling left to complete. It was one of the last items I'd been preparing for the chamber we would share before claiming my bride. The bride that I should never have tried to claim in the first place.

Until today I'd held to the notion that her flight was temporary, that she was merely punishing me for my ill-conceived kiss and was hiding somewhere nearby. But this morning Amitai had sent a messenger, calling me to his home to annihilate my last hope.

The priest himself had greeted me at the door, the last four days having somehow aged the man I'd always considered larger than life. Dark crescents underscored his eyes. He seemed smaller. Stooped. Broken.

Not bothering to invite me inside, he held out a leather parcel. "She left a note behind," he said, the words so replete with loss that the many fissures inside my chest became one gaping wound. "She took Gidal's wedding gifts from the treasury box, but she wanted these returned to you. For your next bride."

"No." Reeling from the blow, I pushed back against the mohar he pressed toward me. "No. I will not accept it, except from her own hands. She can give it back to me herself when she returns."

Tears shimmered in the priest's eyes. "Don't you see, Malakhi? She does not mean to return, or she would not have taken the gifts."

A wave of shock and desolation made my knees wobble, and a rumble of thunder in the far distance echoed the hit, but I drew in a fortifying breath as I backed away, palms raised, attempting to infuse my tone with a confidence I did not feel. "She will come home. Or my father's men will find her. She cannot have simply disappeared. Even if she does not want me. Despises me even." The words gathered into a boulder of humiliation in my gut. "She'd never walk away from her family."

Amitai's fists had gripped the leather bag with white-knuckled desperation as I retreated, and as I turned to walk away, his voice followed me, ragged and hollow. "I pray it is so, my son. I pray it is so."

Every grating pass of the sanding stone against wood since I'd left the priest drove the truth deeper into my soul: she was gone, and it was all my fault. I was grateful Gidal was not here to see what I'd done. If only I'd kept my hands to myself, been satisfied with whatever small piece of her she allowed instead of pressing a grieving widow for more. Perhaps if I'd been patient, given her broken heart time to heal, waited for her mourning to fade before revealing even a portion of my desire for her . . .

No. I should have let her go as soon as she voiced her doubts, instead of clinging to my own selfish desires and trying to change her mind about me. Her final words rushed back, each one more pointed than the last. "*You are the same spoiled boy you've always been, wanting nothing more than to torment me and get your way. . . . I will never want this. . . .*"

I leaned too hard into the next swipe and felt the wood crack beneath the pressure. Numb to the bone, I stared at the destruction. A rift had formed along the wood grain, a snaking crack the length of my palm. Now the entire bedframe was little more than refuse. It would never hold the weight of one person, let alone two.

A large palm came down on my shoulder. The weight and warmth of it was meant to be reassuring, but my brother Eitan's witness to this moment was only one more reminder that I'd failed, yet again.

"Leave it, Malakhi," he said. "We'll fix it tomorrow."

"There is nothing to be done," I said, dropping the sanding stone into the dirt and swatting the sawdust from my tunic until my skin stung. "It cannot be saved."

"Of course it can. I'll show you how to repair it," he said, with far too much understanding. "All is not lost."

My throat clenched tightly, any response I could have formed swallowed up by anger at myself and my ineptitude. Falling back on the habits formed by years of working with my brother, I began cleaning the various tools I'd used throughout the day. Deftly, I avoided his eyes but felt his heavy gaze on my back.

"The gates will be closing soon, and that storm is nearly upon us," he said.

"I should check the hives, make sure they are secure before the wind gets stronger."

"No." My oldest brother's voice hardened, the note of stern command causing me to halt abruptly and look back at him in astonishment. Every day of his eleven-year seniority was behind the glare he leveled at me. "No. You've barely eaten in the last four days, Malakhi. You've spent every spare moment searching. The hives will be fine for now."

It didn't matter that men had combed every cubit of the city's allotted lands or that we'd already looked behind every boulder and tree in the surrounding area. I had not been able to sit still since I'd heard she was gone, telling myself if just one more search revealed a clue to her whereabouts then it was worth the effort.

His tone softened. "Your worry won't bring her back any sooner, brother. You must place her care in the hands of the One Who Sees."

I let my eyes close for a brief moment, stealing a painful breath. "She isn't coming back. She took Gidal's wedding gifts. I don't know where she has gone, but those items can sustain her for years, if she is careful."

"Is there another man?" he asked, vocalizing the question I'd barely had the courage to ask myself.

I shrugged, already having sifted through every conversation, every glimpse of her with other people in the marketplace, and still having no clue as to whether she'd taken up with someone else. "All I know is that I should have released her. She made it very clear that she considered this match a mistake. She does not want me. I am nothing more than a boy in her mind."

Eitan's reflexive response was swift. "Then she is a fool."

A huff of sardonic laughter burst from my lips. "It is I who am the fool."

I loathed the compassion on my brother's face and the furrow of pity between his dark brows, even though he above all people understood the helplessness of not knowing where the woman he loved had gone. But Sofea had been taken against her will to Shiloh before they'd married, and Rivkah had obviously left of her own volition—a last-ditch effort to escape the prison of marriage to me.

He released a sigh and slung his arm around my shoulders. "Come, let's go home before the rain begins. Ima will fill your belly and our sisters will serve you hand and foot out of sheer worry." He gripped the back of my neck playfully. "That may never happen again, you know. You must take full advantage."

I attempted a smile, feeling the smallest bit strengthened by my brother's unwavering support and his pointless attempt at lightening my dark mood. But even though I was confident that he and my family would never turn their backs on me, I'd failed Gidal, destroyed the only means to continue his bloodline, and in doing so, I'd failed all of them too.

TWELVE

Droplets pattered from the eaves in uneven rhythms, the gentle sound of rainfall soothing after the clash of thunder. My mother had opened the windows of the main room as soon as the storm died down, and now the breeze swept through with cool freshness.

Although most of our family meals were taken in the courtyard, the rain had driven us inside. The guests had already been served and returned to their rooms for the evening, and now only my mother and father, Eitan, Sofea, their children, and my three sisters were seated around the woolen blanket upon which the meal was laid. I usually enjoyed these private meals with my loved ones, but now there were *two* empty places that weighed heavily on my heart.

Chana and Abra sat on either side of me, and as Eitan had predicted, were in some sort of competition to see which of them could serve me most often. My cup was never less than half full, my hands never empty of bread, and dish after dish was passed to me with much encouragement to scoop up generous helpings. If they became any more attentive, my sisters might push food directly into my mouth. From across the blanket, my brother's hazel eyes glimmered with amusement as he held his new daughter against his shoulder, softly patting her little back with his large work-scarred hand.

Abra held out the chickpea mash again, shaking the bowl slightly with a silent command for me to take more. I complied, even though I had little appetite. Only the deep concern in her eyes could entice me to eat. "I never cared all that much for her in any case," she said, not needing to signify of whom she spoke.

Chana made a soft noise of agreement. "Remember how she used to fly at you when you teased her, Malakhi? I was always afraid she might hit you."

Knowing that their cutting words were born of protection, and that Chana had always been timid where Rivkah was concerned, I kept my voice soft. "I usually deserved it, sister. I took every opportunity to torment her when I was a boy."

Abra ignored my defense of Rivkah. "It's plain she still holds it against you, or she would not have disrespected you in such a way. She must have a heart of stone to toss you aside like that, without a word. You are better off without her." The ache in my belly swelled, and this time when Chana moved to fill my cup with beer, I placed my hand over the rim.

"Girls," said my mother, the single word causing them both to snap to attention. "Let your brother be. We will not speak ill of Rivkah, no matter what she has done. She was Gidal's wife, and we will honor her as such." Emotion glimmered in her eyes as she looked at me, and I had the feeling she was trying to convey something important. "We do not know the whole of the story. But Yahweh does, and we will trust him with the outcome. Instead we must pray that she is found soon. Unharmed."

I curled my fingers into fists, again fighting the instinct to flee this warm cocoon of familial comfort in order to search for her. She could not have gone all that far. She was one of the most intelligent women I knew; she would not willfully place herself in harm's way.

But where had she taken shelter during the violent thunderstorm that had torn through earlier?

The youngest of my nephews began to cry. Little Yoni had became demanding of his parents' attention since his baby sister had been born and, along with being tired, he was jealous that his older brother Zekai had command of his mother's lap. With a sigh, Sofea gathered the boy close, speaking into his ear in her native tongue. But just as his tears began to abate, someone pounded on the door, startling Yoni into a louder wail.

My mother sprang to her feet, defying the silver streaks in her black hair. It was her custom to greet every guest and wash their feet, even though she employed a number of women who'd taken refuge in Kedesh. It was quite late for newcomers; they must have slipped into the city just before the gates closed at nightfall. But my mother never turned anyone away, regardless of their ability to pay for a room or a meal. A lamp was always left burning in her window, a beacon to refugees and a light to travelers, even on the darkest of nights.

Before she reached the latch, the pounding resumed, and a loud voice demanded entry. From across the room, I saw my father flinch, and then he was on his feet, hauling his wife back away from the door and drawing a bronze dagger from his belt in one swift move.

Confusion swirled in my head. Looking pale and stricken, Eitan carefully transferred his infant daughter into his wife's arms. "Go," he said to Sofea, even as the door shook on its hinges. "Take the children into our chamber. And bar the door securely."

Sofea's blue eyes were wide and her hands trembled, but with admirable calm she shepherded her brood and nine-year-old Tirzah into the next room, muttering falsely cheerful assurances to them as she did so.

Knowing that neither my brother nor my father would be this disturbed by a mere stranger, I hauled up my sisters by their elbows and ordered them to follow Sofea. But they huddled behind me, gripping the back of my tunic and whispering prayers.

"How did he get past the guards?" Eitan hissed, his own bronze dagger gripped in his fist.

My father ignored Eitan's question and lifted his voice to address the man at the door. "Why are you here, Raviv?"

The man's name hit me like a stone to the temple. *Raviv*. My father's brother. The man who had sworn blood vengeance on my mother and Eitan nearly twenty years before. My pulse thundered as I made a swift search for some sort of weapon to wield, finding only a loaded sling one of my nephews had left on the floor. It would have to do, so I snatched it up. I did not care that the man was my uncle; he would not touch my mother or my brother.

"Let me in, Darek!" came the returning bellow. "Where is she?"

Shock, confusion, and curiosity vied for supremacy on my father's face. "Where is who?"

"Where is Nessa?" Raviv yelled. "I know you have her in there!"

My mother took a couple of steps forward, a strangely placid expression on her face and her hand stretched toward the door. "He's not here for me, Darek. Let him in."

He banded an arm around her waist to prevent her from reaching the latch. "I won't take that chance, love. He is not above such deception. You don't know him like I do."

"He vowed to leave Eitan and me alone." She pressed her palm to his chest, her gaze intent on his and her voice gently pleading. "Please, husband. With the three of you to protect us, we shall be fine. He sounds distraught."

"Only *you* would be so compassionate after the things he's said and done." With a mix of exasperation and gentle humor, he pursed his mouth tight as they silently argued her point. Then he nodded and gently steered her toward me and the girls. "Stay behind Malakhi."

She complied, her hand patting my forearm with reassurance as she slipped behind me. I felt the three of them shift position and knew the girls were wrapped in a tight embrace, with our mother's strong presence between them.

Dagger still in hand, my father unlatched the door and flung it wide. Raviv pressed forward, crowding my father and looking down at him with fury. "What have you done with her?"

My father blinked in bewilderment and shifted backward two steps to allow for his older brother to enter the room, giving ground to another person for the first time in my memory. "There is no one here except my family and a small group of traders up from Shiloh, but no one named Nessa. Who are you looking for?"

"My daughter," said Raviv, his eyes seeming to blacken against the flicker of lamplight. "And I know she's here, so stop lying."

"Your daughter is *not* here," said my father. "I have not seen your children since that day at your house eight years ago."

"Your family has already stolen two of my offspring. I won't let you have another."

"Hear me, brother," said my father, his voice strengthening. "You are welcome to search the inn, but I speak the truth, We would not hide your daughter from you."

Raviv's gaze swept around the room, taking in the meal set out on the floor, slithering past my brother, who bodily barricaded the opposite doorway, before moving over my shoulder to the place where my mother stood. It was the closest he'd been to the woman he'd once planned to marry, since her conviction for the accidental deaths of his twin sons. I felt a shudder against my back and grips on my tunic tighten in response to his black-eyed stare.

"Why would you think Nessa was here?" asked my father, trying to draw his brother's attention away from his wife.

Raviv kept his eyes pinned on my mother for a few more skin-prickling moments before slowly turning his head to answer. "I was told she befriended one of your sons' wives."

My father looked at Eitan. "I don't think Sofea knows anyone by that name. Do you?"

My brother shook his head, his expression so grave and his body so tightly strung that I could nearly feel the vibration from where I stood.

"Yoash. Kefa," Raviv called over his shoulder. "Come in here." Two young men appeared in the doorway, and although both of them were of heavier build than my uncle, their submissive expressions gave them the look of chastened sheep.

"My wife's fool nephews escorted Nessa and another young woman to Laish four days ago. The girls slipped away from them somehow and disappeared."

My heart began pounding against my ribs, and my father darted a quick glance at me. "Are you speaking of Rivkah?" he asked the two young men.

"Yes," said one of them. "Nessa said the girls wanted to go to the festival but didn't want anyone to know, so we left at dawn, as soon as the gates opened. But then after the first night they . . . they just disappeared." His cowed expression became a beseeching one. "We looked everywhere, I swear on my own life that we did. We scoured the city, asked everyone."

"Where did you last see them?" asked my father.

The young men looked at each other and then the first one spoke again. "Kefa and I drank a little much during the celebration. We woke up well past noon on the roof of a villa." He lifted his hands defensively. "But we did not know that some of the wine was laced with poppy, or we would not have accepted it. I don't know if Nessa and Rivkah drank any, but they'd made friends with a young woman . . ." His eyes dropped to the floor, his throat working hard for a moment before he spoke again, the words tentative and barely audible. "Lina was recruiting girls for temple work."

Gut wrenching, I stepped forward, my fists clenched and teeth gritted. How could they take Rivkah to such a vile place? Three sets of hands gripped my tunic, holding me in place. Only the regret on Yoash's face kept me from breaking their hold and throttling him without regard for his superior bulk.

"We asked Lina whether she'd seen the girls that morning," he said. "She said Nessa went back to a trader's camp at dawn, but that she hadn't seen Rivkah since she'd taken ill earlier in the evening."

Kefa interjected. "We went back to the marketplace where Nessa had spoken with a tradeswoman the day before, but the group had already left. Packed up their stalls and wagons and just"—he swiped his palms through the air—"vanished."

Yoash grimaced. "No one seemed to know where the traders were headed. And since Laish is a crossroads, they could have gone in any direction. Toward Tyre or Damascus. South to Megiddo, or even down to Egypt."

"We hoped the girls would come here," said Kefa. "Nessa was upset over her recent betrothal." His eyes flicked to Raviv and then away. "We considered that Rivkah may have offered Nessa refuge."

Raviv's shoulders tightened, his lean body going rigid. "If you people are hiding her—"

"They aren't here," my father interrupted, his voice as stony as his brother's jaw. "We have been looking for Rivkah for days—searched the whole city and a few of the villages around here. I didn't even consider knocking on your door, Raviv. Who would have guessed the two girls would flee together or even suspected that they knew each other?"

Raviv's response was terse, his eyes narrow. "Nessa has only been in Kedesh a few times, to deliver our tithe and visit the market."

My father's stance softened as he considered this information. "Rivkah is a scribe. She is involved in keeping records as portions are collected. They must have met then."

Raviv scowled. "I don't care what that woman does or how she convinced my daughter to slink off. I just want her back. *Now.*"

My father sighed, folding his arms across his still-broad chest. "We'll go back up to Laish in the morning together. Someone had to have seen them." My father was in command of a group of spies, commissioned by Yehoshua to ferret out information from our enemies. He and his men were masters of their trade. If anyone could find the girls, it would be him.

"I'm going with you." I stepped forward, shaking off my mother's and sisters' hands.

My father looked over at me, a deep frown on his mouth. After a long pause in which he seemed to weigh the determination in my expression, he nodded. "Just this once. And then not again until you are of military age."

Raviv's brow wrinkled in disdain. "Laish is no place for a boy."

"He is Rivkah's betrothed," said my father, his tone brooking no argument. "It is his right to search for his bride, if he cares to do so."

Eitan stepped forward too. "I'll go as well. I've dealt with some of the metal traders out of Laish before."

"I will go nowhere with *him*," Raviv bit out, every word coated with hatred as he glared with open malice at my brother. It seemed that although he'd accepted my father's inheritance in trade for Eitan's freedom eight years ago, my uncle had not relinquished his bitterness.

My father moved between them, hands lifted to keep them separated, even though neither of them had moved. His chest rose and fell as he stood like a wall between two men I knew he loved more than his own life. "Raviv, you vowed to not pursue my son."

"And I haven't," Raviv snapped. "But that does not mean I want to be anywhere near the murderer of my children."

At the sharp intake of breath behind me, I glanced over my shoulder to find my mother with her palm over her mouth and her silver eyes full of tears. Even after all this time, I knew the deaths of my cousins still weighed heavily on her soul, regardless that her part in the tragedy, and Eitan's, had been purely accidental.

Raviv turned his glare on her. There was so much of my father in the shape of his jaw, the length of his narrow nose, and the reddish tint to his dark hair—all characteristics that also reminded me of Gidal. No matter that Raviv hated us, we were bound by blood, and I knew my father and my mother would never stop praying for reconciliation.

"Eitan," said my father, without looking back at him, "I think it best if you stay here with Sofea. Enjoy your new little one. I'll ask Baz and a couple more of my men to accompany us to Laish in the morning."

Without hesitation, Eitan nodded in agreement and stepped back into the doorway. Every long, lean inch of my older brother screamed protectiveness. Although he'd seen little of combat, nothing more than a few skirmishes with wandering Canaanites over the past few years and one quick battle with a group of Amorites that dared raid a village east of the river, I had little doubt that he would shed every drop of his blood for his loved ones. But he also trusted my father implicitly and would not disobey a direct order, no matter how much it grated. In that moment, I wanted nothing more than to be like him—a devoted warrior, blind to everything else but my duty to my people.

With Eitan's submission, the tension in the room softened.

"We'll leave at first light," said my father to Raviv. "You three are welcome to stay here overnight. Moriyah always has rooms prepared for guests."

"I'd rather sleep in the street," my uncle spat out with an ugly sneer, before pushing past his shocked nephews and back out the door. Yoash and Kefa silently followed, shoulders bowed and heads down. After witnessing firsthand the longevity of Raviv's rancor toward my own family, I did not envy the years of condemnation for the two young men if Nessa was not found.

My father stared at the still-open door for a few long, silent moments before stepping forward to close it and lock the latch. He leaned forward, his forehead pressing against the wood. As if pulled by the sheer force of her love, my mother flew to him, her arms around his waist and her branded cheek against his back.

With his hands perched low on his hips, Eitan squeezed his

eyes shut, shook his head a few times, and then turned to go to his wife and children. Abra and Chana appeared on either side of me, each sliding an arm around my waist, and we watched our parents grieve the old but deep wounds stirred up by Raviv's appearance.

I was thankful that we lived in the safety of Kedesh, and therefore Raviv could not legally retaliate against my mother. And once the High Priest died, she could go free by law. No longer held captive by the conviction of a manslayer, she could travel to Shiloh during festivals, where my grandfather and grandmother lived near the Mishkan. I knew it was her greatest wish to see them both again before they passed from this life into the next. But with Raviv still seething with acrimony, would it ever truly be safe for her to go?

"I am sorry for what I said about Rivkah earlier," said Chana, too low for my parents to hear. "That was wrong of me." She leaned her head against my shoulder. "Perhaps if we'd all been kinder to her she would not have left. If she . . ." She cleared her throat. "*When* she returns, I will make an effort to be a better sister to her."

It infuriated me to think she felt any culpability for something that was my fault alone. No matter how many trees I pruned, how much honey my hives produced, or how much I wished Rivkah would accept me as her husband, I could never have been worthy of standing in Gidal's place. It had been foolish to even try.

"There will be no need for such an effort," I said. "I'll go with the others and search for her tomorrow, as is my duty as her betrothed. And if she does return, I will set her free."

Part II

THIRTEEN

Malakhi

8 Tammuz

1375 BC

Weeds had engulfed the hives since I'd last stepped foot in the quince grove, the day Rivkah had disappeared five years ago. I'd expected the overturned, mud-slathered baskets to be empty of bees, but a low hum greeted me, evidence that despite my absence something of the colonies had survived. However, not only were the hives Gidal had so carefully crafted overtaken by debris, but one had caved in on itself. My brother would never have been so negligent.

A leftover resident of one of the hives rewarded me with a sting on my neck, causing a foul word to slip from my mouth as I slapped at the persistent little assailant.

"You'd best save such language for your fellow soldiers, Malakhi" came Abra's voice from behind me. "If Ima heard you, she'd swat you with her wooden spoon."

I did not bother to help my twin sister push her way through the overgrown tree growth into the glade. If she was determined to invade, she could forge her own path.

"Go home," I said. "You'll get stung."

"By the bees? Or you?"

My shoulders went rigid at the bite in her words, causing a bolt of pain to shoot all the way down to the fingertips of my right hand. Even seven months after I'd been nearly killed during a skirmish on our northern border, I could barely lift the arm that had once wielded a sword with expert skill. The simple task of clearing brush and detritus away from the hives may prove impossible for a man with a worthless arm and especially for one who could barely see out of his right eye.

"Leave me alone, Abra."

My twin moved around to stand in front of me, one fist on her hip. "No. You left Chana in tears, Malakhi. You can lash out all you want at me, I can endure it. But you can't hurt her like that again. I won't have it."

A pang of regret prodded the center of my chest, but I ignored it, my teeth gritted. "Then tell her to stop pestering me about finding a wife."

"She is concerned for you. She wants you to be at peace."

"Then a wife is the last thing she should push on me."

She scowled, her gray eyes narrowed. I returned the expression, aware that my face was a near-mirror of hers. There was little need for my twin to expound on her frustrations with me; we'd always been able to discern the others' thoughts with little effort. She wanted nothing more than for me to scrub Rivkah from my mind and marry someone else.

"She. Is. Never. Coming. Back." Each word was coated in venom, a product of five years of growing resentment toward the woman who'd tossed aside her brother like refuse.

"I am fully aware of this, Abra."

I'd finally accepted the truth the day my father and I had gone to Laish with Raviv and his nephews. We'd searched the entire city, spoken to every merchant, entered every shop, searched out every resident Hebrew, and had even consulted with the priests and priestesses at their vile temple.

Yet even with all the talent my father possessed at coaxing information from a dry well, we'd discovered only two things: Rivkah had been seen leaving the celebration with a Hebrew man who'd mysteriously disappeared since then, leaving behind most of his belongings, and both she and Nessa had been spotted in the back of a trader's wagon the second morning, heading northeast.

We'd pursued the caravan for two days before losing their trail in the maze of intersecting trade roads and finally turned back, determining that wandering aimlessly into enemy territory would only get us killed. Faced with the evidence that Rivkah had likely run off with some other man, I'd pledged to forget her and instead throw myself into preparation for the moment I reached military age at twenty. The fact that I'd served under my father's command for mere months before nearly being killed and sent home to heal was as great a blow as my betrothed's infidelity.

"You say you know she is not coming back," said Abra, "and yet you refuse every possible match Abba proposes."

"That has nothing to do with *her*."

"Oh, it has everything to do with that arrogant, faithless—"

I interrupted her tirade with an aggravated groan. "I am useless to a woman right now, Abra. How would I protect a family with one arm and one eye?"

It was almost a mockery that I'd not been completely blinded in my right eye by the blow I'd received from the flat of an Amorite battle-ax against my temple, just before being plowed over by the iron chariot wheel that destroyed the muscles in my shoulder. Instead, the hazy distortion at the corner of my vision allowed for the smallest portion of excruciating hope.

Abra's tone softened, as if she sensed the depth of bitterness such a thought provoked. "You'll heal, Malakhi. It'll just take time."

My father and Eitan had both told me the same thing, assuring me that I would fight again when I adjusted to my limitations, but I refused to ever put my fellow soldiers in such jeopardy. I could no longer grip a sword tight enough to ward off a direct blow, could not pull a bow or aim a sling, nor could I see an attacker coming up on my side without turning my chin nearly to my shoulder. I would not last a day in combat and they both knew it.

Everything I'd worked for over the last five years had been for nothing. I was back to where I was then—standing in this quince grove, watching my future stride away without a second look over its shoulder.

Ignoring Abra's hollow words and hoping she too would disappear if I turned my back on her, I gripped the small sickle I'd brought with me in my good hand and knelt before the largest of the bedraggled hives. I pushed aside the weeds, earning a few more stings for my efforts. To my great surprise, instead of having abandoned the partially collapsed hive, the bees had filled the remaining space with tiny wax coves replete with golden-brown liquid. Holding my breath, for the hum within the hive had begun to swell, I shifted carefully to study the other mound. There was a tear in one side—perhaps an intrepid coney had discovered the treasure within—but it was even more prolific. Honeycomb burst from the hole near the ground, filling the air with sweetness. A twinge of long-suppressed emotion flickered at the sight. Perhaps I'd not completely destroyed my dead brother's legacy after all. When the time came to harvest the honey, my mother would be overjoyed with the bounty.

Shofarim sounded from the gates of the city, startling me to my feet, sickle in hand. With instinct born of many years of training, my body went on alert, and I cursed myself for not having brought a dagger. There were few reasons such a fanfare might be raised at the entrance to Kedesh, not the least being direct attack. Without much forethought, I grabbed Abra's arm and yanked her down into the tall grass, suddenly glad that she'd not left after all. Who knows what she might have stumbled into at the gates?

"Malakhi! Have you forgotten that I am with child?" she said, struggling to free her wrist from my grip. "Liron would be furious if he saw you throwing me around."

"Quiet," I ordered, knowing she was only a few months along and more durable than half the men I knew. "Let me listen." I cocked my head to the side, breathing slowly as I'd been trained to do. Nothing but the brush of a soft breeze met my searching ears, but I held still, listening for the sound of footfalls, shouts, or metal-on-metal that would signal an attack on our city.

For years we'd heard the rattle of swords from Kushan, the king of Aram-Naharim, who'd crushed many of the city-states between the Tigris and Euphrates and was rumored to be in alliance with some of the Canaanite tribes we'd pushed north out of Israel years ago. In fact, it was a particularly aggressive band of displaced Amorites, armed by Kushan and determined to test our borders, that had nearly killed me. But the intelligence my father's men had gathered over the last few months had not revealed actual movement by the Aramean army in our direction. At least not yet.

Ordering Abra to stay back within the protection of the trees, I edged toward the ridgeline, low to the ground, and looked down toward the gates of the city. Immediate relief sluiced through my veins. There was no enemy invasion. The gates were open wide and no defensive measures had been implemented. But before I could inform my sister of the news, the shofarim sounded again—a familiar but insistent call for the people of Kedesh to gather in the main plaza.

With only one shared look of urgency between us, Abra and I ran down the slope. We did not stop to inquire of the guards at the gate or pause at the inn, heading directly toward the Levite store-house that had once been a pagan Canaanite temple, knowing our family would already be there. The area around the storehouse, as well as the marketplace nearby, was packed full. The overlapping chatter of the crowd made it clear that whatever announcement was forthcoming had not yet been revealed. With the habit of a lifetime of congregating in the same place during festivals and recitations of the Torah, Abra and I threaded our way through the multitude, heading to where my family always gathered in the shade of the three large date palms at the very center of town.

Abra went directly to the side of her husband, Liron, a grandson of one of the elders of Naftali. The man dipped his chin in my direction as he wrapped an arm around her waist and spread his fingers over her gently rounded belly, a nod of gratitude for delivering his wife and unborn child to safety.

My mother and father, always a unit, stood together near the largest of the palms, surrounded by their children and grandchildren. After the argument this morning back at the inn, when I'd emphatically told them both I had no interest in marrying the latest of a long string of eligible young women they'd dangled before me, I avoided their searching gazes. But in doing so, I ended up pinned by a scowl from Eitan, who'd obviously left the foundry in a hurry, as evidenced by the soot covering his face, hands, and tunic. It seemed Abra was not the only sibling frustrated with my less-than-gentle rebuff of Chana's offer to introduce me to her friend Ayala.

I was used to my twin sister's oft-sharp tongue and lack of restraint in sharing her every opinion with me, but my older brother's censure was a rare and weightier matter. Before I could react to the reproach in his expression, the shofarim rang out over the crowd again. The entire congregation went silent, with only the squall of a few babies startled by the ram's horns and the incessant scuffle of sandals carried across the crowded plaza. A contingent of unfamiliar Levites stood on the porch of the storehouse, dressed in the white linen garments worn during festivals or while performing sacred duties at the Mishkan. A frisson of dread traveled up my spine at the solemn expressions on their faces.

Amitai stepped forward. Although he was nearing the age of

retirement from his duties in Kedesh and his face was lined with heartbreak over his lost daughter, the voice he lifted over the congregation was strong. "These Levites were sent from Shiloh," he said. "They carry news from Eleazar, the High Priest of Israel, a message that they are spreading throughout the Land with heavy hearts. It is with great sadness that I announce Yehoshua, son of Nun and successor to Mosheh, has passed from this life to the *olam ha'ba*."

An immediate chorus of wails burst from the lips of many of the women, the mournful ululations filling the air with a thick layer of grief. Although I was certain he had much more to say, Amitai allowed the outburst, his head bowed as the city lamented the death of the man who'd led us out of the wilderness into the Promised Land. As I watched an elderly man kneel in the dirt and rend his garments, two questions arose in my mind: Could anyone ever take the place of a leader who seemed nearly as immortal as the mountains? And what would our enemies do now that he was gone?

FOURTEEN

Rivkah

15 Tammuz
Golan, Israel

Yehoshua is dead?

The news, delivered without even a hint of regret by the young woman surveying goods on my market table, caught me completely by surprise. "How long ago?" I asked her.

"A week, perhaps? At least that is when some priests came here from Shiloh with the news." She shrugged, indifferent as she pawed through my master's stock of finely woven headscarves. Surreptitiously, I adjusted the slippery pile of fabric she'd knocked askew before the precious material could slide off the table and into the dirt. It certainly would not be this flippant young woman bearing the blame if anything were damaged.

I surveyed the bustling marketplace around me, my gaze flitting from one busy stall to the next. There were no women weeping in the streets, no drawn faces or rent garments, no sign that our venerated leader had been laid to rest. There was only the volley of traders and customers haggling prices, vying for supremacy over each transaction in the never-ending battle of commerce.

"Is *no one* mourning him?" I asked.

She wrinkled her nose, kohl-lined eyes full of disdain. "There are better things to do than wail over some ancient warrior." Her complete lack of respect for Yehoshua was astounding. But truly, after five years of living outside Kedesh, nothing should shock me. For as many Hebrews who respected the Torah and held the lessons our people learned in the wilderness in high regard, the same number had traded many of the old ways for the twin shackles of idolatry and compromise.

And yet I had no right to speak. The table in front of me was not only laden with lovely fabrics and pottery purchased from far-flung eastern cities, it also contained an array of jewel-inlaid wood carvings featuring the images of Ishtar and Tammuz. The Babylonian idols fetched high prices within the Hebrew territories east of the Jordan River—a testament to just how far our people had distanced themselves from the Torah, and how far I'd strayed from my father's house. My slavery, however, had been willingly self-inflicted, bartered and sealed with a few misguided swipes of my own reed pen.

Without thought, my hand went to my belt, where a scrap of papyrus lay tucked inside its folds, the ink faded by years of indecision and cowardice. When my master had declared that we were to stop in the market of Golan before heading back to his villa after our weeks-long journey, I'd taken it as a sign that not another day should pass before putting the missive into the right hands—Levite ones.

"How much for this?" the girl asked, lifting a scarf higher to examine the intricate embroidery that scrolled with silvery eloquence over the swath of scarlet.

I gave her a price and her eyes bulged. "For this?" She fisted the fabric near my nose, crinkling the delicate surface.

Summoning my well-worn trader's smile, I gently but firmly

tugged it from her grasp, then spread it on the table in front of her. "This piece was purchased in Damascus, but it was carried there by another trader who brought it from a land that lies at the very edge of the world." I slid my fingers over the scarf to highlight its skillful design and to smooth the wrinkles. "The threads are spun by a certain type of worm and the fabric is woven with a process of utmost secrecy, guarded under pain of death."

"Worms!" The girl's face contorted into an ugly grimace. "Who would wear such a thing?"

I slid my palm across the fabric that glided like water over my skin. Not for the first time, or even the hundredth, I remembered the weight of the silver and jewelry I'd once had at my neck—the value of which could have bought this piece many times over and would have staved off the desperation that had led me into chains.

Each time I allowed myself to think of the bridal gifts I'd left behind in my father's chest, I hoped that the woman who'd ultimately received them was a far better wife than I would have been to Malakhi. Although his handsome features had somewhat faded in my memory, the devastation in his silver eyes as I mercilessly flayed him with my words in the quince grove had not. Thank goodness he would never know just how deep my betrayal had gone.

As was my habit, perfected by five years of practice, I pressed the overwhelming regret as deep as it would go and turned my mind back to the girl and the potential sale. "My master and I have only just returned from Aram, where we purchased this scarf. This fabric is so precious that only royalty wear it there." I allowed envy to lift my brows and sighed in obvious want. "Anyone fortunate enough to cover their head with a scarf like this would rival a queen."

Lust flared in the girl's eyes, and within moments my palm was empty of the fabric and my price met without arguement. I watched her disappear with her purchase into the overcrowded marketplace. Golan was a city of refuge, just like Kedesh. It was surrounded by high walls, and set aside to give asylum to those convicted of manslaughter, but that was where the similarities ended.

I'd expected Golan to be a place like the one in which I'd grown up: quiet and peaceful, and with Levites, townspeople, and manslayers living in relative harmony. Instead, I'd found a hectic center of commerce with a marketplace nearly three times the size of that in the city of my youth. Although there were no pagan altars at the entrance to Golan, a multitude of market stalls greeted visitors, and the cacophony of many traders barking out their wares to any passersby was eerily reminiscent of my disastrous two days in Laish.

Although I'd traveled many places with my master, both inside and outside the Land, this was the first time I'd accompanied him to Golan. When we'd first passed through the gates this morning, I assumed I'd have little problem encountering a Levite, but so far I'd seen only two men who wore the distinctive garments of their office, and neither had approached this large merchant stall at the center of the plaza. They wouldn't, stocked with idols as it was, and I could not walk away from the merchandise or my master would be furious. So I called out to new customers, negotiated prices, and entered transactions on the record my master insisted I keep while he was off meeting with city officials.

I did not bother to pray for one of the sons of Levi to come along. Yahweh's ears were long closed to me. But I watched and waited as the morning meandered lazily into the afternoon, ever aware of the tiny roll of papyrus concealed in my belt.

After weeks of bumping along on a camel through Aram-Naharim and back, I wanted nothing more than to hand off my message and return to my tiny room in the servants' quarters behind my master's villa. I was anxious to ensure that my young friend and fellow slave Anataliah had kept her word to me while I was away—

Someone knocked into my table, jarring me from my musings. Two carvings wobbled before toppling onto their faces, and I scrabbled to save the slippery fabrics from slithering to the ground again.

"You cannot sell those here!" said a man, his gnarled finger pointed at me and his silver brows pulled low. With every word his voice grew louder. "How dare you peddle such blasphemy!"

In wide-eyed shock I stuttered a nonsensical response, mortification rising hot in my cheeks. Here I'd been searching for a Levite all day and the first one to find me was ready to publically cast stones at my head. Everyone within our vicinity stared, no doubt salivating at the prospect of some entertainment at my expense.

"This is a Levitical town, girl. Your gods have no place inside these walls." He kicked the table leg with his foot, making more of the statues wobble before they tumbled onto the cobblestones. The largest of the idols lost a head, its obsidian eyes glaring accusingly at me as I scrambled to pick up the mess. My master would be furious! He'd traded three handfuls of precious Egyptian stones for this lot of gods and expected to profit handily from them.

Pounding a fist on the table now, his face mottled red, the stranger continued to berate me for my "heathen ways," but I could only wonder what Samil would do when he returned. It had been a long while since he'd punished me—years, in fact, since I'd even dared contradict him aloud. I'd learned early on in my indenture that my master was relaxed, gregarious, and even quite generous when his word was obeyed. But if crossed, he skipped right past scolding and directly into threatening whatever was most precious.

I'd watched him order Anataliah's meager belongings be tossed into a flaming brazier after she'd burned a meal during a visit from one of the most powerful elders of the tribe of Manasseh. And in horror I'd been forced to witness the lashing of his steward's oldest son when the wax seals failed on a shipment of wine that was not properly attended. Thankfully, Samil valued my scribal and language skills highly enough that I'd escaped his worst fits of temper, but as I grabbed for the remaining idols this stranger seemed intent on destroying, my blood ran cold.

My master was well aware of what was most precious to me.

"Please," I said to the angry Levite, with as much humility as I could muster. "I make no decision as to what is sold here. I worship Yahweh."

"You are *Hebrew?*" he shrilled. "How can you abide such effrontery to the Almighty? You are *worse* than a pagan. You *know* the truth."

Head down and hands full of splintered idols, I said nothing as he continued to scold me. I did not think it possible for the pit of shame to grow any larger within me, but I was wrong. I'd heard the stories passed down from my great-grandmother Shira about the three days of hideous darkness in Egypt, and somehow it felt as though the same palpable blackness had coated my soul and was slowly consuming me from the inside out.

"You are right," I said, my voice small when he finally paused to take a breath. He blinked at me, startled by my acquiescence. The girl I was five years ago would not have abided such harsh criticism, but the woman I was now knew she deserved every word. Pulling together the last threadbare shreds of courage I had, I lifted my chin, meeting the Levite's confused gaze. "But no matter the stupidity that led me here, I have no choice now but to do as I am told."

The man's face was still flushed from his tirade, but his bearded jaw hung slack. Knowing Samil would return any moment, I dropped the broken idols on the table with a clatter and slipped my message from my belt. Coming around the table, I moved closer to the man, then pursued him when he shuffled back two steps in bewilderment. I was determined not to miss this, my one and only opportunity.

"Please," I said, my voice low and urgent as I pushed the scrap of papyrus into the Levite's hand. "Please, can you find a way to have this sent to Amitai, the head priest in Kedesh?"

Astonishment pushed the man's silver-laced brows together, a sneer of disdain contorting his face. "Why would I do that? Amitai is well respected, a man of impeccable honor and righteousness. He would have nothing to do with the likes of you."

The truth of such a statement was never so clear as this man, consecrated by Yahweh for holy service just as my father was, glared down his nose at me. I had taken advantage of every single moment in my father's presence—every hour spent learning to read and write at his knee, every gentle touch of his hand on my forehead as he recited Shabbat blessings over me, every laugh and smile and endearment. I did not deserve to be his daughter.

"That may be," I said, the blackness inside swelling so high that my words came out in a strangled hush. "But even so, there is something I must say."

FIFTEEN

Malakhi

15 Tammuz

Out here among the hives there were no weeping women still ululating over the loss of Yehoshua, no worry over the future of Israel or her enemies, and no expectations from my family. There was only me, the whispering leaves, the blazing sun, and the buzz of the colony.

Seeking an excuse to escape the inn and the all-too-frequent hints that it was past time for me to take a wife, I'd decided it was time to brave a harvest of honey now that I'd cleared the debris and carefully repaired the worst of the damage. The old Levite who'd helped me rebuild the hives five years ago said harvesting was best done at the peak of the hot season at midday, to allow the sun to do much of the work of extracting the viscous liquid from the combs. I hoped I remembered enough of what he'd told me, because he'd died last year, and without Gidal I had no one else to fill in the gaps.

As the Levite had taught me, I'd wrapped strips of linen around my arms and legs and draped a woolen scarf over my head and twice around my neck, the flimsiest of armor for my incursion. I struck my iron knife against a shard of flint to kindle a spark inside a clay pot I'd placed between the hives. When the flame caught, I used a stick to prod at the dried leaves and grass at the bottom and stirred the embers until smoke curled around my head and stung my eyes. Blowing on the smoldering pile, I encouraged the spooling gray trail to billow and fill the glade.

Once the smoke had done its work to calm the bees and the insistent buzz of the colony had lulled into a gentle hum, I approached one of the hives from the back, so as not to provoke the bees' ire, and lifted the reed mat I'd secured over the hidden opening. Reaching inside, I kept my breaths slow and shallow, hoping the colony would ignore my raid.

I immediately earned two war wounds on my thumb for my efforts. Hissing against the sharp stings, I brought my hand to my mouth, sucking out the stingers and spitting them aside, but the tiny points of pain were nothing compared to the near-constant fire that throbbed in my shoulder. In fact, the stings were almost a welcome distraction from the perpetual ache in my worthless arm.

Drawing on my military training, I pushed aside the instinct to retreat and engaged the enemy again, without flinching at any injuries I sustained. When I was rewarded with a glistening honeycomb, its tiny cavities overflowing with precious liquid, I wished that Gidal were here to see the spoils of my victory. In spite of my foolishness and neglect, something of what he began all those years ago was actually thriving.

Voices drifted up over the ridgeline and I sighed at the invasion. *So much for a peaceful afternoon among the bees.* Eitan, Sofea, and all six of their children threaded through the trees, followed by Chana, who'd been avoiding me since I'd lashed out at her. Guilt nagged at me. I really should apologize to my sister.

I placed my first hard-won honeycomb into one of the goat-skin bags I'd brought with me and approached the group as they reached the edge of the glade, tension pulling my shoulders taut.

"Don't come any closer," I warned, one linen-wrapped palm raised. "The bees cannot be riled." Three points of pain were now pulsing on the back of my neck giving credence to my warning. It seemed the dishonorable little beasts had attacked me from the rear as well. I'd have to swaddle my head and neck much more thoroughly next time.

"Are they on fire?" came the loud question from wide-eyed Zekai, the oldest of Eitan's boys, before Sofea clamped a palm over his lips.

"No. The smoke makes the bees sleepy, so I can steal their honey." I kept my tone even, hoping the children would not sense my frustration. I loved my nieces and nephews, but it had become progressively harder to be around them. I hated myself for thinking it, but their adoring little faces and small voices were a constant application of salt on wounds Rivkah's desertion had inflicted. Wounds I had no interest in probing today.

"They were perishing from curiosity. Begged all morning to watch their uncle gather honey," said Eitan, a faint edge of pleading in his voice as Sofea and Chana herded the brood back into the shade. "I promise we'll stay out of your way while you work." Then, as I opened my mouth to protest the inevitable distraction from my labors, he shut down my argument with a sly expression. "Ima sent food. Come join us when you are ready."

A formidable opponent, my brother. He knew my weaknesses well.

"All right," I conceded with a belabored groan. "But keep them well behind the tree line. The last thing I want is for these bees to swarm your children."

Sofea and Chana had already laid out two wool blankets beneath the canopy of the largest of the trees, where they all could observe me, and were in the process of serving fresh bread, olives, and creamy cheese to the children. The pride that shone in Eitan's hazel eyes as he watched them caused a sting of a different sort in the center of my chest, so I turned away and headed back to the hives.

Once I'd filled all five skin-bags with dripping honeycomb, I headed into the shade, more than ready to slake my thirst and eat my fill of my ima's food. But before I reached the blankets beneath the tree, four of Eitan's children had surrounded me, clamoring for a sample of the harvest. My instinct was to walk away, to guard against the rasping pain that tended to flare to life whenever I spent too much time around Eitan's children, but for the sake of the unmitigated joy on their faces, I took a deep breath and relented.

"You will all have a taste," I said. "But I have a job for you. Who wants to go first?" Seven-year-old Yoni was the loudest volunteer, so I ensured the skin-bag was tied off securely and then, with Eitan's help, I guided the boy to stand atop the bag and squash the combs inside with his feet. With Eitan holding his wrists out to the side, Yoni squealed with delight as he wobbled back and forth, testing his balance on the lumps inside the bag.

"Press down with your heels," I said. "Once we mash up the combs, we'll prick holes in the bag and squeeze out every last bit. The more honey we collect, the more delicious treats your grandmother will make for us, so push as hard as you can!"

He licked his lips with an open-mouthed grin and stomped harder. "But what if my toes get sticky?" His large hazel eyes highlighted the smattering of freckles across his nose and cheeks that he'd inherited from his father.

"Then I will get Toki to lick them clean," Eitan said, looking down at Yoni with a mischievous grin that perfectly matched his son's. "But I warn you, she's been known to bite toes clean off."

The white-and-brown dog that had followed my father's men home all the way from Megiddo last year would do nothing of the sort. Since the moment Baz had tossed a chunk of meat to the stray animal hovering around their campsite, she rarely left the big man's side. They were quite the sight around Kedesh: the hulking giant of a man and the hook-tailed dog forever trotting along at his heels. The idea of Toki, whom all the children in our family fawned over, nipping at anyone inspired peals of laughter from Yoni. With a playful growl, Eitan tossed his youngest son over his shoulder and pretended to take a bite out of the boy's ankle. Yoni squirmed and screamed, calling for his mother to save him from his abba as his brothers jumped up and down, grabbing at their father's tunic, desperate to take part in the game. Rocking their youngest daughter in the shade, Sofea only shook her head at their antics before tossing an indulgent smile toward her husband. Even having been blessed with six children, Eitan and Sofea were still as besotted with each other as they had been when I was a boy.

A sharp but familiar jealousy collided with my affection for my brother's family, followed quickly by a wave of fury. Rivkah had stolen this from me. Not only had she taken with her any chance to honor Gidal with an heir, she'd left me without sons and daughters of my own. I could not even enjoy my nieces and nephews without grieving for what should have been.

Even more infuriating was that whenever moments like these made me reconsider my resolve to put off my family's desire that I marry, it was only Rivkah I could see in my mind, singing her secret songs as she rocked our child to sleep. Somehow, her abandonment and betrayal had done little to excise her from my heart. What a complete and utter fool I was.

As if she'd sensed I could use the distraction from my destructive thoughts, Chana appeared at my side, handing me a cool waterskin. As I accepted the offering from my younger sister and drank my fill, my remorse multiplied tenfold. All she'd done was ask if I might be interested in meeting her friend Ayala, the daughter of one of the Levites who had recently moved to town, and I'd rebuffed her so thoroughly that she'd gone pale and fled to her chamber.

Gidal's death seemed to have hit Chana the hardest, having been the closest of all of us to our brother and the most like him in temperament. Already shy from birth, she now seemed to be even more prone to skittering off into the shadows like a mouse. And I, of course, had fairly stomped on her when it was obvious she had only been trying to help. Would I never stop destroying everything?

Sliding my arm around her narrow shoulders, I pulled her close to my side. "It wasn't you," I said in a low tone, knowing she would understand what I was speaking of. "You did nothing wrong."

"I know," she said, her sweet voice devoid of accusation. "I only want to hear my big brother laugh again."

Her simple statement cut through flesh and bone, slicing across some throbbing artery that began to pulse in my chest. How long had it been since I'd laughed? Most likely before I'd been injured, perhaps in response to some coarse jest by another soldier as we scouted Amorite movement north of Merom. But a true laugh, one that came from the soles of my feet and insisted on bursting from my lips . . . that had been five years, not since that day in this very grove, with *her*.

"I am sure your new friend is lovely, Chana. But you know—"

"That you have no interest in marriage, yes. Yes. We all know. But that does not stop us from wanting to see you joined to a good woman, one who would help you heal."

I scoffed. "There's nothing to be done about my wounds. I will likely always have a useless arm and a half-blind eye."

Her dark-eyed gaze, so much like Gidal's, held steady with mine. "I was not talking about your body, Malakhi. If you keep blaming yourself for what she did, you'll never be whole."

I failed at restraining a flinch from the impact of her words, but she pretended not to notice my reaction and patted my arm with a smile. "I put aside some food for you. Perhaps after you eat I can help you with the harvest. I don't even mind a little honey on my toes." She giggled, her brown eyes sparkling with quiet mirth. Reluctantly, I allowed the smallest bit of my sister's gentle sunshine to permeate my battle-thickened shell.

"Thank you, Chana," I said, hoping she understood that my gratitude was for more than just her willingness to help with the bees. Like Gidal, Chana was always in search of the best in any situation and every person. In fact, I was blessed with an entire family whose love never seemed to wane, even when I came across as a snarling beast.

She squeezed my hand in response and turned to fetch my meal, but after only two steps, she turned back and glanced over her shoulder. "Oh, and Malakhi? Do reconsider Ayala. She is quite beautiful." She flashed a shy but cheeky grin and spun away.

4 Av

Chana had not exaggerated; Ayala was extraordinarily lovely. A fact I was made aware of three weeks later when she and her family joined us for a meal. It was an obvious ruse to introduce us, and one they all did little to hide. With a blatant glint of mischief in her eyes, my mother seated Ayala on my left side at the table and placed a small basket of sweetbread between us, ensuring we'd be forced to share, and giving me the opportunity to appreciate her beauty without the barrier of my distorted eyesight.

"Malakhi harvested the honey I used in this bread, Ayala," she said, attempting to spark a conversation between the two of us. "In fact, his hives yielded so much honey that we'll have plenty to feed guests for months and perhaps even to sell in the market."

"Oh?" Ayala lifted her dark brows, feigning interest with admirable ease. "I'd love to hear how you learned such skills."

I restrained the instinct to scowl at my mother, who seemed all too pleased with her matchmaking as she moved on to serve other guests. "I am simply fumbling along," I said to Ayala. "Trying to figure much of it out on my own. There is not much to tell."

She leaned closer, the hint of laughter in her big brown eyes making it clear that she too was well aware of Chana and my mother's machinations. "Perhaps not, but if you and I don't spend some time talking this evening, they'll never leave us alone."

I chuckled, amused by her honesty. "You too?"

"Chana has not stopped talking about you since the day I met her. I half expected to meet a giant warrior in full armor, with a flock of women bowing at his feet." She laughed at her own joke, and the sound did something pleasant to my insides, as did the ease in which she teased me. Her long braid refused to contain her riot of rich brown curls, so a few tendrils wafted around her face. A dainty mouth complemented the dimples that appeared in her gently rounded cheeks as she indulged in unabashed humor at my expense. I sensed Ayala was in every way the opposite of Rivkah: open, easy, and effortlessly kind.

Why, when most every thought of my formerly betrothed was accompanied by anger and humiliation, was I continuing to hold on to her ghost? Chana was right; I needed to cease torturing myself over Rivkah's decisions. Instead, I should take back what she'd so ruthlessly stolen from me.

Therefore, I willed my muscles to relax and leaned toward Ayala, lowering my voice as if divulging a great secret. "My mother won't allow me to wear armor at the table. And as for the women at my feet . . ." Although the move was rusty, I curved my lips into the crooked smile I'd discovered as a youth had made the girls linger by the foundry. "The evening has just begun."

◆ ◆ ◆

By the time the meal was finished and Chana had steered Ayala off to some shadowy corner to interrogate her about our conversation, which had been surprisingly pleasant, I'd begun to feel a small measure more like myself, as if some long-dormant part of me had begun to unfurl.

Perhaps it was Ayala's relaxed manner and unassuming beauty, or the honeyed wine. Or perhaps between Abra's overt badgering, Chana's quiet encouragement, and my mother's persistence and prayers, I'd been forced to finally open my eyes. But for the first time since Rivkah disappeared, I could see another path. One that might be paved with hope instead of pain. Not once tonight had I dwelt on the weakness in my arm, nor the limitation of my sight.

Leaning against one of the cedar posts at the edge of the courtyard, a fresh cup of barley beer in hand, I surveyed the gathering. Between Eitan and Sofea's growing family, along with that of Sofea's cousin, Prezi, who'd married Rivkah's oldest brother, Tal, there was no shortage of children. My mother was constantly surrounded by little ones begging for treats, their tiny hands tugging at her skirt and nearly always going away full. But as she'd told me many times before, there was "no such thing as too many grandchildren."

Perhaps . . . I lifted my cup to my lips and stole a glance at Ayala across the courtyard. She returned my searching gaze with a fleeting one of her own. *Perhaps* . . .

Long dark fingers curled over my shoulder, and I did not need to look up to know that they belonged to my friend Hakim. "Very pretty," he said. "Excellent choice for a wife."

"I just met her this evening." I scowled, annoyed by the amusement in his tone. "I haven't brokered a betrothal just yet." I willfully pushed aside thoughts of the last time I'd done so and the consequences of that poor decision.

"Ah. But this is the first I see of you spending time with a woman outside your family in years. One can only assume you might finally be considering marriage."

Having only just cracked the door to such a possibility, I tensed at his too-keen observation. "Are you in league with my mother and sisters now? I have made no decisions."

Hakim and I had been acquainted since we were very small. He was one of the sons of Zendaye and Benamin, Ethiopian traders who had befriended and sheltered my mother and father on their flight from Shiloh to Kedesh twenty-five years before. Their caravan came through Kedesh on the way south toward Egypt each year, so I'd played with him often during those brief visits. And in the last few years, the traders had lengthened their annual stops in the city, at times lingering for a month or two, and therefore Hakim and I had maintained a solid friendship as we grew into manhood.

He spread his large palms in mock surrender. "Far be it from me to push, my friend. I only say this because I approve. I have met Ayala. She is a lovely girl."

Built as narrow as a spear, he towered over me by a head, his rich mahogany skin a contrast to my sun-darkened bronze, but something about his quiet, ever-calm demeanor paired well with my more tempermental nature. Even though I'd generally avoided him, along with everyone else since I'd returned home injured and ill-tempered, there was no trace of bitterness in his words.

"That she is," I conceded, then took the opportunity to turn the conversation away from myself. "And what of you? Have *you* chosen a bride yet?"

A grin stretched wide across his face, his white teeth sparkling. "I have." Surprised by the revelation, I stared at him wide-eyed for a moment, speechless. He was two years younger than me, and I'd never once heard him speak of any girl, but perhaps I'd been too wrapped up in myself to notice, or care.

Feeling ashamed that I'd never bothered to ask, I opened my mouth to remedy my lack of consideration, but a commotion on the second level of the inn caught my attention. Eitan and his four boys were up on the roof, along with Tal and two of his own. The men were peering over the city wall at something, and the boys clambered to be lifted in order to see whatever incident was taking place outside the city. Taking the stone stairs two at a time, I made my way to the roof to stand next to Eitan, knowing Hakim would likely follow. My brother said nothing as I joined him because the sight needed no explanation.

A small group of people approached the gates—five men and one woman, all on foot. The woman was leaning heavily upon the man next to her, as if barely able to hold herself erect. Her grief was palpable, even from my vantage point over the city wall. It was a scene all of us had witnessed time and time again over the years. Another manslayer had come to Kedesh.

SEVENTEEN

Without fail, whenever a manslayer arrived to plead for refuge, a crowd of curious townspeople also came to the city gates to witness the spectacle. Not an hour ago, we'd been eating a delicious meal, enjoying sweet wine and light-hearted conversation, and now we were spectators to the imprisonment of a woman convicted of manslaughter.

The rumor, floating mouth to ear among those congregated, was that the young mother had drunk too much wine at a wedding and as a result, had unknowingly rolled over her baby, smothering her only child. The distraught girl, who looked to be not more than sixteen or so, sobbed as a circle of Levites and elders discussed her fate and the rest of us looked on helplessly. She'd been escorted here from her village near the shore of the Sea of Kinneret by two of the town elders who'd adjudicated the trial, two traveling Levites, and her own husband.

My mother had already ordered a room prepared for the girl. As was her usual habit, she was one of the first to arrive at the gates, ready to welcome the convicted killer with open arms. And truly there was no one better to tend the broken spirit of a manslayer than a woman who herself had walked the same journey.

When the circle of Levites and elders had finished their private conversation, they returned to their stone seats by the city gates, leaving a grave and all-too-aged Amitai to announce the familiar terms upon which she would be given safe haven.

"A verdict of manslaughter has been delivered by the elders of this young woman's town. She is to be housed and protected in this city for the remainder of her days, or until the death of Eleazar, High Priest of Israel. Within the two-thousand-cubit boundary surrounding Kedesh, no man or woman shall harm a hair on her head. But . . ." Amitai turned to the young woman, whose red and swollen face was turned to the ground. The priest's voice gentled as he spoke to the top of her head. "If you choose to step past the boundaries of the city, your life can be forfeited to the *go'el haadam* of your victim."

A raw sob broke from the woman's throat, and a few muffled cries of sympathy echoed it within the crowd. A young man standing off to the side wavered, pallor ashen and chest heaving.

"Since your husband is the next of kin to your victim and is therefore a Blood Avenger," said Amitai, "he will not be allowed to remain. May Yahweh have mercy on you both." Echoes of his own losses were heavy in his tone.

Unable to contain herself any longer, my tenderhearted ima strode up to the young mother, tears streaming down her own face, and wrapped her strong arm around her waist. Blindly, the girl leaned heavily on my mother as she led her toward the inn. As she did so, the young father crumpled at the knees and would have landed in the dirt, had the two representatives from his town not caught him about the waist. Faces lined with compassion, they led the man away between them, holding him upright as he stumbled out of the gates, away from the woman he so obviously loved and would likely not see again for years—if ever. He'd lost his only child and his wife in one horrid blow. My wounds paled in comparison.

In near silence, the congregation began to dissipate. Growing up in this city, I'd seen many manslayers beg for asylum at the gates. I'd watched a few of them be hauled away to be tried for murder, and once, as a twelve-year-old, had watched in horror from the walls as a Blood Avenger broke the law and slew a man only one hundred paces from the gates in full daylight. But I doubted that any of us would ever forget the sorrow of this day.

"A sad circumstance," said Hakim from beside me, his low voice rumbling. "I have never seen the like."

"Is this the first time you've witnessed the arrival of a manslayer?" I asked.

"It is. And I would prefer to never see it again," he answered, unapologetically honest but seemingly unruffled, as always.

"I wish the same, my friend. But as long as these walls stand, they will come," I said. "I am just glad my mother was here for that poor girl. And that young man. I cannot imagine . . ." I let the thought trail away, too affected to continue. But Hakim was the sort of friend who felt no need to fill the void with meaningless chatter, so we stood silent and watched Amitai converse with the two traveling Levites who'd arrived with the devastated couple.

Rivkah's father had aged significantly in the past five years. His once-black hair and beard were both threaded densely with silver, and his shoulders bowed ever so slightly, as if invisible weights sat heavily on each side. The man had lost too much: a five-year-old son before I was born, his wife and newborn when I was nine, and then, of course, his daughter.

Still, Amitai bore the mantle of leadership as he tended to the administration of the town: mediation and implementation of the law; Torah instruction for its inhabitants; record-keeping of yearly tithes and their distribution among the Levites; and the responsibility of protecting and providing for the manslayers who had no means to support themselves. I did not know how the man even remained upright, especially with the burden of grief he carried.

I'd barely spoken to him since the day he tried to give back the bride price I'd offered for Rivkah, and I'd never asked for its return, even once I'd accepted that she was never coming back. If I did eventually give in to my family's persuasion and marry Ayala, or someone else, I still never wanted to see those items again. And yet being in proximity to Rivkah's father again nicked at the resolve I'd made to forge a new path instead of retracing the old one.

"Let's go," I said to Hakim, looking forward to making my way to my quiet chamber on the second floor of the inn and succumbing to the oblivion of sleep, but just before I turned away, I saw one of the Levites reach into his pack and pull out a small roll of papyrus, which he then handed to Amitai.

The priest unrolled the scrap, tilting it to catch the waning sunlight behind him as he read whatever words had been written inside. Even from twenty paces away, I watched the color drain from his face and his jaw go slack. When his chin jerked up and his eyes met mine with piercing intensity, I knew.

Somehow, after all this time, word of Rivkah had reached her father.

EIGHTEEN

8 Av

"The tribes of Yehudah and Simeon have marched on Jebus and plan to move on to Hebron and Debir in the coming weeks," said my father. "Apparently, Yehoshua's death inspired them to finally obey his directive to clear the land of heathen influence."

Somehow, over the past few years, the foundry had become the place for him to debrief Baz and Eitan, and occasionally the other men in his company, after meeting with the tribal elders of Naftali. Although I no longer counted myself among their number, I listened attentively as I ran a sanding stone back and forth along the sickle handle I'd crafted from acacia wood. Zekai, Eitan's oldest boy, sat on one of the low stone walls that surrounded the foundry with Toki, Baz's little brown-and-white dog, beside him.

"Where is this Jebus? I've never heard of it," said Eitan.

"A city up in the hills." My father waved a hand dismissively. "A Canaanite one. It's largely destroyed now, though. Judah and Simeon set it aflame. The Jebusites surrendered quickly after that."

"What do you mean surrender?" asked Baz. "They left survivors in that debauched place? The stories I've heard of those people would curdle your stomach."

My father ran his hand through his graying hair. "Just like Asher and Manasseh have done in Tyre and Megiddo, Judah and Simeon agreed to allow the Jebusites to pay tribute, instead of obeying the full will of Yahweh."

Baz shook his head in disbelief. "The tribes are doing half the job and calling it obedience. Where is the outcry?"

"Our people are too busy farming their land, building homes, and settling into complacency," said my father. "Collecting tribute from the enemy among us is much less effort than battle and significantly more prosperous, especially in light of the foreign trade that continues to thrive in the Canaanite cities."

Laish, the Sidonian-allied city to our north, where Rivkah had disappeared, was just such a place. My father was one of the most vocal opponents to the arrangement, but somehow the inhabitants of Laish had convinced Naftali's elders that they were peaceful. They even went so far as to feign acceptance of Yahweh—although that acceptance took the form of dragging our Holy One into their collection of foreign gods. The day we'd looked for Rivkah and Nessa I'd been horrified to see graven images near the temple that included references to Yahweh and his "wife" Astarte. How could the elders stomach such overt blasphemy not a day's walk from Kedesh?

The reminder of my formerly betrothed resurrected the mystery of what news Amitai had received of her. It had been four days since I'd watched him unroll that missive and blanch at whatever had been contained within it. He'd seen me watching and yet I'd heard nothing from him. Had someone sent confirmation of her death? Is that why he'd reacted the way he had? I was too much of a coward to knock on his door and ask—and too much of a fool to force myself not to care.

"Also, the Danites are making preparations to move," said my father, interrupting my thoughts. He leaned against the soot-stained cedar post, arms crossed and brows drawn low. "They are abandoning their inheritance and seeking new land."

Eitan lowered the sharpened blade he'd been examining for nicks to stare at our father in shock. "The *entire* tribe?"

"Possibly, or at least a majority of them. The sons of Dan have been successful in establishing cities in the Ayalon Valley, but they've made little to no headway with the cities by the coast. The enemy tribes there are simply too strong, too well armed, and much better organized than the roaming bands of Amorites we've been dealing with around here."

"Cowards," muttered Baz scornfully, and his entire body went taut, as if preparing to march south and knock their collective heads together all on his own. Years ago he likely would have been happy to do so, but after he'd married Sarai, one of the convicted manslayers my mother had harbored in the inn years ago, his tendency to swing first and ask later had waned. And since the birth of his two girls, now ten and twelve, even more so.

"Where do the Danites have to go?" asked Eitan.

"All I know is they sent out spies months ago, before Yehoshua died," my father said. "And they've begun quietly preparing for a large-scale move. And for battle."

"Will they attempt to steal land from one of our brethren?"

My father shook his head. "I sincerely hope not. But Ephraim, Benjamin, and Yehudah are all concerned. Their cities are closest to Dan's and therefore at risk."

"They would fight their own brothers yet they are too frightened to take on the Canaanites?" Baz snarled in frustration, a string of foul and emasculating names for the Danites exploding from his lips. Toki launched herself off the wall, startling Zekai into nearly falling off too. With her back stiff, the hair on the back of the dog's neck rose in defense against whatever invisible enemy was threatening her master. The ferocity in her growl was a reminder that although she was tame now, she'd come to Baz out of the wilderness, where she'd survived on her own for who knew how long.

Baz squatted his large bulk down and laid a calming hand on her hackles, his palm nearly dwarfing her head. "It's all right, girl. We won't let them succeed."

"A breakdown between tribes would be disastrous," my father said. "What is even more concerning, however, is the news from the northeast."

"The Arameans?" asked Eitan.

"Indeed," said my father. "Kushan of Aram-Naharim has amassed an army. He has vowed to retake the Land, inviting the Amorites, the Hittites, and any remaining Canaanites to join with him."

"But we still have the Ark of the Covenant," said Eitan. "Does he not know what happened to Pharaoh?"

"The tribes have done so little to drive our enemies from our midst. I think perhaps the kingdoms around us have lost any fear they ever had over the Ark—or our God." The sorrow in my father's voice echoed that of my mother, who'd been warning of this very thing for years. Her dreams were full of visions of creeping blackness and retreating, guttering points of light. And she was not the only one exhorting the tribes to repent. During the ingathering festivals in Shiloh, the priests continued to rail against the deterioration of respect for the Law among our people, a clarion call that went largely ignored.

"Have the Arameans begun to march toward us?" asked Baz.

"We are being sent to find out," my father replied. "We must determine if their army is as well organized as the rumors suggest and find out what their weaknesses might be. Once we determine how large the army actually is, we can figure out how long it will be until they are knocking at our gates. It could be months or it could be weeks. But they are coming."

"Finally," said Baz. "A real assignment. I'm tired of spying on other Israelites."

"Yes, and it may very well be one of our most treacherous," said my father. "If the failed attempts by the tribes over the past few weeks are any indication, Yahweh may well have removed the protective covering we fought under when Yehoshua was alive. Instead of enjoying victory, we are hitting our heads against walls and losing more ground than we gain. This mission, and the intelligence we gather, may be the only stopgap between us and eventual annihilation. Kushan seems to be a master of manipulation, using Canaanite resentment as his first line of offense. I've been saying for years that he's been using them to test us, weaken us, and distract us from his ultimate aim. We all saw the way he's armed the Amorites with weapons and chariots."

We had indeed. It was one of those iron-wheeled chariots that had plowed over me, nearly ripping my arm from its socket and destroying any chance I'd had at military glory—or even something as simple as defending myself and my fellow soldiers.

"Are you coming?" my father asked, and when no one else answered I looked up to find his eyes on me.

I suddenly felt the weight of everyone's gaze. "Are you asking *me*?"

"It is time, son."

My muscles went stony. Why was he bringing this up now, in front of Eitan and Baz? Not to mention Zekai, who sat wide-eyed on the stone wall, waiting for me to respond to my father's challenge.

I shook my head and cast a gaze around the foundry. "There is plenty of work for me here. Especially if Eitan goes with you."

The demand for newly crafted weapons had significantly declined in past years, since our people had largely set aside warfare for farming, and now the harvest season was in full bloom. Eitan's reputation for being the most skilled metalsmith in the territory of Naftali, and to a lesser degree my own reputation for carpentry, had brought us more than enough broken tools and plows to mend.

"I need you," said my father.

I scoffed. "Your men are widely known as the most well-trained band of spies among our people. You have no need for a one-armed blind man."

"Sulking around Kedesh is not going to bring you back to full strength, Malakhi."

The glare I leveled at my father was dangerously close to violating the fifth commandment. "I'm not sulking. I am healing."

"Doesn't matter what you call it. You are shirking your duty."

"I. Nearly. Died," I gritted out.

"But you didn't," he said with infuriating calm. "Stop acting as if you did."

I had spent my entire life worshiping at the feet of my father, and while under his command I had not once questioned an order. But I was no longer the soldier I'd wanted to be. For now I was merely a carpenter. A keeper of bees and fruit trees. And I was exhausted by my family's well-intentioned meddling. Between my sisters, my mother, Eitan, and now my father, I had not a moment's peace.

With my blood pounding and a thousand wrongful responses begging to pour from my mouth, I tossed the sickle away from me, ignoring the dull clatter of the wood against the stone anvil. Then I turned my back and walked out of the foundry, suddenly desperate to be out in the orchard. Even though the fragrant smell of the glossy leaves and honey still flooded me with unbidden memories of Rivkah, I'd found peace within its embrace. But I hadn't gone far when the unmistakable thunder of Baz's sandals on the cobblestones caught up to me.

"It's just as I told your father," he said blithely, as if I'd not just stormed out and he was merely continuing a pleasant conversation we'd begun earlier. "I've not seen many with passion like yours, boy."

"What are you talking about, Baz?"

The renowned warrior had been somewhat immortal in my mind when I was a child, but somehow over time my perspective of him had shifted from hero to equal. My flippant question, and the snide way I delivered it, made it clear that although he was still older and wiser, I no longer deferred to him in all things.

"You were a reckless child. Everyone in Kedesh remembers your brainless antics and sneaky pranks. Goodness knows you persuaded Gidal into trouble he never would have conceived on his own. But what we all considered reckless in a boy has somehow translated to a man who fights with his whole heart. A man who charges into battle with courage the likes of which could rival Yehoshua and Calev themselves."

I flinched at the comparison, my mouth gaping slightly. Baz had actually fought alongside those renowned warriors as a young man over thirty years ago. I could not reconcile such an astounding statement, especially when I'd only seen true combat twice before I was wounded.

"So many of our young people don't care enough to defend this Land, Malakhi. They've given in to compromise, like your father said. It's all too easy to sit back and take tribute from the Canaanites, profiting off our disobedience instead of finishing what Yehoshua and Calev started. We need men who will stand and fight with courageous abandon. If your generation does not take heed, we would do better to strap on our sandals and walk right back to Egypt, because the enemies who surround us here have nothing to lose and everything to gain."

A shiver went through me at the image of Kedesh burning, and a ruthless army spilling through the gates, toward my family.

"The Canaanites want this land back," said Baz. "And Aram is salivating over the abundant fertility we've cultivated here over the past twenty-five years, the wealth it would garner, and the important trade routes that cross our territories. If we don't stand now, we will be doomed. Tending bees and trimming trees is surely not going to prevent any of that from happening."

"But Gidal—"

"Your brother was not made to be a warrior." He huffed a chuckle and shook his head. "Sometimes I wondered if he was even made for this world. There was so much of your mother in him, some mysterious thing that I cannot begin to understand . . ." His brows furrowed. "But you, Malakhi, you are your father's son through and through. You are meant to take his place when he eventually retires from service. Don't misunderstand me, he is still the best there is, but he is slowing down. He needs to come home and enjoy his later years. Be with his woman. Enjoy his grandchildren. And when he steps down, so will I."

I could not begin to imagine life when these two men stepped aside for the younger generation to take the reins, but the deepening creases around Baz's eyes and the way gray had overtaken his beard gave testament to the truth of his words.

"But Eitan is older, more experienced," I said.

"Eitan's focus is his metalwork, as it should be. For as talented as he is with a sling, he is not a leader of men. Nor does he have the ambition to be one. He does not possess the single-minded drive, the passion, or the way with people that you do."

I looked into the distance, struggling against the instinct to be flattered by such praise. "I may have wanted that before, but I don't think I am that man anymore."

"Of course you are. You just need to find your fire again, boy. You spent five years learning the how. Now you need to learn the why."

"My shoulder is destroyed. And someone could attack my blind side and I wouldn't know it until my throat was slit."

"Excuses. Look at your brother. He is deaf in one ear. He adapts and so will you. Quit pouting and fight." Resentment warred with the reawakening of my long-held ambitions, so I kept my body still and my jaw locked. Baz rocked back on a heel, bringing his massive arms to cross over his barrel chest. But when he began speaking again, he seemed to shrink. "My first wife died. Do you remember? She died as she gave birth to my . . ." He stopped and cleared his throat. "To my firstborn. My little son, who never took a breath."

It had been long before I was born, but my father had told me of Baz's loss and that it had been the reason he left Shiloh all those years ago to follow my family to Kedesh.

"I was shaken to my core. Everything I loved taken from me in the space of a heartbeat. I wasn't even there," he said, a fragile edge to his deep voice. "I was off on a mission with your father when my wife went into early labor. I never got to see her again or tell her how much I loved her. I never even held my child."

All these years I'd admired Baz's strength and loyalty to Yahweh and to my father, had thrilled at the opportunity to be trained by him before I was of military age, and had even fought alongside him in my short stint as a soldier. But I'd never once taken the time to consider the man *inside* my hero.

"After her death, I told your father I'd never leave Shiloh again. That I would stay there and work in your grandfather's vineyard for the rest of my days. But Darek wouldn't have it. He refused to let me wallow in self-pity. And I've never once regretted taking that first step, even though it burned like a rusty knife to my innards and left me hollowed out. I've spent the last twenty-five years doing what Yahweh wills, under your father's command. As a result, I believe he led me here, to Sarai and my girls, who now fill that empty place to overflowing. You'll never discover what blessings are in store for you if you don't stop hiding here, licking your wounds."

"Malakhi? There you are. I've been searching all over for you." The feminine voice startled me, instinct causing me to attempt a glance over my right shoulder. When I saw nothing more than the usual shadowy barrier, I was reminded why returning to service was such an impossibility, and why I could never step into my father's sandals like Baz insisted. I shifted around until I was able to discern the identity of the woman at my side.

It was Lailah, Rivkah's older sister. I'd known her since I was born, but she was almost six years older, and therefore had had little to do with me. Having been married now for nearly ten years, she had a number of children and was a constant swirl of activity as she tended the wide array of duties she'd assumed after her mother had died. I very much doubted that we'd ever had an actual conversation, so for her to seek me out was a strange occurrence indeed.

She smiled up at Baz, but the gesture was tight, almost pained. "May I speak with Malakhi alone?"

Baz nodded, and with one last speaking look to me—one meant to communicate that I would do well to heed his advice—he walked away, leaving me alone with a woman who looked far too similar to the girl I'd once yearned to marry.

She twisted her hands together, her unease apparent. "My father asked his scribe to come get you, but I wanted to speak with you first, so I offered to come in his place."

The note. Rivkah. I folded my arms across my chest, glad Lailah could not see the pulse that had begun pounding at its center. She bit her lip and looked past me. "My father has received word of her."

"Has he?" I said, my tone admirably even. "She is alive?"

"As far as I know."

Traitorous relief washed down my spine and every one of my limbs. "Where is she?"

"He hasn't told me. All I know is the missive was carried here by a Levite." A flare of frustration tightened her features, and I refused to let my eyes linger on the shape of her cheekbones or the graceful curve of her brow, in some ridiculous attempt at capturing a glimpse of Rivkah there. "He won't tell me anything at all. He came home from the city gates that evening and went straight to the roof. He's been on his knees up there hour upon hour every day, insisting that others tend to his duties while he prays. I've tried everything to get him to at least eat something, but he refuses everything but water."

He'd gone *four* days without food? Whatever was in the missive must be disturbing indeed. "And now he wants to speak to me? Why?"

"I have no idea." Aggravation seemed to have taken up permanent residence on her face, which unfortunately reminded me all over again just how much she and Rivkah resembled each other. "But when you speak to him . . ." She furrowed her brow. "I have a favor to ask of you."

She hesitated, tugging at the seams of her gray tunic. "My father has spent the last five years in mourning. He asks nearly every visitor to Kedesh if they've seen her. He's paid a number of people to search for her. And there have been clues like this before, whispers of someone having seen a girl with similar features in a marketplace, living with another tribe, or in some foreign temple. One man even claimed that he'd tracked her to Hebron and took my father's silver on a quest to return her." She scoffed. "Of course no one ever saw that man again."

I'd had no idea Amitai had been so relentless in his pursuit of his wayward daughter. No wonder he appeared so broken down. Clinging so fiercely to hope all this time must have been exhausting.

"Don't encourage this," Lailah said. "I beg of you. Every time his hopes rise, they are dashed to pieces. At this point it is little more than torture. I fear another crushing blow may destroy him, push him over the edge. Whatever he has to say to you, please find a way to discourage another fruitless search." Her mouth pressed into a hard line. "I loved my sister, but she was selfish and prideful and set on having her own way, regardless of how it affected the rest of us. You know, perhaps even better than I do, that she *chose* to leave. She does not want to return or she would have, years ago. He needs to let her go. For good."

NINETEEN

I returned with Lailah to the home she, her husband, and their children shared with Amitai. She directed me to the roof, where she said her father had spent the majority of the last few days. I took the stairs slower than I would have in other circumstances, pondering how to honor Lailah's request while being sensitive to the brokenness of a man who'd lost a beloved child. After four days without food, he would be weakened, perhaps even faint, but he was still the presiding authority of Kedesh and deserved my honor and respect.

However, it was not a broken man I found on the roof, with shadows beneath his eyes and grief sitting heavily on his shoulders. A man who more closely resembled the Amitai of my youth greeted me with open arms and a wide smile.

"Malakhi! Thank you so much for heeding my summons." Though the big man no longer towered over me as he clasped my shoulders in his meaty palms, the priest who'd governed Kedesh since I was a boy would always seem a giant in my mind. Shocked by the changes since I'd last seen him, pallid and weak-kneed after the Levite handed over the message, I could do little more than stare with my mouth agape.

"Come. . . ." He slung an arm around my shoulders with a chuckle that told me he'd noticed my confusion. "Let's break bread together, and I will explain why I've called you here today."

Lailah must have been mistaken about the fast Amitai had been undertaking, as the spread laid out on a blanket under a canopy was nothing less than regal. And the man who led me to it was full of vigor, not someone who'd been subjecting his body to deprivation. Although profoundly confused, I was never one to turn down a meal, so folding myself down onto a cushion, I accepted a warm round of fragrant bread to dip in the dish of salted olives mashed with spiced olive oil. He filled my cup with barley beer and then spoke a blessing, his rich voice giving thanks to the One who created the grain and the fruit we would partake of together.

Although I expected Amitai to inquire after my family as he usually did, he set aside all niceties in favor of delivering his pronouncement. "I have heard from Rivkah."

I nearly choked on the large bite I'd taken and was forced to wash down the lump with a gulp of beer before speaking. "You've heard news of her? Or from her?"

Amitai's eyes lit with delight. "*From* her."

A pulse of something painful began to tick beneath my ribs. "Where is she?"

"I don't know." His nonchalant reply took me off guard.

"Is she safe?" I asked. "Is she returning?"

"I do not know." With the shrug of his shoulders, his mouth tipped upward in an unmistakable, albeit bewildering, expression of joy. "But Yahweh does."

Dumbfounded, I blinked at him. "What do you mean? I thought she contacted you."

"She did. She sent a message with a Levite who was traveling from Golan to our city. It has been nearly a month since she sent the missive, from what I understand."

"She lives in another city of refuge?"

"The Levite said she was only traveling through, possibly with a traders' caravan."

"The one she left Laish with?"

"One can only surmise." Regardless that Amitai seemed to have little information on her actual whereabouts, his expression was one of unmistakable triumph.

Had this message finally pushed the priest past the brink of sanity, as Rivkah's sister feared? I mulled over my words carefully before I spoke, keeping Lailah's plea in the forefront of my mind, along with her story of unscrupulous men fleecing him during his desperate search.

"Is it possible the note is a deception? Someone presenting false information in hopes that you will pay them to look for her?"

"So." Amitai grinned. "You spoke with Lailah."

I cleared my throat, frustrated with my blatant transparency. "She is concerned."

He laughed and reached for another piece of bread, then scooped a bit of the olive mash into his mouth with a satisfied hum. "This tastes even better after four days of nothing."

After taking a long draft of beer, he continued. "My oldest daughter is so much like her mother," he said. "Which is why she slipped into her role so easily when my wife died, even though she was still little more than a girl herself at the time. The fact that she and her husband stayed with me, instead of moving into his family's home, and have raised their little ones beneath my roof fills my heart with gratitude. She gracefully took on the mantle of responsibility for her brothers and sisters, along with filling the void my wife left as the helpmate of the head priest in Kedesh. She is skilled at ministering to the manslayers and the families of the Levities in my charge but at times can become so entangled in details that she loses sight of the greater picture. Where she sees the theft of a few pieces of silver in my quest for news of Rivkah, I see one step closer toward the goal of bringing her home. It does not matter if I have to sell everything

I own, Malakhi. The mountains will fall into dust before I will ever give up on my daughter."

I ran my hand over my beard, contemplating. I'd left Amitai's house that morning five years ago assuming that the grieving man had accepted his daughter's disappearance as permanent. *I* certainly had. But while I'd been spending my time honing my mind and body for battle in order to bury any remnant of my tattered hopes and dreams, Rivkah's father had spent his days clinging to every shred of hope and dreaming of the day he'd see his daughter again.

"Do you plan to send someone to Golan to search for clues as to her whereabouts?"

"I do," said Amitai. "You."

Like the strike of iron against a stone anvil, his words made my ears ring. I swallowed hard against the bark of confused laughter that lodged in my throat. "Me?"

"There can be no better man to do so than her betrothed."

My jaw went tight. "She left me. Went off with another man. The contract between us was broken."

Amitai watched me for a few moments, his gaze curious. "And yet you have not married."

I thought of Ayala and her pretty round face, her soft curls and gentle laughter. "That is soon to be remedied."

"Yes, there are rumors to that effect." His brows lifted as he scrutinized me, and I wondered how he'd heard such speculation when I'd only seen Ayala twice now. "But it is not to be."

I bridled the instinct to snap at this honored man of Yahweh. "And why is that?"

"Because I have spent the last four days on my knees, Malakhi. I have fasted and prayed. And it is only you Yahweh brings to my mind." He leaned forward, his eyes intent on me. "*You* must go and find her."

"I am injured," I said. "There are plenty of others more capable."

"But none who care for her like you do."

My shoulders went stiff as I met the priest's gaze, portraying outward calm while battling the urge to demand how he could have known the extent of my interest in Rivkah. "She was my brother's wife. . . ."

"And you honored him well, Malakhi. You did. But I am her father. Do you think I did not see how you went from relentlessly pestering her to suddenly following her everywhere with your eyes?"

A flush of embarrassment swept up my neck. "She was . . ." I cleared my throat. "She is very beautiful. And I was only a boy."

"Yes, you were. And I assumed that once you matured, your infatuation would fade and other young ladies would catch your eye, which is why Darek and I agreed to join her with Gidal. I watched with admiration as you smiled and congratulated your brother on his betrothal, even though I suspected you still harbored a small tenderness toward her."

What no one could have known was that I'd hidden on the rooftop of a vacant home for an entire night and half of a day after her betrothal to Gidal was announced, emerging only when I had collected myself enough to wish my brother a blessed marriage with some semblance of sincerity.

Amitai continued, his expression as compassionate as if he'd watched me struggle through those long hours. "When you stood next to him at his wedding with nothing but pride on your face and then found a couple of girls your own age to speak with during the feast, I felt sure I'd made the right decision. But in the weeks that followed I noticed you seemed to be taking deliberate pains to avoid Rivkah and Gidal, so I guessed that you had stepped back purposefully, to guard against dishonoring your brother or my daughter."

My heart thundered louder and louder as all my secrets were laid bare. How had the man with so much on his shoulders even noticed my youthful infatuation with his daughter? Let alone my decision to stay far away from both of them out of respect for my brother?

Something niggled at my mind that I'd thought I had buried. *If you hadn't desired her, you would have been in the orchard with Gidal that day. You would have seen the serpent. He wouldn't have died.*

"I did not say anything at the time because I did not want to embarrass you, son. But I knew my Rivkah would be cared for, even though you were still young. And you were strong enough, even then, to be her match and to win her heart over time, which is why I insisted on the levirate marriage in the first place."

"None of this matters, Amitai. She left. She did not want me." The admission burned my throat. "She saw me as nothing more than a child and a yoke around her neck."

"Perhaps that is true, although I suspect much more was behind her decision to walk away. When her mother died, Rivkah seemed so . . . so lost. So broken. I'd taught her to read and write a couple of years before, and I encouraged her to develop those skills, to throw herself into satiating her keen intellect instead of withering away. And her talent for language was so startling that eventually I could not teach her alongside the other Levites for fear they would be discouraged. But even with the distraction of learning to be a scribe, the wound that formed the day my wife passed from this life never seemed to heal. She curled into herself even further." He stopped, blinking a sheen of tears from his eyes.

"I've come to realize over these years that Rivkah got lost somewhere between my grief and my duties," he said. "Perhaps if I'd listened better to her heart all along she would not have become so bitter and possibly would not have run from us." He paused again to take a drink from his cup before continuing. "Do not misunderstand me, Malakhi. I do not regret betrothing her to you. Yahweh made it clear to me even then that it was the correct path. But I should have explained my reasons better, helped her understand that my decision was born of love."

"You are only human, Amitai," I said. "You did the best you could for her. And you are not Yahweh; you could not know her mind. It was her decision alone to leave."

"I know. And I did everything I could to find her." He turned to the south, unmistakable longing on his sorrow-lined face. "Every day I stand here on the roof before I pray and just watch the road, imagining she will appear. . . ."

The ache in my throat flared hotter, for in those early days of her vanishing I too had stood atop my mother's inn and peered into the distance, hoping to catch a wisp of movement among the trees.

"But . . ." With a loud clearing of his throat, he composed himself. "Enough sorrow and regret. I have spent the last four days up here fasting, praying, begging the One Who Sees for answers. And now I know that, for sure, at least one of my prayers has been heard." He gave me a wide smile, regarding me with amber-brown eyes brimming with inexplicable peace—peace that I was suddenly quite envious of. "And when you find her—and I know you will find her—I have no doubt that more answers will follow."

Amitai reached into his belt and withdrew a narrow roll of papyrus, cut no longer than the palm of a hand. I hesitated for a few breaths before unrolling the strip. On it were only two words written in a hand that even I, with my untrained eye, knew well from the ketubah document that was still hidden in my bedchamber.

FORGIVE ME.

CHAPTER
TWENTY

My family and Hakim's family, along with Baz and his wife and daughters, were gathered around the long table in the courtyard, oil lamps flickering joyfully along its length. Every Shabbat of my life I'd partaken in an evening meal just like this one, replete with overlapping conversations, delicious food, and an air of contented relaxation as we paused our work and celebrated together, even when my father was away on a mission. But as I approached the table tonight, the laughter dried up like a shallow cistern beneath the sun until every eye was on me.

I flicked an accusing glance at Baz, who'd obviously told everyone that Amitai had summoned me earlier. I had not told anyone of what I'd witnessed at the gates the day the young woman was brought into town for asylum—not even Hakim, who'd been standing next to me—but it would not be difficult to guess who the priest and I had been discussing.

Tirzah bounded up to me, her dark hair in wild curls around her upturned face as she gripped me about the waist with both arms. "Malakhi! You have missed most of the meal!" she said, seemingly oblivious to the tension I'd dragged back with me to the inn.

I'd spent hours out among the quince trees after I'd left Amitai's home, puttering with the beehives and clearing out brush, weighing whether I should refuse his request or pursue the woman who'd run from me. Among the many considerations was my father's challenge to return to my place under his command, and Baz's impossible assertions that even with my injuries I might someday move into my father's position. I'd come to the conclusion that even if by some miracle I healed enough to step into such a role in the future, the time was not now. However, in the back of my mind, I wondered whether perhaps this quest to search for Rivkah might be a gauge of whether I even desired that future anymore.

I forced myself to turn my attention back toward my sister. At fourteen she was teetering on the edge of womanhood but stoutly refused to give up the sling she carried with her everywhere, just like I had when I was a boy. With constant scrapes on her shins from climbing trees and ever at the ready to challenge boys her age to shooting matches or footraces, Tirzah would be a force to be reckoned with in the years to come and regularly drove my frazzled mother to her knees.

"Ima had me save your portion," she said.

"Even the honey roll?" I asked, catching a glint of gold on her chin.

Her eyes went wide and she rolled her lips inward, a mask of guilt settling over her features. I forced a halfhearted laugh and kissed her forehead. "You little imp, you still have honey on your face," I said, then leaned down to whisper in her ear. "But you know I can always talk Ima into making more rolls."

She grinned and spun off to return to the table, finding her place among my younger nieces and nephews, who adored her spirited and adventurous nature. I strode forward, ignoring the stares, to fold myself down in my usual spot near the end and take a piece of flatbread to fill with lentils and onions.

The unnerving silence continued as I chewed, until Abra could take it no more. "Malakhi," she growled from directly across the table, "are you planning to leave us in the dark all evening?"

I finished chewing and took a draft of wine, taking a bit of pleasure in drawing out the moment and watching her face contort with annoyance. "I spoke with Amitai."

"And?" she prodded, gritting her teeth. Being with child seemed to have sliced her already short patience in half.

The image of that small scrap of papyrus and the two simple words seemed emblazoned in my mind. "Rivkah sent him a message."

A ripple of gasps went around the table. Only the young children and my mother seemed unaffected by the news. Her silver eyes held only concern for me, so I avoided her all-too-keen gaze. Had she somehow known this day would come? She'd always come to Rivkah's defense in the past, but would she approve of me running off to find the woman who'd stolen Gidal's legacy?

"A message?" Abra's eyes narrowed. "After all this time?" Her husband put a calming hand atop hers, knowing, just as I did, how fiercely protective she was of those she loved. The reason it had taken so long for Rivkah to contact her father, and why now, were only two of the myriad questions that had been buzzing around and around in my head since the moment I'd held the message in my hand.

"She sent it through a Levite," I replied. "One of the men who arrived with the manslayer the other day."

"Why has it taken him until now to speak with you about it?"

"He has spent the last four days in prayer and fasting." I'd avoided Lailah when I left, since I was too much of a coward to explain why I'd been entertaining the notion of trying to find her sister after she'd specifically begged me not to.

Abra lifted her brows pointedly, irritated with my piecemeal information. "Well? Where is she?"

I sighed, knowing if I avoided the question now she'd only badger it out of me later. "Possibly up near Golan, in the eastern territory of Manasseh." I took another sip of wine, savoring the deep flavor on my tongue as I closed my eyes to deliver the rest. "He wants me to retrieve her." The tension around the table stretched and grew, looming in the courtyard like a storm cloud. Even the children held their tongues.

"And you told him no," Abra stated.

"I told him I would consider it."

"No. You aren't going anywhere for that—"

"Stop," I interrupted, lifting a palm. "Not another word. She is Amitai's daughter."

Her lips snapped shut, going pale with the pressure, and the eyes that matched mine flashed with frustration, but Liron's hand tightened around her fingers in silent warning. Surprisingly, the gesture seemed to have the intended effect. Abra took a long, slow inhale before resuming. "Where has she been?"

"I don't know."

"Does she want to return?"

Did she? A plea for forgiveness was not a call for rescue. Perhaps she was married to the Hebrew she'd been seen with in Laish. Perhaps she'd forgotten she was ever betrothed to me and only wanted to clear her soul of transgressions toward her father. "All I know is she is alive and Amitai has asked me to find her."

"Why can't someone else make the journey? You are injured."

I couldn't explain Amitai's reasoning without exposing myself too much, but I'd already made my decision out in the orchard and refused to be swayed by Abra's hostility—especially when I knew it was only born of her deep love for me. So I said the one thing I knew would close her mouth, my tone of voice brooking no more argument. "Because he asked me to, and no matter what she did, her father is deserving of respect."

Silence reigned over the table until Hakim spoke, his dark-eyed gaze on me. "I will go with you, my friend."

Although my instinct was to turn down his offer, I nodded my thanks, since a companion would be welcome on such a trek. Benamin laid a palm on his son's shoulder, his expression warm and approving. "We planned on staying here through the cold season anyhow. You are welcome to one of our wagons, if you'd like."

I shook my head. "Thank you, but we'll walk. It'll give us more flexibility to move off the trade roads when need be." While the territory we had to cover between here and Golan had been settled by the tribes of Naftali and Manasseh, there was always the chance that enemies were about. Bumbling along in a wagon would only draw unwelcome attention. It was best to move quickly and quietly.

"I cannot go with you," said my father, an edge of frustration to his voice. "The threat from the Arameans is too dire. And Eitan needs to come with us this time since we are going so far north. He's been anxious to see Hittite ironworks with his own eyes in order to duplicate their processes, and this may be his only chance to do so. But perhaps Baz can accompany you and Hakim. He's been with us in Golan many times over the years and even has a few contacts there and in the surrounding areas."

My father's most faithful friend lifted his brows, some silent conversation going on between him and my father, but after a swiftly whispered consultation with Sarai, Baz thunked his wine cup on the wooden table with a loud "Agreed." There was no reason to argue. When my father gave an order, Baz obeyed, and there would be nothing I could do to convince him otherwise.

Although I could still feel Abra's disapproval radiating from across the table, emotion pinched the back of my throat as I let my gaze travel over my family and friends. They knew the devastation Rivkah had left behind. I'd been sixteen and not all that skilled at hiding my emotions. I'd been surly and difficult to be around for months. It wasn't until Baz and my father had channeled my anger into weapons training that my wildly vacillating moods had leveled out. And if the sympathetic looks from around the table were any indication, then perhaps they all knew, just as Amitai had, how enamored I'd been of Rivkah. And yet other than my twin, who would without a doubt like nothing more than to thrash the woman who'd wounded me so deeply, they all seemed to understand why I needed to go.

My mother met my eyes, and the peace and pride across her scarred but beautiful face reinforced my decision. I cleared my throat of the lump of gratitude and affection for the loved ones who surrounded me and lifted my half-empty cup in salute to Hakim and Baz. "Well then, we'd best enjoy our Shabbat rest. We have a long walk ahead of us."

◆ ◆ ◆

The journey across Naftali territory took only a day, even with the wide berth we gave my uncle Raviv's valley. I doubted he would know me by sight, especially since I'd only seen him when he came looking for Nessa and he'd paid me no attention as we'd traveled to Laish. But Baz and I deemed it best to avoid contact with him nonetheless.

After our futile search for the two wayward girls five years ago, Raviv had walked away without even a parting farewell to my father, seemingly resigned to his loss, with silent, contrite nephews in his wake. From all that I knew of Raviv, he'd likely written Nessa off as dead and not thought much of her again. Any man who could shut out his younger brother for twenty-five years over a mistake, albeit a tragic one, had no room for forgiveness in his heart.

Now, after days of trekking across the tribal territory of Manasseh, up and over a multitude of hills, through narrow rocky valleys, and crossing a number of streams and rivers, we were finally nearing Golan.

Har Hermon sat to the northwest of the city, its snowy peaks stark white against the green landscape. Fruit orchards, olive groves, and lentil, barley, and wheat fields spread in every direction, and the verdant hills all around were layered with terraced vineyards and thick forests. The land of Bashan, once ruled by the giant King Og, was wealthy beyond what I'd even imagined. No wonder the enemies to the north and east were slavering to wrest it from our grasp. The city itself was built on a hill at the center of the broad valley, and even from our far vantage point at the top of the ridge, I could see the wide-open gates beckoning weary travelers and manslayers to take refuge within its high walls.

After months of languishing in Kedesh as I'd healed, doing little more than helping Eitan cut down a few trees and working in the foundry, I'd initially found the pace Baz set a bit of a challenge. Hakim, with his long-legged stride, had little trouble keeping up, but I lagged behind all too frequently. Only sheer force of will kept me moving forward, and bit by bit I'd begun to relish the burn in my legs and remember the exhilaration of accomplishment as our destination came ever nearer.

Nearer to Rivkah.

Most hours on the trail I'd been content to clear my mind of thoughts about the goal of our mission, but the closer we came to Golan, the more I was flooded with memories of the girl I'd known.

The days after her mother's death had been a confusing time. Even though I'd been only nine years old, I'd never forget the sight of Rivkah's drawn face as she walked behind her father while her mother's body was carried outside the city walls for burial.

I'd had the inexplicable urge to walk alongside her, to hold her hand so she wouldn't be alone, but unable to deal with such heavy thoughts as a child, I'd instead made a face at her in a feeble and immature attempt to make her smile. Her blank-eyed response sobered me instantly. It was almost as if she'd died too.

It had taken weeks for her to react to my teasing after that, but to my childish way of thinking, provoking her was the only way to keep her from being so lifeless. If Rivkah was yelling at me, chasing after me with threats of bodily harm, then at least she was still alive. It was not until that day under the terebinth, her sweet voice lifting up a song I'd never heard before, that instead of goading her into anger I was desperate to have her smile at me. But then, within only a few months, my father and hers had agreed to a year-long betrothal to Gidal. And out of respect for my brother I pushed aside all of my longings, even though at the time it felt like it was *me* who had one foot in the grave.

"What thoughts are making you frown so, my friend?" said Hakim, with a nudge of his bony elbow to my ribs.

I waved a hand toward the road ahead. "Just ready to be done with this."

"And find your woman?"

I inhaled sharply. "She's not my woman anymore." *She never truly was.* "I am doing this for Amitai's sake and then I will return to Kedesh and marry Ayala."

His black brows arched high. "Oh? I thought you had not made this decision yet."

"Why not?" I said. "She's beautiful and kind. Chana tells me she's a wonderful cook. Besides, I think my sisters are deliberately attempting to drive me to the brink of sanity with their nagging."

Hakim tipped back his head and laughed. "Chana is much too sweet for that," he said. "But I certainly would not put it past Abra."

I chuckled, but then admitted I'd taken Chana aside after the Shabbat meal and asked her to hint to Ayala that I would likely approach her father on my return. "They are right; it is time. And I am ready for sons and daughters of my own."

Hakim nodded and clapped me on the back with his large hand. "I am glad to hear it. And perhaps . . ." He paused to take a long, deep breath before continuing. "Perhaps if I can convince your sweet sister to marry me, we will be fathers together."

"You . . ." My jaw dropped open and I stopped in place to gape at him. "You want to marry Chana?"

A shy expression crossed his face, and somehow his dark skin deepened all the more. "Does this displease you?"

"Of course not!" I gripped his forearm. "Does she know you have an interest?"

He shrugged. "We have spoken a number of times at the inn over the past months. She is . . . so lovely. And her heart is pure and generous. I have admired her for years but did not have the courage to say anything until now. Do you think your father will be amenable to the union?"

"I do. Our parents will be thrilled with such a match."

"Even though we are not Hebrew?"

"You are devoted to Yahweh, are you not?"

"We are. Thanks to your mother's influence on my own mother so many years ago, we serve the One True God. No matter where we travel, we obey the Torah and worship him alone."

"If you have committed to taking part in the Covenant, then I do not foresee any impediment to your marriage to Chana. And truly, Hakim, I can think of no better husband for her."

"What are you gossiping about back there?" shouted Baz, his giant paws fisted on his hips.

"Women," I said, shoving Hakim's shoulder with a snicker. "What else?"

Hakim surprised me by pushing back, sending me off balance and into the dirt. I responded by hooking my arm around his knee and pulling him down with me. We tussled back and forth until both of us were panting and sweaty. Toki, delighted by our antics, left Baz's side to run in joyful circles around us, yipping and bouncing, her hooked tail flailing back and forth in glee. Baz had tried to leave her back in Kedesh, going so far as to have Sarai keep her in a locked room until he was well away from the city, but not an hour after we'd departed she'd found us on the road, tail wagging, to take her place at her adored master's side.

With an exasperated growl, Baz threw his hands up in the air. "Enough, you fools. I'd like to make it inside the city before they close the gates."

After a few more playful shoves, Hakim and I caught up with Baz, who furrowed his brows at us but seemed to be pressing his lips together to squelch a smile. "You two are worse than fifteen-year-old trainees," he said. "If we had time, I'd stop right here and make you build a useless stone wall and disassemble it again, but the sun will be setting soon, so let's move."

Although I'd been grateful for the distraction Hakim's declaration had provided, as we neared the entrance to the city all amusement retreated, allowing thoughts of Rivkah to crowd back in. What had transpired over the past five years to bring her to a refuge city so far from home?

We walked by the surprisingly large number of traders' booths and wagons lining the road to pass through the cedar gates. My stomach clenched tight as, after a brief consultation with the guards on duty, we headed toward the home of one of the priests who governed Golan, hoping he might have answers as to Rivkah's whereabouts.

One thing we knew for sure: she had been here only a month before. Her feet had likely trod these same cobblestones. For the past week, since I'd given in to Amitai's plea, I'd been contemplating what I would say to her once I found her, but I still had no answer. What *did* one say to the woman who'd run as far and as fast as she could to escape marriage to you?

TWENTY-ONE

Rivkah

15 Av
Edrei, Israel

I lifted my bleary eyes from the papyrus, rubbing at the ache in my neck after an hour of bending over the faded letters I'd been attempting to decipher. Samil had insisted I determine how the man he'd provided a loan to six years ago had swindled him. But whoever had prepared the agreement guaranteeing Samil a portion of the man's crops was undoubtedly the worst scribe I'd ever encountered. The marks were haphazard and crudely formed, and the poor quality ink so faded in places that many words were nothing more than a guessing game. But such was the nature of my duties as Samil's personal scribe.

I did not relish being the one who must tell my master that, indeed, according to this document, the man owed the original loan amount along with only half the interest the two had verbally agreed upon. Had I been in service to him at the time this contract was written, the borrower would not have gotten away with this. Knowing my master, he would find a way to exact payment anyhow, and the man would regret ever doing business with the richest, most ruthless trader in Edrei. It did not matter that the man was Hebrew and therefore, by Mosheh's directive, should not have been charged interest in the first place. Samil always found a way to profit.

I had completed nearly five years of my indenture contract to Samil, and by Torah law could go free at the beginning of the seventh, but my situation in this household was far better than most, and I anticipated it would be necessary to continue on in his employ. What choice did I have, other than finding some man to marry like Nessa had? That path was one I refused to entertain. When she and I had left Kedesh with our heads full of foolish notions of freedom and determining our own futures, who would have guessed that servitude would be my best and safest choice? At least my master was so wrapped up in his two young, voluptuous Canaanite wives that he had no interest in forcing me to submit to him in other ways.

It had been weeks since I'd seen Nessa, as she lived on the outskirts of Edrei with her husband and two boys. When I had crossed paths with her in the marketplace, her hollow-eyed sadness gutted me, as did the faint bruise along her jawline. The achingly handsome young man with whom she'd been so enamored when we came through this city with the traders five years ago—and the reason we'd stayed after they'd traveled on—had only revealed his true nature after he'd gotten her with child. Now, trapped in a marriage to a man likely far worse than the older man her father had pledged her to, and with a third baby in her belly, Nessa had even less freedom than she had before.

After unfolding myself from the dirt floor to stretch, I crossed the room to the washpot, hoping that a splash of cool water on my face might revive my weary mind. Since we'd returned from our journey past the Tigris River a few weeks ago, Samil had not given me a day to rest, not even on Shabbat. But since the city elders in

Edrei did little to enforce Torah unless it served their purposes, those of us considered slaves had no choice but to work from sunup to sundown if our masters demanded it.

The side door crashed open, slamming against the mud-brick wall, and Anataliah flew into our shared quarters, accompanied by the smell of charred fabric. Whisking off her headscarf, her brown curls sprang free as she held out her arm to me. "I burned myself again!"

I dunked the linen towel I'd been drying my face with into the washpot and ordered the girl to sit on our one three-legged stool. Hissing from the pain, she obeyed and sat with gritted teeth as I applied the cool compress to the burn on her arm. When her body began to relax, I lifted the cloth and inspected the injury.

"It's not nearly as bad as the one on your hand last month," I said. "Dab a little honey there and it will heal quickly." I did not envy Anataliah's grueling job in the open-air kitchen courtyard, shaded only by a threadbare canopy of black wool. My many duties as Samil's personal scribe were nothing compared to the never-ending task of preparing meals for his large and demanding family and for all the many servants and laborers in his employ, as well as serving during the numerous banquets he put on for men whose business or favor he was courting.

"Are you certain?" she asked, peering at me anxiously.

"Yes, it won't leave a scar. How did you accomplish such a thing?" I asked.

She blew out a low, exasperated breath. "I was kneeling to stir the coals in the oven and one shattered and flew right at me. It hit my arm and then landed in my lap." She gestured to the walnut-sized hole in her tunic right above her knee. She groaned. "I've ruined yet another garment."

"We can fix it. I'll ask one of the weavers for some thread and a needle. Don't fret."

"Are you sure? When I spilled pomegranate juice all over that awful sheer linen dress Samil made me wear when those Egyptians dined here two years ago, I thought he would murder me on the spot."

I had no doubt he'd frightened the breath out of the girl. More than once I'd seen Samil turn red as a sunset while berating servants for an offense. And if they had embarrassed him in front of potential customers, all the worse.

"Here," I said. "We can trade tunics. You'd better get back to the courtyard before Dilara notices you are missing."

Samil's pampered second wife, a Canaanite girl he'd met on a trading run to Edom, had little more to do with her days than breeze around the villa, ordering servants to perform additional tasks and reporting any infractions to her husband with the air of a wounded doe. Even though at twenty years of age she was already the mother of two, Dilara was little more than a simpering child herself, dressed in fine Egyptian linens and draped in precious gems, reveling in her power over all of us. And now that she was pregnant with her third child, she was even more volatile than usual.

We traded garments and I sent Anataliah back out to the kitchen, leaving the side door ajar to allow some cool air to filter into the stuffy room and to enjoy the sound of the children playing a gleeful game of chase in the courtyard.

My young Moabite roommate had been sold by her own parents six years ago to satisfy their debts after a devastating crop failure, and although she barely spoke above a whisper to most everyone else, living together in this small room had given me the chance to get to know her well, and we'd come to depend on each other. In many ways her quiet manner and shy smiles reminded me of Chana, Malakhi's younger sister.

Malakhi.

I tended to avoid dwelling on thoughts of the young man who would have been my husband, had I not selfishly walked away from everything good in my life, but the sweet sound of boyish laughter wafting through the back door sparked a memory from when I was nine years old. Gidal, Malakhi, and I had been playing at the stream while our mothers laundered linens together, and the two boys had darted after a rabbit bounding through the tall grass. In my haste to follow them, I tripped on a fallen branch and scraped both of my knees. Malakhi heard me cry out and returned, dropping to the ground beside me. Embarrassed by my tears, I'd snapped at him and told him to leave me alone, but instead he went back to the stream, filled his cupped hands with cool water to wash off the blood, and then helped me stand and return to my mother. Somehow, with all the frustrating childhood memories I had of Malakhi, especially those after my mother died, the memory of when he'd come to my aid, refusing to leave me behind, had gotten buried.

I heaved a sigh, again pushing aside my futile regrets, and retrieved one of the sheets of papyrus I'd saved beneath my pallet, an old inventory report Samil had ordered me to destroy. I also fetched my wooden ink palette—the only item I still owned from my life in Kedesh. Having traveled with me for five years, the surface was cracked, worn, and stained with layer upon layer of black and red ink, but as it had for the years I served my father as a scribe, it continued to serve its purpose well. Now that I'd deciphered the contract, I had a few moments to write down the lyrics that had been trailing through my head since I'd awakened this morning. I folded myself down cross-legged and set my writing board across my lap, wishing I had the one I'd left behind, then turned over the used papyrus and inscribed the words, humming to myself as I did so and hoping I would remember the melody later.

I'd only written three lines when a knock sounded on the front door. Startled, I quickly slipped the filched papyrus beneath our sleeping pallet before putting a hand to the latch. Samil rarely came to my quarters, but I had no desire for him, or anyone else, to catch me using my skills for something that profited him nothing.

I tentatively pulled open the door to find a strange man standing two paces away from the threshold, his face turned toward the large white villa across the courtyard where Samil, his wives, and his nine children lived in luxury. The stranger stood a head taller than me with the broad-shouldered, confident posture of a soldier. His wavy black hair was shoulder length, his beard trimmed neatly at his jaw, and the depth of his sun-bronzed skin attested to a heritage that was not purely Hebrew. He did not seem to have noticed my appearance in the doorway and continued staring at the villa, his arms crossed over his chest and a stony set to his jaw.

"Shalom," I said. "Is there something I can do to help you?"

With a slow turn of his head, the man faced me and unforgettable gray eyes met mine. My knees went liquid and I gripped the doorpost to keep myself upright. His name moved across my lips without sound. *Malakhi.*

"Shalom, Rivkah," he said, in a voice much deeper and richer than I remembered. "Your father sent me."

CHAPTER
TWENTY-TWO

Malakhi

She looked up at me, mouth agape. I kept my arms tight across my chest and my jaw locked, doing my best to appear impassive as I drank in the sight of her. Maturity had only deepened her beauty. Even though she stood in the doorway of what was obviously servants' quarters, dressed in a stained and ratty tunic, her black hair bound in a tight knot at her neck and an ink smudge across her cheek, there still was no one as captivating as Rivkah.

The moment I saw her, the speech I'd prepared during the walk from Golan this morning was wiped clean from my head. So to avoid stumbling over my words and appearing a fool within the first moments in her presence, I kept my lips pressed tightly together as we continued our silent survey of one another, and my double mind battled itself. I refused to allow her a glimpse of the effect she still had on me.

This was the girl who'd stolen my fourteen-year-old heart beneath a terebinth tree.

But this was also the woman who'd trampled that heart and tossed it aside to run full speed into betrayal—of me, and of my family.

A hard spike of anger shot up my spine, and in response my shoulder began to ache, but I kept my posture firm and measured my breaths. She must have sensed my hostility. With a little gasp, she lifted her fingers to her lips and blinked her amber-gold eyes, a glint of moisture in their corners. I dropped my hands to my hips, broke eye contact, and tipped my chin to the side, putting Rivkah in my blind spot as I gathered my wits.

But before I could string together enough words to deliver Amitai's message, and then gather the courage to turn my back and walk away, a small warbly voice interrupted my scattered thoughts.

"Ima, Tarron pushed me down."

My gaze jerked back to Rivkah. A boy of about four years stood at her side, his fingers gripping the seam of her ruined tunic. His little round face was streaked with tear trails, and his lower lip quivered as he looked up at me with curious but somber dark brown eyes. Eyes that I'd seen before.

Gidal's eyes.

I took in the curve of his jaw, the cleft in his chin, the lock of hair above his left brow that refused to lay flat. Everything about the child standing before me was almost the perfect image of my older brother who'd died five years ago.

Before she answered the boy, who'd pressed his face into her thigh with a sob, Rivkah looked up at me, unable to hide the guilty expression that further confirmed the truth. Gidal had a son. An heir. Instead of staying true to her vow of levirate marriage to me, this woman had left two months after his death, carrying with her the only piece we had of him. My mother and father did not know they had another grandchild on this earth, that their beloved son's lineage had not been stamped out after all.

Lailah was right. Rivkah *was* selfish. Set on having her own way without a care for the destruction she caused. She'd taken the trust I'd given her, that my family had given her, and tossed it aside like refuse. I'd been fortunate that I'd not ended up shackled to a woman who would do something like this.

With a slight flinch that made it clear she registered the barely constrained fury barreling through me, Rivkah knelt down and gathered her son—my nephew—into her arms. "What happened, my lamb?" In spite of my looming presence over the two, she somehow managed a gentle tone. She pressed a kiss to his forehead and drew up his chin to look into his eyes.

"We were playing with the hoop and Tarron stole it." His lower lip quivered again. "He is mean."

"Are you hurt?" she asked, her hands smoothing down his arms, checking for injury, and when he lifted his hand, she turned it over in hers. A slight graze at the base of one palm had reddened the skin. Even though there was no blood, I had the sudden urge to find this Tarron and ensure he'd never torment another child again. But instead of flaring with anger like she had whenever it had been *me* tormenting her all those years ago, Rivkah kissed the wound gently and then lifted the other uninjured palm and kissed that one as well. I braced hard against the hit of reluctant emotion the affectionate gesture caused in my gut.

"Better?" she asked, and the child nodded with a sniff. Rivkah pulled the boy's head to her shoulder, running her ink-stained fingers through his tousled hair. "I am sorry. He should not have hurt you."

He pulled back to frown at her, a slight demand in his tone that reminded me of how Gidal had chided me whenever I took my antics too far. "Tell his abba to make him not mean."

Rivkah's grimace was a poor attempt at a comforting smile. "I'll see what I can do," she said, then wiped the dirty tear trails from his cheeks and kissed his sweaty forehead. The boy peered up at me again, his gaze sharply inquisitive and so like his father that I was nearly knocked backward with a rush of longing for my brother.

Gidal should be here right now, watching this tender moment between his wife and child. Not me.

"Who is that, Ima?" he asked.

Rivkah ignored the question and delivered a swift distraction. "I know what will make your hand feel better, Amit. One of those dates we brought back from Damascus." She nudged the boy with a finger to his belly. "Go see if Ana has one left." With a spark of anticipation in his brown eyes, he nodded and then slipped out the side door and into the walled courtyard beyond, both wound and stranger seemingly forgotten.

Amit. She'd named her son for her father. Still on her knees, Rivkah watched him go, then dropped her chin, eyes closed as if in prayer. I'd come here to deliver a message, put my hurts behind me, and instead I had discovered that Rivkah's betrayal had been far worse than I'd even imagined. My breathing was labored as I gripped the nape of my neck with a trembling hand, drawing on my military training to contain the outrage that begged to spew from my lips.

Finally, Rivkah ran her palms down the length of her thighs and stood. "Come inside." Both her posture and her tone spoke of unequivocal resignation. "I am sure you have many questions."

An understatement if ever there was one. I had five years' worth of questions.

She stepped aside to allow me entrance through the small doorway. And although I was not nearly as tall as Eitan, I was still forced to stoop and tilt my shoulders to fit through the narrow opening—and to avoid any contact with the woman I'd once dreamed of touching.

Rivkah stood as still as a cedar post as I entered, then peered outside, her swift glance sweeping to the right and left before she closed and latched the door. She crossed the tiny room and shut the side door that led out to the courtyard as well, enclosing the two of us in complete privacy for the first time in my memory.

The light from the high window illuminated one large pallet made from a few meager layers of wool blankets, along with one stool and Rivkah's inks and reed brushes next to some sort of document on the floor. My eyes flicked back to the bed, noting that it was large enough for three. Was she married? The thought threw me into another confusing sea of emotions, so I looked away as she sank down on the pallet, cross-legged. I leaned back against the wall, arms folded over my chest, head down and ankles crossed, feigning calm.

"So my father received my message, then?" she asked.

"He did. We traced you back to Golan through the Levite who delivered it."

"But how did you know I was here?"

"We asked around in the marketplace for information about a woman scribe. Someone said they'd seen you with this Samil, whom we discovered lived in Edrei." I waved a vague hand toward the enormous white-plastered villa outside. "It took little effort to discover your whereabouts once we arrived this morning. Your unique position is well known."

"A woman scribe is rare," she agreed. "Although I have met a few on trading runs with Samil in the East and South."

I lifted my brows. "You have traveled outside Israelite territory?"

"I have," she said. "I have crossed the Tigris and Euphrates and been as far south as Avaris."

She'd seen Egypt? I'd once journeyed with my father and his men up to Tyre and Sidon and gone north of Laish while searching for Rivkah, but to travel back to the country our people left sixty-five years ago? To see the Black Land of the pyramids and the Nile? With admirable restraint I kept my expression calm. Now was not the time to ask the flood of questions such a revelation provoked, especially since Amit was the much greater surprise.

"The boy is Gidal's," I stated.

"He is."

"And you knew you were with child when you left."

Her eyes went wide and she shook her head. "I did not, Malakhi.

I promise you. It was not until three weeks after Nessa and I left Laish that I understood the . . . changes that were happening to me." Her cheeks reddened. "If I had known . . ."

My blood heated with a rush and I pushed off the wall. "What, Rivkah? You wouldn't have run off? Devastated my family and yours? You would not have stolen my brother's heir from his grandparents?" *And left me broken and bleeding behind your sandals?*

She'd gone from blushing to pale as I ranted. "No. I would not have left."

Bitterness welled in my mouth. "And when you discovered your situation you did not try to return?"

Head down, she shifted on the pallet, tugging at the hem of her tunic. "No. I couldn't. I could not leave Nessa. It was too late."

"What do you mean?"

"Shortly after we arrived in this city with the traders we'd be traveling with, she . . ." Rivkah sighed. "She met a man. She insisted that he cared for her and would provide the two of us a place to live. She went to live as his wife, but he refused to give me shelter unless . . ."

"Unless?" I prompted.

"Unless I provided him with some"—her eyelids fluttered—"incentive . . . to do so."

Fury curled my hands into fists as I discerned the underlying meaning to her statement, and every muscle in my body slipped into battle-readiness. No matter what Rivkah had done, any man who would dare suggest such perversity deserved to be torn limb from limb.

Taking my physical response for anger at her, she threw up her palms in defense. "I refused! I swear to you. Nessa was horrified that she'd put the both of us in such a situation. Without a place to live, I had nowhere else to go and no way to provide for Amit when he was born. The traders made it clear I was not welcome to continue on with them either."

Although her explanation helped to file the rougher edges from my rage, I could not keep the sharpness from my tone. "You left Kedesh with a bag full of jewelry and silver. Why did you not simply use that to return home?"

Her chin dropped again, as if she were loathe to meet my gaze. "It was stolen from me. In Laish." The words were barely above a whisper, the current beneath them making it clear there was much more to the story. But for now I'd settle for more immediate answers.

"How did you come to this household?" I asked.

"One of the traders heard that Samil's personal scribe had recently died. She negotiated my indenture contract with him. For a profit, of course."

A huff of air burst from my lungs. "You are *enslaved*?"

Her head jerked back at the force of my words. "Malakhi. Look around you. Are these the quarters of a valued wage earner? I had no *choice*. I was with child. Alone. And desperate."

"You sent a message to your father a month ago. Why not back then? We would have come. Especially had we known about . . ." I waved toward the courtyard where my nephew was laughing with some other child. The date must have done its job, since he was no longer crying. I lowered my voice so he would not overhear through the open window, although my words came out like daggers. "We would have moved earth and sky to bring him home. You know we would have. And instead you *sold* yourself?" I could not keep the revulsion from my voice as I jabbed a finger toward the pallet she sat upon. "Does this *master* of yours exert his rights of ownership here too?"

A gasp slipped from her mouth. "No, Samil has never approached me in that way. He has two beautiful wives less than half his age who keep him . . . occupied."

Relief was swift, but it took a few more moments for the rush of my pulse to calm.

"We have been treated well here," she said. "We are provided with shelter. Food. Clothing. And because Samil relies on me so heavily for all his dealings, I am afforded some luxuries that other servants in this household are not."

Scoffing, I waved a hand toward her stained and charred tunic. "Such as these fine garments?"

"Anataliah, the young woman who shares these quarters with us, burned her tunic in the kitchen. We traded so she could go back to work before one of our mistresses noticed her absence." Her expression softened. "What I mean is that Amit is allowed to play with Samil's children and even to participate in some of their household celebrations. He is not forced to labor, but instead is allowed to be a child. I don't think he even realizes that I am a slave. At least not yet."

I'd seen the sharp scrutiny behind her son's eyes. He was small, but if he was anything like Gidal, I was almost certain he noticed differences between himself and his wealthy playmates. The thought of my nephew living in slavery made my stomach roil, but he did seem to be healthy and cared for, in spite of the situation Rivkah had trapped them in. And it was plain to see that for all her transgressions, she adored Amit.

Uneasy silence poured into the room as I stared wordlessly at the woman I'd wanted so badly. It had not only been her beauty that had drawn me to her, nor even the honey-sweet voice I'd heard in song, but the way she never backed down when I provoked her. And once I'd stopped seeing her like a sister, I'd begun to admire her quiet strength after the death of her mother, and the way she spent every morning bent over potsherds with a reed pen or practicing letter shapes with a stick in the dirt, and the way she hovered around the foreign traders in the marketplace in the afternoons, soaking up their languages like a thirsty sea sponge.

Although her outward beauty had bloomed into a richer shade of loveliness, the broken woman who sat before me barely resembled the girl I'd known. With shoulders hunched, her expression unsure, and her hands wringing themselves white in her lap, it was as if her once-bright flame had been snuffed out.

She lifted wary eyes to meet mine. "You have changed."

Surprised and unsettled by the way she'd reflected my own thoughts, I volleyed back with her own last words to me. "I am not the same spoiled boy I used to be."

Her entire body jerked. And although I felt a tinge of regret for my harshness, I could not forget that she'd brought this on herself. She'd left. Stolen Gidal's son. Kept him from us for five years.

I was not here to rekindle the desire I'd once had for her. I was here to deliver a message. I reached into the pack at my hip, pulled out the small roll of papyrus Amitai had given me when I'd agreed to make the journey, and held it out to Rivkah.

Her hand trembled as she took the offering. She ran a finger over the grooves her father's signet ring had pressed into the clay seal before breaking it to unroll the missive. After only a moment of taking in whatever her father had written, she lifted her golden eyes to mine, tears shimmering. "I can't go back," she said, her tone mournful. "There is a year and a half left of my indenture contract."

I stood blinking at her, weighing the implications of her statement, but before I could respond, a loud knock sounded at the door. "Rivkah," shouted a man's voice. "Samil wants you. Now!"

With surprising speed, she tucked the note from her father beneath her pallet and sprang to her feet. Then she brushed past me to grab a document off the floor. "You must go. Now. He cannot see you here." The vehemence with which she delivered the command was nearly like the old Rivkah, but the panic beneath the words was not.

"What would he do?" I demanded as she snatched a threadbare over-garment from a hook on the wall and slipped it over the burned tunic she wore. The messenger outside banged on the door again, and her expression went stony as she placed her hand on the latch.

"Just go, Malakhi," she whispered, without looking over at me. "Don't come back." Then she slipped outside and slammed the door behind her.

TWENTY-THREE

Rivkah

My hands would not cease trembling. I forced myself not to look back over my shoulder as I walked away from the servants' quarters, and from Malakhi. As soon as I passed through the rear door to the villa, I scurried over to peer out a nearby window from an angle that would ensure he'd not catch me watching. I never should have left him there, so close to Amit. I held my breath, waiting for him to emerge from my room and walk away from my son.

I could not wrap my mind around Malakhi's appearance here in Edrei, nor could I reconcile the drastic change in both his appearance and his mannerisms. The Malakhi of my childhood, the smiling, jesting mischief-maker, had been replaced by a scowling, snarling stranger. A stranger with a frame that barely fit through the small door to my quarters. Nothing about him was the same, except those silver eyes, but instead of dancing with amusement like they used to, they now steadily regarded me with five years' worth of bitterness.

Full-bearded and radiating contempt, his presence had filled the room to the point of suffocation. I'd nearly exhaled a relieved sigh when Estebaal, Samil's bodyguard, called for me. What better excuse to flee Malakhi than to heed the summons of my master?

But I should not have left Amit in the courtyard, since Malakhi could easily slip through the side door and abscond with my precious boy and take him back to Kedesh, back to the family that in all likelihood had far more legal right to him than I did. The way he'd locked his attention on Amit's face the moment he'd appeared in the doorway, I'd known that he'd seen what was more than obvious: Amit was every bit Gidal's son. And after what had transpired in Laish, I was glad of it. I would never want his heritage questioned because of my recklessness. But still, it had taken everything I had in me to not snatch Amit in my arms and run the moment Malakhi's keen gaze had landed on him.

I caught my breath as Malakhi exited my home, his head ducking to pass beneath the lintel. He paused, his face turned toward the villa, his chin tilted as if he were listening to the sounds of Amit and his friend Bensam playing together in the courtyard. My heart beat a double rhythm until he turned and walked away, and I slumped against the wall, relief coursing through me.

"Rivkah!" Estebaal's voice made me jump and spin away from the window. His muscular arms crossed over his chest and his deep blue eyes were locked on me from the end of the corridor. "Samil is not happy that you've taken so long. I'd rather not be taken to task for it as well."

"Apologies," I said, dropping my chin in a gesture of submission, and then followed the tall Aramean to my master's chamber. The man was Samil's most trusted personal bodyguard, and as such, dressed in clothing nearly as fine as our master's. One could almost mistake him for a rich man himself were it not for the thick copper ring in his right ear, the sign that Estebaal had taken a vow of lifelong service to Samil. Without knocking, Estebaal opened the door to usher me inside before taking his usual station outside the doorway.

For the first few months of my service here, I'd quaked whenever I crossed this threshold, worrying whether Samil would ultimately dishonor the contract Nessa's trader friend had negotiated, for I'd insisted on the stipulation that I'd not be considered a wife, nor a concubine, and that it was only my skills as a scribe that were to be sold, not my body.

But as the months progressed and even as I grew heavier with child, Samil always spoke to me as he did his male servants—with condescension but lacking indecent suggestions. Once I realized that he valued me solely for my skills and their ability to build his wealth, I'd gradually eased into my role.

Besides, one look at his two young Canaanite wives, Ofira and Dilara, and it was evident that his tastes ran toward the exotic, the flamboyant, and the well-endowed. Even now, halfway through her pregnancy, Dilara sat on Samil's lap, stroking his beard with her henna-tinted fingernails, dressed in little more than a few strips of linen that barely covered her ample breasts. The manservant who was trimming Samil's hair was forced to move around them as he worked, his well-trained eyes locked on the razor he wielded against our master's graying brown curls. Dilara glared at me as I entered the room but continued scraping her fingernails up and down her husband's cheek.

"Rivkah," said Samil, pushing aside Dilara's hand and waving off the manservant, who scuttled out of the room without a word. "What took you so long? What have you learned of the contract?"

I explained my findings, not coating my words with honey. I'd discovered that Samil valued my honest opinion and was much less apt to lose his temper at me if I spoke straight facts rather than trying to placate him. He tensed as I laid out the terms of the document, and by the time I'd finished relating the wording the scribe had used to cheat him out of his expected due, he'd pushed his vexed young wife off his lap in order to stand and pace the room. Dilara's hands went to her shapely hips, and she scowled at me with nearly as much vitriol as Malakhi had done earlier.

I cared nothing for Dilara's obvious contempt. I was used to it, since for some reason she seemed to blame me for Samil's single-minded focus on trade. Whenever he turned his attention from her to business, she whined and fussed like a child, as if the gold and jewels that dripped from her neck and ears had come from underneath a rock and not her husband's conscious efforts to build a lucrative trading conduit between Israel and the lands in the east.

However, Malakhi's disdain was another matter. He may have teased and taunted me as a child, but he'd never glared at me like that, as if his piercing gray eyes saw right into the ugliest part of me and hated what they beheld. The longer I'd been in his presence, the higher my shame roiled in my gut, and deservedly so.

Halting at the other end of the room, Samil turned his sharp gaze on me. "What is his weakness?"

Still thinking of Malakhi, I blinked at my master for a moment, scrambling for comprehension. Then I realized he was speaking of the man who'd defrauded him of six years' worth of interest.

I'd spoken to the farmer in question when Estebaal and I were sent to deliver Samil's demands a few days ago. Like my master, he was of the tribe of Manasseh, and older than I'd expected. When I questioned him about the contract, he was relatively defiant, insisting that the scribe the two of them hired that day had written the terms exactly as discussed. But by the sweat that lined the edge of his brow and his upper lip, I guessed he was fully aware of the deceit.

Even more telling was the way his gaze kept flitting to his wife, where she lay on a low bed in the corner of their one-room home, pallid, unmoving, and obviously deathly ill. Samil's methods were well known in Edrei; it was clear the farmer feared his sick wife might bear the brunt of any retaliation.

"*Please,*" he'd pleaded, his tone slipping from insolence into fear when he realized I'd discerned the truth. "*All I have left must go to the healers.*"

"His oxen," I said, offering up something that might profit Samil instead. "He has a fine pair, purchased with your loan, I would guess." Without the animals, the farmer's lentil and chickpea crops would be difficult to put in the ground next season. He'd be forced to plow by hand again, like he'd done before he came to my master.

Samil paced again, contemplating, then called for Estebaal. "Take his oxen, tonight. Don't be seen. I know a buyer who might be interested." He paused. "And destroy his plow."

The farmer would likely be ruined by losing the most important tools of his trade, but at least Samil would not guess that barring the healers from giving the man's wife comfort in her final days would inflict a far greater toll than losing his livelihood.

Estebaal and I exchanged a look behind Samil's back. He'd seen what I had in the farmer's home. As head bodyguard, he was charged with carrying out Samil's commands, to whatever lengths necessary. Would he contradict me? Reveal the man's true tender spot? I held my breath until Estebaal nodded and returned to his post.

Thankfully, Dilara had distracted Samil from the silent exchange between his bodyguard and his scribe by wrapping her body around him and speaking intimacies in his ear, doing little to lower her voice as she did so. Nauseated by their shameless display, I turned my gaze to the ivory inlay table beside me, feigning interest in a depiction of the goddess Ishtar I'd seen hundreds of times, but unable to go until Samil gave me leave. I cleared my throat softly.

"Have you finished the contract for the new overseer?" Samil's question drew my unwilling eyes back to the man and his scowling wife, still unrepentantly entwined in each other.

"Nearly."

He kissed Dilara's neck. "Go then. The one I dismissed last week was useless. At the rate his crew was going, the final addition to the villa wouldn't be finished for years. I want it done by Sukkot, so we can celebrate properly."

"Of course."

"And let it be known that I desire more carpenters as well. That shipment of cedar logs arrived three days ago, and I want construction to begin immediately. Hire as many men as necessary. There are less than two months until the festival."

Knowing that it was useless to argue whether the extravagant project could be completed within that time, I dipped my chin in submission, but Samil did not notice, since he'd been drawn back into Dilara's caresses. He'd already told me to leave, so I spun away, gratefully fleeing the room.

But as I passed Estebaal outside the doorway, he gripped my wrist and murmured, "I heard a man's voice in your room."

A hard knot formed in the center of my chest. "A messenger," I said, attempting a casual air and digging up pieces of a conversation I'd had in the marketplace yesterday in order to appease him. "Delivering a missive from Ishtallah. She acquired a new lot of fabric from Ur and thought Samil might have interest in a trade."

He lifted a black brow, his dark blue eyes narrowed as he mulled my lie.

"I forgot to tell him." I tried to look frustrated with my apparent oversight, then darted a look back at the closed door, unable to conceal my disgust. "However . . . I'd rather not go back in there just now."

Estebaal watched me for another moment, and then one corner of his mouth turned up, the closest I'd ever seen to a smile on the burly Aramean. When he spoke, it was in his own language. "She is relentless, isn't she?"

Since Samil had never bothered to learn any language but Hebrew, he would have no understanding of our exchange, but I dropped my voice anyhow. "You'd think she would at least let him conduct business in peace."

He huffed a low chuckle.

With a silent gesture of farewell, I continued a few more steps down the hall. But just before I turned the corner, Estebaal spoke in his own tongue again. "Take care, Rivkah. Our master guards his possessions well."

TWENTY-FOUR

Malakhi

"A son?" Baz repeated. He gaped at me, slack-jawed. The stick he'd been whittling with his knife dangled loosely in his big palm. "Gidal had a son?"

He looked nearly as stupefied as I had been by the news. Baz had been a part of our family before I'd even been born, and although I knew he held all of us in deep affection, there was something special about Gidal, something otherworldly about his connection to creation and, through it, to Yahweh. Baz had been right when he said it was as if my brother had not been made for this world. The sheen in eyes he quickly averted spoke to just how affected he was by the news.

"He is the very image," I said, thinking back to the open curiosity in the boy's gaze, and my chest ached at the reminder that he saw me as a stranger instead of his uncle.

Walking away today when I had so many questions had been nearly impossible. Rivkah was no fool; she could have found a way to return home or to send a message to her family, no matter what

Nessa had chosen. Something else had kept her here and driven her to such desperate measures. I'd wanted nothing more than to chase her into that villa and demand answers, demand she tell me why she'd done this, why she'd hidden Amit from us, and what had drained the life from her amber eyes.

If she'd not been so adamant that I not be seen by her master, I would likely have done so. But I would not risk putting her and Amit in more of a precarious situation than they were already in, so I'd stayed in her tiny, sparse chamber until she'd disappeared into the villa before slipping out.

Even as I'd walked away, wrapped in a swirl of anger and surprise and frustration, I could not help but ponder how she'd sat on her bed with shoulders bowed and eyes on the floor and the dispassionate way she'd spoken to me, as if we were barely acquainted. As if we'd not dug in the dirt together as children and played chase around the goats in the fields. As if we'd not squabbled and poked fun and tattled on each other hundreds of times. As if she'd not been married to my brother. As if we were not still legally betrothed.

"What do you plan to do?" Baz asked, startling me from my silent revelation.

"Take them back, of course." My parents would be beside themselves with joy to hold the child in their arms, regardless of the devastation of discovering he'd been kept from them. And based on my interaction with Amitai on the roof, he would be thrilled to have his daughter back.

"I thought you said she was indentured."

I ran my fingers through my hair with a snarl, thinking of Rivkah signing her life into another man's hands. "She is."

"Then we smuggle them out," said Baz, as always ready to plow into battle.

I shook my head. "Lawfully, she is bound to that contract. And that villa is a fortress. Her *master*," I said, the word tasting of bile, "employs a number of well-trained guards, some nearly as big as you."

Baz scoffed. "Never stopped me before."

I had little doubt of that. He'd been on the front lines of the incursion into Canaan under the command of Yehoshua and had his fair share of clashes with giant Anakim like King Og of Bashan, who'd built Edrei, the same city whose walls towered in the near distance. The copper-plated gates glowed in the light of the setting sun, hinting at the extravagant wealth Og must have enjoyed before the forces of Israel crushed him.

"Can you not purchase her freedom?" asked Hakim from where he lay on his back, watching the clouds scurry overhead.

"It's possible. But I have nothing to offer. And from the way Rivkah describes her role in the household, buying out her contract would be a costly proposition."

The three of us went silent, mulling the situation. We'd set up camp last night within a well-protected ravine at the foot of the rocky hill upon which Edrei was perched. Toki snuffled around in the weeds, staking her claim on the territory, and cornered a bevy of quail twenty paces off.

Her tail went still, her body rigid. Only her little black nose twitched as she watched the birds shuffle to the side, feathers ruffled, and gather into a huddle against a low outcropping of limestone. Suddenly she darted toward them, making the flock scatter, squawking and chattering their displeasure as they fluttered in all directions.

Baz chuckled at his brown-and-white companion. "She's a determined little thing. She'll likely make one her dinner and come back covered in feathers. Too bad she hasn't learned to retrieve them; I'd enjoy having a meal delivered to me." My stomach rumbled at the thought of fresh meat, and I dug into my pack for some of the dried figs we'd purchased in Golan and handed some to Baz and Hakim as well.

I'd been glad to shake the dust from my sandals when we left that place. We'd spent only one day in the city of refuge, searching out answers about Rivkah's whereabouts, but that was enough, in my opinion. Golan seemed to stand directly opposite of everything I loved about Kedesh: the way everyone worked together to bring in the fruit and nut harvests, frequently accompanied by joyful corporate song; the way the manslayers were folded into the city in such an easy manner; the feeling of familiarity, safety, and camaraderie within its walls.

In contrast, the Levite quarter in Golan was situated on one side of town, delineated quite obviously from that of the manslayers, and it was made clear to us that any interaction with those convicted of manslaughter was forbidden. Although the justification for such an edict was the safety of those who might be pursued by Blood Avengers, the explanation somehow didn't quite ring true.

Also, apart from the bustling marketplace where goods from all over were sold by both Hebrew and foreigner alike, the streets of the city were strangely devoid of any good-natured banter between neighbors. I wondered whether without my mother and her inn, or without generous and just priests like Amitai and his father, Dov, before him to govern it, Kedesh too would be a place where commerce outweighed kindness.

Toki barked, pawing at a large pile of rocks where the bevy of quail had been huddled before. Perhaps one of the smaller birds had taken refuge there before the flock retreated. As Baz had said, Toki was nothing if not determined, or she would not have found her way out of a locked room to follow her master.

Baz called out a command, but she ignored him, her digging becoming almost frantic as dirt flew up from her insistent paws. "Strange," he muttered. Tossing the meat skewer he'd made to the side, he headed over to see what she was after with such resolve. After a few moments of watching her, he squatted down and pulled at a few rocks as well, tossing them off to the side. "Malakhi. Hakim. Come see this."

With something like a satisfied grin on her spotted face, Toki trotted off with a feathered prize clamped between her jaws, her hook tail wagging as she headed into the trees to devour her meal in solitude. But she had uncovered a large hole in pursuit of her prey, one that looked to go down at an angle into the limestone.

"Is it a cave?" Hakim asked.

"Perhaps," said Baz, his tone thoughtful as he tugged at another large rock. "Or a tunnel. Look." He pointed to the limestone along the sides. "This is no natural formation. These are chisel marks."

"Who would build a tunnel out here?" I asked.

Baz sat back on his haunches and surveyed the area, knuckles rubbing at his thick beard. "The more important question is, where does it originate?"

"Perhaps it is merely an abandoned cistern?" offered Hakim.

"Could be," said Baz. "Although I've heard rumors about such tunnels in these parts."

"What did the two of you discover in the marketplace after we parted ways?" I asked, anxious to bring the conversation back to Rivkah, but Baz seemed too wrapped up in the mystery of the hole to answer. He tugged at another large stone and it created an avalanche underground, the sudden clatter of tumbling rocks and debris indicating that the pit was indeed larger than I'd guessed.

"We spoke more with Ishtallah," said Hakim, "the woman who told me where to find Amitai's daughter this morning. She is a fabric merchant from the Far East. Our family has crossed paths with hers before. She is well acquainted with Samil, your Rivkah's master."

I did not correct him, but the thought of her as "mine" caused that sharp pain to once against flare beneath my ribs. I pressed the sensation away with my fingertips.

"He is Hebrew. Of the tribe of Manasseh. Well known as the most prosperous of merchants in Edrei, mainly for his connections with Damascus, Ur, and Avaris. He is also famous for ruthless dealings that skirt the edge of Torah's boundaries."

The way Rivkah's face had paled as she'd insisted Samil should not see me made it clear that her master was not a man to be trifled with. The unease that had taken hold of me as she'd explained her predicament only deepened at Hakim's words. "She mentioned he has two Canaanite wives."

Hakim nodded. "Yes, I heard this too. It seems that he has taken up the custom of flaunting his wealth with multiple wives."

Along with disregarding the law of Mosheh by marrying Canaanites, I thought. It was becoming all too common for men of power to broker peace and prosperity with enemy tribes by intermarriage. And from what I'd seen of Edrei, there seemed to be as many Canaanites as Hebrews living side-by-side in the city.

"His villa is certainly proof of his flourishing business. It is larger than my mother's inn, and it looks as though he is building on another wing of rooms. There is an enormous amount of rocks, bricks, and cedar logs assembled at the site already, and while I waited at Rivkah's door, another wagonful of mud-bricks was delivered."

"There is your answer," said Baz as he tugged at a clump of vines that swirled down into his mysterious hole. "Go build his house."

"What?" I asked.

Baz looked over his shoulder. "Have you learned nothing from training with your father, boy? You need to get close to the girl. Determine the safest way to get her and the little one out of that household. So take a job as a carpenter, which you are already skilled at, and do what we do best. Spy."

Baz's idea had merit. I'd slipped out the villa gates quickly, keeping my head down. It was unlikely that anyone would have noticed me speaking with Rivkah. The guards at the gate had barely taken notice of me when I'd asked to speak to my "cousin" in the servants' quarters—after they painstakingly checked me for any weapons, of course. And if anyone had seen our interaction, I could certainly frame it as petitioning for work, asking if she'd help me find employment with her master.

If I worked at the villa, I could ensure that she and Amit were safe, and it would give me time to plan. Hopefully I wouldn't dig myself into a hole as deep as the one at Baz's feet. But for the sake of my brother's child, I'd move any number of obstacles until he and his mother were free.

TWENTY-FIVE

Rivkah

It had been two days since Malakhi had walked out of the villa, but nearly every moment since then had been spent in torment. Every knock on the door made my heart race, every deep voice out in the courtyard strangled the breath from me, and every moment Amit was out of my sight caused my body to vibrate with fear. The truth was that Malakhi could return at any moment to assert his rights as the uncle of my child, and there was every reason to believe that the elders of Edrei would stand behind him. I was a woman. A slave. There would be no recourse if he chose to take my son away.

But despite my fears, I had no choice but to leave Amit in the care of Ana in the kitchen courtyard while I performed my duties. So with my legs folded beneath me and a thin slab of wood balanced on my knees, I recorded the skill and agreed-upon wage for the bricklayer who stood in front of me. I'd already hired fifteen men just like him, as well as three carpenters and five new stonemasons, and the line of men searching out employment still stretched twenty long, at least.

As I gestured for the next man to step forward and state his skills and experience, I was reminded of the days I'd spent recording tithes for my father in Kedesh, specifically the first time I'd been given the task.

Although I'd received a few scowls—and more than one leer— from a number of the men that day, by the time I'd called forward the last person in line to record their tithe and thank them on behalf of the Levite families like mine who relied on the generosity of the Hebrew people for sustenance, I'd already been anticipating the next morning. Back then, utilizing the skills my father had taught me felt as natural as breathing and nearly as life-giving, but now the act of putting ink to papyrus was mundane, a drudgery instead of a joy. The only time I felt even a flicker of contentment was when I snatched a few secret moments to scribble down lyrics on stolen pieces of papyrus, and even then most of my words tended to be woven from sorrow and regret.

I completed hiring the bricklayer, then another, and then a stonemason, without even looking any of them in the eye, but when a familiar and yet somehow altogether different voice responded to my rote query about carpentry skills, the freshly loaded tip of my reed skidded across the rough papyrus sheet, marring my otherwise perfectly executed list.

I pulled in a shaky breath before I allowed my eyes to slide up Malakhi's changed form. Even after seeing him the other day, the transformation was still a shock. This was *not* the boy I'd known. Not the affable, charismatic young man whose crooked smile made the girls of Kedesh flutter and preen. This man was dangerous. Eyes like the frost that gathered in shadowed places narrowed as I met his cold gaze.

A thousand questions flooded my mind, not the least of which was why he was here asking for employment as a carpenter at Samil's villa. But acutely aware that Estebaal stood only a few paces away, I could do nothing but ask Malakhi's length of experience, although I knew the answer full well.

"Ten years" came the curt reply.

Helpless to ask anything of real meaning, or to plead with him to go back to Kedesh and leave my boy alone, I asked for the name and tribal affiliation I knew as well as my own, then outlined the expected wages of a carpenter with his length of expertise. Then, with my stomach twisted into knots, I nodded my head as if he were dismissed. He stepped to the side and a dark-skinned man stepped forward, one who looked vaguely familiar, and gave a reverent dip of his chin. A strange gesture, for I was certainly in no position to deserve such respect.

"Your skill?"

His mahogany eyes flicked over to Malakhi, who lifted a brow at him—a silent command.

"Carpentry." Hakim's discomfort was nearly painful to watch. This man did not like lying. And one glance at the callus-free fingers twitching at his sides made it obvious that it *was* a lie. He was so tall that I was forced to crane my head back to see his face. His arms and legs looked plenty strong, but Malakhi's muscular build gave witness to his trade. Those shoulders had wielded an ax and an adze for years, hauled heavy logs all over town, and felled trees on countless occasions. I met Malakhi's cool gaze, one that communicated quite clearly that I should swallow any concerns. Hakim was no carpenter, but for some reason Malakhi wanted me to accept that he was, without question.

My pulse fluttered, and sweat beaded at my hairline. My panic must have been on full display, for Malakhi suddenly shifted his stance, his expression softening, his silver eyes conveying encouragement instead of the palpable disdain that had so far defined him. Had I been wrong to assume that his appearance today meant he was here to steal Amit? The tension in my gut loosened ever so slightly, and I prayed that the letters I wrote down next would not be ones I regretted for the rest of my life.

"Name and tribal affiliation?" I asked his friend.

Hakim ben Benamin. He designated no tribal affiliation, so I looked up with curiosity.

"I come from a line of traders. Although we are in Covenant to Yahweh, we are not bound to a tribe—"

"Naftali," interrupted Malakhi, with a pointed look toward his friend.

With an unnamable emotion shimmering in his dark eyes, Hakim dropped his chin. "Hakim ben Benamin. Naftali."

I wrote down the words, fascinated by the exchange and watched the two of them walk toward the half-constructed wing of Samil's villa, where the replacement overseer was directing new laborers in their tasks for the day. I hoped Malakhi would guide Hakim well; my master did not tolerate lazy or inefficient workers, a distinction the last overseer should have heeded or he would not have lost his position on Edrei's largest construction project in years. Samil's business had grown to nearly three times what it was when I came into service, and through the expansion and renovation of his home, he'd made sure everyone was aware of his status as one of the most respected and powerful men in the city.

With a sigh, I dipped my reed pen in my inkpot, but just as I gestured for the next laborer to come forward, Estebaal caught my eye. His expression and the brow he raised made it quite clear that he'd seen my silent but meaningful exchange with Malakhi.

Alarm slithered through me. It would be imperative that Malakhi show himself to be a loyal worker. Because if Estebaal sensed that he was here for me and divulged such suspicions to Samil, he could very well be in danger. So I threw myself into my task and did not turn my eyes back to the man who'd walked days to find me—a monumental achievement when he was only twenty paces away and curiosity was gnawing a hole in my stomach.

When the line had dwindled to only five men searching for positions, two little arms wrapped themselves around my neck as a small body latched itself to my back. "Ima!" announced the most precious of voices. "I came to help Ana!"

I turned to find Amit grinning down at me, freckles on full display and his dark hair a windblown mess. Wild adoration for my boy thumped in my chest. Gidal had given me the best of gifts within our short marriage. Although the discovery of my pregnancy had been a confusing and frightful time, one when I'd made the desperate, unwise, and irrevocable decision to enslave myself, I'd never regret protecting my sweet child. Being Amit's mother had changed me for the better and made the years of servitude bearable. Every breath I took was for him.

"Now, Amit," said Anataliah, as she approached with a large dripping waterskin slung over her shoulder, "give your ima some room while she finishes up with these men. You and I will make sure the laborers' thirst is quenched."

Three other women from the kitchen carried water as well, along with clay cups and baskets of fresh bread. Samil ordered that his workers were well watered and sated, ensuring they'd remain motivated to work longer and faster for the wages they were promised. My master was the king of seemingly magnanimous, yet shrewd gestures. After planting a kiss on my cheek, Amit scrambled off to follow the young woman he regarded as a second mother, whose complicated name he'd shortened to Ana as soon as he could speak.

The group moved from laborer to laborer, filling and refilling the cups with water and handing out bread. Ana tasked Amit with delivering the filled cups and then holding the empty vessel as she refilled it for the next man. When Amit and Ana neared the place where Malakhi and Hakim swung adzes to skim bark from one of the giant cedar logs, Malakhi halted his work and signaled for Hakim to do so as well, then lifted a palm to keep Amit from getting too close. The protective gesture caused my throat to swell, but when Amit held out a cup of water to Malakhi, my trepidations roared back to life.

Malakhi knelt on one knee, looking straight into my son's eyes as Amit pointed to the workers behind him and asked a question. My grip on the reed pen tightened, my knuckles whitening and my attention hopelessly divided between their conversation and my job. I was forced to ask the man in front of me his tribal affiliation three times before I could successfully record his response.

Surely Malakhi would not be so foolish as to reveal his identity to my son, who could not understand the danger an innocent remark might inspire. Nausea churned in my gut. I'd made another horrible error. I should not have let down my guard and hired him and his friend today. I should have called out to Estebaal and had them ushered out of the gates with orders to never come back.

Abruptly telling the last man in line that all positions were full for the day, I ignored his startled protests and jumped to my feet, leaving my inks and pens behind on the ground as I headed for my son.

"Amit!" Hands shaking, I pulled him backward, closer to me. Away from the man I'd once vowed to honor and obey.

Startled, my son looked up at me. "Ima! Malakhi said he would teach me how to use an adze."

"What?" My gaze fell to the sharp tool on the ground nearby.

Malakhi's lips twitched with humor. "I said I would teach him when he is *much* older." Then he grinned at Amit with wicked conspiracy in his eyes. "But perhaps in a couple of years I can talk your ima into a small whittling knife."

Squelching the hysteria that threatened to pour from my mouth, I glared at Malakhi, who suddenly looked far too similar to the teasing boy of my youth.

"Go back to the kitchen courtyard, Amit," I said.

"But Ima, Malakhi—"

"I said go back. Now." I felt Amit's shoulders stiffen beneath my palms. I rarely had to chastise my son, so my snappish response must have startled him. Gently, I turned him around and kissed his forehead in apology. "Go, lamb. Find Bensam and play until it's time for your afternoon rest."

He nodded, deferring to me easily. Along with inheriting Gidal's natural inquisitiveness, he also had his father's calm and compliant tendencies. I gave him a reassuring smile as he walked away, but instead of looking back at me, my precious son gave the man he did not know was his uncle a large grin and a wave before trotting off to find his best friend, Dilara and Samil's five-year-old son.

Still on bended knee, Malakhi watched him go, then peered up at me with such intensity that my heart began to beat a murky, disjointed rhythm. I spun, heading back to the canopy where I'd left my tools, determined to put as much distance between me and the guilt-inducing expression on his face. Yes, I'd kept Amit from him and the family who would undoubtedly adore him, but I would not be separated from my boy, not for one single day.

"I believe you have something to tell me," said Anataliah, who'd appeared at my side while I was kneeling to gather my inks and reeds.

I stood, brushing the dirt off my well-worn tunic. "What do you mean?"

"You know exactly what I mean." She glared at me, hands on her hips. "Who is that man? Why does your son know him? And why did you drag Amit away in such a panic?"

"I did not *drag* him away." I glanced around to ensure that Estebaal had not heard her, but he was engaged in a conversation with the new overseer. The constant thud of axes against wood, shovels into hard-packed ground, and the tapping of chisels on stone would muffle our conversation. And although I was loathe to discuss this here, it was likely the best time, when Amit could not overhear.

Ana knew few details about my past in Kedesh. I'd told her I'd been widowed shortly before I left, but not my reasons for leaving, only that I was looking for a way to sustain myself and my child.

After nearly five years of holding in the truth from the young woman I'd come to rely on and see as a younger sister, it was time to confess.

"Malakhi is . . . was . . . my betrothed. I was promised in levirate marriage after Gidal died."

Her lips parted and her eyes grew twice as large. "Is? Or was?"

I cleared my throat. "Truly, I do not know. He is more than likely married now. I left behind the bridal gifts when I departed. And my abandonment was certainly grounds for severing the betrothal." As was my reckless behavior in Laish, but mercifully Malakhi did not know about that.

"Amit started talking to him as if he already knew him," Ana said. "I was so stunned I did not know what to do."

"He came to our room the other day, carrying a message from my father."

"What message?"

The roll of papyrus sat ensconced in my belt, in the exact same place I'd carried my plea of forgiveness for almost three years. My father had responded to my two words with two of his own.

COME HOME.

"He asked me to return," I said. "But of course that is impossible."

Ana let her gaze drift toward Malakhi, but I kept mine on her face. "And what of him?"

"I don't know. I told him that I am under contract and cannot leave. I'd hoped that he had left the city. I was very shocked to see him today." I pulled my ink palette closer to my chest. "I am afraid he means to take Amit."

Her response was sharp. "Why would he do that?"

"Amit is Gidal's heir, Ana. If Malakhi asked the elders to return Amit to Kedesh, especially after my deception, I have little doubt they would comply." My voice trembled. "I could lose my sweet boy."

She brushed a soothing palm up and down my forearm. "No, my

friend. Amit asked how Malakhi knew you and he told him that he was your friend from long ago. When Amit bragged about your scribing skills, Malakhi said he remembered watching you practice letters for hours and hours and how much he admired you for how hard you worked to learn. He even remarked that Amit should be proud to have such a skilled mother. A man intent on separating a child from his mother would not say such things, Rivkah."

Eyes burning, my words came out strangled. "I pray you are right. . . . I could not bear . . ."

She squeezed my arm in a reassuring gesture. "You must speak with him, find out why he stayed."

"Yes, but I cannot let Estebaal know that I am doing so or he may tell Samil." I glanced over at the bodyguard, who was no longer speaking with the overseer but staring our way. "I should go back to our room and see to a few other tasks before I return to disperse wages at the end of the day."

She and I parted ways, and I turned to head toward the servants' quarters. It was then that I noticed Estebaal's eyes were no longer on me, but instead on Ana as she made her way back to the kitchen courtyard. I stumbled, shocked by the obvious longing on his face. His gaze darted back to me before he turned away with a guilty jolt.

Samil's loyal bodyguard was also the most feared. Dark rumors passed from servant to servant in the household—of men with severed limbs, of houses set aflame, and even of one trader who'd disappeared completely after somehow betraying Samil. Estebaal had always been respectful toward me, but he was anything but safe.

I resolved to keep a closer eye on my innocent young friend, as well as search for some way to speak to Malakhi alone. I would not breathe easy until I knew what his intentions were here in Edrei and likely not even until he walked out those gates and back to Kedesh.

Alone.

TWENTY-SIX

Malakhi

I'd given up on finding a comfortable position on my sleep mat and instead glared at the inn ceiling, waiting for exhaustion to overtake my ever-churning frustrations with Rivkah. I wanted answers. And although I reported to her every morning before beginning my labor and every evening when she doled out wages, I could say nothing with Samil's large and attentive guards standing watch. So every night I seethed at the impossible situation she'd gotten herself into and my helplessness to do anything about it.

The stench of this place was gag-inducing. I'd decided days ago that the innkeeper rarely, if ever, cleaned the room, nor did he care that the last guest had used the corner to relieve himself. If I'd not been determined to stay within the city walls, to be close to Rivkah and Amit, I'd not have bothered to keep a room but instead camped among the trees with Baz and Toki.

This inn was the very opposite of my mother's warm and hospitable abode. There were no clean and aired rooms awaiting guests, no carefully spiced and lovingly prepared dishes to fill their bellies, and no laughter, good-natured banter, or bright and happy voices of children floating in from the courtyard. Instead, the Edomite who owned this place had ushered us to this cell, demanded nearly a full day's wages, and informed us that we'd be responsible for all of our own meals before walking away without another word.

"Are you ever going to sleep?" asked Hakim from his own miserable pallet two paces away from mine. To his credit, my friend had not said a word about the accommodations. Neither had he complained about the labor we'd endured for the past week, nor the blisters that had risen on his palms, ones he'd been forced to wrap in linen in order to keep working. He must truly be enamored with my sister.

"She won't let the boy near me," I said, my aggravation boiling over. "Not since that first day." Those few moments I'd had with my nephew had left me aching for more, but it seemed Rivkah had other plans. Amit had not accompanied the women who brought us food and water again, and she kept him within arm's length whenever he visited while she worked. "He is my brother's child. I have every right to see him, to know him. He should be in Kedesh with my family."

"Perhaps she is fearful," said Hakim.

"Of what? I would never hurt Amit."

"Of course not, but what about her?"

"She is the one who ran, Hakim."

"And she wounded you, I know. But she is not the girl who ran anymore, is she? She is a mother who adores her child."

That much was true. The flat demeanor I'd noted in Rivkah was washed away completely in the presence of her son. Although I could not hear the conversations that passed between them over the noise of mallets and chisels and adzes, the corners of her rose-colored lips tipped upward the moment he threw his arms around her neck from behind, her eyes dancing as he prattled and gestured, and I'd even twice seen her throw her head back and laugh.

Regardless that I could not hear the sound, both times it brought to mind the one last carefree moment we'd laughed together in the quince grove. The fact that I still wished to hear that laugh with my own ears only served to remind me of what a fool I'd been over a woman who'd never wanted me and added tinder to the aggravation that smoldered hotter every day.

"Why did you come here, my friend?" Hakim asked.

"Because Amitai asked me to."

Hakim's silence was an accusation. I let it spool out too long, the loops wrapping around my neck, so my next words were strangled. "Because I wanted to know why."

"Not to punish her for going?"

Had I wanted to punish her? Make her suffer the way I had when she left? Perhaps, if I was honest with myself, I'd felt a certain measure of satisfaction that first day at seeing her brought low, but the sight of her with her son had washed those merciless thoughts from my mind. I may still be angry with her for discarding me and hiding Amit, but my first instinct was to protect her, and that is what I planned to do, whether she begged my forgiveness or not.

A tap at the door saved me from responding to Hakim's question. The tap was followed by an insistent scratching near the ground that made it clear who our vistors were. I lifted myself from my pallet to open the door, groaning at the dull ache in my shoulder but noting that it did not hurt quite as much as I'd expected after a week of heavy labor.

Baz blew out a disgusted breath as he stepped inside the tiny room. "Did one of you die in here?"

I ignored him and checked outside before latching the door behind him. "What are you doing here so late?"

"I've attempted to catch the two of you early, but you're gone at dawn. Figured this would be my best chance of sharing news without being overheard."

Toki snuffled around in the room for a few moments, then did her part to cover up the stench in the corner before shaking her entire body, as if sloughing off water. Dust and debris flew in all directions.

"Why is your dog covered in dirt?"

Baz grinned. "That's part of why I'm here. And how I got past the gates after dark. I found the other end of the tunnel."

My jaw dropped. "You mean to say you've spent these last few days burrowing underground?"

"I have. What else was I to do while the two of you were fooling around with sticks and stones? Toki and I followed the entire length of one of the tunnels, which comes out not too far from here into one of the deep cisterns beneath the city. Luckily the water level is low enough that we were able to climb right up the stairs and into the street."

"You said tunnels. There are more than one?"

"I counted at least five branches, and there are entire caverns down there. Some look to be natural and some are hand-carved. This city was well prepared to withstand an invasion. It must have taken decades for King Og or his predecessors to have these pathways dug out. Although the majority of the tunnel was surprisingly unobstructed, I did have to push through a couple of areas of cave-in, but it seems to be fairly passable."

"Did our armies not discover these tunnels when we took this city from the Amorites?"

"I did hear rumors to that effect, but I was not yet twenty then. I did not fight my first battle until after we'd crossed the Jordan River nearly a year later. Jericho was my first."

It was hard to imagine Baz younger than me, a time before he worked and fought alongside my father. A time before he was the fearless, bold, and heavily scarred warrior he was now.

"Although this is all quite interesting," I said, "what made you so intent on braving that tunnel tonight to find us?"

"I have to leave," he said, a deep frown on his face. "In the morning."

Although I did not expect him to stay for my sake, his urgency unsettled me.

"I've spent some time in the marketplace when I wasn't in the tunnels, gathering information from vendors or just wandering around with my ears open. This afternoon, I overheard disturbing news. Apparently, some sort of uproar has sparked serious tension between the tribes. There is concern that an intertribal war may be on the near horizon."

My father had warned for years of this very thing. How could we possibly stay united under the banner of the Torah when so many Hebrews no longer respected the Covenant and the tenets that bound us together? With so many fractures between the tribes, and now without Yehoshua to lead us, how could we possibly stand against the enemies around us?

"I must get back. I need to share what I've learned with Darek and determine what he and Eitan discovered up north. Between the threat of the Arameans and this new issue, things are very precarious."

"I agree. You must go. I'll be fine."

"You are staying?"

"I am not leaving Edrei without Gidal's son." Or Rivkah.

Baz clapped a palm on my shoulder. "I thought you'd say that."

"I'll stay with you," said Hakim from his prone position on his mat. The poor man was so exhausted he'd not even bothered sitting up when Baz came in, nor when Toki began licking his face in earnest.

"You should go back with Baz, Hakim. There is no need for you to stay."

"I can't leave you alone," he said, rolling to his side.

"I'll be fine. I'll be working at the villa until I can find a way to get them out, for however long that takes. And you need to ask for Chana's hand before my father departs again."

Baz lifted a thick brow with a low whistle, and I felt sure that if Hakim's skin were not so dark it would be blazing red. For a man so extraordinary tall and imposing, Hakim was unusually shy. He cleared his throat. "And what should I tell Chana about Ayala?"

Crossing my arms, I let out a sigh. I'd come to Edrei with every intention of returning to marry the girl, and although my resolve to guard myself against Rivkah's effects on me remained intact, I could not in good conscience ask Ayala to wait for me. It could be days until I found a way to bring Amit and Rivkah home, or it could be months. And as much as I did not anticipate making a home here in this dank and cheerless room, I was resolved to stay near Amit. Even if I had to wait out the rest of Rivkah's indenture.

"Tell Chana that I am sorry, but Amit needs me. Ayala is a lovely young woman. I am sure there will be another who is more than willing to make her his wife."

Within only a short time after their arrival, Baz and Toki were gone, and Hakim with them, heading back down into the tunnel where they would use an oil lamp and the charcoal markings Baz had left on the walls to guide their way out of Edrei.

The next morning when I reported to Rivkah at dawn, she looked up at me with surprising concern in her amber eyes and asked about Hakim.

"He has returned home," I said.

"Oh? Will he be back?" she asked, dropping her eyes back to her papyrus record, as if she were merely making pleasantries with a stranger.

"No."

She drew a line through Hakim's name on the list. "Will you be staying on then?" Her demeanor was impassive, but I was fully aware that she was anything but indifferent.

The question hummed between us for a few moments before I answered. "I have no plans to leave."

She slowly lifted her gaze back up to mine. "For how long?"

"As long as it takes to complete the job," I replied. From the way her eyes widened and her knuckles went white where she gripped her pen, I knew she comprehended my true meaning, and for some reason it terrified her.

Although consumed with the urge to question her odd reaction, I looked up to see that the tall Aramean guard I'd noticed on the first day of my employment was watching the two of us with sharp interest again. My desperation to speak with Rivkah alone would have to wait a little longer. With Hakim gone I'd have nothing to occupy my mind, so I'd likely spend the entire day of work plotting out the best way to speak with Rivkah and attempting to squelch the simmering ache that always seemed to flare to life whenever I stood within ten paces of her. This day would be long indeed.

TWENTY-SEVEN

Rivkah

5 Elul

The renovation to Samil's home had seemed interminable, but with the addition of the new workers, Malakhi included, I wondered if it actually might be finished by Sukkot as he'd ordered.

In the second year of my indenture, we'd traveled to Avaris, and Samil had been so enthralled with the wealth and extravagance of the Black Land that as soon as we returned he ordered his large home to be transformed into an Egyptian-style villa, complete with a garden pool filled with lotus, a white-plastered exterior, and a small sanctuary at the back of the property to house his wives' gods.

From the brightly painted and ornately carved beams that were installed in the private courtyard at the center of the villa, to the claw-footed bedsteads built in the swooping Egyptian style, to the expertly woven linen carried back with us on our camels, the effect of the transformation was impressive.

Samil had even bullied all the surrounding neighbors to sell their homes to him as well and incorporated those he did not raze inside the enclosing mud-brick fence that surrounded his new larger property. This final addition of rooms had been added onto the plans a few months ago, a response to my master's ever-expanding family and the many foreign visitors he entertained.

As I'd been ordered to do, I ensured that the laborers received their daily wages but also aided the overseer with correspondence to and from material suppliers. Therefore, when Tarron, Samil's oldest child and exalted heir, walked into the center of the construction area, I was only fifteen paces away.

The boy was a menace. Entitled and nearly as pampered as his mother, Ofira, he was forever tormenting Amit, and I could do nothing but hold my tongue. And since no one else had any power over the young master either, the ten-year-old strode past the stonemasons, the bricklayers, and the carpenters directly into the chamber he'd been told by his father was designated as his alone.

With panic on his well-lined brow, the overseer darted toward the child with a feeble warning to take heed of the carpenters, who were even now positioning cedar support beams overhead. But he'd not reached the threshold of the chamber before a series of shouts rang out, followed by the thud of heavy wood on stone, the billow of dust from inside the half-constructed room, and then an ominous silence.

Then everyone seemed to be yelling at once, and even though I held no affection for Ofira's firstborn, my heart contracted painfully. Anataliah appeared at my side, both of us silent and wide-eyed as we awaited the outcome of such a disaster. No matter Samil's proclivity for manipulation, and even at times violence, losing a child was nothing I wished upon him. The overseer disappeared inside the room alone, but appeared with another man by his side, one carrying a sobbing and bleeding Tarron.

Malakhi.

My formerly betrothed had a scrape down one cheek, and dust and wood shavings coated his skin and hair, but he looked to be intact. He hoisted Tarron into a more secure position against his chest, his face contorting in obvious pain. He'd been favoring his right shoulder over the past two weeks, and it looked as if whatever injury he'd suffered before had been aggravated by this incident. But still he strode forward, his lips moving. He seemed to be comforting the foolish child as he carried him toward the villa, led by the overseer. Estebaal met them at the doorway, and after a brief exchange between the three men, the overseer led Malakhi with his sorrowful burden into the house. Estebaal looked back, catching my eye with a speaking glance before he too entered our master's home and shut the door behind him.

As the workers jolted into motion and Ana headed back toward the kitchen courtyard, I stood locked in place, desperate to know what was happening inside and consumed with fear that Estebaal might say something about Malakhi and me.

What would I do if Samil discovered that we knew each other? Or, may Yahweh forbid, that we were at one time betrothed? Samil was relentless in pursuit of wealth and I was integral to that goal. He'd told me for years now that he'd never had a scribe, not to mention a female one, who was so valuable. He would no sooner hand me over to Malakhi than he would hand him the deed to his villa, no matter that our ketubah contract had been drawn up before the indenture. The Torah meant little to Samil, unless he could skew its regulations in his own favor. Estebaal's warning from the day Malakhi arrived rose again in my mind.

As I'd expected, one of the housemaids soon called me inside, her blank countenance giving no clue as to what I was walking into. So I braced myself as I tapped on the door to my master's chamber, breath trapped in my chest. I feared our connection might be discovered, but I also feared Samil might blame Malakhi for this incident with Tarron and demand that the elders charge him with negligence. Injury to the master's son would require restitution Malakhi could ill afford to pay. Perhaps he too would be forced into servitude to pay the debt. The door swung open, and Estebaal ushered me inside, his expression also unreadable.

"Rivkah!" said Samil. "I require your help." He swept an arm toward Malakhi, who stood in the center of the room, a trickle of dried blood still tracking down to his beard from the gouge on his cheek. "This is Malakhi," he announced, with a tone of admiration that caused me to blink in surprise. "He saved Tarron! Jumped through the open rafters to shield my boy from the beam that rolled away from one of the carpenters. If he had not put his own body in the way, my son may well have been crushed!"

"I am pleased to hear that, my lord," I replied cautiously. "How may I be of service?"

My master gestured toward the table in the corner where I performed many of my duties under his watchful eye. "Do prepare a sheet of papyrus. I would like to reward this young man for his quick action in rescuing Tarron today."

"That won't be necessary, my lord," said Malakhi as I moved to do my master's bidding, and I hoped I was the only one that heard the tension beneath the designation of Samil as his authority. "I am just thankful the boy is relatively unharmed."

Samil dismissed his argument with a wave of his palm. "Tell me, Malakhi, from where do you hail?"

Malakhi kept his eyes trained on my master. "From Naftali territory, my lord."

"Yes? Our Rivkah does as well."

"Is that so?" Malakhi asked, his gaze barely flickering over to me.

"Indeed," said Samil. "And how did you gain expertise in carpentry?"

"My brother is a noted bronzesmith but dabbles in carpentry when metal is scarce and whenever tools require carving. I learned most of what I know from him beginning at age twelve."

"What brought you here?"

"I heard there was wealth to be built in this city."

Samil nodded, accepting that explanation easily. "And tell me, what happened today? Why did that beam fall?"

Malakhi shifted his weight from one foot to the other, his posture communicating wariness.

"Please speak freely," Samil urged. "I must know that my work site is safe."

Malakhi kneaded his right shoulder absent-mindedly. "There are a number of carpenters working on the villa who have not participated in a cooperative project of this scale. The overseer is doing a fine job of managing the many workers involved, but there is no leadership over the carpenters themselves. We spend more time quarreling over the best method to hoist the beams than actually doing so. The men are skilled, my lord; they only lack firm direction to ensure efficiency and safety for all involved. Unfortunately, your son entered the room just as a disagreement broke out over the most secure way to join the crossbeams, and the men were distracted. It was simply a terrible accident that no one could have anticipated."

Samil scratched his chin thoughtfully. "As I suspected." He turned to me. "This man is now the head carpenter. Please ensure that his wages reflect his position."

My chin jerked up to catch Malakhi's reaction. His jaw slackened and he took a small step backward. "That is not—"

Again, Samil waved off his protest. "Do your wife and children have accommodations nearby?"

My fingers gripped my reed pen far too tightly. Which of the beautiful and doting girls in Kedesh had captured Malakhi's attention? And did Amit have silver-eyed cousins? I had no right to care either way, but I found that I did, and held my breath until the answer came.

"I have none," he replied, not looking my way.

Samil looked shocked. "Truly? A handsome young man like you? I would think you'd have a girl on each arm."

"I was betrothed." Malakhi's smile was tight and grim. "But she left me."

Heartbeat pounding in my ears, I laid my pen atop the papyrus and gripped my knees beneath the table to prevent myself from jumping up and running from the room to find somewhere to deposit the contents of my rollicking stomach.

"I am sorry to hear that," said Samil, patting Malakhi on the shoulder with true empathy in his tone. "But there are plenty of lovely ladies here in Edrei." He leaned in closer and lowered his voice. "And with your higher wages now, I'm sure you'll have little lack of company at night." He winked, laughing at his own crude humor.

Although Samil had not made any advances on me, he did nothing to shield me from his proclivities. Many times I went back to my quarters at night desperate for a cool, fresh stream to wash away the filth I was subjected to in his home and within the homes of those with whom he conducted business. Egypt had rubbed off on Samil in more ways than one, as had the depravity of his wives' heritage.

For his part, Malakhi did nothing more than acknowledge the crass jest with a tight dip of his chin.

"I'll leave you with Rivkah. She'll outline your wages and make a record of your new position here in the household, as well as explain your duties." Samil glanced at me over his shoulder. "Include meals in his wages, Rivkah. I want the rest of the workers to see what rewards loyalty provides."

"Yes, my lord," I said, doing my best to keep my voice from warbling.

"Excellent," he said with a clap of his palms that ended the conversation. "Now come, Estebaal, I have a task for you. Do you remember that Moabite . . . ?" His voice trailed off as he left the room, his attention already on to other matters, assuming his bodyguard would follow. But Estebaal stopped at the threshold and gave Malakhi and I both a stern look that communicated quite clearly he'd understood much of the silent current that had transpired in front of our oblivious master. Then, to my astonishment, he shut the door.

Both of us stared at the doorway for the count of thirty breaths, as if in agreement that we should not speak until there was no chance of being overheard. Although still reeling from the revelation that Malakhi was as yet unmarried, the bloody trail on his cheek reminded me that he was in pain.

"You are injured," I said. "Samil employs a healer, I can call her—"

"No," he interrupted, once again massaging his right shoulder. "It is an old injury. And the beam did not land on it anyhow. It glanced off the wall and rolled down my back instead."

"But your cheek . . ."

"The boy scratched me with the pointed stick he was carrying. It's nothing. The worst of it was that he bit his own lip when I landed on him. Frightened him more than anything."

"That child could do with a little fear," I mumbled.

A hint of reluctant amusement quirked his lips. "The same boy who was tormenting Amit?"

I nodded. "Tarron bullies all the children, but he especially delights in poking at my sweet boy until he cries."

His jaw worked, as if his teeth were grinding together. "And you are helpless to do anything."

"The child himself is above me in this household. I am shackled in every way." I cleared my throat as I picked up my reed pen, dipped it in the inkpot, and outlined Malakhi's reward. "When were you injured?" I asked.

"I served under my father for less than a year once I attained military age," he said. "We came across a group of Amorites up north who were surprisingly well armed. Apparently, I was hit in the head with a battle-ax, then trampled by an iron-wheeled chariot. I awoke three days later with a half-blind eye and my shoulder feeling as if it had been shredded to pieces." He scoffed. "Five years of training wiped away in one moment, and I don't even remember it happening."

"You are unable to fight?"

He scowled and placed the edge of his hand just to the right of his pupil. "Not only is my sword arm practically useless, this part of my sight is severely limited. I would be far too easy a target on the battlefield. My presence would only endanger fellow soldiers."

The despair within that statement was hard to ignore, but what could I say? I'd never lifted a sword or faced down a chariot, and it made me quail to even contemplate Malakhi doing such feats. "And yet you seem to be managing this job well."

"I've been working on developing the strength in my left arm," he said. "And using the right only when necessary."

"Perhaps in time . . . ?"

He sighed. "I'd rather not have this discussion again. Baz and my father refuse to let it go."

"Fair enough." I tried not to bristle at his brusque manner. "Then tell me why you stayed."

"I'll not leave Edrei without my nephew," he said.

Anger and fear entwined to wrap my backbone in iron. "You *won't* take my son from me."

His brows furrowed in confusion as he stared at me. "Of course not."

"You won't separate us?"

"Why would I do that to Amit? You are his mother." His expression was incredulous. "Don't you know me at all, Rivkah?"

Dropping my pen, I put my head in my hands as I stifled a sob, but tears dripped onto the papyrus below me anyway, pooling and smudging Malakhi's name.

"I told Baz I would stay until we find a way to free you," he said, his voice near to a whisper. "I took this job to watch over you both and to evaluate the best way to get you home safely."

I wiped away my embarrassing tears and busied myself with pulling a clean sheet of papyrus from the basket beneath the desk instead of looking up at him. "I told you, I am still bound for many months. If I tried to escape, Samil would find me. He is relentless, Malakhi. The things I've seen . . ." I shook my head, trying to blink away some of my memories. "No. Amit and I would be in far more danger outside the walls of this villa than within it. I must finish out my contract."

He said nothing as I rewrote the lines my tears had destroyed, so when I finally looked up I was surprissed to find that he was in front of the narrow table directly across from me. I'd finally adjusted to him being much taller than me and the strong build that he'd developed over the years, but the bitter slant to his mouth and the cool stare that met mine were still jarring.

You did this.

The thought startled me. He was obviously angry over my deception about Gidal's son, but I felt the icy fury the moment I opened the door the first day he arrived, before he even knew of Amit's existence. Was it because I'd dishonored Gidal that he was holding on to such bitterness? Or was his resentment more personal? *"She left me,"* he'd told Samil.

A memory from our last conversation in the quince grove arose in my mind. Our shared humor at his expense. His quick slide into quietness as he watched me dissolve into laughter. And then the sudden, intense resolve that came into his eyes as he reached for me. I'd accused him of manipulation then, but perhaps . . . perhaps I'd been wrong.

"Why are you unmarried?" I asked, then silently chastised myself for letting the words slip from my mouth.

He let out a slow breath but held my gaze beneath half-lowered black lashes, his lips drawn tight. "Because I am still betrothed to you."

Just as my vision blurred and my pulse took off at a gallop, one of Samil's Moabite servant girls swung the door open, her expression startled as she took in Malakhi's proximity to me. "Oh, forgive me. I came in to gather the master's linens for washing."

"That's all right. We are nearly finished," I said, dropping my attention back to the papyrus document that I'd barely begun and hoping she wouldn't notice that my hand trembled as I formed the letters. "Do you understand the terms of your employment?"

"Yes," Malakhi replied.

"Good. And are the wages to your satisfaction?"

"Yes."

I planned to be especially generous with those wages. Samil rarely, if ever, questioned my judgment in such matters anymore. "You will be expected to arrive before the men and not leave until the last one vacates the jobsite. All meals will be provided. Anataliah will make sure you are served in the kitchen courtyard."

He lifted his brows in question. I knew he was curious about whether I wanted him near Amit.

"All the servants and their children eat together at mealtimes." I fabricated a smile, even though my insides were still churning. "You will be welcome to join us."

A bit of the iciness melted from his expression. "Thank you. That is . . . I appreciate that."

As Malakhi turned and passed the servant girl to exit the room, the girl's jaw dropped open. She craned her neck to follow his form until he'd disappeared around the corner of the hallway, then flashed a wicked grin at me. "Please tell me that one isn't married."

Unbidden, the word whipped from my mouth like a stone from a sling. "Betrothed."

TWENTY-EIGHT

Malakhi

6 Elul

Ceding to the demands of my stomach after a long morning of labor on the villa, I finally made my way to the kitchen courtyard to search out Anataliah. One of the servants directed me to the slight young woman who was elbow-deep in a dough trough. The process of making bread for such a large household must be a never-ending task.

"Shalom," she said as I approached. "Rivkah told me to expect you for meals. She also hinted that your appetite is quite impressive." Anataliah looked to be around the same age as Chana but her cheerful demeanor and wild brown curls made her seem nearly as youthful as Tirzah.

I smothered a smile at her gentle tease. "Well, growing up with a mother whose main goal in life is to prepare the most delicious food in all of the Hebrew territories, I had a duty to consume as much of it as possible."

"A worthy endeavor." With a flour-covered finger, she pressed a coil of hair that had escaped her headscarf back behind her ear and grinned up at me in a way that made me wonder what else Rivkah had said about me.

"Why don't you fetch some water from the cistern and then rest over there?" She gestured toward the corner of the courtyard where a small cluster of date palms offered a reprieve from the direct sun—a spot that was very near the room she shared with Rivkah and Amit. "I'll bring you some food while I let this dough rest."

Gratefully I obeyed, slaking my thirst with three dippers-full of water, then headed over to sit in the shadows with my back against one of the tree trunks and massage the morning's ache from my right shoulder.

Not wanting to distance myself from the carpenters with whom I'd been working for the past three weeks, I'd continued hefting beams and swinging the adze alongside them, even as I directed their efforts. I was determined to earn their loyalty and respect instead of demanding it from afar, as I'd seen other men in high positions do. Jumping from the rafters and shielding the boy had aggravated my injury, but not as much as I'd expected. Perhaps Baz's assertion that my shoulder would heal in time was not as unimaginable as I'd once thought it to be.

As I reveled in the cool shade and breathed in the homey smells of smoke and yeasty bread that wafted through the kitchen courtyard, I surveyed the assortment of servants gathered to partake of the afternoon meal. Samil's household was an odd mix of Hebrew and Canaanite. Clusters of indentured Hebrews sat on the ground together, evidenced by the tzitzit on the corners of their simple tunics and the blessings spoken over their food. But nearly as many foreigners were interspersed between them, likely those who'd been forced into labor after our people swept into the land of Bashan.

Anataliah approached to hand me a basket of food and a fortifying cup of barley beer. I was surprised by the assortment of fruit and cheese that accompanied the steaming hot bread and commented that I'd expected more meager fare.

"Samil is generous with us, for the most part," she said. "He feels that it breeds loyalty."

"So you are content, then, to be part of this household?"

She narrowed her eyes. "I had little choice. I was purchased like a sack of grain when I was twelve, and my small bundle of belongings was burned in front of me the one and only time I dared question an order."

Rivkah had hinted a number of times about Samil's tendency toward ruthlessness, and I feared that burning belongings was the least of the man's transgressions against those who flouted his authority. She'd said that he had not demanded her body, but her insistence that she and Amit were safer inside the villa than outside of it did not sit well with me.

"Why did she leave you?" she asked, the blunt question making me nearly choke on the gulp of beer I'd just swallowed.

"Has she not explained why?"

"The only thing she's ever told me is that she was married and that he died. Only when you appeared did I discover she'd even been betrothed to another man."

"The two of you seem to be good friends. Why has she not confided in you after all these years?"

"I don't know." Anataliah chewed on her lip. "It wasn't until after Amit was born and she was forced to rely on me to care for him during trading runs that she even told me that much. She keeps her thoughts to herself. It is only love for Amit that shines brightly on her face. Everything else is buried beneath layer upon layer of guardedness."

I had to agree. Rivkah had always been adept at hiding behind a mask of indifference, which is why as a child I'd made such a game of drawing her emotions to the surface. Seeing her weep out of sheer relief when she realized I was not there to steal her son had gutted me. It had taken all the restraint in my body to keep from rushing around the table and scooping her into my arms. I'd then spent the entire night flipping back and forth on my pallet, wondering what could have been.

"All I know is that she did not want to marry me," I said. After all this time, the words still stung.

"Why not?"

"I was only sixteen years old at the time. And she was grieving Gidal."

"Do you plan to fulfill your marriage contract?" she asked, again shocking me with her plainspokenness.

"Ana!" Amit barreled into Anataliah, slinging his arms about her waist with a joyful greeting, saving me from supplying an answer I did not have.

"Shalom, little jujube," she said with a tweak to his nose. "Is your belly rumbling?"

"I have plenty to share," I said, gesturing to the basket near my feet. Rivkah may soon fly in and bustle the boy away, but I would enjoy at least a few moments with Amit before she did. Without reservation, the boy folded himself down into the dirt to reach for an apple and some bread.

"I must return to my duties," Anataliah said, apparently not sharing Rivkah's wariness of my spending time with the child. "If you two need more food, come find me."

Amit spoke around a large bite of apple. "Ima said you saved Tarron when the roof fell down."

Although pleased that Rivkah would offer any word in my favor, I forced a stern look in lieu of the smile that threatened. "If he had not been in the wrong place, he'd not have been injured. *You* will stay away from the workers, won't you?"

He nodded, his solemn expression a mirror of Gidal's. Now that the shock of discovery had worn off, I'd begun to enjoy looking for scattered pieces of my brother in this small child.

"Did you fall too?" He pointed at the scrape Tarron's stick had inflicted on my cheek.

I ripped the loaf of bread down the middle and handed him half. "No, but building can be very dangerous. All of us must be very careful or someone could get hurt or even die."

Amit's eyes grew very round. "My abba died."

My lungs constricted, and the bite of bread I'd just taken went down my throat like a clump of straw. "Yes, I know."

"You knew my abba?"

Obviously Rivkah had not explained who I was, so I must be careful in my answer. "I knew him very well."

"He was very brave and good," he stated, as though the words were deeply ingrained in his mind.

"He was," I said, overwhelmed by the knowledge that in spite of all she'd done, Rivkah had still lifted Gidal high in his son's regard. A glut of emotion ached in my throat. "I admired him my entire life and always wished to be more like him."

"You did?"

"Yes. In addition to being brave and good, he was one of the kindest and most generous people I've ever known." No matter how I pushed my brother, he'd rarely flared with temper, and even when I cajoled him to join one of my ill-conceived schemes and landed us both in trouble, he never pointed the finger of blame. He'd accept the consequences with astounding grace, which usually made me feel more convicted than if he'd laid all the responsibility at my feet, as he should have. "Would you like to hear about the time he and I climbed to the very top of the storehouse?"

"Yes!" Amit scooted a little closer, his smile growing wider as I launched into the first of three stories about adventures we undertook as boys. With each one, the child's eyes grew larger, and I imagined his estimation of his father did as well. By the time I'd finished telling of how Gidal rescued me from falling into the deep cistern at the center of town—after I'd insisted that I could walk the edge with my eyes closed—I guessed that Gidal may well be ten cubits tall in Amit's eyes. He'd peppered me with questions throughout the telling and had moved so close our knees touched.

"It is time for a rest," said Rivkah, startling both Amit and me. We'd been so wrapped up in stories of Gidal that she'd come up beside us unnoticed. I wondered just how long she'd been listening to my tales.

"But, Ima, I want to hear another story about Abba," Amit said, even as a yawn stretched across his lips.

"I must return to my work." I stood and brushed the dirt from my tunic. "I wish I could take a rest like you. But perhaps if your ima gives her permission, I will tell you more stories tomorrow?" I directed the question to his mother.

To Amit's satisfaction Rivkah agreed, then with a kiss to his forehead sent him inside with instructions to lie down on the pallet. She began to follow him inside but paused at the threshold.

"I have something for you," she said to me, with a hint of hesitation. "Wait here a moment."

She disappeared into the room, admonishing Amit to lie still and then offering a muffled promise of some sort before she appeared back in the doorway. "This is for your shoulder," she said, handing me a small alabaster jar. "I've been told it works miracles."

I pulled the stopper from the top and peered inside. The smell of the balm within was a heady mixture of spice and wood pitch. "What is it?"

"An unguent made from a certain tree that grows only in this area."

"Where did you get this?" I asked, knowing that such a fragrant ointment must be costly.

"My duties put me in contact with those who can procure certain items," she said, her tone making it clear that she was not interested in explaining such a cryptic statement. But the idea that she'd done something like this, had even taken my pain into consideration, raised a lump in my throat that was hard to clear away.

"Thank you," I said.

She swiped a hand through the air, brushing away my gratitude. "It is nothing."

It was not nothing at all. Rivkah earned no wages for her labors, so the only way she could have procured this item was by a trade of some sort. Although I wanted to demand she tell me what she'd given up in order to alleviate my discomfort, I let it go for the moment.

"I thank you not just for the balm, although I am grateful," I said, "but also for telling Amit of Gidal. For making my brother a hero in his eyes."

"He was always kind to me," she said. "It was important that Amit knew."

"I hope you do not mind my stories."

"Of course not," she said. "I want him to know more of Gidal. I have only scattered memories of our childhood, and our time together was short."

A familiar emotion flared to life at her words, one I'd thought I'd buried.

Jealousy.

No matter that his time with her had been fleeting, Gidal had been her husband. He'd gotten to hold her and touch her. She'd not run from him like she had me.

Uneasy silence settled between us, but with Amit only a few paces away, this was not the time to address our unfinished conversation. She must have felt the same because she turned and walked into her room, latching the door behind her without another word. Rooted to the spot, I stood staring at the door, my thumb stroking the smooth surface of the alabaster jar. How much had this gift cost her? And why had she done it for me?

Just as I willed my feet to move, a voice began, the sound so low I nearly missed it.

Rivkah was singing Amit to sleep. She must have thought I'd already walked away—and I should—but instead I moved closer to the window and folded myself down to lean my back against the brick.

The song was familiar, a lullaby that my mother had sung to me, but instead of reviving memories of my own childhood, the melody ushered me back to my fourteenth year and the day I'd followed Rivkah with every intention of teasing her and instead found myself under her spell.

That morning, Gidal and I had been charged with working in the fruit orchard to the south of Kedesh, cutting back brush after the late-season rains had caused an abundance of overgrowth. Tired of the monotony after working since sunrise and nowhere near as enthralled as my brother with tending the various fruit trees around the city, I'd made the excuse of being desperate for a drink and wandered over to the spring that flowed beneath Kedesh and burst free just past the eastern wall.

Kneeling in the tall grass on the bank, I lapped the cool water like a pup, then wiped my chin and laid back, arms folded behind my head to watch the clouds, hoping Gidal wouldn't seek me out. I loved my brother, but the older he'd gotten, the more serious he'd become, sometimes going quiet for hours as he puttered in the dirt around tree trunks. His fascination with the earth and its fruits was not one I particularly shared.

At first, I thought the pale yellow fluttering in the corner of my vision was a butterfly dancing in the weeds, but when I sat up, I saw Rivkah darting across the open area, skirting a stone sheep pen and heading for the tree line with swift purpose. Curiosity compelled me to follow.

Dodging trees and ducking beneath branches, I followed her to where white limestone markers were set in a perimeter, a clear delineation of the boundaries of the refuge city—the line past which a Blood Avenger could not pursue an accused manslayer and past which my mother, who'd been sentenced as such, was banned from crossing. Although Rivkah checked over her shoulder twice, I slipped behind a tree both times and she did not slow her steps. She lifted her hand to her eyes, scanning the horizon beyond the tangle of olive trees. For a moment I considered whether she might be running away, but then she sat down on a nearby boulder, beneath a terebinth blooming in vivid shades of red. Pulling a piece of papyrus and a reed pen from her satchel, she scribbled something down on her page. Then she gazed off into the distance, her slender body still and quiet, and then, to my surprise, she began to sing.

The sound startled me, its crisp, sweet notes blending with the birdsong and the blossom-scented air in perfect harmony. Using the silent movements my father and Baz had taught me, I crept forward, keeping my body low in the knee-high weeds.

Finding a vantage point just out of her sight line, I crouched on my heels, keeping my body behind a tree trunk but peering around so I could see her face. I'd hoped to discern her words, yet found that the distance swallowed their shape. But even so, all thought of teasing her dissipated and I was held captive. I'd never heard anything as beautiful as the sounds emanating from her lips. Lips that in that moment somehow became the most intriguing thing in my world.

The hair I'd yanked too many times to count shone in the sunlight, trailing down her back like liquid obsidian. Her amber eyes were closed as she sang, chin tilted upward as if to worship the feel of the sun on her golden skin. Thick black lashes brushed her cheeks where I knew a few freckles lay. And knowledge hit me like a boulder falling from the heights—the girl I'd spent a lifetime provoking was the most beautiful creature I'd ever seen.

Thrown off balance, I wobbled and dropped a knee to the ground, cracking a twig. Her song broke off and her attention snapped to me. Heart pounding and face on fire with embarrassment, I ran. Behind me, Rivkah shouted my name—along with a fairly violent threat to maim me for spying—but even as I flew through the olive grove, my laughter trailing behind me as I dodged the pebbles she lobbed at my back, I determined that someday I'd make her mine.

With Rivkah's unexpected gift clutched in my fist, I rose and headed back toward the construction site. For as lovely and gentle as Ayala was, it had been easy to dismiss the thought of marriage to her from my mind. No matter that Rivkah had fled Kedesh, lied, stolen Amit, and who knew what else, there was still no one else I wanted as my wife. I still was just as much a fool for her as I'd ever been.

TWENTY-NINE

Rivkah

I pressed down on the point of my reed pen with such force that it split up the center and blotched ink all over Samil's latest correspondence. Groaning, I tossed the now-useless tool to the ground and dropped my head into my hands, massaging the ache in my temples that had taken up residence during my earlier visit to the marketplace today.

Never in my life had I wanted to throttle anyone before, but I'd been sorely tempted to strangle Nessa today. And once I finished shaking some sense into her, I'd make sure the man she called "husband" suffered a slow, painful death. The woman refused to listen to reason, and instead clung to a lecher whose frustrations were once again displayed on her arms and neck in shades of blue and purple.

Gaunt, ragged, and with an infant at her breast, she'd been hawking a paltry assortment of wilted vegetables on a blanket in a neglected corner of the town plaza. Her twin boys were with her, but even as they crouched together drawing in the dirt with sticks, they were eerily silent.

Over the years I'd tried everything to persuade Nessa to leave the man who was not only chronically unfaithful but who also wielded his fists as weapons. I'd begged her to petition the town elders, hoping at least a few of them might be compassionate and concerned for her safety and that of her children. However, fear that her husband might cast her out with nothing outweighed her trust in the men who were supposed to govern Edrei with fairness.

I knew, without question, that were we in Kedesh and my father presiding as judge over a man such as her husband, the consequences would be severe. My father always deferred to Mosheh's law, insisting that a wife was to be treated as a husband's own flesh—to be cherished, protected, and loved—and that a man who would even dare to defame his wife in public was a coward of the lowest character.

"What is bothering you?" Malakhi's voice had once again become familiar to me, but unlike when I was a girl, it now made frissons of sensation spike to my fingertips. Somehow over the last couple of weeks, I'd lost all ability to guard against the new way his presence affected me.

"Nessa's husband," I said, avoiding eye contact as I collected my shattered pen and covered my inks. When I finally gathered enough courage to look up, the silent fury on his face sent a wave of confusion through me.

"Did he proposition you again?" The silver of his eyes deepened to the exact shade of a thunderstorm, his voice rising. "Did he touch you?" Two servant girls stopped their conversation to watch us, their tilted chins making it clear they were anxious to overhear our conversation.

I feigned a smile, hoping to dispel their interest. "No. But we cannot discuss this here."

Malakhi flicked a glance around the courtyard. "Meet me in the garden then."

"We can't—"

"Unless you want someone to see me going into your room," he said, "there is no other place we can speak privately. And I have questions."

Of course he did. The tenacious boy who had prodded me until frustrations spewed out of my mouth would in no way give in until he knew everything. And truly, he did deserve answers. Resigned, I blew out a slow, trembling breath. "All right. I'll put my tools away first so it does not seem that I am following."

He nodded and made a show of walking to the cistern for a drink, then speaking to one of his workers before slipping into the garden. I finished the lines I'd been attempting to compose, then took my ink palette into my room and tucked the ruined papyrus beneath my pallet to be used later. After checking twice to make sure no one in the courtyard was watching me, I headed through the open garden gate.

This early in the afternoon the pool was shaded by the palms, lily pads and lotuses undulating gently on the surface of the water. Samil had patterned his garden after one he'd seen at the governor's palace in Avaris, right down to the ornately carved cedar doors of the pagan sanctuary where his wives worshiped their gods. Thankfully, the stench of incense emanating from within was mitigated by the heady mix of floral fragrances contained within this oasis.

Following the narrow stone path that meandered through oleander, flax, and lemongrass bushes, I continued peering over my shoulder every few steps. I'd never set foot in this quiet place without my master, and if Malakhi and I were seen here alone, I'd have no viable explanation. A large hand darted out from behind an oleander bush and pulled me into the shadows. Even knowing that it was Malakhi, I slapped a palm over my lips to keep from crying out.

"Now tell me what that worm did to you." His gaze bore into mine. Five years ago I'd have been annoyed by this flare of protectiveness, thinking it was some sort of proprietary claim, but now his obvious concern made something warm settle into the center of my bones—something I should *not* entertain but did nonetheless. It had been a long time since I'd felt safe and cared for.

"Nothing. I promise." I reined in the urge to reach out and smooth the outrage from his brow. "I am only concerned for Nessa. I have not seen that *worm*, as you so aptly called him, for years. He sends her into town to sell their farm goods and then drinks and whores away the majority of the proceeds."

The unmitigated relief on his face made the delicious warmth burrow even deeper. "Tell me what happened."

"I saw her in the marketplace today with bruises on her body and her soul in pieces." My throat pinched tight. "Here I am the one who sold myself, and yet she is treated lower than a slave."

His body stiffened. "What can we do?"

"We?"

"She is my cousin, Rivkah. No matter what her father has done, I do not want her to suffer."

My jaw gaped. "Your cousin?"

"You did not know? She is Raviv's daughter."

"No, she said nothing." I was well aware of the blood feud within Malakhi's family, but Nessa had revealed little of her past, and I'd been so wrapped up in my own worries that I had not thought to ask about her heritage.

"So you ran off from Kedesh with a woman you barely knew?"

I was sorely tempted to defend myself, but with the wisdom gleaned from hindsight I was well aware how reckless my behavior had been. Leaving my home with a stranger and her two male cousins had been the height of foolishness, and it was only by the grace of Yahweh that Amit and I had arrived safely in Edrei. "I have no excuses for my actions. I'd struck up a friendship with her but knew little more than that her father had sold her into marriage with some old farmer. And that he cared more for silver than his own daughter."

"You didn't see him when he burst into the inn looking for her, ready to tear our home apart with his bare hands. We all went *together* to Laish to search for you."

Thinking of Malakhi and his family searching for me in that wicked place dredged up a slew of guilt-laden memories. I turned my face away to hide the tears that suddenly sprang to my eyes. "I was such a fool," I whispered.

"Why?" he asked, the strangled sound of that one word peeling back so many layers of shame that I could barely breathe from the raw pain it uncovered. I'd dreaded this conversation from the moment I'd opened the door to him. I'd never even told Nessa the full truth, although I suspected she guessed that the night of the festival had gone awry when I returned at dawn, reeking of pig filth.

"What did I do to make you go?" he asked, his words taut and tortured. My head jerked up as my stomach dropped to my feet. He was looking toward the pool, his arms crossed and his lips pressed tightly together. One thing was evident—this question was not from the soldier and leader of men before me. It was from the sixteen-year-old he had been.

"It wasn't about you," I said, attempting to soften the truth.

"You made it very clear you did not want me."

"You were so young—"

"True. I was young and had much to learn, but I was old enough to be a husband, Rivkah. I would have taken care of you. Provided for you and Amit. I would have . . ." He shook his head, his words sliding into silence.

"What?"

He paused, his jaw working back and forth. Then he seemed to make a decision as he stared into my eyes. "I would have loved you."

My heart pounded furiously, my thoughts a swirling confusion as he continued. "I'll never forget the day you married my brother. I stood there, watching you pledge your troth to him and felt like someone had taken a dagger to my chest. I couldn't breathe."

My knees wobbled. Everything I thought I knew about Malakhi was being turned on its axis. Then he continued, his tone so bitter I could practically taste it in my own mouth. "And then he died, and I was the lowest of the low to be thrilled when your father asked that I marry you. I hated myself nearly as much as I hoped that you would see me, even in your grief. I deserved your desertion."

"No! I was selfish. Arrogant and prideful. Determined to have my own way. It would not have mattered who my father betrothed me to, Malakhi. I still would have run."

He scoffed. "You told me I was a spoiled child and did your very best to push me to break the betrothal for weeks before you left. You cannot say it wasn't about me."

"I thought you were just bowing to my father's command. That I was an obligation. And you seemed to take such pleasure in tormenting me when we were children—"

"Because I wanted you to be alive!" he said, his voice spiking too high. Without thinking, I closed the short distance between us and pressed my palm over his mouth, terrified someone might hear, but as soon as I touched his lips I dropped my hand, flushing from head to toe, my skin tingling.

Malakhi drew in a deep breath, then continued in a softer tone. "When your mother died, it seemed like you did too. The only time I ever saw fire in you was when you were yelling at me. So I did all I could to get you to snap. I was a boy, Rivkah. It was all I knew how to do. I couldn't tell you that your silent sadness made my stomach ache. It was easier to pull your braids or put crickets in your bed to make you flare your tail feathers at me so I didn't have to worry that you were going to lie down next to your mother and wither away."

I blinked my eyes, swept back into memories of those days when I had indeed felt like there was nothing to live for without my ima, when my father had been so caught up in his own grief and my sister too busy filling my mother's sandals that I'd been forced to press the hurt down deep or be consumed by it. To think that even at nine years old he'd seen my pain and tried to help in his own, misguided way . . .

If only I'd not closed my ears to my father's wisdom, had listened when he'd encouraged me to give Malakhi the chance to grow into the man who now stood before me. We would have been married all these years. Amit would have known Malakhi as a father. I would be free. Instead, I'd destroyed everything with my selfishness, so wrapped up in pointing out his faults that I'd not even attempted to know his heart. I'd run away from the boy I'd imagined him to be, not the young man whose strengths my father had seen from the beginning.

"I'd planned to set you free from the betrothal when we found you," he said. "When you did not return, I pushed all thought of marriage aside. Threw myself headlong into training with my father. Into war. It was less painful—" He cut himself off with a shake of his head.

"Than what?" I dared to ask.

He pinned me with his silver-eyed gaze, his tone layered with a shade of abashment that I'd never heard from his mouth before. "Than hoping someday you would come back . . . to me."

I gripped the seams of my tunic to hide the trembling of my hands as a caravan of memories surfaced, filtered through these new revelations: the abrupt change in the way he'd treated me in his fourteenth year; how he'd watched me from afar after my first betrothal with frustration in his eyes; how he'd then suddenly encouraged the attention of the other girls; how easily he'd agreed to my father's demand for levirate marriage—as if he welcomed it.

The kiss in the quince grove.

True, at the time that kiss had been unwelcome, but perhaps it had been the plea of a young man unsure how to express his heart to the woman who'd once been married to his brother. I cringed, remembering how afterward I'd accused him of manipulation, trampled on him, and then tossed him aside. How had I been so blind? So spiteful and cutting?

His bitter laugh broke into my turbulent thoughts, all remnants of his earlier self-consciousness having been wiped away during the silent moments between us. "Believe me, if my mother and sisters had their way, I would already be married by now. When I came home after being wounded, there was a constant flow of young women at nearly every family meal."

I had little doubt of that. Malakhi the boy had been attractive and charming. Malakhi the man was nothing less than devastating. I swallowed the acid on my tongue. "And none you considered?"

"Ayala," he said. "I decided to marry her right before your note arrived."

Now I understood the pain he'd spoken of earlier. The woman's name felt like a dagger between my ribs, one with serrated edges and slathered in poison. And I had no right to feel this way. None. He deserved a faithful, constant wife. One who had not willingly stepped into chains and dragged her child with her. Besides, it was plain to see that whatever affection Malakhi once held for me had been dissolved by my betrayal.

My throat was on fire, but I managed a feeble smile. "You will make her a fine husband, Malakhi. Your willingness to stay here, to take on this work to protect Amit, not to mention the way you treat him with such patience and kindness, tells me just what kind of man you've become."

Although I did not expect him to forgive me—especially if I ever told him the entire truth—perhaps I could try to make amends, build new bridges for the sake of my son. Because even when Malakhi married Ayala, Amit would still be his nephew.

Approaching voices drifted into our private space. Without a word, Malakhi plunged between two palm bushes, their fronds barely moving as he slipped into them with the skill of a man trained by expert spies. I stood rooted to the spot, unsure whether I should attempt to flee out the gate or try to follow Malakhi. Peering around the oleander, I realized that my indecision had left me in the path of

Ofira and Dilara as they moved toward the pool, an assortment of their children swarming behind them like a flock of unruly sheep. I held my breath as they passed me, praying for invisibility, but to my chagrin, Bensam spotted me and called out a greeting.

Samil's wives turned with matching scowls on their faces.

"Why are you hiding in here?" said Dilara. "Don't you have work to do?"

I willed my voice not to shake. "My hand was cramping and it was quiet in the garden, so I took a short break here by the pool."

Dilara's gaze swept around me, as if she somehow sensed that I'd not been alone, but I held a mild expression on my face. Ofira said nothing, turning away with her usual cool haughtiness. She'd always ignored me, as if speaking to a servant were far beneath her. But Dilara, the more calculating of the two, tipped her head to the side and regarded me with suspicion. "This garden is not for your personal use. Get back to work, or I'll make sure my husband knows you've been squandering time instead of tending to your duties."

Biting the inside of my cheek with a force that nearly drew blood, I gave a subservient nod and shuffled away. After a few paces, I braved a swift glance over my shoulder to find her still watching me, eyes narrowed. She would run to Samil with this morsel in all haste, desperate as she was to remain at the center of his affections. Most likely she feared he would lose interest in her as he had done with Ofira when he brought a younger, more nubile wife into the household. I upped my pace and fled the garden, praying that Amit and I would not end up as burnt sacrifices to her vanity.

CHAPTER
THIRTY

14 Tishri

Amit and Bensam worked together to drag a tree branch across the courtyard, intent on being of use to the men building *sukkahs* for the upcoming festival. The friendship between my son and Dilara's oldest child had never settled easily with me, but I had no reason to prevent it. And since Samil encouraged their pairing, even going so far as to include Amit in family meals and special events, it would be difficult to counter his generosity.

Now that the addition to the villa was complete, even in advance of the date Samil had demanded, Malakhi had been asked to oversee the building of temporary shelters for the Feast of Sukkot. Everyone—masters and slaves, Hebrews and foreigners—would spend seven days feasting in the shelters, remembering the time our forefathers spent in the wilderness after fleeing Egypt.

Tomorrow evening would begin the first day of the annual celebration, which would start with a day of rest; but today there was much to be accomplished, and Samil had directed me to put aside my written work to aid the other servants with preparations. Malakhi's men were assembling ten sukkahs, and the women had been charged with decorating them with palm fronds, flowers, and vibrant fabrics that would put Samil's wealth on display for all of Edrei to covet. As the law prescribed, he directed that everyone in the household be included in the banquet, dancing, and games—not only to foster devotion, but also to demonstrate his Torah observance to the elders of the town. This front would ensure that later they'd turn a blind eye when he bent those very same laws to his favor.

"Ima!" yelled Amit, waving a dirty palm at me from across the courtyard, dark hair sweeping over his eyes. "Malakhi used *our* branch for the top!"

With a purple lotus in hand, I returned the wave, smiling at my sweet boy's enthusiasm. He took pride in every small task Malakhi gave him, whether it be fetching a mallet or gathering twigs, and begged daily for more chores just to be near the man who had known his father. Then later, with hero worship glittering in his dark eyes, he regaled me with story after story of Gidal, some that included me as a girl and some that made me understand my late husband better than I ever had while we were married.

Even unaware of the true nature of their relationship, Amit was naturally drawn to his uncle, and once I'd pushed past my uneasiness and accepted that Malakhi had no intention of stealing my son away, I'd become grateful for the affection he had for him. And in all honesty, I deeply regretted that Amit had never gotten the chance to call Malakhi "Abba" and that I'd wasted the opportunity to call him "Husband." Instead, Ayala would enjoy that privilege, and I would strive not to resent the faceless woman who would benefit from my stupidity.

"When are you going to tell Amit the truth?" asked Ana as she tucked a spray of white lilies into the gap between two palm branches. She gestured toward Malakhi, who had lifted my son onto his shoulders and was teaching him to tie a knot that would hold the crossbeam secure. "The two of them are enamored with each other."

"It is too dangerous right now." It was conceivable that my master had already heard of Malakhi's particular attention to us, since Amit was not in any way subtle about his infatuation with the head carpenter, but I shuddered to think what Samil might do if he discovered we'd been connected all along. "Perhaps when he is older and can understand the need for secrecy."

Besides, I was unsure how to explain to a four-year-old that his foolhardy mother had placed him in danger for her own selfish reasons, and that my twin failings of pride and shame had kept me from running back to my father's house before it was too late. Ana made a small noise of frustration, but when I refused to explain myself more thoroughly, she walked away, answering the loud summons of the head cook from the kitchen courtyard.

Absently, I hummed the song that had been forming in my mind for the past few days and tucked the lotus between the quince branches the men had tied to the sukkah frame, the fragrance causing a fleeting reminder of my last moments in the grove with Malakhi. A few paces away, he gave low-toned directions to his men as they stripped the trees, dug holes to anchor the shelters in place, raised the corner poles, and then filled in the tops and three sides with all varieties of branches and limbs. Samil had demanded that his sukkahs be the most beautiful in Edrei, and Malakhi had risen to the challenge. I'd be loath to see them disassembled in a week's time.

The master himself had visited the courtyard a number of times and praised the efforts, clapping Malakhi on the shoulder as he outlined the progress they'd made. A ridiculous swell of pride had filled me as I watched the man I'd been betrothed to receive such accolades. The charms of the boy who'd been so skilled at convincing others to participate in his games and acts of daring had translated into the confidence and persistence of a natural-born leader. Even the older laborers deferred to him with surprising ease.

Once the flowers were tucked into place across the leafy wall of the sukkah, I retrieved one of the long, narrow lengths of blue linen to decorate the entrance to the shelter. I found a sturdy basket to stand on and began interlacing the fabric in and around the branches, palm fronds, and flowers.

I heard a crack as the basket wobbled beneath my sandals. With a gasp, I instinctively grabbed the crossbeam above my head to steady myself, but since it was not made to support the weight of a woman, the branch snapped in two. Just as my makeshift stool gave way and I began to fall, strong arms wrapped around me from behind and gently placed me on the ground.

"Are you all right?" came Malakhi's voice from directly next to my ear, his arms still around my body. Everything went still inside me as I restrained the urge to lean back into him, to indulge in the undeniable comfort of this embrace.

"Rivkah, have you hurt yourself?"

I cleared the uncertainty out of my throat and shook my head. "I am whole."

He dropped his arms, but a deep chuckle vibrated against my back. "Well, your basket is not. And neither, for that matter, is my sukkah. You didn't have to swing from it."

"I did no such thing." I whirled around. He was so close that I nearly stepped back, but found myself bereft of any desire to do so. He loomed over me, blocking out the rest of the courtyard behind him. But instead of being menacing, his presence was all-encompassing, as if I were wrapped in a cocoon of warmth and protection. Malakhi was no longer a boy—he was a broad-shouldered man whose once youthfully beautiful face had become only more artfully defined with age. And yet, no matter how handsome he was, it was the kindness he showed my child and his faithfulness to stay in Edrei for us that made me more aware every day of just how stupid I'd been to walk away from him.

"It . . ." I blinked to reassemble my wits. "It happened so fast. I grabbed on without thinking."

He looked down at me with a glint of amusement in his eyes, as if he knew the pathway of my thoughts and reveled in them. "Perhaps next time you should pick a sturdier stool."

"And perhaps *you* should use sturdier limbs," I snapped back.

His lips twitched. "You never could let me get the last word could you?"

Taking the bait, I quirked a brow as I suppressed my own smile. "Why, when mine were so much more clever?"

He brushed the long hair from his eyes as he gazed down his nose at me with the smirk I remembered so well, and then, to my delight, he laughed. A full-throated, deep, rich laugh that I felt from the soles of my feet to the tips of my fingers.

Amit appeared at my hip. "Ima, you broke the sukkah!"

"She did," said Malakhi, not taking his gaze from mine and laughter still tugging at his mouth. "You and I will have to mend it, won't we?"

"But the beam is broken in half!" said Amit.

"You'd be surprised what can be restored, with the right motivation," said Malakhi, his silver stare holding mine captive in a way that made me wonder whether he was speaking of the sukkah at all.

Although I'd spent the last five years regretting my flight from Kedesh, I'd counted Malakhi as having benefited from my leaving. But since he'd appeared in Edrei, regret for having wounded him had taken up residence in my soul, growing larger every day. I didn't see how the destruction I'd caused could ever be made right, but I desperately wanted to try.

Spindly arms wrapped around my hips. I looked down at my son, whose face shone with joy and contentment in Malakhi's presence. I would do anything to keep that expression there. I brushed back the tangle of hair that threatened to hide his beautiful brown eyes. "You, my sweet boy, need a haircut. I'll have to borrow a razor from one of the men."

Amit pouted. "I don't want one. Can't I tie it like Malakhi?"

I glanced up at the man in question. Indeed, his hair had grown quite long over the weeks, and he'd taken to tying it up behind his head to keep it out of his eyes as he worked. One black hank of hair that had come loose nearly touched his shoulder. It reminded me of the time I'd shorn him out of spite. Maybe restoration could begin with something as simple as this.

"Perhaps Malakhi would like to go first," I said. "I do owe him a proper haircut."

Malakhi playfully narrowed his eyes at me. "You think I'd let you near me with a razor? I had to have my mother take the sheep-shearing scissors to my head. Took months to grow in properly."

"You still had every girl in Kedesh following after you like a puppy."

"Not the right one," he said quickly, and before I could respond, he looked down at Amit. "I'll get my hair cut if you do, but first we must finish our work. Why don't you and Bensam go find me some rope and we'll fix this mess your ima made?"

Amit bounced off, calling to his friend, who'd joined his mother in the shade on the far side of the courtyard for refreshments. It was then that I noticed Dilara watching Malakhi and me with a keenness that made the hair on the back of my neck prickle. I took two steps backward, affixing a bland smile on my face. "It would be best if you came to our room after the meal for your haircut," I said. "Dilara retires early."

He didn't follow my gaze, but instead turned to inspect the damage I'd caused the sukkah. "Is she watching us now?"

"Yes."

"She seems to have a particular disdain for you," he said, tugging at the flower garland that had once been wrapped around the crossbeam.

"She resents Samil's reliance on me and how much time he spends in my presence because of my duties. She has nothing to fear, of course, for I am far too old for Samil's tastes, but all the same, she's been extraordinarily disagreeable these past few weeks."

"Then I'll come after sunset."

"All right. Anataliah and Amit will be there, so there should be no hint of impropriety."

He looked over his shoulder at me, and the intense expression on his face made my skin flush. "Yes, it would be best if we were not alone together."

Flustered by the sudden huskiness of his voice, along with the distinct shift in his attitude toward me, I excused myself to offer help to a group of servants who were twining flower garlands around corner posts. But I could not help but look back numerous times as Malakhi instructed Amit and Bensam in gentle tones while the three of them bound the broken branch securely and then rewrapped the linen and flowers to hide the fracture I'd caused.

Once the sukkahs were sufficiently decorated, Ana called for all of us to gather for a meal. Amit slipped through the crowd of servants and laborers to find me. Sweat had plastered his wild dark tangles to his forehead and neck, but the smile on his face could light the night sky. A pang of fear hit me dead center. No matter what he'd said, Malakhi could not possibly stay here for an entire year and a half to wait for us. What would Amit do when his hero returned to Kedesh—and what would I do when he returned home to Ayala?

Brushing away the unbidden thought, I accepted a small basket of food from Ana in the kitchen courtyard and then led Amit to a spot in the shade near our room. As we ate, I let him chatter away in his excitement about the festival and how high in the air he'd been when on Malakhi's shoulders. I surveyed the various groups of workers and slaves clustered together as he talked.

Estebaal stood off to one side of the courtyard, leaning against the mud-brick wall, his posture seemingly casual but his attention fixed on Ana. Unaware that a wolf had her in his sights, my friend bantered with the other kitchen workers, her deep dimples making an appearance whenever she laughed, and her rebellious coils of brown hair slipping from their mooring time and time again. Estebaal never looked away. A deep sense of foreboding curled in my gut. He was a handsome man, blue-eyed and finely chiseled head to toe, but Ana was in no way safe at the center of his attention. Her body may have grown into that of a woman in the last few years, becoming nearly as shapely as Dilara, but she was an innocent, trusting and guileless.

The Hebrew in Laish must have seen me the same way—nothing more than a wide-eyed lamb eager for slaughter. He'd preyed on my naïvety, stroked my vanity, and fed my appetite for affection that night. Although the wine had dulled my senses and warped my judgment, it had not muddled the memory of the way I'd practically begged for his touch. That one of my own people had used my drunkenness as an opportunity to take his own pleasure with my body and then abscond with everything I carried made him the worst kind of villain.

Apart from his violent behavior in service to Samil, I had little knowledge of Estebaal's character, nor of his tendencies with women. But in case he might be anything like the unscrupulous Hebrew who'd used my own weaknesses against me, I had to do something. I refused to let Ana suffer any of my own regrets.

"Amit," I said, "it's time for a rest. Please go lie down. I'll be in shortly."

"But Ima," he whined, "Malakhi has to tell me a story of Abba first."

"Not today, son."

His lower lip pushed forward, but he complied, a wide yawn on his lips before he'd even made it to the door of our room. I strode over to Estebaal, driven by a rush of fierce protectiveness. "Leave her be," I said, my usual caution around the enormous man pushed aside by the thought of Anataliah being harmed in any way. She'd become more than a friend; she was a sister, and I would guard her as such.

He looked down at me, expression cool and tone detached. "Pardon?"

Ana was kneeling in the dirt, speaking to one of Samil's children. The sight of her sunny, untainted smile gave me the courage to continue. "I've seen you watching her, Estebaal."

A flicker of shock registered in his eyes, but he did not contradict me, nor question of whom I spoke.

"She is young and fairly ignorant to the darker element within this household. Your attentions would not be safe for her."

"I know." The words were so soft I barely heard them as his gaze moved back to her. "And I will do anything to ensure that she is safe."

My breath lodged painfully in my lungs as I absorbed both his statement and the deep sorrow painted across his face as he watched her. Not because he meant to harm her. But because he had come to love her from afar.

"I saw her first," he said, his tone low and mournful, "in that market. Samil did not have any interest in purchasing a slave that day, but she looked so lost, so small standing there with her little bundle, dressed in rags. . . ." He sighed. "I reminded the master that one of the cooks had died and we were in need of more kitchen help. I was so relieved when he bought her, took her away from the Moabite who had her up for auction like a sow."

Anataliah had told me of that day as well, of her terror over who might purchase her to satisfy her parents' debts and her profound relief when Samil ordered her to the kitchen instead of his bed.

"I felt responsible for her. So I kept an eye on her from that day onward. And over time"—he shrugged—"it became less of an obligation and more of a . . . necessity."

"And you've never approached her?" Slaves within a household were allowed to marry, given the master's permission. Samil held Estebaal in high regard; I doubted he would object to the match.

"I have no right. She is not for me."

Even though I'd said nearly the same thing a few moments ago, curiosity drove me to ask, "Why not?"

"Look at her," he said, and I followed his line of sight to the object of his reluctant affections. Bensam and a few of Samil's other younger children now surrounded her as she placed a plump date into each of their eager hands.

"Even though everything has been stripped from her, she is still a bright flame," he said. "When Samil ordered me to burn her belongings, she stood there without a tear in her eye, bowed her head to our master, and apologized for questioning his wisdom. And then she turned to me and smiled."

He paused, the most affected I'd ever seen him in the five years I'd known him. "I wanted to vomit on the ground, Rivkah. I've broken fingers and smashed toes. I've burned homes. I've stolen animals in the dead of night. I've killed. But the sight of her sweet, brave smile nearly brought me to my knees."

He shook his head. "No. She is not for me. I would never drag her sunlight into my dark world. But I will bathe in it from afar, for as long as I can."

Although I hadn't done a fraction of the things Estebaal had, I understood the creeping blackness he spoke of. The constant roil of shame in my gut as I huddled in the back of the traders' wagon on the road away from Laish. The ever-cycling words of condemnation in my mind that kept me in Edrei once Nessa had abandoned me for her snake of a man. The conviction that no one in Kedesh would ever forgive me, which had driven me to sign that indenture contract.

In that moment, I found my opinion of the imposing man wholly altered. He was nothing like the Hebrew who'd stolen so much from me. For all the evil he'd participated in at the behest of our master, there *was* honor in this man, and admirable restraint in his refusal to even approach the woman he loved, for her sake.

"I have lived with Ana for nearly five years now," I said. "And one thing I know is that she would never shame you for anything you've done. She is one of the most openhearted and generous people I've ever known."

"Which is exactly why she is over there, and I am over here. There is nothing on this earth that could ever make me deserving of her." He took one last look at Ana and then walked away.

CHAPTER
THIRTY-ONE

Malakhi

After casting another glance over my shoulder to ensure that I'd not been spotted creeping through the courtyard, I knocked on Rivkah's door for the second time since coming to Edrei, and received a far different welcome than I had upon my arrival.

Before Rivkah had even fully opened the door, a well-trimmed Amit had slipped through the opening and dragged me inside, telling me his mother had already cut his hair and now it was my turn. He pulled me over to the stool in the center of the room and insisted that I sit in the place he'd only recently vacated, as evidenced by the dark waves of hair on the dirt floor. Ana was cross-legged on the pallet nearby, quiet amusement dancing in her eyes.

I untied my pack from around my waist and handed Amit the leather satchel in which I usually carried a number of essential carpentry tools, then attempted to situate myself on the short stool with my legs stretched out awkwardly in front of me. Once he'd hung the pack on a hook by the door, Amit ran back and slung his arms around my neck. With his little face close to mine, he asked if the sukkahs were finished.

My chest contracted sharply. From the moment I'd said I knew his father and began to tell him stories from our childhood, Amit had trusted me implicitly. He asked a thousand questions a day—about his father, about my work, about being a soldier—but tonight was the first time he'd physically embraced me. I swallowed hard before responding and noticed that Rivkah had tears in the corners of her eyes as she sharpened the razor on a whetstone.

I ruffled his hair. "Yes, my friend. Thanks to your help and Bensam's, we are well prepared for Sukkot."

"Malakhi will tell you more tomorrow, lamb," said Rivkah. "It's late now. Go lay with Ana while I cut his hair." The boy complied, curling his back into Ana like a kitten but keeping his eyes on his mother and me, even as he yawned and settled deeper into her embrace. The sleepy smile he gave me was one of pure childlike contentment, and the adoration in his brown eyes, as well as their distinct resemblance to Gidal's, nearly brought me to tears myself.

This remarkable boy should have been my son. And his mother, who with all her faults still drew me like a bee to an apple blossom, should have been my wife. We should have grieved Gidal together and then spent the last five years growing into love and building our own family.

As my bitterness toward her waned, in no small part due to her fierce devotion to Amit, I'd begun to realize just how much of a mirage I'd conjured in my youth. Yes, we'd known each other as children and I'd watched her and desired her from afar, but she'd never allowed me close enough to truly know her. I'd built Rivkah up in my imagination, expecting that she would mold herself to my expectations—and then I kicked the pedestal out from beneath her when she did not conform.

This afternoon, when she'd snapped back a mischievous retort about the broken limb, the icy shell around my heart had cracked, gushing out five years' worth of dammed-up longing, the playful tease in her voice invoking more hope in me than any breathless declaration ever could. And although she still had yet to explain what happened in Laish and her connection to the man she'd been seen with, by law she and I were still betrothed.

However, I'd simply have to wait until she trusted me enough to explain all her reasons for leaving Kedesh and until she was ready to reveal her true self. From the tantalizing glimpses I'd gotten over the past weeks, I was eager to uncover more, to separate fact from my own inventions. I'd been enthralled with a girl of beauty and intelligence as a boy, but the woman who stood before me now, who'd endured five years of trial with the backbone of a warrior, was well worth the wait.

Rivkah came nearer to me with the small razor in her hand and I glanced at it, remembering the last time I'd trusted her with such a tool. "It's well sharpened," she said. "It won't pull."

I adjusted myself on the stool, eyeing her with feigned trepidation. "Perhaps I should find a barber . . . or do it myself."

She poked me in the shoulder with a quiet laugh. "Hold still, or you might have cause to worry."

Another surge of hope pressed upward. She seemed almost completely at ease now, as if no debris littered the long and jagged road behind us. Perhaps my wait would be shorter than I'd anticipated.

"How much shall I cut?" she asked as she combed her fingers down the length of my hair.

I repressed a groan of pleasure at the contact of her skillful fingers and pushed against the hot stone that seemed lodged in my throat. "Whatever you think looks best." I clamped my mouth shut as she worked a wooden wide-tooth comb through my tangles, determined to keep my mind on anything other than her nearness or how I wanted to wrap my arms around her waist and pull her even closer. But I refused to make assumptions or force her hand ever again.

Ana and Amit had fallen asleep, the boy's head tucked into the young woman's chest and their soft breaths rising and falling in tandem. Shadows dodged between the flickers of the oil lamps, lending an intimacy to the silent room, making me even more aware of the sweet almond fragrance of her skin and every inadvertent caress as she wielded the razor with the deftness of an experienced barber. Testing the length of the portion at the back of my neck, her palm tracked from the crown of my head downward, her skin meeting mine for a brief moment that caused me to brace against a shiver. I closed my eyes and measured my breaths.

"Thank you for the balm," I said, keeping my voice low to not wake the others. "I cannot believe how much the pain has lessened since I began using it every day." The sharp tearing that had been such a constant since the chariot plowed over me had become a dull ache, even after a long day working on the villa. If the healing continued, Baz's insistence that I could revive my deftness with a sword might well be realized. And since working as a carpenter had forced me to rely more on my left hand, it too had become much more dexterous, which would be an advantage in battle instead of a hardship.

"When you need more, let me know. I have a direct connection to a man who raises the balsam trees from which the ointment originates."

"What did you trade?" I asked.

"What do you mean?"

"You have no wages, Rivkah. What did you trade for that balm?"

She shrugged. "Nothing of consequence. I only agreed to take on some extra work for a few months."

"Don't you have enough to do?" My response was too loud, and Amit shifted on the pallet restlessly, so I lowered my voice. "Every time I see you, your head is bent over a sheet of papyrus, or a clay tablet, or a shard of pottery. Samil works you too hard as it is."

She waited until the boy had settled back into stillness before she continued. "I am fine, Malakhi. It's nothing that I cannot handle. Besides, it is worth it to hear that you've gotten some relief." Had she truly come to care for me? Or was her concern simply born from regret?

"Why, Rivkah?" Emotion swelled in my throat, causing my words to come out on a harsh rasp. "Why would you do that for me?"

She breathed deeply, her gaze traveling over her child, her friend, and then touring the room in a slow sweep before coming back to me. "Because you were hurting. I didn't . . . I hated seeing you in pain."

"I was a soldier," I said. "Injury was inevitable, especially with my father's unit, which seeks out danger. And carpentry is no safe occupation either." *And losing you hurt worse than the injuries anyhow,* I wanted to say.

"You were struggling, Malakhi, and I wanted to help alleviate your pain." She gently placed her palm on my wounded shoulder, and the warmth of her hand did nearly as much to soothe the ache as did the ointment. If only she would continue touching me, allow us to forge something new together from the broken pieces of our past. Her willing presence in my life would be far more healing than any balm.

"What of your eye?" she asked.

"Not much has changed. It is still blurry at the edge of my vision. But working here has forced me to rely so much on the other one, as well as my other senses, that it's become more of a mild nuisance than an impediment."

"I am glad to hear that." She brushed the remnants of her trimming from my shoulders and then my neck. Did I imagine that her fingers lingered there for longer than was necessary? Could I dare hope that my infatuation was no longer one-sided? Our eyes met and held briefly before she snatched her hand away and set herself to sweeping up the hair on the ground with a straw hand broom.

I stifled a smile. This haircut had taken much longer than any I'd ever received from my mother or sisters. But I'd gladly be shorn bald like Eitan had years ago after his nazarite vow if it meant she'd keep her hands on me.

She glanced over at the pallet and then spoke in an even quieter tone. "I caught Estebaal watching Ana. I am concerned for her."

"I've seen the same thing." For as keenly aware of his surroundings as the bodyguard was at all times, whenever Ana chanced by, an army could invade and Estebaal would see only her. I knew the feeling well.

"I spoke to him about it. He vows he has no intentions of approaching her, and although I no longer believe he means her harm, I've seen too much to be completely at ease."

I could only imagine what she'd seen since she walked out of the gates at Kedesh. Laish had been a pit of wickedness, and Edrei, though Hebrew at its core, was not much better. Levites walked in the market with tzitzit at the corners of their garments discussing points of the Torah while passing stalls offering idols and amulets that broke those same laws. And Samil was not the only Hebrew with a heathen sanctuary on his property. The holy alongside the profane—this city was the epitome of everything Mosheh had warned against.

"And yet again . . ." She dropped the hair trimmings she'd collected into a refuse pot near the door. "Something he said makes me wonder whether he is more trustworthy than I'd first guessed."

"What is that?"

"He said nothing on this earth would ever make him deserving of her."

"And why does that make you think he won't go near her?"

"Because Samil has asked him to do things . . . heinous things . . . to protect his wealth and instill fear in the people of Edrei. The elders may be officially in charge of this city, but my master owns it, and much of that is due to orders Estebaal has carried out. I'd always thought those terrible duties were meted out with cool callousness, but he carries a heavy weight of shame. Feels like there is nothing but blackness at the core of his soul and that nothing can wash away the stain of it. He does not want to taint our sweet Ana with such wickedness."

"I can understand such a feeling."

"You have done nothing for which you should feel ashamed, Malakhi. You have been honorable in all things."

I huffed a quiet laugh. "I killed my brother."

Her eyes flared wide. "You did nothing of the sort. He was alone when that serpent bit him."

"Exactly. And if I'd been with Gidal that day, instead of off sulking, I would have been there. Whenever he was deep in thought or focused on his work, he paid little attention to his surroundings. I would have seen it. I could have killed that snake before it sank its fangs into his hand."

Her eyes shimmered. "I blamed myself too," she whispered. "That day I wielded my sharp tongue against him, for some reason that I cannot even remember, and he left early to go tend his trees instead of putting up with me. If I'd been a better wife . . ." Tears tracked down her cheeks. "He was so kind, Malakhi, so patient with me. He was my friend, and I did not treat him with anything resembling love because I was so incredibly selfish. And he died because of it."

Forcing myself to stay firmly seated on the stool, I reached for her hand, and to my surprised delight she allowed me to wrap my fingers around hers. Her admission made me see my own in a different light. "It seems as though both of us have been convicting ourselves of a crime we did not commit. Gidal made the choice to go to the grove that day by himself. He could have asked someone else to go, even if I was avoiding him. And he could have stayed with you that morning and worked to reconcile instead. Perhaps no matter what choices you and I had made, that snake would still have found its way to him. Who are we to question the ways of Yahweh anyhow?"

"I thought all of you blamed me for Gidal's death. Especially your sisters."

Reluctantly, I released her hand. "None of my family blamed you for an accident, Rivkah. Chana least of all."

"I can only imagine what Abra thought of me . . . after I ran from you."

Although tempted to sidestep the issue, I did not want any more untruths between us. At some point she would have to deal with Abra. She might as well be prepared.

"Abra has been the one pushing me to marry most of all," I said. "Although I never shared all of my reasons for going through with the levirate marriage, she's my twin. She knew."

"And she hates me for leaving."

"I don't think she hates you, Rivkah. But the . . . aftermath of your flight was likely hard for her to watch. There was a reason I threw myself into training with such fervor. Spying on the enemy or engaging in combat kept my mind off other things . . . off you. When I came home wounded, it only sharpened her anger."

"I wish . . ." Her words trickled off.

"What?" I prodded.

She lifted her eyes to mine on a small sigh. "I wish I'd known that you . . . cared for me in such a way."

"I wish I'd been brave enough to tell you."

"I'd likely still have thought you were too young and did not know your mind."

"I've known my own mind since I was fourteen and spied on you under that terebinth tree, Rivkah."

Her breath caught.

"I heard you sing, and it dragged me over a cliff that I did not even know existed."

Her response was breathless. "All that time?"

"Apparently even your father knew. He thought I'd grown out of it by the time he proposed marriage between you and Gidal."

"He did?"

"It's why he sent me here."

She clutched her hands together in the center of her chest as if to hide an ache that lived there. "Is he . . . is he well?" This was the first time she'd asked me about her father in all these weeks. I'd thought it strange at first, but just as I had plunged into war to keep the loss of Rivkah at bay, I guessed she'd likely focused all her energies on her duties and her son to keep her own pain at arm's length.

"I will not lie, mourning you has changed him. These years of not knowing what happened or where you were grieved him deeply. But he has never stopped looking for you with whatever means he could. When he called for me to let me know you'd written, it was as if the grief had melted away like snow beneath the sun. He's waiting for you."

Her chin trembled and her voice dropped low. "If I could return, I would. I'd be a slave in *his* house if it meant I could repay him for the hurt I've caused."

"You will return. And when that day comes, I'll be with you."

"But Ayala . . . you must go back now. I appreciate that you want to watch over Amit, but he is safe here with me, and you cannot make her wait any longer."

"There was never an understanding between us. And I asked Hakim to relay where I stand. She is a lovely girl and will make someone a fine wife. But she isn't you."

She clamped a palm over her mouth, her golden eyes teary. Her startled reaction poured fuel on my once-smoldering hopes, making them burst into a bright flame. I stood, retrieved my pack, and withdrew the parcel I'd carried from Kedesh—a gift wrapped in the papyrus roll I'd kept tucked between the wall and my bed for the last five years. One I'd waged a battle with myself over bringing in the first place.

Chin dropped as if in defeat, she accepted my offering with a trembling hand but did not look up. I thanked her for the haircut, pressed a kiss to the top of her head, and then left her with the reminder that long ago I had chosen her.

I prayed this time she would choose me.

CHAPTER
THIRTY-TWO

With my head full of Rivkah and whether she'd understood the meaning of my gift, I turned the corner toward my miserable room back at the inn. At the same moment, a well-muscled arm slipped around my neck and yanked me backward against a barrel chest. I grabbed the wrist that threatened to cut off my air, but my assailant's strength was beyond mine, and I could not budge the chokehold.

"Perhaps you should be more aware of your surroundings" came a growl in my ear. "Rivkah's *master* will not be pleased to hear that you are coming out of her quarters well after dark."

"I was not alone with her. Anataliah was there," I replied. "Which you must know since you've obviously been waiting here for the past hour to waylay me."

"Someone needs to watch you, boy. You are out of practice. I taught you to always be on your guard. Too bad that woman has always been your weakness." Baz let up his grip on me and I slipped away, but not before jabbing a retaliatory elbow into his gut.

"Why are you here?" I asked.

"Your father sent me with a message."

"I can't return, Baz. Rivkah and Amit need me here. Her master is ruthless, and I won't leave them alone to finish her indenture. I've worked my way into Samil's good graces so I can watch over them."

"The message isn't for you—although you definitely need to know what is happening. It's for the elders of Edrei." Foreboding snaked its way up my spine. Even in the dark I could see the deep frown on his face as he said, "The Arameans are on their way."

"Here?"

He nodded. "Darek and his men returned with news of movement by Kushan's forces, but it seemed as though they were headed westward, possibly with a destination of Laish. But then they abruptly turned southward, sending an advance force that can move faster than the bulk of the army. Edrei is directly in their path."

"How long?"

"Two weeks at the outside. I'll be meeting with the elders in the morning. Defensive measures must be taken and the people outside the walls given notice of what is coming."

With fortifications that hailed back to King Og—thick walls, sturdy gates, large cisterns, and the well that reached all the way down to the spring beneath the city—Edrei could certainly withstand a short siege, but unless the tribes of Israel banded together to defend their brothers, eventually this city would fall.

"Are reinforcements on the way to defend Manasseh's territory?"

"Your father is working to drum up support among Naftali," he said. "And messengers have been sent to all the rest of the tribes. But it's doubtful that we'll be able to unify successfully, especially after what happened with the Danites."

I thought back to the conversation in the foundry so many weeks ago, when my father warned of discontent within the sons of Dan. "Did they stir up war with neighboring tribes?"

"You haven't heard?"

"I've been busy building an addition to Rivkah's master's villa. There's not much opportunity to focus on other things when I am responsible for seventeen men."

Baz raised his eyebrows. "You are in charge?"

"Of the carpenters, for the most part," I said, noting the pride with which he asked the question. "Although the overseer recently asked that I direct the bricklayers as well."

His smile was as wide as the Jordan River. "See now? I told you leadership was in your blood."

I brushed off his praise with a shrug. "It suits my purposes in watching over Rivkah and Amit. Now, tell me about the Danites."

His pleased expression turned solemn. "They've taken Laish."

"Laish? But their allotted territory is far to the south!"

"It is, but you know they've never been able to get a firm hold there," he said, frustration evident in the way he pawed at his thick beard. "The enemy cities on the coast are well fortified, so the cowards gave up. But somehow, and we aren't even sure how they accomplished it beneath our noses, Laish fell effortlessly. They've already reestablished their clans throughout the foothills of Har Hermon and along the headwaters of the Jordan."

"It is a fertile area; I can see why they chose it. But our elders must be furious."

Baz nodded in agreement. "It's been contentious, without a doubt, although those fools have no rock to stand on. Laish should have always been our territory; then Dan would not have even considered such a brazen move. The elders of Naftali left it vulnerable by allowing the Canaanites to remain, a decision that your father was firmly against, if you remember."

"Yehoshua would be appalled at the fractures among us," I murmured.

"Agreed. Few Hebrews are willing to come to Manasseh's aid. Most of your generation has forgotten how the eastern tribes fulfilled their vow to Yehoshua during the Conquest of the Land. They lived up to their promise to fight alongside their western brethren, even though they'd already claimed their inheritance on this side of the Jordan. It seems as though the favor will not be returned."

"Is there no hope then?"

"Unless something drastic has happened in this city since I left you a few weeks ago, Edrei is highly vulnerable. And even if your father succeeds in bringing reinforcements, Manasseh's army is greatly depleted. The number of men your age who even know how to fight is pitiful. They've been too busy farming, trading, and who knows what else to bother with learning how to wield a sword or shoot a bow. This city will fall without the help of Yahweh."

And as I'd observed over the past months, few here were crying out for that help. Samil was far from the only Hebrew to have taken foreign wives, nor was he the only one who manipulated the law for his own gain. The elders in this city had turned a blind eye to the rot before them and would now reap what they had sown.

"I have to get Rivkah and Amit out," I said, already turning to make my way back through the gates.

"Wait," said Baz. "I have something for you."

He pressed a leather satchel into my hands, one weighted with treasure, if I was right about the cool clink of metal inside. "What is this?" I untied the purse strings, and moonlight glinted on gold and silver within.

"Amitai sent the mohar you gave to Rivkah," Baz said. "Along with as much silver as he could pull together. Darek and others added a few pieces of gold jewelry as well."

Rivkah's father's words rang through my mind. *"It does not matter if I have to sell everything I own, Malakhi. The mountains will fall into dust before I will ever give up on my daughter."* This would be more than enough to buy Rivkah's freedom.

"And you told them of Amit?" I asked, as I placed the priceless gift within my carpentry bag, where it would stay on my person until I was able to determine how best to negotiate with Samil.

"They are thrilled," he said. "Your mother wept with joy when I told her and Darek. Neither can wait to hold that boy in their arms. It's like a piece of Gidal has been resurrected."

Indeed it was. And yet Amit had also inherited some of Rivkah's traits as well. He'd already shown me how to draw all the Hebrew letters with a stick in the dirt and displayed a tenacity that was much more like his mother than his father. I thought of his drowsy smile as he drifted off while his mother cut my hair and decided to allow the two of them one more peaceful night's sleep before I delivered the news that would change everything.

Baz whistled for Toki and she bounded toward us, her white patches dancing in the night as she joined her master from wherever she'd been ordered to wait. "I'll be back in the morning to meet with the elders, as well as the commander of the forces stationed here."

"You and Toki are welcome to stay with me tonight. I'll speak to Rivkah tomorrow."

Baz made a sound of disgust. "Not unless your room smells a heap better than it did before. I'll take my chances outside the walls. Toki knows the tunnels so well now she leads me right through."

There was no use arguing with that. I was acclimated to the reek of the inn by now, but if I'd had the freedom to sleep under the stars in the fresh air instead of a tiny cell with only one miserly window slit, I'd have been happy to do so. However, proximity to Rivkah and Amit was worth any discomfort.

THIRTY-THREE

Rivkah

Sitting on the pallet after Amit and Ana left the room just after dawn, I once again unrolled the parcel Malakhi had given me the previous night, examining it beneath the morning sunlight streaming through the window. Even though the finish was five years old, the little mahogany box gleamed as if someone had continued to oil and polish the wood in order to maintain its near-to-new condition.

Opening the latch, I lifted the lid, still as astounded as I had been last night when I realized that Malakhi had bought and kept the box of brushes and inks that I'd admired in the market so long ago. He must have returned that very day and purchased it for a wedding gift, even after I'd been so rude to him. I could not believe he'd kept it all this time.

His admission about the day he'd caught me singing under the terebinth tree had made my long-held beliefs about him entirely unravel. I remembered that day well. I'd been missing my mother, which always drove me to solitude and to song. She'd loved my voice, comparing it to that of my great-grandmother Shira, who was reputed to have a voice that would put a skylark to shame. My mother always asked me to sing songs of my own creation whenever we were alone, since I was timid about singing in front of others. After she died, her memory was closest in the fields, beneath the blue sky, as I lifted my voice in praise to Yahweh and wrote down the words that came to me on scraps of papyrus or shards of pottery.

When I'd seen Malakhi spying on me, I'd been humiliated, wondering what all he'd heard and whether he would spread the tale of my private indulgence among his friends. For days I'd waited for him to taunt me about it or to hear whispered rumors from his friends or sisters. To my surprise I'd heard nothing and after a while forgot the incident. To think that a brief moment I'd brushed into the recesses of my mind had been such a turning point for him.

Now, looking back to that time with new eyes, his avoidance of Gidal and me made sense. Even as a very young man, his honor had risen above his strong attraction to me. I'd misjudged Malakhi for years. I'd maligned him and discounted his honest efforts to transform the strange situation of our betrothal into one based on friendship. The day he'd taken me to see the honeybees, he'd spoken of building trust between us and of his commitment to faithfulness, and I'd thrown it all back in his face.

Setting the box of brushes and inks aside, I lifted the papyrus that he'd wrapped the gift in. The ketubah, written in my own hand, outlined the terms of our betrothal and the vows I'd taken, to be a wife to Malakhi and to attribute my first son to Gidal. The creases in the papyrus made it clear that it had been wrapped around the scribe's box for a long time, but the ink was worn by more than just time. Had Malakhi come back to this ketubah whenever he thought of me? Had he followed the curves and lines of my handwriting with a finger in order to keep my memory alive, the way I'd once done with my mother in my songs?

This document was as much a challenge from him as it was a reminder of the contract between us. When he'd revealed that he was not betrothed to Ayala and that it was me he still wanted even after everything I'd done, it had taken a monumental effort to even continue standing. As soon as he'd walked out the door, I'd collapsed into a puddle of silent tears. He'd remained faithful to me all these years, and it seemed he still considered us bound together and hoped that I would be his bride, in body and spirit.

My heart quailed at the thought. I'd never expected to be so drawn to Malakhi, to feel so protected in his presence, to crave his voice and touch and attention the way I'd come to over the past weeks. He should be Amit's father—and still could be—if by some miracle Samil gave permission for such a union.

I imagined a number of outcomes, wondering if perhaps we could marry in secret and wait out my indenture. Or perhaps Malakhi could petition the elders on the grounds that our betrothal was confirmed before I'd entered service. I would vow not to leave and honor my word if only they might allow us to stay together. To be the family we should have been. Perhaps Ana could move in with another slave and we could live here. Samil would undoubtedly have plenty of work for Malakhi—

All my fanciful musings skidded to a halt as the true obstacle to a marriage between Malakhi and I reared its head.

Laish.

Once I revealed the consequences of my reckless behavior with the Hebrew man there, Malakhi wouldn't just walk away—he'd *run* back to Ayala. And for as much as I'd come to desire what I'd once thrown away so thoughtlessly, I did not deserve it. Yet, no matter the outcome, I owed him the truth.

Running a palm over the words I'd written with a misguided heart full of anger and resentfulness, I prayed that for Amit's sake, Malakhi would have mercy. For if he concluded that my actions were infidelity, he could very well call for my stoning.

◆ ◆ ◆

I'd seen Malakhi a few times today, and he'd seemed inordinately agitated. Samil had given him a few last-moment tasks before the festival began at sundown, including hauling three stone incense burners from the sanctuary to place near the sukkahs. Whenever we exchanged gazes I had the distinct feeling he wanted to speak to me, but with so many people bustling around, there was no opportunity. As much as I craved his presence, my conviction about telling him the entire truth was a heavy yoke around my neck, so I was grateful for the temporary reprieve. Cross-legged near the garden gate, I bent over the correspondence Samil asked me to prepare this morning and did my best to pretend Malakhi did not exist in order to focus on the task. It was a fruitless endeavor; I'd only written three lines in the last hour.

In contrast to the roiling in my stomach, the atmosphere around the villa was light and jovial. Amit and Bensam had found a shiny red pomegranate that they were tossing back and forth with a few other children, making the distance wider and wider with each pass.

Their bright laughter blocked out the wailing so thoroughly that it took a few moments for my ears to pick out the distinct sound of mourning from somewhere outside the walls of the villa. One of the neighbors must have suffered a loss in the family.

Suddenly more loud voices lifted on the breeze, and then a ram's horn call from the central plaza cut through all the noise. The hair on the back of my neck lifted at the mournful stutter of the shofar. There was little need for such a signal during times of peace. It was the call for the heads of households to gather immediately.

Two servants rushed into the courtyard, their faces pale from whatever news they carried. Everyone halted their tasks to congregate around the messengers. My pulse raced as I surveyed the courtyard for Amit, but the children seemed oblivious to whatever chaos had erupted in Edrei and were gleefully continuing with their game.

Just as I rose to join the crowd, Malakhi appeared in front of me. "Meet me in the garden," he said as he brushed past, urgency thick in his tone. For as desperate as I was to follow him and find out what was happening, I forced myself to stay still, remembering that the last time we'd met there we'd nearly been discovered. Thankfully, all eyes and ears were on the servants across the courtyard and Samil's wives were nowhere to be seen. Once I was satisfied no one would take notice of my absence, I spun and plunged into the garden, heart pounding.

Following the stone path that led around the back of the pool and by the sanctuary, I whispered Malakhi's name a few times but heard nothing over the overlapping chatter of the people in the courtyard and the sounds of distress outside the walls. The city was in an uproar.

Just past the stone sanctuary, a callused hand grabbed my wrist, pulling me off the path and into the space between a young almond tree and a prolific jasmine bush. Surrounded by honey-sweet leaves and a profusion of tiny white blossoms, I could not help but inhale the medley of fragrances, along with the headiness of Malakhi's nearness. There was little more than two handspans between us. "What is happening?" I breathed, imbalanced by his proximity.

"The Arameans are coming. They will be here within only a matter of days."

Terror sizzled through me. "The Arameans?" I repeated.

"We need to get you and Amit out. Tonight. City officials will leave the gates open for a couple of days I would guess, to allow those living outside the walls to take shelter, but once they close, they will stay that way."

"Samil won't let us go."

"Rivkah, do you hear me? An entire army, rumored to be among the most savage in the world, is making its way toward us. This city is well fortified, but I doubt they can sustain a lengthy siege."

"Most of the cisterns are at least half full and there is a spring beneath the city. Edrei has plenty of water."

"It does, but with the number of people who will take refuge within the walls, resources will soon be scarce. Edrei exports more crops than it retains for its people. This city will fall. It is only a question of when."

"But the armies of Israel . . . ?"

He shook his head. "There has been difficulty in rounding up reinforcements, and Manasseh's army is unprepared for such an assault on its own. We must get you to safety."

"It doesn't matter that we are in danger. Samil won't release me, Malakhi."

He reached into the carpentry bag at his waist and drew out a leather purse.

Bewildered, I accepted the pouch, surprised at its weight as it shifted in my hands. I untied the drawstring and peered inside, nearly dropping it from shock at its contents. Digging into the treasure, I came up with a copper necklace that looked very familiar. *The mohar.* The betrothal gifts Malakhi's family had given me were inside this purse, but although they'd been generous, there had been no gold jewelry exchanged during the ceremony and only half the silver contained here.

"Your father sent this to negotiate your freedom. My father and others in Kedesh contributed as well. They all want you to come home."

The value inside this small bag would be many times the worth of a normal slave. I knew this because I'd prepared many indenture contracts for Hebrews and participated in negotiations for foreign slaves as well. But Samil had made it abundantly clear that he valued my skills as highly as he did Estebaal's. Would he accept this payment in exchange for my freedom?

"You are worth far more than this in my estimation, Rivkah, but you know as well as I do that Samil will do anything to build his wealth. He can purchase five more scribes with such a sum." A smile twitched on his lips. "Though none quite so beautiful."

How could such a simple statement cause every misgiving I had to crumble into a thousand pieces?

"I would pay any price to keep you and Amit safe." His silver eyes met mine and held. "Please come home with me. Be my wife."

Feeling as though a whirlwind had swirled me into its embrace, my knees wobbled and I dropped the purse, hearing the jangle of the gold and silver spilling into the dirt. Instinctively I reached to steady myself and found my hands wrapped around Malakhi's wrists, and those two handspans cut into one. Unable to fight the pull of this honorable, beautiful man any longer, I lifted on my toes and pressed my lips to his. He hesitated for only a moment before gathering me close and taking up where his hopeful kiss in the grove had broken off. But this time, I had no desire to push him away. *This* was where I should have been for the last five years, in the circle of his arms.

His lips moved to my cheek and then my forehead as he brushed one hand down the length of my hair, again and again, as if soothing a small child. "We will go together to Samil and buy out your contract. I know a way out of the city. We can be in Kedesh within the week, before the Arameans even arrive here."

I laid my head on his chest, breathing in the smell of his skin and taking comfort in the warmth of his embrace. "What if he refuses?"

"I'll never leave you," he said, his vow rumbling against my cheek.

The truth burned a fiery trail up my throat, yet I could not look at him as I spoke the words. "I betrayed you."

His body stiffened, but he did not pull away.

"In Laish. There was a Hebrew man and too much wine and I was so wrapped up in my rebellion against my father. . . ." Tears slipped down my nose into the neckline of his tunic. "I could give you a thousand excuses, but I made the choice to be there, to be swayed by his flattery. And when I awoke the next morning, he'd stolen Gidal's mohar. I couldn't come back after that. Couldn't face my father after what I'd done. Nor could I marry you and sully your family's name. If it wasn't for Amit, I don't think I would have even fought to survive. I was not worthy to be your wife, Malakhi. I still am not. I am an adulterer and deserve death."

He was so still, his arms like iron bands around me, but his heart thudded against my cheek like a signal drum, and his chest expanded again and again as if he were working to control his breathing. Too much of a coward to look into his face, I began to pull away. But he refused to let me go.

With one arm keeping me pressed against himself, he lifted my chin with his other hand to look straight into my eyes. His visage went blurry as I stared back, terrified and trembling. He'd shown himself to be forgiving for my abandonment and even my deceit over Amit, but this was too much, even for him. Would he have me stoned? Or just take my boy and leave me to my fate with the Arameans?

"I knew," he said.

My jaw dropped open. "You what?"

"When we went to Laish with Raviv to search for you, one of the servant girls told us you'd been seen with a Hebrew who was doing his best to lure you. But in her position she could say nothing to stop you." He cleared his throat. "I expected when I arrived in Edrei that I would find you with him."

A sob built in my throat as hot shame spread across my skin. "And yet you came anyway?"

"I respect your father, Rivkah. He asked me to come."

"But you brought the ketubah. And the mahogany box. Why? If you guessed that I'd dishonored my vows to you, why would you bring them with you?"

He shrugged. "Because the sound of your voice beneath the terebinth tree followed me everywhere I went, even into battle. And when I closed my eyes at night, I could see only you. No matter what I did to squelch it, I could not help but hope."

I shook my head. "I am not worth—"

He interrupted. "Did you give yourself to this man of your own volition?"

"I—" Blinking my eyes, I tried to once again pull the hazy memories of that night into clarity. "I don't think so. There were . . . bruises on my body, and my tunic was torn." My skin flushed. "I think perhaps I tried to defend myself, but I remember very little."

Fury gathered in the eyes he lifted over my shoulder and his chest heaved, as if he were holding back a cry of rage. "May Yahweh's judgment fall heavy upon him."

"I should have left that rooftop, should have refused the wine—"

"There is no excuse for any man to do such a thing, Rivkah, especially a Hebrew under the Torah. From what we learned from Yoash and Kefa, the wine likely contained poppy juice as well, which would have made you even more compliant. He knew what he was doing, and from the rumors in Laish, he'd done it before."

My stomach curdled at the thought that any other woman had suffered from such a thing, but at the same time knowing that I'd not been the only one to fall prey to his schemes eased the ever-present sting of self-blame.

He peered down at me. "Has there ever been another . . . ?"

I shook my head with vehemence. "No. I never considered marriage, even after I realized I was with child."

"Then I hold nothing against you. You've suffered too much of your own condemnation, I would imagine. It is time for us to move forward—together—and stop flogging ourselves for whatever lays behind."

He took my face in his hands, his thumbs stroking my cheekbones. He pressed another gentle kiss to my lips. "It doesn't matter what Samil's contract says. You are mine. And I am yours, forever."

"Forgive me," I whispered as I slid my arms around his waist and pressed my tearstained cheek against his chest, praying that he understood that the plea encompassed every one of my many sins against him. He held me close, stroking my back and murmuring merciful assurances I did not deserve as I allowed the sorrow to finally pour free.

"Isn't this precious" came a voice from nearby. My blood stilled and then turned to ice. Dilara moved into view, her hands braced on her hips and a feline smile curved across her crimson lips.

She wrinkled her nose in wicked delight. "Won't my husband be *thrilled* to discover what the two of you have been up to while the rest of the villa is in a panic over some army?"

CHAPTER
THIRTY-FOUR

"After all I have done for you, *this* is how you repay me?"

I stood in front of my master, head bowed and pulse fluttering in my throat. Dilara had wasted no time in running to Samil after finding Malakhi and me in the garden, but it had been a long while before I was summoned.

Wondering how I could possibly stave off my master's fury, I'd sat in paralyzed panic on my pallet, clutching the bag of gold and silver left behind in the confusion after Malakhi had been escorted from the villa at Dilara's loud and vehement insistence. The sight of the man I'd too late realized that I loved being dragged through the gates, his impassioned pleas for an audience with our master roundly ignored, refused to leave my mind. Would it be the last time I ever saw him?

Samil paced the room. "I have given you unfettered access to my business dealings. I have given you freedoms far beyond what any other servant in this household enjoys, other than Estebaal. Your son has been welcomed at my own table!"

"Yes, my lord, and I am grateful for it. If not for your generosity, we would have been destitute."

"And yet not grateful enough to be truthful." His glare speared me. "You have been given the utmost respect in this house, Rivkah. You know as well as I do that most masters would have had you in their beds. I have not laid a hand on you. I have boasted of your skills and treated you no differently than I would have a man in your position. Better, in fact."

"All of this is true. You have been most kind."

"And yet you brought a spy into my house!"

My head reared back. "Malakhi is not a spy." At least not in the sense Samil thought him to be.

"Then why hide your connections to him? Was he sent by Hanoch in Golan? Have you been trading secrets to my rival?"

"No! I would not break your confidences, my lord."

"Why else would you sneak around in my garden with your lover? Dilara says she suspects you've been meeting him there for weeks. Do you accuse my wife of lying?"

"No, my lord. I did meet with Malakhi, but it was only so he could deliver something to me." I touched the leather pouch that now hung around my neck, still awed by its weight. "There is silver inside, and some gold jewelry as well."

His brows arched as his eyes followed my gesture. "Gold? My secrets are worth so much to Hanoch?"

"It is not from Hanoch, nor any other tradesman, my lord. The offering was sent by my father."

"Your father? I thought your people were dead."

"I allowed you to believe that so you would be willing to take me on as your scribe."

"So you lied from the start," he said, his eyes narrowed.

"Only to protect my child, my lord."

He peered at me, curiosity edging out fury in his gaze. "Did your father set you out of his home when he discovered you were with child? Is Amit your lover's son? Is that why he's been lurking around my home?"

"Malakhi is not my lover. He is my betrothed."

Samil's face wrinkled in confusion. It would profit me nothing to hide my past any longer, so I took a deep breath and laid it all before him, leaving only a few of the more shameful details out of my story. "When it was made known that I was in this city, my father sent Malakhi to find me. But I swear to you, upon my own child, that I told him I would keep my word to you and would not leave until the end of my indenture."

Samil frowned. "Then why the bag of treasure?"

"Malakhi's father sent one of his men here with the purpose of paying off my indenture contract and also to warn Edrei of the coming Aramean invasion."

He brushed a dismissive hand through the air. "We will be fine. I have been assured by the elders that they will surrender peacefully. I've done plenty of business with the Arameans, and I have you and Estebaal to translate any necessary negotiations. We may have to pay tribute to Kushan, but he won't raise a finger against us."

I was shocked by his cavalier attitude. "There are *thousands* marching toward us. They will burn the city. Kill all of us. I have to get my son out before its too late! *All* of us need to go, your family as well. Malakhi says he knows a way—"

"No. We stay. And your contract is not up for negotiation."

"Please, my lord. It may not seem so after what Dilara saw, but I *have* been loyal to you for nearly five years. You have my eternal gratitude. But Amit is everything to me. I *must* protect my boy. I could not bear to see him slaughtered." I slipped the strap over my head and held the bag out to him, my hands trembling. "This is enough to purchase the remainder of my contract ten times over, perhaps more. I beg you to release me so I can return to my home and save my son's life."

Samil's eyes flared and went to the purse. I could see that he was gauging its weight and perhaps calculating its value in the uncanny way he guessed weights in the market without even handling the items. My only hope was that his lust for wealth would outweigh his desire for my skills.

"Please. My father has not known where I was for five years. He has grieved all this time, thinking I was likely dead. If there is any mercy in you, I beg of you to free me so I can go home and make amends for my sins against my family."

He regarded me for a few long moments and then strode across the room to take the treasure from my hands. Untying the purse strings, he peered inside and made a noise of approval. Hope fluttered at the gates of my heart as he placed the bag on the table with a metallic jangle. *Please, Yahweh. If you hear me at all, soften Samil's heart.*

"All right. If you are so very determined to leave, then I will take this in lieu of the reminder of your contract."

My knees wobbled and tears burned my eyes. "Truly? You will let me go?"

"You have been a good scribe. I don't know how I will ever replace you, but perhaps if this city changes allegiance I would be better off with an Aramean to tend my business connections anyhow."

Relief flooded into every part of me. "Thank you, my lord. Thank you."

"You are welcome to write up the agreement today and be on your way before the guards close up the gates."

I clutched my hands to my chest. "Won't you reconsider leaving Edrei? You and your family would be far safer in Golan, or even farther south."

"I spent ten years building this business, Rivkah. And the last three making this villa worthy of an Egyptian vizier. I will not give up my property so easily."

I bowed my head. "Yes, my lord."

"Go on, then," he said, patting the bag that had bought my freedom. "You'll want to be on your way before dark, I assume."

"I have learned much here, my lord. Although my own foolishness brought me to Edrei, I have found satisfaction in working for you and will never forget the kindnesses you extended to me and my son."

His smile was tight, but he nodded acceptance of my gratitude. I turned to leave the room, my mind whirling and a new song bubbling up in my heart. Free! I was free!

"Oh—Rivkah," he said. "Before you go, I'd like to show you something."

I turned back to find him near the window. He gestured for me to join him. Confused, I did so, but as I stood beside him I saw nothing of note, except a large number of servants scurrying about, doing all they could to secure food and water to prepare for the siege, and the group of children playing at one end of the courtyard. I wondered how many of them would survive the upcoming onslaught. Would Ana be safe? Would Estebaal protect her? Perhaps I ought to ask Malakhi to explain the system of tunnels and caves to him before we left so he could hide her and the rest of Samil's family in case his plan to appease the Arameans failed.

"Look at our sons," said Samil, pointing toward Amit and Bensam with a note of pride. "They have become wonderful friends, haven't they?"

My heart panged with regret. Amit would be devastated to leave his friend. Perhaps going with Malakhi would soothe a bit of the hurt though, and I knew my boy would be thrilled with his many cousins. The place where I'd grown up had become my own elusive version of the Garden of Eden during these last years I'd been away. I longed to walk in the orchards with my son, show him the groves his father tended, let him run free, climb trees, and chase after the lambs and goats in the fields around the city.

"You can be sure that Amit will be well cared for. I will have him moved to the room with Bensam and the other children. He will want for nothing."

His words scattered in a thousand directions inside my head, none of them fitting together. "My lord?"

"Perhaps in a few more years he too will be ready to be a scribe. Wouldn't that be lovely? To take up the place his mother left? He's a smart boy, Rivkah. You've done well with him. And I know he already can read many letters. He's shown me."

My vision blurred. "But . . . no. Amit will be with me."

"Oh. No, my dear. You gave birth while you were contracted as my slave. He belongs to me. Our agreement was only for your release. Not his."

Did the Torah say that? Surely not. Although Samil rarely kept the true letter of the law. "But . . . but I was with child when I came to you! He is my son!"

Samil lowered his brow and clucked his tongue. "Oh, now I don't believe the elders would see it that way. Who is to say he is not my child anyhow? As I said, most masters would have not have hesitated to exert their rights, lawfully or not. And the timing of his birth could be . . . shall we say . . . altered?"

Horror eddied in my bones. Half of the elders in Edrei owed Samil for loans he'd extended to them. They would undoubtedly rule in his favor, and I would have no recourse. My response was as weak as my position. "No. You can't have my son."

"Oh, I will do what I please, my dear." He reached out to slip an arm around me and pulled me to his side with a grin that chilled me to the core. I shuddered, my teeth chattering. He lifted a finger to gesture toward Estebaal, who was in the courtyard, not five paces from where Amit and Bensam knelt in the dirt, drawing with sticks. "And if you try anything foolish . . ." The lack of emotion in his voice was more menacing that any explosive threat could ever be. "Well, I'm certain you know what my bodyguard is capable of."

"What do you want?" I choked out, feeling as though every drop of blood had pooled into my feet. "I'll do anything."

He smiled, petting the length of my hair as if I were his own daughter. "I am certain we can come to an understanding."

THIRTY-FIVE

Malakhi

I'd paced the room for hours after I'd been dragged from the villa, hoping that Baz would arrive soon so we could plot Rivkah's rescue. When finally a knock sounded, I hurried to open the door. But instead of my father's enormous friend at the threshold, it was Estebaal, his mouth set in a grim line.

"Just could not stay away, could you?" he said. He shook his head, his expression chagrined, as if I'd disappointed him somehow, which was ridiculous since he and I had exchanged no more than a few words in the many weeks I'd worked for Samil. "I'd hoped you could rein yourself in, knowing what the master would do."

"She is my betrothed. By law she was mine long before she came here."

"Quiet," he said, with a wary glance around the inn courtyard. Then he pressed a meaty palm against the center of my chest and pushed me backward. Stunned by the odd command, I retreated a few steps as he shut the door behind him and then leaned back against it. "Your woman has been kind to me. Far kinder than most of you Hebrews. And it is only for her sake that your jawbone is not in pieces already."

"So you've been sent to deal with me?"

He nodded. "And to extract the information Samil desires."

"What does he want to know?"

"Who are you and what do you want with Rivkah?"

Having no reason to hide anything from him, I told Estebaal the truth. He listened in silence, arms folded across his massive chest.

"He won't let her go," he said. "No amount of gold or silver would make him release her. He hinted months ago that even when her contract was fulfilled he had no intention of letting her walk away."

How would he circumvent the Torah command that she go free to go in the seventh year?

"Rivkah has been a key part of why Samil is as wealthy as he is," Estebaal continued. "He would no more let her go than he would me, even if I desired so."

I'd seen the ring in his ear, the mark that made it clear Estebaal was not only a lifelong slave, but that he'd chosen to submit himself to that position by having an awl driven through his earlobe at the doorpost of his master's house. A Hebrew tradition that the Aramean had chosen to submit to.

"You have this city living in terror of you, Estebaal. You could likely walk right out of the gates and no one would raise a finger to stop you. What keeps you here?"

"Samil saved me," he said. "I was ten years old and he found me half alive, living in the charred shell of what used to be my home after a rival tribe attacked, the bodies of my family rotting around me. He'd been on his very first trading run to Damascus. He took me in, treated me more like a son than a slave."

"And so you maim, destroy, and murder for him?"

He shrugged. "I owe him everything."

"Will he hurt her?" I asked, my bones going cold as I considered the savagery of the man.

"Not physically."

"What does that mean?"

"She's not your concern anymore. You should have kept your hands to yourself. You will not be allowed back inside the villa walls. Once we are done here, it would be best if you took yourself out those gates before they close and go back to wherever you came from. You'll only do her more damage if you stay."

"There is an army coming," I said. "Thousands are making their way south, and the advance force is nearly here. She and Amit are not safe. No one is. Isn't your master planning to flee anyhow?"

"Samil believes he's made enough contacts with the Arameans to negotiate his safety in case the city falls. He's dined in the home of the very king who sent the forces in the first place. And of course, he has me to speak for him. Rivkah and her son will be as safe as anyone in the villa. I'll watch over them. I promise you."

For such a brilliant tradesman and master negotiator, Samil was a fool. He and his family would burn along with the rest of the city once the gates were breached. I'd heard the stories of Kushan, and there was a reason we Hebrews called him the King of Double Wickedness. I had to find a way to get my family out of this city. Baz would help me, I was certain, and there were few warriors fiercer than him.

Estebaal stepped forward. "I need to get back to the villa and report to Samil. You can either take what you've earned without a struggle, or I can apologize later to Rivkah for making it harder on you than it had to be. What is your choice?"

I heaved a sigh, knowing that even with all my training, Estebaal was at a distinct advantage. Not only did he far outweigh me, I'd seen him sparring with another of Samil's bodyguards from the roof one day and had been shocked at his speed and agility. "Would you at least avoid my right arm and eye? I'm finally getting some use out of both of them and would rather not be set back months of recovery time."

"I'll do my best." He cracked the knuckles on one hand as he approached. "Shield that pretty face."

THIRTY-SIX

I swiped at my bloodied face with the grimy scrap of linen Baz had begged from the innkeeper. The mercenary Moabite had, of course, demanded a fee for such a "luxury."

"Looks like you've been run over by a chariot. Again," Baz quipped, chuckling at his own jest.

"The man certainly knows how to conduct a beating." I moved an arm to support my torso, my bruised ribs screaming. Toki licked my hand, her large yellow eyes following my every twitch. She'd been stationed at my side since she and her master had discovered me facedown on the dirt floor shortly after Estebaal had left. I scrubbed between her ears, grateful for a distraction from the throbbing pain in my torso and jaw.

"I thought you said he went easy on you for Rivkah's sake."

"Apparently, in Estebaal's opinion, this *was* going easy." Groaning from the effort, I forced myself to sit up. I could not take time to wallow in the pain. Rivkah needed me. "What did you learn from the elders? Do they actually plan to capitulate like Estebaal says?"

"A bigger pack of fools I've yet to meet." He shook his shaggy head in disbelief. "I recommended that they give the people enough time to evacuate the city and head for Golan or somewhere else, but they have announced that the gates will close tomorrow at midday. They insist they have plenty of stores to withstand a siege and assured the people that the gates will hold. I suspect it is only a means to placate everyone until they hand over the city to our enemies."

"Samil may be advising them in this. Estebaal said his master seems intent on staying. Thinks he can negotiate with the Arameans."

Baz cursed the man for his arrogance. "Kushan doesn't negotiate. He means to take control of our territories. We are not the only spies who keep a close watch on the enemy. He knows we are divided and means to use those fractures against us. It is no coincidence that he is striking in the midst of this uproar over Laish. Even if the elders get on their faces and stretch out their necks for his sandals to tread, this city will burn, and its inhabitants, especially the women and children, will suffer unspeakable horrors."

My protective instincts roared to life at the thought of my woman and the child I loved as my own anywhere near such atrocities. I twisted to retrieve the dagger Baz had brought me from beneath my pallet but could not restrain a gasp when a wave of pain clenched my side.

"You aren't going anywhere right now, boy," he said, frowning in displeasure as I tried again to reach the weapon and failed with a furious growl.

"I won't leave them here." I gritted my teeth against both the ache and my frustration. "Even if by some miracle Rivkah and Amit survive this invasion, I don't believe Estebaal's claim that Samil won't harm her. He demands absolute loyalty and offers no second chances."

Baz scrubbed at his grizzled jaw with a deep sigh. "I can try to get in. But it'll be risky getting both her and the boy out without notice."

"There are guards at all the gates and a few stationed near the villa, but if you climb into the garden behind the sanctuary, Rivkah's chamber is easy to find—"

A quiet knock halted my instructions. Toki leapt up to snuffle at the crack beneath the door, a low growl building in her throat. Baz slipped his knife from his belt. "Your friend coming back to finish you off?"

"Possibly. Perhaps Samil decided it was best to eliminate me altogether."

Baz nudged his dog aside with a knee. She complied but stood at attention, her tail twitching and her luminous eyes on her master as he slowly opened the door.

It was not Estebaal standing at the threshold, but Rivkah, with Amit's little hand gripped in her own, both of them wide-eyed at the sight of Baz and his dog. Rivkah's gaze swept from my father's friend to me, and with a small cry, her hand went to her mouth. Pushing past Baz, she rushed toward my pallet and knelt down. "Malakhi! What did he do?" Toki whined, likely wondering whether I was under attack.

"I am fine," I said, hoping both females would be placated by my casual tone. "Baz says nothing is broken."

The dog settled, but Rivkah wasn't fooled. She gingerly placed her palm on my right cheek, her gaze moving from injury to injury. "I cannot believe he did this to you," she murmured as tears gathered in her eyes. The sight of her worrying over me should not cause such bone-deep satisfaction, but it did. I'd spent so long dreaming of the day when she'd care about me like this that the furrow between her brows made me feel like crowing with victory.

"Does Samil know you left the villa?" I asked.

Her hand dropped from my face, her lips pinching tight. "Yes. He gave me permission to come."

"Why?" That made no sense after sending his bodyguard to pummel me.

Her mouth trembled, and she reached for Amit, who'd been standing near the foot of my pallet, his attention divided between me and Toki, who'd now relaxed and lay two paces from the boy's sandals, chin on her paws.

Rivkah pulled Amit close, wrapping her arm around his waist. "Little lamb," she said, lifting a note of false happiness into her voice as she gestured across the small room. "I want you to meet Baz."

Shrinking against his mother, the boy's eyes went round as he stared at the hulking man near the door. "He's bigger than Estebaal," he whispered.

"He is." She gave him a little smile. "Baz knew your father too."

"Truly?" His jaw dropped open.

"I did," Baz said. "I watched him and your uncle there"—he pointed to me—"grow from tiny sprouts into boys about your age, and then into men."

"My uncle?" Amit's incredulous gaze traveled back and forth from me to his mother.

I wondered if she'd be upset that Baz had revealed my identity, but instead she nodded. "Yes, my lamb. Malakhi is your father's younger brother. They were two years apart. And Baz is a close friend of your grandfather, Darek."

Although I was thrilled she was finally telling Amit the truth about his heritage, foreboding whispered in my ear. Something had changed drastically for her to suddenly be so forthcoming.

"I have a grandfather?"

"Indeed you do," said Baz. "And he is the commander of a group of men who spy past enemy lines to make sure our people are protected."

Amit's face was the portrait of wonder, all fear of the giant man seemingly wiped away by the declaration of such heroics. "Is that your dog?" he asked.

"Yes, it is." Baz knelt down and snapped his fingers at the animal, who immediately jumped up and rushed to his side. "This is Toki. Would you like to pet her?"

After asking permission of his mother, the boy sidled closer, and after only a brief hesitation had his little hands deep in her thick fur, chattering away at Baz as if he'd known him his entire life. My father's friend answered every question in the same deep, patient tone with which he'd answered Gidal's and my questions when we were boys. Rivkah watched the interaction, her expression so troubled that I longed to pull her close and demand answers, but I would not press while Amit was in the room.

Baz must have sensed the need for a few moments of privacy. "Why don't you and I go find Toki something to eat? I'll tell you about the time your grandfather and I had to swim across the Tigris to escape a group of women who mistook us for thieves."

Amit ran to Rivkah, his big brown eyes pleading with her. "May I?"

"Of course. I've known Baz since I was a little girl too," she said, giving the big man a meaningful glance over his head. "I trust him with my life . . . and with yours." Her lips trembled as kissed her son's forehead. "My sweet boy," she murmured. "You know how much I love you, don't you? I would never leave you with anyone who would do you harm."

The cryptic words caused unease to creep up my spine, as did the smile that came nowhere near her eyes. "Toki does look very hungry. You and Baz had better find her something to eat, and I'll stay and talk with Malakhi."

Amit complied but looked back over his shoulder twice as he followed Baz out of the door, his hand on the curve of Toki's back. It seemed Gidal's son was just as perceptive as he had been; he too knew something was very wrong.

The moment the door closed behind the three of them, Rivkah crumpled, her face in her hands, her shoulders jerking with silent sobs. Caring nothing for the burst of pain in my ribs, I slid off the pallet and pulled her into my arms, her anguish spearing me completely through.

"Rivkah. My love. Tell me." I kissed her hair as she clung to me, her face buried in my chest and her body trembling. "Did he hurt you?"

She dragged in a heaving breath. "No. But you have to take Amit. Now. Tonight."

"What?"

"He must go with you and Baz. Take him to Kedesh. Away from the Arameans." Another sob heaved from her lips. "I won't watch him die, Malakhi. I won't."

"Shhh." I tightened my grip around her, pulling her close. "We are *all* leaving tonight. Baz was headed to you when you knocked at the door. He knows the tunnel that will lead us out of Edrei. We will be safe at home before the army arrives."

She shook her head back and forth against my chest. "No. I cannot go."

My body jerked from the shock of her statement. "Of course you are coming with us. Amit needs you."

"I kept him safe for as long as I could," she said. "And now you will. I trust you. I should have trusted you five years ago." Her body trembled. "I was so wrong. Please tell my father I was childish and desperate and just . . . so very wrong."

I pulled back to look into her face. "Rivkah, you are not making any sense."

Her eyes were swollen and red, her entire body wracked by shivers. She peered back at me with such sorrow that I felt its echo at the center of my being. "You have to leave me."

"Never." My response was fierce as I placed my hands on her face and drew her to me. "Never," I repeated against her lips and then kissed away her ridiculous statement. Immediately inebriated by her nearness, I slid my fingers into her sleek black hair and took my time in claiming her mouth. She yielded to me and pressed closer, her arms slipping around my neck.

I broke the kiss and murmured her name, moving my lips along the line of her jaw and losing myself in the intoxicating scent of her skin. "I won't be parted from you again. We marry the day we return to Kedesh."

Her body went stiff. "I am not returning."

I slid my hand up one side of her neck and pressed another kiss to her lips. "Of course you are, as soon as Baz and Amit return—" I stopped speaking when my palm met the curve of her ear, my breath catching. With my heart thudding against my rib cage, I pulled back her hair to stare at the metal ring embedded in her earlobe.

"No," I gasped, my mind spinning with rationalizations for why Rivkah had a hole in her ear, still red and swollen from the piercing. One just like Estebaal's. "What did you do?"

She untangled herself from my embrace and jumped to her feet. "What I had to. It was this or my son."

Too shocked to care about my ribs, I stood. "What do you mean?"

"Samil took the bag and gave me my freedom, but he said I could not take Amit. He said my boy was his property and that the elders would do nothing to refute his rights of ownership." Her eyes fluttered as her chest heaved. "I . . . I had to, Malakhi. It was the only thing I could do to ensure his freedom."

"You let Samil pierce your ear at the doorpost? Bound yourself to him?"

She nodded her head, her eyes dropping to the floor. "He let me bring Amit to you, but Estebaal is outside, with three other well-armed guards, watching the inn and waiting for me." She dragged in a grief-laden breath, her amber eyes glossy with despair. "You must leave now, go to the tunnel. Before Samil changes his mind. Please. Save Amit. For Gidal's sake. Go."

Paralyzed by shock and anguish over the irrevocable vow she'd taken to enslave herself for life, I stood staring at her, as much impressed by her astounding courage as I was devastated by the reality of what she was asking of me. She'd been mine for less than a day and now she wanted me to take her son and leave her behind?

The door swung open and Toki bounded inside, Amit close behind, laughing at the way the dog's tail whisked against his face. Baz followed, his expression grave as he took in the strained silence in the room.

Rivkah winced, a tremble going through her as she turned toward

Amit, her lips pulled into a pained smile. "You are going to stay with Malakhi and Baz tonight, my lamb. They have a wonderful adventure planned. A secret tunnel to explore." Her voice was raspy and everything false.

Amit read right though it, his smile immediately wiped away. "No, Ima. I'm coming with you."

Crouching, she swept his hair back from his face and looked into his eyes. "Not right now, sweet boy. I have to return to my work. Your uncle and Baz will take good care of you, just like Ana does when I go on a trading run."

"But I want to be with you, Ima." His words came out on a whine, his arms going around his mother's neck.

Rivkah squeezed her eyes tight, then looked up at me, imploring. "I have to go," she said. "Or Estebaal and his men will come for me. . . ."

After the emotionless way he'd beaten me, I feared Estebaal might terrify Amit by bursting in to collect Rivkah. The boy would likely never recover from the sight of his mother being dragged away into the night. So I braced myself for doing what I must by pulling a breath into a chest that refused to fully expand.

"Baz and Toki will show us the way," I said, doing my best to work a note of excitement into my voice, even though my mouth tasted of bile. "It'll be just like when my abba goes spying on the enemy."

Amit clung to Rivkah, rightly disbelieving my lies. "No. I don't want to go."

Rivkah stood and disentangled herself from Amit, pressing him toward me. "I have to go, little lamb. Have courage."

He cried out and bucked against her outstretched hands, grasping for her. She sobbed my name as a plea and pushed him toward me. Although my own searing-hot tears obscured my vision, I caught him up in my arms, holding the weeping, writhing little boy tightly to my chest as his mother fled the room, giving her own life for his.

CHAPTER
THIRTY-SEVEN

Rivkah

19 Tishri

Anataliah led the way through what used to be the market but now housed the multitude who'd taken shelter behind the thick gates of Edrei. Instead of the brisk trade that had characterized this place only a few days before, the main plaza was now crammed with a restless and terror-stricken crowd. Infant wails mixed with the lowing of crudely penned livestock and the constant murmur of men and women discussing rumors of the ruthless army that was steadily making its way toward us.

Each horror I overheard as I stumbled along behind my friend was more gruesome than the last, making me profoundly grateful that I'd ripped out my own heart and sent it with Malakhi. The Aramean king seemed to take pleasure in the prolonged suffering of those who stood against him, and children were in no way exempt from the tortures he used to subjugate his enemies. If the elders of this city did not pay tribute to the invaders, it would be a mercy for all inside these walls to burn. Yes, I'd made the right decision in sending my son away with warriors who would gladly give their lives to deliver him to safety.

If only the image of my boy's precious face contorted in panic and the sound of his confused wail as I ran from the inn would stop slamming into me hour after hour. The hollow in my chest would likely never stop bleeding. *Please, Yahweh, please* was the only prayer my grief-addled mind could compose for the past three days.

"Rivkah." Ana tugged at my elbow, bringing me back to my senses. In my haze, I'd slowed to nearly a standstill. "We have to hurry," she said, pairing her urgency with another yank on my arm. "Shabbat is nearly over, and I'll be expected back in the kitchen to serve the meal."

I gave in to her coaxing without argument. I'd already forgotten where we were going, but I truly did not care. Until Ana had badgered me to come with her on some errand across the city, I'd been taking advantage of the unexpected day of rest Samil had given me, spending Shabbat curled on our pallet, breathing in the remnants of Amit's little-boy scent on the blankets, my arms wrapped tightly across my chest in a failed attempt to cover the gaping hole there.

The maze of makeshift tents strung between wagons reminded me that today should have begun the fourth day of Sukkot, but instead of feasting in beautifully decorated sukkahs, the people of Edrei were living out an unwitting, ghastly imitation of our ancestors' flight from Egypt.

Near the edge of the plaza, I caught sight of two boys walking hand-in-hand, twins with unruly dark curls that I recognized. I pulled Ana to a stop. "Those are my friend Nessa's sons. I should speak with her."

"We don't have time." Ana tossed an anxious glance over her shoulder.

"I must make sure she and the children are safe," I said, already veering off to follow the boys into an alleyway between two shops, knowing Ana would follow.

Clogged with yet more people taking refuge within the narrow space, the alley turned sharply to the right before emptying into a small courtyard off the back of a two-story home. Nessa's twins raced through the gate and up the stairway to the flat roof. I followed, curious why boys a few months younger than Amit would be allowed to wander through the glutted marketplace alone. Cresting the last stair with Ana two steps behind, I soon discovered why.

Nessa was seated in the corner of the roof, her babe at her breast and her head resting against the stone parapet, exhaustion evident in the deep shadows beneath her closed eyes. At least today her skin was free of bruises, as far as I could see. The twins had already claimed another corner of the small, secluded area and were devouring the figs they'd more than likely stolen, juice tracking down their chins and their wary eyes on me. As for her husband, he lay on his back in the only patch of shade available, fast asleep.

Kneeling down by Nessa's side, I grazed a palm over her forearm, hoping to wake her without disturbing the baby or the worthless man a few paces away. Her eyelids fluttered open immediately, likely having only been resting her weary eyes as the little one suckled. She regarded me impassively, as one would a stranger, without a shred of emotion moving over her features.

"Are they here?" she asked, detached, as if it were not an army bent on annihilation barreling toward us. A whisper of guilt moved through me. My child was safe, while hers were directly in the path of atrocities the likes of which I could only imagine.

"No," I said. "But runners brought news this morning that it won't be much longer." Although Samil had assured me that the elders planned to surrender fully and offer up tribute, envoys had yet to arrive with terms from the Arameans, and every hour they tarried stoked my fears higher and higher. Perhaps Kushan had no intention to offer such terms to Edrei.

I said none of this to Nessa, instead choosing to do anything I could to conjure even a spark of emotion in her dead eyes. "My master is convinced that Edrei will fall peaceably. You may very well be back safely in your home again within the week. Although we'll be under the rule of the Arameans, at least we will live."

"It doesn't matter anyhow," she said, and her apathy wounded me. I had the irrational urge to shake my friend into a reaction until she raged over the fear that a merciless army might slaughter her babies. Now I understood why as a boy Malakhi had been so determined to goad me into a flash of emotion after my mother died.

I cast a glance toward her husband. "Why is he here? I thought all able-bodied men were called to arms."

Her mouth contorted. "They were. Why do you think we are hiding up here like a nest of rats?"

Not only was he a monster, he was a coward as well. Fury surged through my limbs. "Come with us," I whispered. "I'll find someplace to hide you all. Let's go now, while he is sleeping, and he'll never know where you've gone. I refuse to leave you behind." Perhaps I could sneak them into our chamber. It would be uncomfortable with six of us jammed into the little room, but it was better than staying out here in the elements. And if she was willing to come now, she may finally yield to my pleas to flee for good. She was not enslaved here. She could go home.

"I can't, Rivkah. This is my lot."

"No, don't say that. Do you remember the man . . . the boy that I was betrothed to? Malakhi? He came for me. He was here to bring a message from my father, begging me to return."

She huffed a scornful breath through her nose. "It must be nice to have a father who cares."

"But you don't understand. Malakhi said your father was distraught when he discovered us missing. He risked coming into Kedesh, with Yoash and Kefa, and practically threatened to tear down the inn stone by stone if they were hiding you inside."

Nessa's jaw had slackened as I spoke.

"He went with them to search. Put aside his long-held bitterness against their family on the chance that they would find you. A father who does not care would not do such things."

Her eyes fluttered, the barest sheen of tears glossing her dark brown eyes. Finally! A hint of emotion!

I clasped her hand in mine, a surge of conviction rising in me. "There is still hope. If there is a way for you to return home, then we must believe that Yahweh will reveal it." Surprisingly, my own words inspired something hopeful in me as well, a whisper of assurance that Amit was safe in the palm of the Almighty. It was a tiny drop in a bottomless cistern of grief, but it was welcome nonetheless.

She slid her finger over the round cheek of her baby, a gentle touch that caused the infant to sigh in her milk-induced sleep. For as rash and headstrong as she'd been five years ago, and in spite of all the suffering she'd endured within that time, Nessa obviously loved her children.

"Come with us," I said. "There's no time to waste."

"My woman isn't going anywhere with you" came a caustic voice behind me, the words squelching the fragile sprout of hope I'd been nurturing for the last few moments. "And I'll thank you to leave us now."

I glared over my shoulder at the man for whom Nessa had given everything up, including me. His handsome visage did nothing to distract from the rottenness in his soul. I'd only had that one interaction with him, when he attempted to use my desperation to his own sordid advantage, but I'd never forgotten the way his green eyes had slithered over me. "Your wife and children are in a precarious position here," I said. "I'll find them shelter while you go do your duty."

He scoffed and called me a foul name, then stood to his feet and crossed the rooftop to loom over me. "Leave," he said, the word coming out with the stench of stale wine. Ana let out a little squeak and shuffled backward. The twins huddled in the corner, their sticky faces pale with terror. My stomach turned over as I wondered how many times these children had witnessed scenes like this one.

Before I could make sense of the movement, Nessa's husband had been swung around and lifted nearly off his feet by the neck of his tunic, his face nearly level with Estebaal's. Samil's guard spoke low, the words almost polite in their effortless delivery. "Touch either of them and you die."

Of course Samil had sent Estebaal to follow me. He'd made it abundantly clear that the trust he'd once had in me had been erased by my association with Malakhi. What he did not understand was that I would not go back on my word to him, no matter how much I longed to be with my boy. I'd broken too many vows in my lifetime—at least in this I would be faithful. Only Samil's death, or my own, could free me from the prison I'd built with my own hands. But in this moment, as Nessa's husband rasped a strangled plea, I was thankful for my master's mistrust.

Clutching her now-wailing daughter to her shoulder, Nessa stood to her feet, her eyes darting back and forth between her husband and Estebaal. "Call off your dog, Rivkah. My place is here."

Silently I pleaded with her to make the right choice this time, but she returned my plaintive stare with a shake of her head. "Five years is a long time," she said. "I know my father. Even if there was ever any love in his heart, it's passed into oblivion. We stay."

THIRTY-EIGHT

Malakhi

28 Tishri

Dagger in hand, I crouched near the entrance of my hiding place in Baz's tunnel, listening to the approaching footsteps and rationing my breaths. This cave reeked of waste and rot seeping down from above, which, when mixed with the dankness of an underground chamber that had not been used for years, made every breath for the last two weeks down here a practice in controlling the instinct to gag. At least the stench of the inn had been limited to one corner and offset by a window, the sole miserly airhole in the ceiling of this small cavern offered little in the way of fresh air and only a feeble shaft of light.

Although I'd heard a few echoes of voices down here in the past few days, likely others taking refuge within this maze below ground, it wasn't until now that I'd heard the shuffle of feet approaching my hiding place. Whoever was making their way upward through the hand-hewn passages toward me was not alone.

Baz and I had worked hard to disguise the entrance with brush, but perhaps instead of a full-out assault on the gates, the Arameans had heard about the tunnels and meant to use them to infiltrate the city from below. If so, I may be the first line of defense—and therefore the first casualty. My body taut, I prepared for both, cursing my inability to reach Rivkah and praying that if I died now, Yahweh would guard her.

The distinct snuffle of an animal and the scratch of claws upon stone reached my ears three heartbeats before I realized the truth. A brown-and-white muzzle pushed into my cave with a little yip of joy. Toki wiggled around me, licking my face. Laughing, I fended off the assault with both arms.

Baz's booming voice echoed off the walls. "Where are you, girl?"

"We're here," I answered for her, emerging from my hiding place.

Baz's familiar form came around a corner, his bearded face marked with dirt and split by an enormous grin. "Found the mole!" he called out, and then to my surprise, my father, Eitan, and his friend Chaim, the captain of the guard in Kedesh, appeared behind him.

"What are you all doing here?" I asked, incredulous.

"What else? We're here to get you and your woman out of Edrei," said Baz.

"Where is Amit?"

His grin widened all the more. "With Moriyah."

Sending Amit on to Kedesh with Baz had been almost as gut-wrenching as watching Rivkah tear herself open and lie down on the altar for her son. But I could not leave her. And every time I doubted that I'd done the right thing, I'd held the image in my mind of my mother gathering yet another chick beneath her capable wings. The confirmation that he was exactly where he was meant to be inspired a warm swell of gratitude.

My father gripped me by the shoulders. "Son," he said, a world of relief and affection contained within the word. "Thank you for sending Amit to us. He is . . . he is so much like Gidal."

"What is the plan?" asked Eitan, without even a hint of censure for my insistence on rescuing the woman who'd once dashed me to pieces. His unwavering support infused me with a rush of confidence. He handed me a bundle that, when unrolled, was revealed to be my armor and my best sword.

"I've been waiting for the fighting to begin so I could sneak over the villa wall during the uproar," I said as I slipped the bronze-scaled leather breastplate over my head. "Samil's guards are well acquainted with me, so I certainly can't go strolling through the gates in plain sight."

"We'll create a diversion," said Baz. "Shouldn't be too difficult in the chaos. We'll be out in plenty of time to join the battle."

"You've brought men with you, then?" I asked my father.

"We have."

"How many?" I asked.

"Not enough," he replied, his expression grim. "And it was a struggle to even round up the ones we did."

"But the other tribes are coming?"

"We've sent word to all Israel." He frowned, disgust thick in his tone. "But so far only Gad and Reuben, along with as many as we could gather from Naftali, have answered the call to aid Manasseh."

"There aren't even that many from Manasseh's tribe on the west of the Jordan willing to stand up for their brethren," said Baz with a sneer.

"How much time do we have?" I asked.

"A few hours at most," said Eitan. "They struck before the sun arose and have nearly made it through our defenses at the foot of the hill already. They'll be up the road and at the gates all too soon.

"We have to get her. Now."

Toki jumped to her feet, padding a few paces back the way they'd come, the hair on her neck bristling and a growl emanating from her throat.

All five of us were instantly armed and alert. A scattering of stones and a shuffle announced yet another pair of sandals approaching. My father and I met eyes, a silent accord forming between us. I gestured for Baz, Eitan, and Chaim to shrink back against the sides of the cave, and my father and I each took our places in the shadows on either side of the tunnel.

A dark-haired, bearded man came into sight, illuminated by the meager light from one of the air shafts. My father reached for him, his dagger to the man's throat. The man did not struggle but stood with his palms up.

My father growled and pushed him backward. "Raviv. What are you doing here?"

"My daughter is here," he stated. My father must have sent word to Raviv about her situation after Baz returned to Kedesh with Amit. "I saw the four of you sneaking out of camp well before dawn and assumed you knew a way inside. Just as you won't leave your son here alone, neither will I leave Nessa."

My father stared at the brother who'd caused him so much pain over the last twenty-five years with a mixture of frustration and sympathy. "All right. First we find Rivkah, since we already know where she is. And then you and I will search out Nessa together. I have no less desire to see that my niece and her children are safe."

Raviv pursed his lips, then nodded—a pact between estranged brothers, born of desperation but rooted in mutual understanding. Both men would do anything for those they loved.

THIRTY-NINE

Rivkah

Ana and I had been ordered to stay in our room, like two trembling mice awaiting an army of lions. Samil had sent his own envoy to the Arameans yesterday with a message written in my hand, declaring the city's willingness to submit and pay tribute to Kushan. The man had returned without a head, my crumpled message still clutched in his fist.

And yet Samil still insisted that all would be well, that Estebaal would somehow ensure our safety. But from the clamor of battle being waged not far from the gates, it would not be long before the Arameans crashed through. Samil's arrogance would be his downfall, and that of everyone within his villa. His wives, his children, his slaves. We would all die.

"I used to dream," said Ana, "that some kind man, another slave in this household perhaps, would ask for my hand in marriage. But I am glad that my dream never came to pass." Little did Ana know how close her fantasies were to reality, except of all the things I could say about Estebaal, kindness was not included among them.

"Why are you glad?"

"Because I don't know that I would have had the courage to do what you did, Rivkah, sending Amit away like that. I couldn't have done it if I had my own children."

Pain lanced through my body, as did the image of my boy, screaming for me, fighting against Malakhi's secure hold. "You could have. Because a mother will lay her life down for her child every time, or she is not worthy to be called a mother at all. Amit is safe. He is loved. That is all that matters to me."

Ana slipped her arms around me, and we sat together on the pallet, dry-eyed, waiting for the death that would soon be plowing through the gates.

Commotion floated through the window, shouts and calls for help. Perhaps the elders had thrown open the gates to the invaders already, hoping to stave off wholesale slaughter by capitulation. In my bones I knew it would all be futile. The people of Edrei were no more than pebbles on the path to war. Those not hauled off to slavery would be eliminated to make room for his men. If Kushan meant to take on the tribes of Israel, this city would be the perfect place to station his army and stage his invasion.

"Do you hear that?" Ana slid free of my grip, pulled the stool to the window, and peeked over the sill. A gasp slipped past her lips. "The sanctuary is burning!"

I joined Ana on the stool, both of us perched precariously on the rickety seat, watching in fascination as a number of guards and male servants ran by, eager to help. Perhaps it was a welcome distraction from the reality that was closing in upon us moment by moment.

Another set of sandals approached, the sound coming from the kitchen courtyard, and then without warning, our side door burst open, the wooden latch flying across the room and causing both of us to tumble off the stool into a confused heap.

I sat on the ground, dazed at the sight of the silver-eyed man I'd never thought to see again in this lifetime, along with the gleaming bronze sword in his grip. "How are you here?"

"I told you I won't be parted from you," Malakhi said. "Five years was long enough. I've been in a cave below the city."

A little sigh broke from Ana's lips at Malakhi's declaration, but I could only focus on one thing. "Amit?"

"With my mother."

My eyes dropped closed, an ocean of relief swallowing me whole. "Thank you," I whispered.

"We have to go. Now."

Startled into action by the urgency in his tone, I crawled across the floor to my pallet. There was only one thing I could not leave behind. I slid my hand beneath our bed and grabbed the mahogany box, still wrapped in the ketubah. But just as I gripped the treasure to my chest, Samil strode through the door, Estebaal close behind him.

With a hand over her mouth, Ana flattened herself against the wall as our master took in the scene in front of him. "You burned my sanctuary," he said to Malakhi. "My wives are not pleased."

"It will all burn, Samil," Malakhi responded. "You must get them out of this place."

My master shook his head. "Estebaal will make sure we are safe. He is one of them. Besides, I've never lost a negotiation. Rivkah of all people knows this." It was true that Samil was the master of commerce, but this was a bad bargain, and from the desperation on his face he knew it.

"Estebaal, give me your dagger," he said. Was I the only one who heard the tremor in his voice?

When his bodyguard hesitated, he spat the order again, eyes wild. After flicking a glance of apology at me, Estebaal slipped an iron blade from its sheath and handed it over. But instead of attacking Malakhi or going after me, Samil stepped to the side, grabbed Ana's wrist, and yanked her close to his body, one arm around her waist and the dagger beneath her chin.

My heart seized. "Please, Samil. Let her go. She is innocent."

"You thought you'd bargained away your only treasure, my dear.

But this one is almost as precious to you as your Amit, isn't she?" He pressed the tip of the knife into her skin and blood trickled down her neck as she shuddered in his grip. "Tell your lover to surrender or she dies. I won't lose my scribe, especially now that the Arameans are taking the city. I need your language skills. I need your pen. You are my *property*." He jerked his chin toward my pierced ear. "Just like Estebaal, you vowed to remain faithful until death."

The madness in his eyes made it clear that Ana's life breath was meaningless. His wealth, his survival, surmounted all. I lifted my palms in surrender. From the moment I awoke covered in pig filth I'd known that all was lost, that I'd never return to my father's house. At least my precious boy was safe.

"All right," I said. "Just let Malakhi take Ana to safety. I will stay."

Samil laughed, pressing the dagger farther into Ana's skin. "She's my property too. I'll do with her as I please." He slid his hand up her torso until his palm was curved over her breast. "Now that Dilara is getting tiresome, perhaps this one might make a sweet little concubine." He whispered something into Ana's ear that made her entire body flinch. "But if he doesn't lay down his weapon, she dies. I can always find another to take Dilara's place. Makes little difference to me."

Estebaal moved so quickly that Samil was still mid-sneer as his body crumpled forward, the knife he'd been holding at Ana's throat clattering to the ground. Hazy from shock, I sat back on my heels, staring at the pool of blood flowing from my master's side as he twitched and gasped for breath on the floor. Samil's eyes went to the bodyguard he'd so highly valued and trusted, a question for the boy he'd rescued from certain death twisting his brow.

"I will guard your family to the best of my ability," Estebaal told the man to whom he'd vowed a lifetime of service. "I owe you that much. But you will never touch Ana again."

CHAPTER

FORTY

Malakhi

Leaving Samil's body on the floor of our room, Estebaal walked the three of us to the gates, then nodded to the guards, who let us pass without question. "Come with us," Rivkah said to the Aramean. "Malakhi knows a way out of the city."

"No," he said. "I will keep my vow. His wives and children have no one else to protect them." Regardless of the cold-blooded thrashing he'd given me, there was a deep vein of honor beneath the surface that I could not help but respect. And I owed him for protecting the life of my Rivkah, so I gave him the only thing I had to offer.

"There is a tunnel." I crouched down and drew a map of the city with my finger in the dirt, hoping my feeble markings would make sense. "It opens here"—I pointed—"into the cistern right next to the stables. If you follow the charcoal markings my friend Baz made along the length"—and here I drew the symbol of a dog with a hooked tail—"you will find yourself outside the walls and near the river."

Estebaal nodded his thanks, then gestured toward the women. "Get them out of here. The gates will soon be breached."

I curled my fingers around Rivkah's wrist, tugging her forward, eager to get her to my father and brother and then on to safety. But Ana hung back, her focus on the menacing bodyguard who'd killed his master for her sake. She went to him, blood still trickling down her neck from where Samil had held the dagger, and reached for his shoulders. She was so small before him, almost childlike next to his massive form, but she tugged him down and placed a kiss on his lips. Then she whispered in his ear before darting toward us, tears trailing down her cheeks. Rivkah reached for her hand and we walked away, leaving the Aramean to fulfill his last vow to the master who did not deserve such faithfulness.

Once we rounded the corner, the rest of our group joined us, weapons in hand. "Get them into the tunnels," my father said to me. "We'll find Nessa."`

"I know where she is," said Rivkah, attempting to tug out of my grip. "I'll show you."

"You will not." My fingers clamped tighter on her wrist. "You are going in that tunnel. Now."

"How will they find her without my help?" she said, her tone high and beseeching. "That marketplace is a sea of confusion. We have to rescue her. Her babies . . . We cannot leave them. . . ."

Her despair wrenched at my resolve to personally escort her to safety. But there was no one I trusted more than Baz to take my place. "Tell me where she is, then. I know the city well."

"No." Tears brimming, she gripped my tunic. "Malakhi, you can't leave me."

I bent to look her in the eye, my palms curved around her cheeks. "I told you we won't be parted, and I vow that it will be so. I was trained for this. We will find her, and then we will meet you in the tunnels." I poured assurance into the words, confirming them with a sincere promise in my eyes. Then I curled my lips into my most enticing smile. "You won't be rid of me so easily, my sweet mischief-maker. You still owe me an edible meal."

She huffed a small, tearful laugh, and then nodded. "She is hidden on the roof of a house tucked behind the shop that sells musical instruments. Do you know it?"

"I do."

Ignoring our audience, I pulled her close, memorizing the scent of her hair and the feel of her body against mine, wishing I could linger there for an eternity. Instead, I kissed her forehead and pushed her toward Baz and Chaim. "Go. They'll keep you safe."

She complied, but hesitated when she noticed Raviv standing off to the side. Rivkah's brow furrowed in confusion.

"Nessa's father," I said.

Understanding dawned in her amber eyes, and in spite of the swelling sounds of battle now being waged at the city gates, a smile curved her rose-colored lips. "I told her you'd not stopped caring," she told my uncle. "And that somehow Yahweh would show her the way home."

Raviv went still, looking as if he were struggling to take a breath, but his chin dipped in a gesture of silent gratitude.

Rivkah and Ana followed Baz, with Chaim walking behind them, and fully assured the two of them would protect my love with their lives, I turned to lead the men of my family into battle.

Gut-wrenching sounds of agony emanated from the marketplace. Every drop of blood in my body cried out to do something, to take a stand against the soldiers plowing through the square, destroying every soul in their path. Under the command of their wicked king, they were deaf to the pleas for mercy from the women and blind to the innocence of the children they slaughtered.

Baz had informed the elders about the tunnels below the city when he first brought news of the invasion, but from the screams rending the air, few had taken shelter below. I hoped the cowards who'd allowed Edrei to slide into such compromise and then thought they could bargain with evil were among the first to be put to the sword. They'd offered up the people of this city on the altar of their arrogance.

Before, when I'd been involved in skirmishes, I'd fought for the glory of battle and to keep Naftali's territory intact. But regardless that Edrei was of the tribe of Manasseh, these were *my people*— brothers and sisters by blood and covenant. This land was ours, given to us by Yahweh himself and won beneath his holy banner. Baz had been right to call me out. Slinking away to lick my wounds had been nothing less than cowardice. It had taken Rivkah's balm to heal my arm, but it was righteous anger that gave me fresh purpose and burned away any latent worries over the limitation of my sight. I vowed that these snarling dogs would not snatch away the promise of Avraham so easily. If the generation before me would not do its duty, then I would inspire my own to take up the cause.

Yet as horrified and enraged as I was by the carnage before me, Nessa and her children took precedence. They were my own kin, and I'd made a promise to Rivkah that I was determined to keep.

My father allowed me the lead as we slipped through a back alley toward the instrument shop, Raviv and Eitan trailing behind. At the sound of sandals approaching around a corner, I raised a fist, a silent order to halt, and we pressed ourselves against the mud-brick walls.

A foolish young Aramean whipped around the side of the building, his eyes going wide at the sight of the four of us. Before his mouth could open to call for aid, my dagger had lodged in his throat. Pushing the body aside, I pressed on, battle-rush flowing through my limbs, searching for the stairway Rivkah had described.

A sudden clash of swords and loud grunts behind us caused me to swing around, a weapon in each fist. Two more Arameans had snuck up behind us in the narrow alleyway, Raviv and Eitan engaging them. One enemy swept Raviv's leg from underneath him, raising his sickle sword to slash my uncle's torso, but Eitan, having knocked his own opponent senseless with an axe, plunged his dagger beneath the attacker's arm, driving the bronze blade deep where his scaled armor did not hinder the blow. Then, before the soldier could recover, Eitan brought the axe down and ensured that he would not rise again.

Blood-spattered and wide-eyed, Raviv sprang to his feet, his chest heaving. A brief but weighted moment passed between my brother and uncle as Eitan's actions stretched an olive branch across a twenty-five-year-wide gap. Without a word, Raviv nodded, accepting the gift.

Reeling from the implications but unable to pause, I moved on, pushing aside any thought but finding Nessa and knowing the rest of them would follow. The instrument shop was on fire, smoke billowing from the windows and flames consuming the brightly striped awning that once shaded its wares. I breathed a prayer of thanks for the smoke that concealed our climb up the back staircase. Although the battle raged out in the market, we reached the rooftop without being seen.

I'd never met Nessa, but there was a woman huddled here with her three children. She lifted eyes full of resignation at our approach. But when my uncle pushed by me, her expression transformed into profound confusion.

"Abba?" She clutched her baby closer to her chest.

He reached for her, placing a kiss on her forehead. "Are you hurt?" he asked, then grazed two fingers over the cheek of his tiny granddaughter with a look of awe.

Dazed, she shook her head. "How . . . why are you here?"

"There's no time. We must get you out." Raviv grabbed one of the boys, who looked to be twins, and held him out to me. The child did not struggle but clung to me, trembling and smelling of fear. A pang of longing for Amit struck my chest, along with gratitude that it was not him witnessing such brutalities today.

"Where's your husband?" Raviv asked his daughter.

"He fled this morning," she said without emotion. The coward had abandoned his family? I consoled myself with the thought that if he wasn't dead already, he soon would be.

Once the other twin was in my father's arms, Raviv aided Nessa to her feet. Eitan led the way down the staircase, my father and me coming next, and Nessa and Raviv directly behind.

Unfortunately, the fire in the instrument shop had already burned itself out, dissipating the cover we'd had before. Within only a few moments of our descent, a group of three Arameans came up behind us. With a loud cry, Raviv spun, slamming one of the soldiers against the wall with his sword. Helpless to do anything more, I yanked Nessa closer to me and shielded the infant between our bodies. After passing the child he held to Eitan, my father pushed past us to go to his brother's aid. As Raviv tussled with the second man, the last and largest of them held firm, staving off my father's every blow. Then, to my horror, the Aramean caught my father by the edge of his breastplate and threw him against the wall. Although over the ruckus I could not hear the sound of my father's helmeted head slamming into stone, the reverberation traveled all the way through me. Dazed and bleeding, he dropped to his knees and slumped to the side.

The Aramean sneered, spitting blood on the ground and setting his sights on Nessa, as if a weeping woman clutching her innocent babe were some great battle trophy. I tried to push my cousin behind me, but her son grabbed for her neck, frantically calling for his ima and clinging with the strength born only of sheer terror. Tangled between the two with my back against the wall, I was helpless to move. Three paces away, the large Aramean stumbled to the side as Raviv pushed him from behind with a roar. But although he managed to disrupt the enemy's charge toward his daughter and grandchildren, my uncle was unable to defend himself against the axe that crashed into his chest. He went down, his torso covered in blood.

At the same time, my father flew at the Aramean, as if the sight of his brother being felled had given him a burst of supernatural power, and was joined by Eitan, who'd dropped the second twin next to me to join the fight.

Tears streamed down Nessa's face as she swayed into me, calling her father's name. I gripped her close, glad that the boys were both hiding their faces from the ghastly sight of their grandfather gasping for breath on the ground.

When the last opponent was finally overcome, my father dropped to his knees beside Raviv and gripped his face in his hands. "Brother," he said, "hold on. We'll get you out."

Raviv shook his head, his eyes wheeling toward his daughter. "Nessa," he gasped, blood bubbling at the corners of his mouth. "Twins—promise—"

"Of course. We'll get them to safety. Just breathe," said my father, his face nearly as pale as Raviv's and his voice full of sorrow. After all these years of separation, these few moments would be all they had together. He brushed his palm over his older brother's face, as if to smooth away the pain, muttering assurances and pleading for him to live.

"My—family—"

"I vow that I will care for them as I do my own, brother."

Raviv's eyes fluttered closed as his body convulsed and he exhaled one last word. "Forgiven—"

A sob burst from my father's throat. "Yes," he said, dropping his forehead to Raviv's. "All is forgiven between us."

"Abba," said Eitan, his tone somber but urgent. "We must go. More will come."

As if in a daze and looking years older than he had an hour ago, my father gently laid Raviv's lifeless body on the ground, then stood and picked up one of the twins, clutching him to his chest. I gripped Nessa's hand, and regardless of her sobs and cries for her abba, dragged her behind me as we followed Eitan back through the maze of alleyways, heading for the tunnel and praying that Yahweh would blind the enemy to our flight.

FORTY-ONE

Rivkah

Huddled inside the small cave where Malakhi had hidden himself away for the last two weeks, Ana and I clung to each other, listening to the war raging above our heads. We'd been down here far too long already. A few paces away, Baz and Chaim discussed whether to press on through the tunnels, fearing that the exit might be blocked by the time the men returned.

If they returned at all.

Although airshafts dotted the ceiling of the tunnels every so often, the smoke from above and the foulness from within ensured that the deeper we'd ventured into this stone fortress, the more effort it took to snatch a full breath. Thankfully, Baz had prepared for our retreat weeks ago by leaving a few oil lamps in ancient niches along the way, but nothing could dispel the dread whispering from the shadows.

The thought of Malakhi engaged in combat made my bones turn to water. Somehow over these past two months, I'd discovered that life without the man I'd once thrown away was unthinkable. Neither did I want to consider Amit's life without his strong influence. He needed Malakhi as his abba. So there in the dimness, with my back against the cold limestone and a battle overhead, my heart finally bowed to Yahweh as I pleaded for the life of the man who'd come for me—twice. And in that same desperate moment, I saw a vision of my own abba kneeling on his rooftop so far away, even now pleading for *my* return.

Overflowing with grief for my transgressions against him and against the God who'd somehow protected me over and over again in spite of my rebellion, I leaned into Ana and wept. When I realized that she too was trembling and her tears had mingled with mine, I pushed aside my own concerns and drew in a shaky breath to console my sister in spirit.

"Did you know?" I asked. "About Estebaal?"

She nodded. "I saw him watching me, even though he never spoke a word. But he frightened me, so I did nothing to encourage him. Perhaps I should have. . . . Was I was too hasty in my judgment of him?"

"No," I said, gently combing my fingers through her tangle of curls. "No, you did nothing wrong." I should tell her the full story, but it was more than likely that Estebaal would not survive this day. Someday I would reveal it all, but not while death breathed down our necks.

Near the entrance of the cave, Toki jumped to attention, her hackles raised and a growl building in her throat as she stared up into the black void of the tunnel.

"Someone's approaching," hissed Baz as he and Chaim took positions in front of us, daggers drawn. But if the Arameans had somehow discovered this tunnel, there was little chance we would survive, even with these two fierce warriors to protect us.

I was flushed with a strong wave of gratitude that my boy was far from here, safe in his grandmother's arms. I owed Moriyah and

Darek a profound apology just as much as I owed my own father one, but if I could never deliver those words in person, I prayed that Amit's return would be the restitution for my sins.

Yet it was not a group of vicious Arameans who stepped into the feeble light of Baz's oil lamp, but Darek himself carrying one of Nessa's boys, desolation written across his brow with a heavy hand.

Everything in my world went still and silent. *Not Malakhi.*

Nessa emerged next from the gloom, her face pale and her baby tight against her breast. I untangled myself from Ana and ran to her, checking to see that the baby was unharmed before tugging her close. The infant was wide-eyed but quiet as I cradled the two of them in my arms.

"Are you wounded?" I asked.

She shook her head against my shoulder.

"Your husband?"

"Abandoned us," she said without a hint of regret. A coward at the last, her man, but at least she was finally free of him.

"Yes, but Raviv did not." From directly behind me, the beloved voice brushed the curve of my ear with warmth. "He gave his life for her. For all of us."

My entire body shook as I spun to face Malakhi. Blood spattered his face and his tunic, but he looked to be whole. Although he held the other twin on his hip, I collapsed against him and sobbed my relief into his chest. He swept his hand down the length of my hair and then pressed me closer, a heavy sigh coming from deep within him. Eitan stepped into the light as well, and for Sofea's sake, as well as for their children, I whispered another prayer of gratitude.

"Come," said Baz. "These tunnels will eventually be discovered, if they haven't been already. We may have to fight our way out at the bottom as it is."

In silent acquiescence, our group, led by Toki, pushed downward into the tunnel. Malakhi went ahead, with Nessa's trembling son wrapped around his torso. His low assurances to the frightened child echoed off the narrow walls. "Just a little while ago, I came through here with my nephew," he said. "And he's only a few months older than you. I'll bet you are just as brave as he is, aren't you?" The little one nodded his head and wiped his face against Malakhi's tunic.

For what seemed like hours, we picked our way past boulders, squeezed through narrow crevices, sloshed through a number of tiny streams that cut across our path, crouched when the roof dipped low, and gaped in awe at the large echoing caverns we passed through. Through it all Malakhi continued speaking to the boy in gentle tones, telling stories and asking him questions to keep his mind off the number of bones that littered the path, both animal and human, as well as the peril that might greet us once we emerged from this dreary maze. I had no doubt that he'd comforted my own child in the same way only two weeks before.

Just when it seemed as though we'd descended into the very center of the earth and would never emerge from this tomb, the ground sloped upward. One by one we climbed out of the hole Toki had discovered weeks ago and stepped into the afternoon, blinking at the brutal sunlight. Baz had hidden the entrance to this tunnel well. Neither Aramean nor Hebrew was anywhere within sight.

The men herded us to the southwest, up a steep embankment, and past the tree line, where Darek and Baz finally gave us leave to rest beneath a canopy of oak and sycamore. From our high vantage point we could clearly see the city of Edrei perched atop the rocky plateau, as well as the thick smoke that emanated from within its walls. My gaze went to the place I'd spent the last five years, hanging on to a small bit of hope that Estebaal had worked a miracle and fulfilled his vow, but dark plumes billowed at the place where Samil's villa had stood.

His great home and all his wealth—and more than likely the large family he'd taken so much pride in—would be nothing but ash. And regardless of what he'd done or the way his wives had treated me, I mourned every soul within the place that had been my prison,

Estebaal the most. For a man who'd done such dark deeds for his master, his death would be nothing less than heroic.

Malakhi joined me on the ridge as I watched Edrei burn. Sliding his arm around my shoulders, he drew me close to his side. "The tribes have retreated. They've probably pulled back to Golan. We'll be there in a few hours to meet with the men of Naftali before going on to Kedesh."

Even as I calculated the moments until I could hold my boy in my arms again, dread swirled in the pit of my stomach at the thought of entering the gates I'd once been so glad to escape. How could I even face my father, my sister, and all those whose love I'd been so reckless with? Malakhi had been forgiving, but I could not expect the rest of my family, nor his, to be so merciful. I'd betrayed them all and would return still dragging the chains of five rebellious years behind me.

Somehow divining my thoughts, Malakhi turned me toward himself. "I will walk beside you," he said, his silver eyes full of sincerity. "Every step of the way."

He lifted his other hand to brush the hair away from my ear. With gentle fingers, he removed the ring that Samil had pressed into the hole he'd drilled into my flesh at the doorway to his house. Malakhi kissed my wounded lobe and tossed the last link of my slavery into the dirt before taking my hand and leading me toward home and toward my son.

FORTY-TWO

8 Heshvan

We spent three long days in Golan as Darek, Malakhi, and the other men organized a long-term strategy of defense against the Arameans who now firmly held Edrei. Very few managed to flee the stronghold once the gates were thrown wide to the enemy, and those who did brought stories of annihilation that caused me to grieve all over again for the people of Samil's household, kin and slave alike. Kushan had delivered his swift and terrible warning with an expert hand. Whether the tribes of Israel would stand together against him or bow to the threat out of fear, one could only guess.

After a week of walking alongside the wagon the men had procured for Nessa and the children, whom we'd already delivered safely home, the walls of Kedesh finally came into sight. But regardless that the road to the city of refuge was kept clear of debris, the last climb up to the city felt like a slog through wet sand. My flight had been swift, the steps between the city of my birth and the city of my downfall far too easy, but the journey home seemed to drag on forever, each footfall more eternal than the last.

Five years' worth of doubts clung to me as I trudged upward, weary in body and mind. My father had never been a hard man, but I'd spent every one of my first eighteen years listening to his teaching of the Torah and knew that he counted each word as sacred. I may have only been his headstrong daughter when I left, but I returned now a thief, a liar, and perhaps in the minds of many, an adulteress.

Surveying the last two thousand cubits on the road between myself and my home, the culmination of those lingering doubts solidified into one burgeoning fear. My feet tripped to a stop near the white boundary stones that marked the farthest reach of the city as a vision rose in my mind of the gates of Kedesh being slammed shut before me and my own family members securing the latch.

Having never left my side for the entire journey, Malakhi slipped his hand into mine. "Rivkah, what is it?" His soothing tone reminded me how he'd assuaged the fears of Nessa's son in the dark tunnel. Would I ever be worthy of this man's steadfast kindness?

My fingers tightened around his as my greatest fear tumbled out of my mouth. "What if they turn me away?"

Instead of answering, he gently tugged me to the side of the road, beneath the shade of a sycamore, to allow the rest of our group to pass by. From the bed of the wagon, Ana's concerned gaze landed on me, but she offered an encouraging smile as they ambled by, the grizzled mule's ancient pace having slowed even more on this last day of climbing toward home. The other men kept stride with the wagon, eyes trained on the city, no doubt anticipating joyous reunions with their loved ones and wishing they could sprint alongside Toki, who'd run ahead to herald our arrival.

Malakhi pulled me close, wrapping his strong arms around me, eyes full of compassion. "They won't turn you away." When I opened my mouth to argue, he interrupted me. "But even if they did, beloved, my family is yours. They love who I love. And as the mother of Gidal's child, and my wife, you hold a place of high honor within our home."

"But after what I did, surely they will not forgive—"

He surprised me with a fervent kiss before pulling back with a twist of mischief on his lips, a reminder of the Malakhi of my youth. The rascal certainly knew how to distract and silence me. The coiling tension that had been winding ever tighter in the center of my chest began to slowly unfurl as he stroked the sides of my neck with his thumbs in a soothing rhythm.

"Have you forgotten who my mother is and the reason she lives in a city of refuge?" he asked. "Has it slipped your mind that Eitan too had a hand in the deaths of Raviv's sons? Our family was built atop the ruins of tragedy, Rivkah, each brick fashioned from mercy. You will find no stones in their palms."

As his reassurances poured over me like fragrant oil, I surveyed the city that lay before us, drinking in the beauty of my home set high on the hill. Although five years had passed between my flight and my return, very little had changed. Flocks of sheep and goats dotted the rocky landscape, the silver-fingered olive trees and varied fruit orchards in every shade of red, green, and gold still lined the road, and the thick cedar gates remained open wide to visitors and manslayers alike.

On our last day in Golan, the Levite who'd shamed me in the marketplace so many months ago knocked at the door of the kind family who'd given us shelter, asking to speak with the daughter of Amitai. My stomach full of dread, I'd met him in the street, where he asked my forgiveness for his harsh words and hasty judgments that day.

It seemed my simple plea for forgiveness had brought the prideful man to his own knees, repenting of driving his own son from his home when he'd gotten caught up in the wickedness that had seeped into Golan. The Levite wept before me as he spoke of the young man's death and the tragic irony of a priest whose charge it was to bestow mercy on killers but who'd refused to extend grace to his own child. *"I'd give anything to hold my son in my arms again,"* he'd said.

The Rivkah who'd walked away from this sanctuary city and taken advantage of the safety within its embrace was not the same prideful, foolish girl, and whether anyone in Kedesh deigned to accept my sincere contrition or not, I *would* hold my son today.

Gratitude welled in my heart as I lifted a smile to the man who loved my child as his own and who had waited so long to be my husband. My feet began to move of their own volition, their pace accelerating in my desperation to close the gap between Amit and me; but even so, Malakhi did not let go of my hand as we passed the others and pushed toward the city.

It was nearing sunset, so when one of the guards emerged from the gates, the flare of sunlight to the west disguised his features. But as the lone figure began to move toward us more quickly, I saw that his mantle was flying out behind him as he advanced. My breath became trapped within my lungs. This was no guard, but a man with silvering hair and beard and a familiar form who, despite his years, was sprinting down the road in our direction.

Stunned by the sight of my father racing toward me, I came to a halt, heart thundering. His message had asked me to return, and he'd sent gold and silver to retrieve me, but had my transgressions forever severed the once-sweet connection between us?

My name shouted across the distance, replete with overwhelming relief, was the answer to my question.

Malakhi squeezed my hand before gently guiding me forward with a palm on my back. "Go," he said. "Don't make him wait any longer."

And then I was moving, running, with tears searing my cheeks and blurring my vision. I stumbled twice but kept pushing toward the outstretched arms I did not deserve.

Nearly plowing me off my feet, my father slung his arms around me and clasped me to his wide chest, repeating my name over and over. I was engulfed in his familiar scent, one that brought to mind a hundred memories of snuggling into his embrace as a little girl, listening to the rumble of his voice, and falling asleep in perfect security.

"Abba," I sobbed. "Abba. Forgive me."

He pressed a flurry of kisses to my cheeks and forehead, salty trails on his own face as well. "Oh, my precious daughter. It is already done."

"But you don't know . . ." I choked on my confession. "I can never make up for all that I did."

He shook his head as he placed his large hands on either side of my face, looking into my eyes. Hot shame rose in my cheeks as I felt the gaze penetrate through five years of layer upon layer of compromise—through my desperate and foolish decision to enslave myself, through the choice to flee Laish instead of returning home, through my self-indulgence and reckless behavior with the Hebrew in Laish, down to the very moment I'd chosen to walk away from his love and protection.

"You are my beloved daughter, Rivkah." The wrinkles around his brown eyes deepened as he smiled through his tears. "There is nothing you have done or will do that will ever erase the love I have for you. It is enough that you have returned to me."

Could it be so simple? Could my return to the arms of my abba be all that was required to wash away the blackness that had consumed me for so long? I'd thought I'd left the last vestiges of my slavery behind in Edrei, but here on the road to the city of refuge, safe in my father's arms, I dropped the final link of the chain that had bound me. Then I laid my head against his chest as he stroked my hair and whispered endearments until my weeping ebbed. Even as I stood there, basking in such unmerited forgiveness, a new song welled up in my heart, replacing the cold laments of the last five years with words that spoke of new seasons and fresh joy. My fingers itched for my reed pen and inks to record them.

"Ima!" called the most beautiful voice in the world. "Ima!"

I yanked myself from my abba's embrace and dropped to my knees as the missing half of my heart ran into my arms. Like a drunkard I imbibed the sensation of his arms wrapped tightly around my neck, his little-boy smell, and the feel of his body trembling against mine. Then I kissed his head, his cheeks, his forehead, his chin, and his freckled nose. "Oh my sweet lamb." I tightened my hold on him and closed my eyes, gratitude for his safety brushing aside every other thought.

"We've been waiting for you," he said as he tangled his fingers into my hair. "Up on the rooftop. Grandfather and I have been watching, every day. And he was right. He said you would come home."

FORTY-THREE

"I simply do not understand why we are celebrating this way," my sister Lailah said. The sound of her voice on the other side of the door was muffled, but her derisive tone was unmistakable. I paused with my hand at the latch, startled at the venom in her voice and yet curious as to what she and my father were discussing. I stood perfectly still, not wanting the copper bracelets I wore on my wrists to clink together and give away my presence.

Although the rest of our family had seemed overjoyed when I'd arrived home two weeks ago, Lailah had not. Her response had been tepid, although she'd kissed my cheeks and welcomed me back, but I'd hoped that once I'd stood before the family at our first meal together, told my story with sincere contrition, and then pleaded forgiveness, that she, like the rest, might offer a small measure of mercy. But she'd said little more than ten words to me since, going about the preparations for my wedding feast with cool detachment. The gates of Kedesh may not have been closed to me, but my sister's heart certainly was.

"And why not celebrate? After five years of waiting, do they not deserve to celebrate their marriage?" asked my father.

Her answer was too soft to distinguish.

"Of course she does. She is my daughter, Lailah. Your sister."

"So we are to pretend that she did not run off and sell herself? Put her own child in peril? Who knows what else happened with her." Her accusations struck me dead center. I'd been forthcoming about everything except for the man in Laish, since Malakhi asked that I keep that between him and me, for my own safety and for Amit's sake, but somehow Lailah must have guessed there was more to my story than I'd let on.

"She has admitted her faults," said my father. "And humbled herself in front of the entire family."

She scoffed. "Yes, she made an admirable show of it, didn't she?"

"Lailah . . ." My father sighed.

There was a pause, and I pressed my ear closer to the door, only partly ashamed for listening in on their conversation. They'd seemed to have forgotten that I was dressing for my wedding night in the next room.

"Even if she is truly repentant," she continued, "and I have my doubts, why Malakhi and his family would be eager to not only put together a wedding feast but also invite the entire town is beyond my comprehension."

"It was my idea," my father said. "Malakhi was ready to take her as his bride the moment they passed through the gates, without fanfare, but I asked that he wait until a proper celebration could be organized."

"*You* did this?"

"Of course!" he said. "Should we not shout from the rooftops that our prayers have been answered?"

"She doesn't deserve to be lauded," she hissed. "She is a liar and a thief, Abba. She took more from you than just silver. I watched you mourn for five years. I worried while you wasted away, fasting nearly as many days as you ate, and spending hour upon hour on that roof scanning the horizon for an ungrateful girl who cared more about herself than her family. *I* took over the duties you were too broken to handle, alongside raising my own family."

"That is true, daughter. And you have been a faithful helper to me over these last years. Your mother would be so proud of you."

Lailah made a noise of disgust. "Not that you've noticed all I've done."

"Of course I have—"

"No. You were too busy weeping over your wayward daughter to see the weight of everything I've carried. I've always obeyed you. Did *everything* that was asked of me, and more, without any complaint, and yet Rivkah comes home after five years of recklessness and rebellion and now we have a *feast?*"

I'd not wanted this public event any more than she did, but the elation on Malakhi's face when my father insisted on a grand wedding celebration had driven away my misgivings. And over the past week I'd grown more amenable about the prospect. When I'd married Gidal I'd been a vain, self-important girl going through the motions of marriage, but this time I would be bound in covenant to a man who I was more than eager to cleave to for the rest of my life. And Amit was beside himself with joy when he discovered that Malakhi would now be his abba, so that was certainly cause for celebration. But hearing my sister's resentment sheared my excitement in half.

"Come now," said my father, and I imagined he was drawing her close to himself. "There is not one of my children that I love above the other, nor have I missed the heavy load you have endured in the absence of your mother. You have honored her in every way and have been a blessing to not only me but also your entire family. What greater reward than a husband who raises you high in esteem and children who adore you and will pass on your legacy of service to Yahweh to the next generation? But Rivkah is home. She is returned to us as from the dead and brought us Amit as well. And we will celebrate this new beginning together. Yes?"

Her muffled response made it clear that she was pressed against his wide chest, but a loud knock from outside cut off any more discussion they might have had. The knock also had the effect of wiping any worry over my sister's resentment from my mind.

Malakhi had arrived.

I shuffled backward, then darted across the room to sit on the bed, fidgeting with my bracelets, the pleats on my linen gown, and my sheer crimson veil until my father opened the door to collect me. He did look thin—those days of fasting *had* whittled away at him—but the broad smile on his face, as well as the sparkle of his amber-brown eyes, made it clear that whatever valley he'd walked in during my absence now overflowed with streams of joy.

"It is time," he said.

I slipped my hand into his outstretched one and allowed him to lead me to the front of the house, grateful for the renewal of our bond. We'd spent many hours on the roof together since my return, both of us repenting of missed opportunities to hear each other's hearts and miscommunications born of self-inflicted isolation after my mother's death. Now that I understood the reasons for Lailah's cold reception, I vowed to repeat those same apologies to my sister.

She was nowhere to be found, but her husband and children stood in the main room, smiles of encouragement on their faces. Although her absence pinched, I could not fault her for such resentment. There was much work to be done on rebuilding what I had torn asunder.

My father paused at the threshold in order to lay both hands on my head and speak a blessing over me, one I'd heard thousands of times. But this time the words of profound and abiding shalom washed over me like ink over finely woven papyrus, slid into my hair and my skin, and burrowed into my bones, filling tiny cracks and even soothing the sting of Lailah's rejection. Then, after pressing a kiss to my veiled cheek, my abba flung the door open wide to my bridegroom.

Torchlight danced against the night sky as I took a step toward Malakhi, drinking in the sight of him after ten days of separation. He'd insisted he needed time to prepare our new home, although I was not sure what renovations could be made to his tiny room on the second level of the inn, but the time apart made this moment all the sweeter. He stepped forward to meet me, Amit's hand clasped in his.

Along with Malakhi's entire family, a large group of townspeople stood behind them, shifting and jostling for the best position, making me glad for the veil that concealed my face. Thanks to the public announcement my father had made, all of Kedesh was aware of my return, and it seemed most of them had shown up to witness this spectacle. My palms went clammy and my stomach soured as I wondered how many of them judged me in the same manner as my sister, or worse.

"Ima!" said Amit, his small voice pitching high with jubilation. "We've come to bring you home!" A number of chuckles floated from the crowd, soothing a bit of my discomfort. And truly, what did it matter how anyone saw me when I had been reunited with my precious son?

Grinning, Malakhi bent to whisper something to Amit, who then ran back to stand in front of Moriyah. Gidal and Malakhi's mother wrapped her arm about my boy's chest, tugging him close, and nodded to me with a look of such affection and gratitude that the rest of my nerves faded into nothing as her youngest son moved to stand in front of me, cutting off my view of everyone but him.

Warmth spread down my limbs as he lifted the veil from my face, folded it behind my head, and then brushed his palms over my shoulder blades to gather me closer. "Hello, my beautiful bride." He sighed and pressed a lingering kiss to my cheek. "I have waited so very long to say those words." That enticing smile curled his lips, reminding me exactly why all the girls of Kedesh had always whispered and giggled in his presence. But none of them knew that the depths of his faithfulness, kindness, and generosity far outshined his exquisite face.

"And *I* cannot wait to hear you call me *wife*."

"Only . . ." He kissed my other cheek, then leaned to whisper in my ear, his warm breath ghosting over my skin and sending a pleasant shiver down my spine. "If you promise to sing for me."

CHAPTER FORTY-FOUR

Malakhi

The main plaza of Kedesh overflowed with chatter and laughter, music echoing off the buildings and dancing firelight fending off any hint of gloom. My mother had lamented that the courtyard of her inn could not accommodate so many wedding guests, but she'd soon thrown off her disappointment for the joy of organizing a community feast that would last for seven days. She flitted around the square, blissfully overseeing the service of food and drink, but still never too absorbed in busyness to embrace a grandchild or spend a moment chatting with a friend. This was Moriyah shining in her element, a light to the town and especially to those of us who were blessed to call her Ima.

"Do you think Golan will fall next?" Eitan asked my father, who'd been silently tracking my mother's every move with his eyes, as if even after twenty-five years of marriage he still could not get enough of the sight of her.

My father shifted to face us, all longing for his wife wiped away by thoughts of war. "Enough men from Manasseh, Gad, and Reuben are stationed there that I don't anticipate Kushan will attack soon, at least not until the cold months have passed. His army is well entrenched in Edrei, though. It's only a matter of time."

"And the other tribes are still refusing to come to their aid?"

"Unfortunately, yes. They are too mired in their own squabbles to care that our brothers to the east of the Jordan are in serious danger of being completely overrun."

"What can we do?" I asked.

My father laughed. "*We* are going to work on calling up more men to arms, and then we will fight to keep the rest of our cities out of Aramean hands. *You* are doing nothing."

My body stiffened in defense. "I am ready and willing. My arm is nearly back to full strength, and I've learned to adapt to my sight limitations. You and Baz were right that I should not have hidden away."

He clapped me on the shoulder. "I know, son. And I am thrilled that you've gotten over your sulk." He grinned and then gestured to the crowd all around us. "But have you forgotten that this is your *wedding* feast?"

"After hounding me for months to take up my sword beside you, you would have me sit on my thumbs while you all fight Kushan?"

"One year, Malakhi. The Torah says no military service for an entire year."

Eitan jammed one of his sharp elbows into my ribs. "Quit scowling. You've waited *five years* for that woman, brother. Enjoy your wife. Give Amit a sibling. There'll be no hardship in that."

His teasing wink coaxed a grin out of me. "It certainly will not," I said. "We have a ways to go to catch up with you and Sofea, but Rivkah and I will eventually close the gap. Twins *do* seem to run in our family."

My brother threw back his head and laughed. "That they do. Abra seems to be expanding mightily and getting more surly by the day. I would not doubt there's a pair of warriors squabbling in her belly."

My own twin had been less than thrilled when I returned with Rivkah, but she'd been admirably cordial and for my sake had put aside her pregnancy discomfort to pitch in with my mother's flurry of wedding preparations. She and Rivkah were almost too much alike, strong of spirit and opinion, but with time I hoped they would make peace.

As soon as he'd returned from Edrei, Hakim had asked for Chana's hand. I'd seen them a while ago, whispering in a corner, and my heart swelled with gladness over the pairing. A beautiful circle would be completed by their marriage, one begun two and a half decades ago when my mother and father stumbled across a trader's caravan with a bleeding man carried between them. Together, Hakim and Chana had taken over the care of the hives while I was in Edrei, and I found it a fitting tribute that the honey that sweetened the bread and wine during my marriage feast came from Gidal's bees—a blessing from beyond the grave from my older brother.

"I do have a job for you," said my father, "while you bide your time in Kedesh with your lovely wife."

As much as the prospect of a year with Rivkah appealed, and as much as I enjoyed carpentry, I was already restless at the thought of waiting around while the men of my family went to war. "Anything," I said.

"I need someone to train new men. Baz and I are getting old," he said, then lifted his palm to silence my argument against the statement. "Unfortunately, there is a dearth of young men with skill enough to fill the sandals of those who fought alongside Yehoshua. We've been training you since the moment you could grip a wooden sword, son. I have every faith that you can take the lead in bridging that gap."

I'd not told anyone of my revelation in Edrei—that I felt called to be an inspiration to the men of my generation—so his declaration snatched the breath from my lungs. "It would be my honor," I managed to push past the knot of emotion in my throat, "to follow in your footsteps."

My father gripped my shoulder, pride glinting in his eyes as he looked at Eitan and me. "Excellent. We'll discuss the details later, along with bringing you up to pace with the latest intelligence we've gathered on the Arameans. This will be a long fight," he said. "One that may well determine the survival of our people."

Then, with a lift of his brows, he tipped his head toward Rivkah, who was seated on the ground ten paces away, head bent together with Ana. The two were recovering from the vigorous dance that had left them flushed, laughing, and gasping for breath. "But for now, I do believe you have a bride waiting for you."

I took his suggestion without argument and strode across the gathering. All conversation ceased as I approached, although I heard a few giggles as I stretched out my hand to Rivkah. "I've come to steal my bride."

"And if I am not finished dancing?" Rivkah's lips quivered as she pressed back a smile, but she contradicted her tease by allowing me to draw her to her feet. Ana grinned in encouragement, dimples flashing. The young woman had already slipped into the rhythm of our family—just one more refugee welcomed into the fold of Kedesh.

"You're done," I affirmed, then pressed my lips to the soft skin beneath Rivkah's ear before whispering, "Run away with me."

Her only answer was a surprised laugh and a quick rasp of breath on my cheek, but I turned and pushed through the crowd, holding her hand tightly in mine as we fled our wedding feast together, ignoring the good-natured teasing that floated behind us as we ran past the boundaries of torchlight.

"What about Amit?" she said, giggling and stumbling along behind me, inspiring a brief memory of a long-ago game of chase through a blossoming apple orchard.

"He's with Sofea. Eitan vowed to allow us a full seven days alone." I paused in the abandoned street to kiss her rose-colored lips. "Don't fret. He's having so much fun with his cousins that he'll likely not even notice we are missing."

"All right," she said, squeezing my hand with affection. "I trust you."

Those three simple words branded themselves on my heart, making the past eight years of yearning worth every prolonged moment. My youthful infatuation for a beautiful girl singing under a terebinth tree had matured into a deep and abiding love for a woman who had laid her own life down for her child. There was no one else I would ever want to bear my own sons and daughters.

"Come," I said, tugging her along behind me toward the inn. "I have something to show you."

Our sandals tapped out an urgent beat on the cobblestones as we raced through the empty city, and by the time we reached the door to our family home, both of us were breathless. Once inside, I lit an oil lamp and carried it as I led her out into the courtyard and up the stone steps to the second level of the inn. Myriad stars decorated the moonless night, and a cool breeze ruffled stray tendrils of Rivkah's black hair as we entered the small room I'd once shared with my brothers.

Leaving the door ajar, allowing starlight to spill in, I lit another oil lamp, hoping two flames might be enough to fully illuminate my surprise. Rivkah's gasp of disbelief and expression of astonishment caused a jolt of pride that was every bit as satisfying as my younger self had hoped it would be.

"Oh, Malakhi. It's beautiful." She shuffled forward to examine the smooth curves of the bed. "It looks similar to the beds in Egypt, and those Samil commissioned for his villa. How could you possibly have done this in such a short time?"

Over the past ten days I replaced the crossbar I'd cracked years ago with the weight of my anger, and then I sanded and polished the cedar to a silken glow. Her finger traced the pattern of leaves I'd carved along the length of the footboard.

"I built this five years ago," I said gently, hoping my answer would not wound, but the rueful huff she released told me that those bruises were still tender. I wrapped my arms about her waist and pulled her close, breathing in the herbal scent of her intricately braided hair. "Let it go, *ishti*. I told you back then that I wanted to build a life with you, and that has not changed. Like Gidal's hives, we've weathered some damage, you and I, but in spite of it all Yahweh brought forth something sweeter than I could have ever imagined."

Teary-eyed, she reached up to caress my face, the feel of her skin on mine making my pulse quicken. "It is an honor to be called your wife, Malakhi." Her palms slid down my chest, a sudden mischievous tilt on her lips. "I see you received my wedding gifts as well."

I glanced down at the finely woven green wool tunic Chana had delivered this afternoon. "That I did. I found a new obsidian knife rolled inside. An excellent replacement for the one you maimed."

"Amit helped me pick it out in the market. Of course now he wants one too," she said, rolling her eyes skyward.

I forced a playful frown. "I was hesitant to eat the bread and lentil stew that accompanied the gifts, however. I've not forgotten the last time I suffered your cooking."

"I *did* owe you an edible meal." Her bright laughter worked its way beneath my skin, and I vowed to provoke that particular melody every day for the rest of my life. "At least it was not fish stew."

"Anything but that," I groaned, earning myself another precious giggle.

"What is on the bed?" she asked, craning her neck to see the rolled parcel I'd placed atop the linens, but I refused to release her.

"A stack of fresh, clean papyrus."

Her mouth dropped open. "Truly?"

"Of course. *My* wife will have no lack of materials to write me poetry. Even if I have to gather the stalks and weave the fibers myself."

I covered her laugh with my lips, still astounded that she was here, warm and content in my arms, and finally mine. I'd never stop thanking Yahweh for watching over her and bringing her back to me. Without relinquishing my hold on my bride, I reached over her shoulder to push the door closed.

"Welcome home, beloved."

Epilogue

Moriyah

Taking a moment to massage the ache that had been plaguing my lower back for the past few hours, I surveyed the crowd gathering in the plaza as the women of the city completed the final preparations for tonight's meal. The last of the choice wine from my father's vineyard had already run dry, so there would be far fewer wedding guests on this last evening of feasting than there had been on the first, but it would be no less fulfilling to serve those who'd spent the last week celebrating my son's marriage. We'd seen little of him and Rivkah, too wrapped up in each other to make more than a few short appearances before disappearing into their chamber or wandering out into the orchards together, but I hoped they would join us for a while this evening.

It had been difficult to trust Rivkah's reappearance in our lives after her abandonment of my boy. And, in all honesty, for the first few days after their return, I'd feigned enthusiasm for their long-awaited union. But after Rivkah came to me privately, pleading forgiveness for her treatment of not only Malakhi, but also Gidal, my maternal resentment began to fade. Her self-sacrifice for Amit, along with the child's resemblance to the missing piece of my heart, smoothed over the rest of my misgivings and made it easier to pluck rose petals from the ashes.

Tirzah passed by with a giggling Amit clinging to her back and a parade of nieces and nephews at her heels. My grandson was already smitten with my youngest daughter and reveled in her talent for creating new games, shimmying up trees, and slinging rocks as far as any of the boys in Kedesh. Although her propensity for mischief was nearly as frustrating as Malakhi's had been, and though she was still much more likely to be found passing time in the foundry with her brothers than with girls her own age, she'd finally begun to blossom into womanhood. It was hard to believe that our youngest would likely be married in the next few years as well. Darek and I had much to be grateful for, even if thoughts of Gidal caused my chest to throb and burn just as much as the day we'd lost him. *I place him in your hands, Yahweh. Again.*

I scanned the gathering for Nessa, wondering if she and her family would join us on this last night. Although Darek had walked down into the valley to extend an invitation to Raviv's widow, we'd all been astounded when a large group of her family members had actually appeared in the city plaza, full of thanks for the safe return of Nessa and the children.

Their appearance made it clear that the rift caused by my accidental killing of Raviv's sons was truly mended, even if a silent current of grief yet lingered beneath my skin. I doubted that the sight of Zeev and Yared dying by my hand would ever fade from my vision. *Have mercy on Raviv, Yahweh, for the sacrifice he made.*

Zendaye strode up to wrap her arms around me in a brief embrace. "Shalom, my friend. How can I be of service to you this evening?" Her steadying presence in Kedesh over the past few months had been an unexpected blessing, and I selfishly hoped that once Hakim and Chana married, their family might not travel as widely. Shuah, the old Midianite who'd once led their caravan, had long passed away, but Zendaye and Benamin, along with their six sons and daughters, still carried on his tradition of inviting traders from many different nations to join their travels. Over the years, a number of foreigners had bound themselves in covenant with Yahweh because of the couple's kindness, generosity, and example of Torah faithfulness. They were a light to all whose paths they crossed.

"I believe the girls and I have the food and drink well in hand," I said. "But might you be willing to stay close to Margalit tonight? The longer this wedding celebration has gone on, the more withdrawn she has become."

I gestured to the poor girl standing a few paces away, who was still deep in the throes of grief over the death of her baby, the separation from her distraught young husband, and her conviction of manslaughter. I'd done my best to offer comfort over the past few months, to empathize with her, and to keep her occupied with tasks at the inn, but she still walked through the days in a haze, barely speaking and neglecting to wash her body or comb her hair. Whenever Abra came to the inn, Margalit would flee to the room she shared with Chana, seemingly desperate to avoid the sight of a pregnant woman.

"I certainly will," said Zendaye, who was familiar with the young woman's plight.

I squeezed her arm in thanks, remembering how she'd cared for me during my own time of desperation. "If anyone can draw her out, it would be you."

She pressed a kiss to my cheek, her white smile dazzling against her dark skin as she gripped my shoulders. "Now you, my friend, will go sit down for a few moments and rest. You've been on your feet for seven days. You are no girl of twenty anymore."

I laughed at her tease. "That, I am not. But this wrinkled old grandmother refuses to lay down her weary bones during a feast. I'll rest tomorrow."

Her next words were lost to me as a shriek tore through the air, followed by a number of exclamations and then a rising murmur among the wedding guests. Confused by the furor, I watched Eitan dash across the plaza toward Sofea and pull her away from her children to whisper something in her ear. Her hands went to her mouth and then her gaze flew straight to me.

Not five paces away, Margalit, the young woman who'd been so flat and distant since her arrival in Kedesh, began to sob, her knees buckling. Releasing me, Zendaye ran over to kneel and gather the distraught girl in her arms. Then my husband was suddenly in front of me, pulling me close, his familiar warm, brown eyes filled with tears.

"Darek," I said, trembling in confusion and fear. "What is happening? Are the Arameans coming?"

He lifted his hands to cradle my face, his thumb gently stroking the brand-scar on my cheek. "No, my love. Eleazar, high priest of Israel, has died. You are free."

A Note from the Author

In many ways this book has been the most personal for me to write. There was a time in my life when I, like Rivkah, turned my back on my family and my spiritual heritage and squandered my own blessings. Of all the lessons I learned during that time of reckless self-centeredness, the greatest was that not only does my family love me unconditionally, but my heavenly Abba refuses to let me go. He was always there, waiting for me to run back to his arms and to remind me of his extravagant and marvelous grace. My hope for this story is that we will all be reminded that no matter how far we've run, no matter how we've wasted the days and talents we've been gifted with, there is no place we can go to hide from the One Who Sees, and there is no pit we can dig deep enough that he won't graciously climb into to rescue us and carry us to safety.

As with both of the first two books in the CITIES OF REFUGE series, *Until the Mountains Fall* is based in the time period after the Conquest and before the Judges. There is little known about this time, except in the biblical account it is clear that once Joshua died, things went downhill fast. The tribes of Israel were not one united kingdom at this point. They were a confederation of tribes connected by shared heritage and the Torah, and just like during the lifetime of Jacob's twelve sons, there was very little smooth sailing and not a small amount of tension between the tribes.

And not only were the Hebrews already sliding into idolatry, but they'd pretty much given up on getting rid of the Canaanites, who still lived among them. Moses's admonition to keep themselves as a holy people focused on God's Word went largely unheeded. The archeological record shows that there were, in fact, many idols of Yahweh and references to his "marriage" to different goddesses. Obviously worship of Yahweh became entangled with worship of the Canaanite gods in a fairly short period of time, and syncretism (mixing of worship practices) twisted God-given rituals into something that angered him so much that he gave them over to subjugation by the Arameans for eight years (a period that will be explored in the conclusion to the CITIES OF REFUGE series, *Like Flames in the Night*). It was the beginning of the sad cycle of compromise, idolatry, subjugation, desperation, repentance, and salvation that dominates the timeline of the Judges.

It was fun to explore some new settings in this book. I had the pleasure of seeing Tel Dan (ancient Laish) with my own eyes in the winter of 2017, and as I walked those timeworn cobblestones, saw the gorgeous lush beauty of the forest all around, and hopped from rock to rock over many tiny tributaries that gather into the headwaters of the Jordan, I knew I wanted to place my heroine in that beautiful, yet historically wicked place. I also had the pleasure of standing on a mountaintop in the Golan Heights and looking over the valley where many believe Golan, the Levitical city of refuge, may have stood. There is a reason why this small patch of land has been fought over for thousands of years, even to this day. It's beautiful, fertile, and in an important strategic position, which is why I chose to place the first battle with the Arameans here.

Edrei (modern Daraa) is in Syria and sadly has been ground zero for some of the worst atrocities in that war-torn country, so little to no archeological work has been done there. However, I stumbled across information about a man named Gottlieb Schumacher, who was an engineer, surveyor, and architect in the late 1800s and was part of building a railway in the area around Daraa. Schumacher published detailed descriptions of the land, its people, and archeological interests, along with a fascinating account of the place locals informed him was ancient Edrei. Beneath the ruins of the city was a maze of tunnels carved into the bedrock thousands of years before, the perfect place to hide during a siege. Schumacher's descriptions of shimmying along on his belly through the dank blackness underground gave me lots of fodder for my own imagination about Malakhi and Rivkah's flight through the tunnels. Edrei seems to have been in Hebrew hands for only a short period of time after they captured it from the giant King Og (Deut. 1:4), and it's very conceivable that it could have been one of the first cities to fall to Kushan.

We don't know much of anything about King Kushan, except that he was most likely a king of Mesopotamia (although think of a "king" more like a governor over a city-state) from the area of Aram-Naharim, which is between the Tigris and Euphrates. His name wasn't even Kushan. In Hebrew, *Kushan Rishathayim* (or *Cushan-Rishathaim*) meant roughly "the king of double wickedness," so it was basically a not-so-nice nickname for a really bad guy. The Arameans were known for their brutal war tactics, some of it so disturbing that it was difficult to read about, and likely the fall of Israel into the hands of Kushan was a horrific and bloody one.

Rivkah's occupation as a scribe is not quite so farfetched as it may seem; there were accounts of women scribes in both ancient Egypt and Babylon, and as one scholar pointed out, we cannot tell the gender of the scribe from the writing on parchment. So it may have been a much more common practice that we might even guess. Who knows?

We tend to view the ancient people as vastly more primitive than we are, but not only does the Bible make it clear that written contracts were common (in fact, the entire Torah itself is a written covenant between Yahweh and his people), but the Code of Hammurabi, which dates well before the Exodus, lays out a complex set of legal codes that dictate interest rates and lending practices. International trade was well established in this part of the world, so scribes would be necessary to conduct commerce and correspondence between buyers and sellers, as well as government officials. A good and honest scribe would have certainly have been in demand by wealthy traders like Samil.

I hope that you have enjoyed Rivkah and Malakhi's story, which, of course, was loosely inspired by the parable of the Prodigal Son, as told by Jesus in Luke 15:11-32. We tend to be quick to judge that reckless son who squandered his inheritance and ended up eating with the pigs, but aren't we all far too easily compromised by our own idols? Isn't it so very tempting to waste our time, money, and attention on things that aren't eternal? How simple is it to grow complacent and forget the price that was paid for us on Calvary and the blood that was shed to buy our freedom?

Thank goodness for a God who keeps pursuing us and loving us, even when we are caught in the same destructive cycle the ancient Hebrews were swept into time and again. But our Abba is always there, isn't he? Standing on the roof. Hand shielding his eyes as he searches the tree line for any movement. Ready to run to us with arms outstretched, robes flying, to welcome us home. *Selah.*

I would like to give special thanks to my mom, not only for her constant prayer when I was in the throes of my own prodigal wandering, but for her unfailing support in this writing endeavor. My deepest appreciation also goes to my writing and plotting partners: Nicole Deese, Tammy L. Gray, Christy Barritt, and Amy Matayo, whose insight transformed this story from a tiny wisp of an idea into a fully-bloomed plot line in the space of ninety minutes, and whose continual support makes this sometimes overwhelming writing life into something truly special.

Thanks also to my eagle-eyed beta-readers Joannie Schultz, Ashley Espinoza, and Jodi Lagrou and my go-to grammar girl Elisabeth Espinoza. I am also blessed to have Tamela Hancock Murray, my gracious and encouraging agent, in my corner. Many thanks as well to the entire team at Bethany House: my editors Raela Schoenherr and Jen Veilleux, Noelle Buss and Amy Green and the rest of the marketing team, Jennifer Parker and the design team, and all the hardworking people who have their hands and eyes on my books from start to finish. I cannot even begin to express the depth of my gratitude for such a supportive publishing house behind me as I travel this fantastic journey.

I'd also like to thank all my friends in Waxahachie, Texas, for the support and encouragement over the past few years. It was so hard to move away from a community that has shown my family and me so much love. From my fellow homeschool mamas at ECCHO and MomHeart, to my neighbors the Lapusans and the Matthews, who always made my kids feel so at home while I was writing like a madwoman, to the sweet librarians at Sims Library, to every one of you who showed up (sometimes in costume!) for my book release events, I miss you all and am so very grateful.

Thanks also to Adam Barnes, the Bee Guy of Nashville, who enlightened me on ancient beekeeping practices and shared his extensive knowledge of honey and its many applications, both edible and medicinal.

And lastly, I'd like to thank my precious family, Chad, Collin, and Corrianna, for their unfailing love as well as their patience with my writing-hangover mornings, my tendency to suddenly slip into storyworld and stare into space, and also for being my greatest cheerleaders as I pursue the path God laid out for me. I love you three to the moon and stars and back.

Questions for Conversation

1. This book was inspired by the parable of the Prodigal Son in Luke 15:11–32. What similarities do you see between Rivkah's journey and that of the reckless young man in Jesus's tale? What differences?

2. The concept of arranged marriages and levirate marriages (Deut. 25:5) is pretty far from our cultural and modern norms. What, if any, benefits do you see in such unions? What complications might arise? What would our society look like if arranged marriages were still customary?

3. The definition of *prodigal* is "reckless or wasteful." Have you, or someone you love, ever spent time wandering from your spiritual and/or familial heritage? In what ways were you (or they) reckless during that time? What, or who, influenced a change? What lessons were learned during that period of your (or their) life?

4. Rivkah and Malakhi change drastically over the course of the book, due to both circumstances and simple maturation. What contrasts do you see between Rivkah at the beginning and Rivkah five years later? What about Malakhi?

5. When have you, like Rivkah, made harsh judgments about a person and then come to realize that you did not have all

the information and were perhaps wrong in your assessment? How did that change your relationship with that person?

6. When have you, like Malakhi, mistakenly put someone on a pedestal or imagined them to be something more than who they actually were? How did you come to understand the truth? How did that new insight affect your relationship with that person?

7. Have you ever made a decision out of desperation, like Rivkah did when she sold herself into slavery? What effects did that have on your life or on those around you? What good came out of that situation?

8. Which secondary characters are your favorites in *Until the Mountains Fall*? What about the other books in the series? Why are you drawn to them?

9. How has Moriyah's influence shaped the town of Kedesh? What do you think she and her family might do now that she is free to leave?

10. We met Tirzah as an infant in *Shelter of the Most High* and encountered her as a spunky, energetic young girl and then as a feisty, adventurous teen in *Until the Mountains Fall*. Since she will be the heroine of *Like Flames in the Night*, book four in the series, how do you think her character might develop over the eight-year interim? What kind of hero do you think would be a good complement to her spirited nature?

Connilyn Cossette is the CBA bestselling author of the Out from Egypt series from Bethany House Publishers. Her debut novel, *Counted with the Stars*, was a finalist for both the 2017 Christy Award, INSPY Award and the Christian Retailing's Best Award. There is not much she enjoys more than digging into the rich, ancient world of the Bible, discovering new gems of grace that point to Jesus, and weaving them into an immersive fiction experience. She lives with her husband of twenty-one years and a son and a daughter who fill her days with joy, inspiration, and laughter. Connect with her at www.ConnilynCossette.com.